# Mechanical Failure

ALSO BY JOE ZIEJA

Forthcoming:
*Communication Failure*

EPIC FAILURE
BOOK I

# Mechanical Failure

JOE ZIEJA

1230 AVENUE OF THE AMERICAS, NEW YORK, NEW YORK 10020

This book is a work of fiction. Any references to historical events, real people, or real places are used fictitiously. Other names, characters, places, and events are products of the author's imagination, and any resemblance to actual events or places or persons, living or dead, is entirely coincidental.



Also available in a SAGA PRESS paperback edition
The text for this book was set in ITC New Baskerville Std.
Manufactured in the United States of America
First Edition
2 4 6 8 10 9 7 5 3 1
CIP data is available from the Library of Congress.
ISBN 978-1-4814-5927-3 (hardcover)
ISBN 978-1-4814-5926-6 (pbk)
ISBN 978-1-4814-5928-0 (eBook)

**To my wife, for whom my military life wasn't always this funny. Thanks for sticking with me.**

# Asses to Ashes

"I don't like the looks of this, Rogers," Dorsey said in a sort of depressed whine. "There are pirates here."

"Of course there are pirates here," Rogers said, looking out the window at the formation of ships floating in front of them. "I invited them. I invited *two* groups of pirates here. How the hell else do you expect us to make money off this transfer?"

Dorsey looked at him, mostly expressionless except for the heavy-lidded stare that he seemed to have been practicing all his life. He punched a couple of the instruments on the panel and sighed.

"I don't like pirates," Dorsey said.

Dealing with intergalactic space pirates was difficult enough; dealing with intergalactic space pirates with the most cowardly copilot Rogers had ever hired was a whole new level of ass pain.

"They don't really advertise themselves as likeable people," Rogers said. "And I didn't hire you to like them. I hired you to help me make a lot of good money off a lot of bad people. So just keep the controls steady while I work my magic."

A beep on the panel told him that he had an incoming transmission, and Rogers keyed it in. A gruff, inarticulate voice crackled over one of his several independent communication systems—Rogers had it configured so he could hear everything at once but had to switch channels to transmit. He didn't want either of the two groups to hear what he was saying to the other.

"You sure this is the right place?" asked a member of the Purveyors of Vitriol, one of the pirate groups.

"Of course I'm sure it's the right place," Rogers said with a practiced scoff of indignation.

He wasn't sure it was the right place. The military had trained him in navigation a bit, of course, but he was an engineer, not a pilot.

The Fortuna Stultus galaxy had been humanity's home for a thousand years or so—since they'd accidentally collapsed the Milky Way—but that didn't mean he knew it like the back of his hand. If he was reading the charts correctly on his holosphere, this *should* have been a desolate little location on the edge of Meridan territory, just outside of an Un-Space drop point that nobody ever used because it led to absolutely nowhere. And if there was one place that Rogers preferred to do hard work—like brokering a deal between two of the system's most devious pirate groups—it was absolutely nowhere.

"Just give them time," Rogers said, though he wasn't sure if he was reassuring the Purveyors or reassuring himself. "They *need* these supplies. The Garliali will be here."

A terse grunt was the only reply, which didn't surprise him at all. The Purveyors of Vitriol weren't known for their eloquence; they were a pirate organization, after all. They were decent chaps once you got to know them, and Rogers knew them well enough. He'd been pretending to be a spy for them for months.

The Garliali Mercenaries for whom they had been waiting, on the other hand, were not fine chaps. Some of them had been trained by the military, but most of them were just common thugs and cutthroats looking for a quick buck, and were pretty indiscriminate when it came to picking targets. Rogers would know; he'd been pretending to be a spy for them for months too.

"The *Garliali*?" Dorsey asked, his lilting voice cracking with nervousness. "You invited the *Garliali Mercenaries* here?" His face might have been flat, but his body looked like it wanted to jump out of his seat.

"Were you not even listening when I briefed you on this mission?"

"The Garliali are the biggest pirates in the system! They've knocked over armed Meridan patrol units."

"Yes," Rogers said, "and they're dangerously low on medical supplies precisely because they keep knocking over Meridan patrol units."

"How do you know they're low on supplies?"

"Because I stole them. Then I gave them to the Purveyors to sell back to the Garliali so that we can get a kickback."

Dorsey moaned like a cat that couldn't find its litter box. Rogers wanted to throttle him. Of all the pilots in the Meridan system, he had to hire Dorsey. Rogers wished more than one person had responded to the Help Wanted ad.

"Are you sure you know what you're doing?" Dorsey asked.

"I spent ten years in the Meridan Patrol Fleet," Rogers said. "If you can't learn how to con someone in ten years in the MPF, you can't learn anything."

Dorsey looked askance at him again, then sighed and went back to the controls.

"I don't like pirates," he said.

The space around them remained empty for another long few moments, and Rogers had the uncomfortable feeling that he might have made a miscalculation somewhere in his plan. He leaned back in his chair and swallowed the discomfort. He just needed to relax, wait, and resist the urge to lean forward and send a call to his contact in the Garliali Mercenaries.

Rogers leaned forward and sent a call to his contact in the Garliali Mercenaries.

"What's taking you so long?" he cried.

As if on cue, a thin blue line emerged in the backdrop of black space, out of which spewed a handful of Garliali ships. Unlike the Purveyors, they took a bit more pride in the way their ships looked; their shimmering chrome surfaces shone brilliantly in the reflections of the Meridan solar star. The Purveyors, on the other hand, looked like they had assembled their ships from space refuse dump points. Rogers knew better than to judge either of them by their looks. Once those plasma cannons started firing, nobody was really concerned what they looked like.

"Sorry we're late," a thin, feminine voice came over the comms. "A little trouble with the authorities," she said. "But asses to ashes, and all that."

"I'm pretty sure it's 'ashes to ashes,'" Rogers replied.

"Go back to the place we jumped from," the Garliali woman said—Rogers didn't recognize her voice—"and you tell me if you can find any asses left."

"You see? You see?" Dorsey said, shaking his head. "They're going to take our asses! We're not going to have asses!"

"Shut up, Dorsey. If you can't keep your cool, I'm going to eject you. I need you to trust me, alright? We'll get through this."

"I don't—"

"Like pirates, I know. I don't like them either. But sometimes you have to work with people you don't like so that you can make a ridiculous amount of money."

Rogers swallowed. Would they really make it through this alright? Maybe he should have stuck to running gambling rings and moving contraband between new recruits.

Looking out his cockpit window and through the many video cameras mounted on the hull of his ship, Rogers could see the two opposing squadrons moving into battle positions. At least, they certainly looked like battle positions; he was pretty sure pirates didn't have a wide variety of formations. But they weren't going to fight each other—not if Rogers could help it, anyway—but that didn't mean that a lot of shiny silver cannon barrels weren't pointed at a lot of other shiny silver cannon barrels. He'd hate to be in the middle of them.

Unfortunately, he was directly in the middle of them.

"If they try anything," the Purveyor said over the radio, "we're gonna see us some fried Garliali."

"Fried calamari?" someone else on the Purveyor channel said.

"No, I said fried Garliali."

"They won't try anything," Rogers said.

"They won't try anything with what?" the Garliali woman asked. "Who's trying anything?"

Rogers swore and switched the comm system back to the Purveyors' channel.

"They won't try anything," Rogers said again.

"Why not? Fried calamari is good. You won't know if you like it until you try it."

"We ain't fryin' no calamari!" the Purveyor leader roared. "Get the wax out of your ears and get off the radio or I'm gonna come down from the bridge and rip—" The comms cut off.

Rogers shook his head and sighed. "Pirates . . ."

He looked over at Dorsey, who was still shaking his head and mumbling as he did his control checks. Could he really trust him if this got heated? Rogers didn't need someone that was going to freak out at the first sign of trouble. He needed someone that could help them bug out if people started shooting. Rogers thought it would be a good idea to calm him down a bit.

"Dorsey," Rogers said, sighing. "Don't worry about anything. This is going to be simple, just like I told you. I know this is your first mission with me, but I'm going to take care of you. All we have to do is be the intermediary for the cargo and the cash. The Garliali are going to start sending us the credits, and then the Purveyors will let us release the cargo. They'll pick it up, and we'll go home. Does that sound so hard?"

Well, it was a little harder than that. Rogers wasn't just planning on getting a kickback; he was going to steal the credits, too. He left that part out. He didn't want to spook Dorsey any further. That and he'd gave to give Dorsey a bigger cut if he was honest about the amount. Honesty didn't pay.

Rogers *also* left out the part about the Garliali getting giant packets of baking flour instead of medical supplies. The . . . unlucky family he'd met at the transportation terminal on Merida's second moon had convinced him that maybe pirates didn't deserve to get patched up properly. That and the hospital there had been willing to buy them. At a discount, of course.

Dorsey looked at him, clearly dubious. "I guess it doesn't sound that bad."

"It'll be easy. Like, uh, what did you used to do before I hired you yesterday?"

"Postal work."

"It'll be like postal work. Just delivering packages. See? You're already an expert. Nobody is going to shoot us."

After a moment of looking at Rogers with open distrust, Dorsey visibly relaxed. He was still shaking his head, but at least he wasn't muttering about not liking pirates anymore.

"Great," Rogers said. "Now, you're in charge of maneuvers while I manage the communications and the cargo. Just like we talked about. Okay?"

"Okay."

Rogers took a deep breath and wiped his hand across his forehead. It was now or never, he supposed.

"Alright," he said to the Garliali over the radio, making sure to switch the comms channel this time. "Get your cargo ship in position and start the transfer."

"Way ahead of you."

A small tugboat-like ship had already separated from the

Garliali group and was heading toward the *Awesome*—Rogers' ship—its heavy-lifting engines emitting an eerie blue glow. It looked like a giant beetle, with two mandibles below its flat cockpit. The Garliali fighters maintained a tight wedge formation, the tip of which pointed right across Rogers' bow and toward the Purveyors, whose formation was more like space popcorn.

"Credits first!" the Purveyor leader belched over the radio.

"Relax," Rogers said. "I'll let them know not to get too ahead of themselves."

Reaching forward, he keyed in the frequency for the Garliali representative.

"Listen up," he said. "You can route the funds through the computer on my ship. I'll remove any traces from the credits so they can't be, uh, traced, and then I'll route them to the Purveyors. When it's halfway done, you can start picking up the cargo. Got it?"

"Got it, Rogers," the female said. "You're a good man."

Rogers had been called a lot of things in his life, but a "good man" wasn't one of them. If the two groups he was tricking were anything but notorious criminal organizations, he might have felt a little bit bad about it. Mostly, though, he was one careless sneeze away from peeing in his pants in fear.

His digital interface changed as he was notified that the credits were incoming. With a couple swift button presses and an authentication code, the money started flowing.

"That's kind of strange," Dorsey said. "Why are they sending us the money?" He made some trim adjustments on the control panel and checked his instruments, fiddling with buttons. Some of the nervousness had already come back—Rogers could see him sitting more stiffly.

"It's complicated," Rogers said. "Lots of, um, really technical finance stuff about money laundering and all that. Just pilot the damn ship and make sure we don't run into the cargo after we release it, alright?"

The "technical finance stuff" was a spoofing program that

would funnel all the credits into Rogers' account. The Purveyors would be receiving empty data packets, but if the finance tech he'd known from his military days had programmed this correctly, they wouldn't know about it until he was relaxing on a beach on Dathum under an assumed name.

A quiet moment passed as the sequence started working. Rogers saw a lot of code running from his command console—he even understood most of it—and his heart felt like it was trying to climb up his throat and out his nose. Just one over-observant Purveyor, and people would start shooting.

"There's the credits," the Purveyors squawked over the radio. "You're a good man, Rogers."

A good man, twice in one day? Something about that made his skin crawl a bit.

Rogers smirked to himself as the transfer reached fifty percent completion. Now all he had to do was unlock the cargo magnets to release the crate, sit back, and collect the best kind of money there was—someone else's. He flipped the switch to disengage the cargo and watched the open, empty space through the window.

"Beautiful," Rogers said. "Just beautiful. See? I told you this would be easy."

The tugboat's mandibles cinched around the crate and began its flight back to the Garliali escort, and Rogers reached for a bottle of Jasker 120, the finest Scotch in the system. Now was a time for celebration.

A beep came from his instrument panel, which he promptly ignored just like he did most beeps that came from his instrument panel. This was not a time for beeps.

"What's that?" Dorsey asked.

"It's nothing. Ignore it. Never believe computers. Just keep your eyes on the controls and keep us steady. We're going to jump back out of the same point we jumped in from as soon as we're done."

The beep sounded again.

"Rogers," Dorsey said. "There's a ship coming in."

"That's ridiculous," Rogers said. "We're in the middle of nowhere. The Meridan Patrol Fleet doesn't even bother scanning this sector—that's why I picked it. It's probably just a late pirate cruiser or something."

Just to prove him wrong, a void opened in Un-Space and disgorged a bright silver ship bearing the markings of the Meridan Patrol Fleet.

"You've got to be kidding me," Rogers said.

"It's the MPF!" Dorsey yelled. "I don't like *them*, either!"

"What the hell?" the Purveyor yelled over the radio.

"It's a setup!" the Garliali shouted.

"Cancel the calamari and get to the guns!"

"Wait!" Rogers said, but it was too late. And he wasn't sure what channel he was talking on, anyway.

Everyone from both sides started to talk into their radios at once, creating such a cacophony of panic that Rogers felt like he should be shooting something. But shooting something would immediately reveal to whatever side he shot that he was not their ally. Running away would do the same thing for both sides. So, Rogers did what he did every time he was in a battle: nothing.

Because in ten years in a peacetime military, ex-Sergeant R. Wilson Rogers had never been in a battle. And he was already pretty sure he didn't like it.

"All fighters, break formation and engage the Purveyor ships! We'll teach them to cross us!"

"Take down that Garliali freighter! Those sons of bitches won't get away with this!"

The Garliali wedge charged toward the Purveyors' motley formation, engines flaring to life as they converged on the center position that was, unfortunately, the *Awesome.* A rainbow of cannon fire lit up space like some kind of deranged slot machine in the Heshan casino, and stuff started blowing up.

"Oh god, oh god," Dorsey said, devolving into an utterly useless stream of babble as he sat back uselessly in his chair and held his hands awkwardly in front of him. He shook his head, his bland expression rapidly approaching panic.

"Snap out of it, Dorsey," Rogers said, "and get ready to boost us toward the Un-Space point when you can. Who is in that damn patrol ship?" He still knew people in the Meridan Patrol Fleet. Maybe it was a buddy of his and he could convince them to jump back into Un-Space and stop ruining his swindling.

"This is ex-Sergeant R. Wilson Rogers of the *Awesome*," he said, keying in to a known Meridan patrol code. "You're, uh, interrupting me! Interrupting this! Go away! Who is your captain? What's his favorite beer?"

There was no response. Rogers brought up a command console and started doing research as fast as he could. Maybe if he could find out the ship's name, he could contact someone he knew on board directly.

"The *Rancor?*" he said incredulously when the name popped up. "What's the *Rancor* doing here?"

"Who's that?" Dorsey called from under the seat. "Can they help us?"

"Probably not," Rogers said. "They're all supposed to be dead. They flew into an asteroid when I was on duty."

"Oh god," Dorsey said, "now we have pirates *and* ghosts!"

Rogers wasn't entirely sure he disagreed with Dorsey's assessment. If he hadn't been covered in a panicked sweat, he might have gotten a chill up his spine.

"*Rancor*," he called, not knowing what else to do. "Abandon your course and jump back to the fleet! You're *blocking my exit*!" Rogers paused. "Please?"

The *Rancor* didn't do anything at all. He expected at least for it to call for more ships, but nothing else came out of Un-Space. It simply floated in the middle of a torrent of gunfire, its shields flaring to life every time it took a glancing blow from one of the pirates' cannons, like a brain-dead animal that didn't know where its dinner was. The crew on board the *Rancor* should have recognized his name at least—Rogers had beaten the *Rancor*'s captain at several rounds of underhanded card games. But the captain was also supposed to be dead, so maybe that put a damper on conversation.

It was all falling apart in front of him, the space quickly filling with the debris of destroyed ships as the battle raged on. Behind the *Rancor,* ships started flying out of Un-Space as the two groups called for reinforcements. Even though the Meridan ship was blocking the exit, that didn't mean that a horde of pirates couldn't jump in, take a quick evasive maneuver, and then move to engage the other pirates. And that's exactly what they were doing.

Where were they all coming from? It seemed as if both pirate groups were summoning every ship in their respective fleets to come to their aid. This wasn't a cargo transfer anymore; it was a space battle. And Rogers needed to get out of here fast.

"Aren't you going to pilot this ship?" Rogers screamed at Dorsey.

Dorsey shook his head and mumbled.

"Ugh! You're fired!" Rogers shouted, and grabbed the controls.

Equipment crashed around behind him as his frantic yanking of the controls put a couple gee's worth of force into the ship. Dorsey tumbled sideways out of the chair from the force, and Rogers lost sight of him as he focused on getting the *Awesome* out of harm's way. In the background, the comm chatter from the pirates grew even more frantic as each issued orders to its fighters.

"Punch those cannons out of the frigate! They're tearing our fighters apart!"

"Grab that damn cargo and get back to the fleet so we can get out of here!"

But the tugboat, still dutifully dragging the crate of medical supplies, fell to pieces as it was hit by a barrage of blue cannon fire. The space battle seemed to halt for a moment as Rogers stared at the cracking hull of the tugboat and started counting the seconds until both pirate groups turned on him. He also learned what several hundred pounds of baking flour looked like expanding into open space. In a weird way, he found it kind of pretty.

"Protect the *Awesome*! All fighters cover his exit!"

"Get Rogers out of here! He's our best man!"

Rogers sucked in a breath as every fighter in both fleets started charging toward him. To protect him. From each other.

"They're going after Rogers!" both pirates said simultaneously.

The battle became a massive furball as the two groups of fighters made a valiant effort to simultaneously defend the same target from absolutely no one attempting to attack it.

"Um, guys?" he said over the comms, only to realize that he was still talking to the unresponsive *Rancor*, who still had done nothing at all. It wasn't moving to intercept. It wasn't even issuing any warnings to the two pirates to cease and desist and prepare for boarding, which was standard for all interdictions.

Warnings flared to life on his display as the plasma wash coming from the pirates' fighters' engines and cannons slammed into the *Awesome*. Rogers fell out of his chair as his scheme of evasive maneuvers was roughly interrupted by a stray shot. Luckily, since nobody was actually aiming at him, his shields were absorbing most of the impacts. His brain, on the other hand, didn't have shields, and he was quickly learning the value of seatbelts.

Rogers crawled back up to the seat and hit something on the communications panel.

"Everyone just relax!" he shouted to nobody.

"Rogers!" one of the Garliali called in a mess of static. "We're sorry we couldn't protect you! You were our best—"

"Run, Rogers!" a Purveyor screamed as his ship disintegrated. "Those bastards'll kill you! Wait, is that flour? What the—"

As suddenly as it had begun, it was over. While the fighters had been distracted killing each other to get to Rogers, the two command ships had brought their giant guns to bear, turning each other into balls of scrap with just a few well-placed shots. The space that had been host to a simple cargo exchange was now a graveyard of gray specks and space dust. The radio went utterly and completely silent.

"Oh," Rogers said stupidly.

Rogers turned his ship and fired his engines to full. With enough time, he might make it to another Un-Space point or lead the *Rancor* away, pull a few maneuvers, and double back to the one the *Rancor* was still blocking.

A beep sounded from his instrument panel.

"What now?" he shouted, looking down, then froze.

This particular warning was one he actually recognized. Two guided shots had been fired from the *Rancor* at the *Awesome.* The computer blared a warning: impact in thirty seconds.

"Oh shit," Rogers said. "Oh shit, oh shit, oh shit."

The *Awesome* had a single escape pod that was set to launch at a moment's notice, rigged with all the equipment needed for a short trip in space. Rogers got up, grabbing his bottle of Jasker 120, and shouted at his copilot.

"Dorsey, we need to get to the—"

The computer notified him that the escape pod had been safely jettisoned just as he saw the trail of blue light cross the viewscreen.

Dorsey was no longer in the cockpit.

"You worthless, cowardly, backbiting—"

A thunderous impact shuddered through the entire ship, interrupting what would have been a brilliant stream of insults. Rogers closed his eyes and wished he had never left the military. At least then he wouldn't have had such a good chance of being killed.

After what seemed like an eternity, warning sirens blared from the instrument panel, and Rogers came to the unbelievable realization that he was still alive. Opening his eyes, he saw that the *Rancor* had fired two disabling shots right into his engines with a precision he had never seen in all his days in the fleet.

The damage assessment popped up almost immediately: the engines had been ruined. But why would the *Rancor* sit there for the entirety of the fight, then just shoot out Rogers' engines? And why wouldn't they *say* anything?

Then Rogers knew. The Meridan fleet had discovered the missing ship—the *Awesome*, which Rogers thought he had so carefully erased from the fleet's inventory before leaving with it—pinpointed Rogers as its new owner, revived the *Rancor* and its crew from the dead using voodoo and a lot of Scotch tape, and sent them after him. Any moment now, they'd come across the radio, tell him to prepare to be boarded, and he'd be on his way back to the closest Meridan magistrate for sentencing. What an end to a relatively short, relatively successful post-military career.

Instead, the *Rancor* promptly turned around and jumped back into Un-Space.

This was it. Rogers was going to become a rotting corpse on a perfectly good ship with no engines in the middle of nowhere. Nobody had come to pick him up. No ships had transited to which he could send a message. Maybe a spot this remote hadn't been such a great idea, after all. His life support systems were on their last reserves, and it was only a matter of time now before the oxygen tanks gave out and he started to feel that uneasy, sleepy feeling that foretold a slow and hypoxic death.

He'd been in hypobaric chambers before in training; he knew the signs. First he'd start to taste funny things, then he'd be unable to perform basic mathematical equations. He'd start mumbling incoherently. The last traces of his intellect would vanish as his body no longer put oxygen into his brain. Then he'd be promoted to colonel and run the personnel squadron. It was an inevitable chain of events.

Rogers was an engineer, damn it, and a good one! He should

have been able to fix those engines. But the compartment that held his Vacuum Mobility Unit and tools had been sealed when the *Rancor* blew a hole in it. Maybe if he held his breath long enough when he went outside . . . he'd been a pretty strong swimmer in his younger days . . .

Rogers shook his head. What was he thinking? Was he getting cabin fever, or . . . He checked his life support systems. He had less than half a standard day's worth of oxygen left.

Dorsey. Horror vids couldn't describe the litany of physical violence Rogers would hire someone else to inflict on him.

The instrument panel gave him another warning about the life support systems, and he almost threw the long-since-empty bottle of Jasker 120 at it. He would have, actually, had he not already done so two days before and missed completely, putting a dent in the storage locker that held the rest of his bottles of Jasker 120 and rendering it unopenable. He'd never had very good aim.

When the panel beeped again, he thought he was going to pry it open with his fingers and start ripping out wires. But the sound was different. It was the sound he'd heard right before the *Rancor* had come out of Un-Space and started this whole idiotic escapade.

Moments later, a hole opened at the Un-Space point, and two ships popped out like the pus from a black pimple. Two MPF ships.

"Attention, *Awesome*—wait, is that really the name of this ship?"

Rogers flicked the comms switch and responded in a hoarse, tired whisper.

"Yes."

The name on the registry was sort of a happy accident; Rogers had been messing around with ideas and had typed "I am awesome" into the terminal. He'd accidentally hit return, and the name stuck. Right now, though, he didn't feel very awesome.

He heard muffled laughter over the radio. "Attention, *Awesome.*

You, your crew, and your ship are subject to seizure under Code 9 of the Meridan Laws of Free Space. You will power down your engines and prepare to be boarded. Any resistance will be treated as authorization for the use of deadly force."

"My engines are disabled," Rogers replied. "I can't power them down."

"Well, at least flip the switch," the Meridan ship responded. "We have protocol."

Rogers reached forward and flipped the switch, then flipped the bird. He hated protocol. But not nearly as much as he hated dying from asphyxiation.

# Second Chances

The brig of the Meridan Patrol Ship *Lumos* wasn't exactly a palace, but it could have been much worse. A relatively comfortable bed, a fresh change of clothes—something that Rogers greatly appreciated after spending all that time floating around in the *Awesome*—and three meals every standard day. Even if those meals were actually Standard Edible Wartime Relief (STEW) meals, which were really more like protein cardboard than anything else, they were still food.

Rogers couldn't remember the last time he'd eaten a STEW ration—or SEWR rats, as anyone who ever actually ate them called them. When he'd asked the guard for a martini and filet mignon, however, Rogers had been laughed at, which didn't make any sense. Rogers never joked about filet mignon.

But now that he was standing at the docking hatch, ready to be transferred, Rogers wasn't thinking very much about any kind of food.

A young officer, by the look of him and the rank on his epaulet, chatted affably with him as they waited for the docking technician to finish checking the systems.

"Mr. Rogers," he said smugly. "It seems you've reached the end of your tenure on our ship. I won't say we'll be sad to see you go."

"Oh, really?" Rogers asked, giving an exaggerated frown. "I was expecting a lot of tears and hugs."

"Still waiting for clearance, sir," said the docking tech. "Shouldn't be more than a minute or two."

The officer—an ensign—nodded and put his hands behind his back in what Rogers thought was a very arrogant pose. His uniform was just as crisp as everyone else's Rogers had seen, and he even wore a small disruptor pistol at his side. What use he'd ever have for it, Rogers had no idea. The last thing anyone in the modern military ever expected to do was shoot a gun.

"You mind telling me what's happening?" Rogers asked.

"I think you know."

"Yeah, I spend all of my breath asking questions I already know the answers to. I hope to one day metamorphosize into medical paperwork."

The ensign scoffed. "You're being taken to Magistrate Tuckalle for your trial and sentencing. After that, you'll probably spend the rest of your life in the salt mines on Parivan if you're lucky."

Rogers shifted uneasily, eyeing the hatch like a poison viper. The name of the magistrate sounded vaguely familiar, but he couldn't remember where he'd heard it before.

"That doesn't sound very fun," Rogers said.

The ensign looked mildly offended. "What do you mean? Have you never been to Parivan? It's a great place. I was born there. That's why I said if you're lucky."

"I guess you're a real salty sailor, then, aren't you?"

"That joke," the ensign said, "was in very poor *taste.*" He raised his eyebrows up and down rapidly, grinning like a fool.

"Please stop talking."

"Anyway, I was only saying that you'd spend the rest of your life there because it's got great real estate prospects. Once you're done with your community service, you'll probably want to stay."

Rogers frowned. That didn't make any sense. Were they charging him with the theft of a Meridan ship or weren't they?

"Community service?" Rogers asked. "Not jail time? What kind of war crime are you charging me with?"

"War crime?" The ensign looked genuinely confused. "What are you talking about? We're not at war. Yet, anyway. We picked you up for littering."

"Wait . . . *Littering*? You mean you didn't arrest me for . . ." Rogers swallowed what would have been an astronomically stupid confession. "You mean that's it?

"Well, sure," the ensign said. "You dropped a cargo crate in the middle of open space, then blew it up. We try to keep a clean system around here, you know. You can't just go dropping your garbage wherever you feel like it, even if it was in the middle of that refuse heap."

He must have been talking about the debris from the space battle. It certainly had looked like a garbage dump by the time the MPS *Lumos* had shown up.

"But if it was a refuse heap," Rogers said carefully, "what's the problem?"

The ensign grabbed a datapad from the docking tech's workstation and tapped on what was presumably the report about Rogers' arrest.

"No permit," he said. "Can't dump without a permit."

Rogers' heart settled down a little bit. This would be a piece of cake, if a little inconvenient. For him, getting out of a littering fine was as easy as pulling the "got your nose" trick on a marine private first class.

"We're all set, sir," the technician said. "Opening the hatch."

The hatch to the bridgeway opened, revealing a short corridor with no windows to give Rogers any idea of where exactly he was being transferred. Three days of traveling could have put them almost anywhere in the system, but that was assuming that the *Lumos* had made a straight line. They could have finished a patrol route before bringing him to this outpost, or, more likely, they had spent three days doing beer runs and making sure the ship was fully stocked with their favorite snack foods. That was what Rogers would have done, anyway.

Regardless, they were clearly still in free space; Rogers hadn't heard anything about making a landing planetside, nor had he felt the jolting atmospheric impacts that always used to make him clutch the nearest piece of furniture.

A pair of mean-faced Meridan Marines stood on the other end of the hatch. marines didn't bother him so much—they were some of the best drinking buddies in the galaxy—but he couldn't say the same for the loaded disruptor rifles they had at the ready. One of them held a datapad, which he showed to the ensign, who pressed a few buttons on his own. The pad emitted a pleasant *ding* followed by a pleasant feminine voice that said:

"Congratulations! Your prisoner has been transferred, and the system is now a safer place because of your actions. You are entitled to one free round of nachos at the *Lumos* Lanes, courtesy of Snaggadir's Sundries. Happy bowling!"

"Sweet!" The ensign pumped a fist in the air. "He's all yours, boys. I have a date with the lanes." He turned to Rogers with a surprisingly genuine smile. "Enjoy Parivan! If you go to the Birddog Restaurant in the capital, don't get the fish. It's very . . ."

"Salty?" Rogers offered.

"Exactly! How did you know?"

"Just a guess."

The sergeant with the datapad motioned for Rogers to move ahead of them, staring daggers at him the whole time. Rogers felt very uncomfortable with these two grunts at his back, their disruptor rifles humming with their signature low-pitched rumble.

As they emerged out of the bridgeway and through a second hatch, Rogers immediately recognized where he was. It wasn't another ship—it was an administration station, an organ (most similar to the intestines, for various reasons) of the Meridan government, located on the fringe of the system. He'd passed through here once during a station transfer, though he hadn't stayed long enough for him to remember the name of it. He *had* stayed here long enough, however, to make off with a couple extra hundred credits, thanks to a little card game he had organized with the personnel in the armory. Those credits had bought him his first bottle of Jasker 120.

Rogers was marched silently through the station for a short while, passing through corridors packed with people going about their daily business. Rogers couldn't shake the feeling that there was a sort of tension in the air. Like the kind of tension that was generated by having two armed guards at your back—maybe that was it.

They passed a group of paper-pushers doing customer service drills in a small room off to the side; a group of fresh recruits was practicing looking busy while drill sergeants sat in chairs and looked at them expectantly.

One of the recruits, unable to take it any longer, broke and looked up. "Can I help you?"

"No, no, no!" a drill sergeant exploded, jumping out of his seat and bearing down on the unfortunate recruit. "How do you expect to inconvenience people if you're asking them if you can help them all the time? Give me twenty pushups and then *ignore me properly*!"

Administration stations were always a little weird.

Only after the last turn in the hallways did Rogers notice that the almost-pleasant hum of people had died down to a whisper. An unsettling silence crept up from the polished metal of the walls, and for a moment, Rogers could only hear three sets of footsteps, the beating of his own heart, and, strangely, the clucking of a chicken. They came to a door, and, without saying anything, one of the sergeants opened it and roughly shoved him inside.

"Hey," Rogers said. "You could have just told me to go in."

"Shut up and sit down," one of the sergeants said. "They'll be with you shortly. And someone get this chicken back to the zoo deck!"

Without saying who "they" were, the grunts locked the door behind him, and Rogers was left alone in a small room that was clearly built for either interrogation or a very serious game of checkers. Some welcome for a guy who was only being charged with littering. A square, plain table in the center of the room was bolted to the floor, with a pair of chairs on either side. The room was devoid of decoration, but Rogers did notice the security cameras mounted on the ceilings in all four corners. Their unblinking eyes made him want to find a stick to poke them with.

Sitting down with a heavy sigh, Rogers stared at the surface of the table and ran his fingers through his short beard. He hadn't had a chance to trim it since he'd been arrested. He wondered how it looked now. A fair-skinned man with a cherub face, he had taken quite some time to grow it, and taking good care of his beard was Priority Number One. Well, maybe Priority Number Fourteen; he had lost his list somewhere on the *Awesome* (and he rarely paid attention to it, anyway). Maybe he could get "them" to bring him a trimmer and a mirror, whoever "they" were. By god, he hated putting pronouns in imaginary quotes.

The room was eerily silent, and after a moment, Rogers realized it was soundproof. He didn't really want to think about why, but for some reason, rubber hoses kept popping into his head.

For that reason, he didn't hear anyone coming before the door slid open to reveal two men in uniforms—sector police this time, not Meridan military. One of them, a grizzled older man with a pale, pockmarked face and yellowed, watery eyes, barged into the room in a huff and, before Rogers could say anything, began shouting.

"You scum," he snapped. "You worthless pile of trash. How dare you show your face in our facility?"

"You brought me here!" Rogers said, but the man didn't seem to hear him.

"You are a disgrace to Meridan society!" The officer pointed a long, bony finger at him, inches from Rogers' nose. "In fact, you're a disgrace to all humanity. People like you make me wish we had stayed monkeys!"

Inexplicably, the other man, a younger officer with charcoal skin and dainty little eyebrows, stood at the doorway politely and rapped on the edge of the doorframe.

"Hello, Mr. Rogers. May we come in?"

Rogers wordlessly gestured to the other officer who had been shouting at him. The younger man took this as acceptance of his request and tiptoed gingerly inside the room, smiling the whole way.

"It's *so* good to finally meet you," he said. "I'm Officer Atikan, and this is Officer Brooks from the sector police. I've read so much about you from the report."

"I've read your report," the older officer—Brooks—spat. "I wiped my ass with your report, and it *added character.* How can you look at yourself in the mirror?"

Rogers didn't know what to do. He looked back and forth between the two police officers, clutched feebly at the arms of his chair, and hoped he never touched Brooks's datapad.

"But," he said, pointing at Atikan, "he just said . . ."

"I don't care what he said," the mean officer shouted. "I don't care what anyone says. I know what you're about. I've seen hundreds of so-called 'men' like you. I know your type."

"And we could use more men like you," Atikan said.

"You . . . need more scum?" Rogers said.

"Oh no," the younger officer said. "No, we need more men of valor and honor, with the constitution and fortitude you displayed."

"That's right," the older officer said, and Rogers thought it had finally been settled until he continued. "You *are* scum. You only look out for number one, and you'd stab your mother in the back for an extra dime."

"Well," Rogers said, bristling a little, "who the hell else is going to look out for number one? Who is number two? How many numbers are there?"

"Don't get arithmetic-ish with me," Brooks said. "I know how to count!"

"Oh yeah? Let's use our fingers to find out. Here's one—"

"I should explain," the younger officer broke in.

"I wish you would!" Rogers shouted, his face red. Who was this idiot to come in here and start telling him who to look out for? And who the hell used dimes anymore?

"You see," Officer Atikan said, "you're being commended."

"You're in deep shit," the older officer said. "Neck deep. Eyeball deep. You'll be wearing shit for mascara."

Rogers pointed at the younger officer. "He just said—"

"Don't talk back to me!" The older man slammed his hand down on the table. "I ought to bust you right on the lips if I could find them behind those dog shavings on your face. What kind of glue did you use to get that stuck on there?"

"You watch your god-damn mouth," Rogers said, pointing at the police officer, but before he could defend his facial hair any further, Atikan waved a hand in the air.

"The Meridan judicial system is in a bit of a pickle," Atikan said.

"And you're in hot water." Brooks snorted.

"The intelligence gathered from where you were picked up showed that both the Purveyors of Vitriol and the Garliali Mercenaries were nearly totally obliterated in a space battle at which you were the center. The records on your ship filled in only some of the remaining details."

"Dealing with pirates," Brooks said. "Despicable."

"Hang on a second," Rogers said. "I thought I was picked up for littering!"

"Littering, too?" Brooks said. "On top of the rest, you're an

eco-terrorist! I've got your number, Rogers. I've got it right here."

Brooks slid a piece of paper across the table with "40R" scrawled on it.

"What the hell does this have to do with anything?" Rogers asked.

"I found it in your personal effects. What do you have to say about that?"

"It's my coat size?"

"It's your number!" Brooks said, a smug smile blossoming across his face. "And I've got it!"

"But, on the other hand," Atikan said, not at all moved by the mood of his compatriot, "you *did* rid the system of two very dangerous groups of people that had been plaguing the Meridan fleet for some time. Really, brilliant work. Just stupendous."

"I don't understand," Rogers said.

"Like hell you don't!" Brooks leaned over the table, the intensity in his eyes so fierce, Rogers thought he might be set ablaze. *"Talk!"*

*"You haven't asked me any questions!"* Rogers squealed.

"We're having a difficult time, as you can see," Atikan said. "It's not fully clear what your motives were; they don't know whether to prosecute you or reward you." A wide grin split his face and he put both palms out in a gift-giving gesture. "So, until we figure this out, we're doing both!" Atikan looked absolutely thrilled.

"This is your number!" Brooks said, pointing at the tag again. "I've got it!"

Rogers shook his head. "Wait a minute. So, you're not going to prosecute me for littering. You're going to prosecute me for dealing with pirates and then give me a medal for destroying them?"

"Now you've got it!" Atikan said.

"The gallows," Brooks muttered.

Leaning forward in his chair, Rogers looked between the two officers helplessly. "But that doesn't make any sense! Don't I get a trial or something? What about my due process?" He paused. "And how am I going to wear a medal on a prison uniform?" He turned to Brooks. "Did you say *gallows*?"

"Oh, don't worry," Atikan said. "We're only doing both *right now.* I'm here to congratulate you and treat you with the utmost of honors."

"And I'm here to tear your pirating heart out with my bare hands!" Brooks roared as he made a vicious tearing motion with his hands. "Do you know how many innocents have died in Garliali raids? The blood of children is on your hands, Rogers. How does that make you feel?"

Rogers thought it was a rhetorical question, but both of the officers seemed to be looking at him expectantly. Atikan folded his hands in his lap and smiled pleasantly.

". . . Bad?"

Atikan clapped his hands and laughed. "And a pure conscience, to boot! You really are a marvel, Mr. Rogers. A real marvel."

Rogers put his face in his hands for a moment and tried to squeeze his head hard enough that he would pass out and maybe both of these people would leave him alone.

"Don't I get a lawyer or something?" he said.

"Oh, lawyering up now, are you?" Brooks laughed. "A sure sign of a guilty conscience. What do you need a lawyer for?"

"The magistrate is coming to see you in a moment," Atikan said. "Until then we're here to interview—"

"Interrogate!"

"—you. What made you finally decide to rid the system of these pirates? Did something happen to you in your childhood that involved the Purveyors or the Garliali?"

"No, it wasn't—"

"How much were they paying you? Was it worth selling your soul, you bastard?"

"They didn't—"

"How did you come up with such a brilliant plan? The records didn't tell us everything. I want to hear it in your own words." Atikan whipped out a datapad and began typing.

"It was just—"

"Talk!" Brooks slammed his fists on the table again.

"You won't let me!" Rogers shouted. "This is insane! I want to see the magistrate. I don't want to talk to either of you."

"Clamming up, eh?" Brooks said. "A sure sign of a guilty conscience."

"I don't have a guilty bone in my body," Rogers said, glaring at the officer.

"Oh, now we're bringing anatomy into it, eh? A sure sign of a guilty conscience."

Atikan was typing furiously on his datapad, despite Rogers' not saying anything of substance. He wondered if this pair of officers was his karmic payment for all the things he'd pulled in his lifetime. It was starting to make him wonder if any of it was worth it.

"Great," Atkins said cheerfully. "Absolutely wonderful. Good stuff. This will all appear in your commendation records, of course, and the news media. They'll want to interview you on live broadcasts, when your parade schedule lightens. There will be lots of parades!"

Atkins put down the pad and swung his arms in what was either an approximation of marching in a parade or an attempt to scratch his back on the chair.

"I don't want a parade," Rogers muttered. "I want to see the magistrate. What was his name again?"

The door slid open.

"Tuckalle," came a voice that Rogers recognized. "Magistrate Tuckalle, you slick son of a bitch."

In the doorway stood the magistrate, resplendent in an official uniform that had golden cords wrapped around a black double-breasted coat bearing the Meridan symbol in the middle of the chest. A sash around his waist showed a golden picture of an ancient glyph of justice, a tipped weight scale with a dagger through the middle of it.

"Tucky!" Rogers said, brightening. He knew he'd recognized that name. The last time he'd heard it, however, it had the word "colonel" in front of it. Finally, someone he knew from his military days. What a stroke of luck! Tucky would get him out of this; Rogers was sure he would.

The magistrate, his hair gone from salt-and-pepper to full gray in the year or so since their last meeting, made a dismissive gesture toward the two officers.

"I have all I need to know. I'll take it from here."

Atikan stood, tucking his datapad under his arm, and reached across the table to vigorously pump Rogers' hand.

"It's been a pleasure, sir, a real pleasure. Wow, a genuine hero. I have goose bumps!" He and Brooks swiftly exited the room. "I'll see you on the parade grounds!"

*"I'll see you in hell!"* Brooks called as the door closed.

Rogers let out a tremendous sigh of relief and made to hug his old mate. "Thank heavens it's you, Tucky. I thought I was space dust. You won't believe—"

"Sit down, Rogers."

The magistrate's face was something resembling a stone slab, if a stone slab also had a big nose, thin, crescent lips, and thick-rimmed spectacles around a pair of beady black eyes. Rogers tried to picture this old, ruddy-looking man back in his marine uniform.

Rogers slowly sat down. "Come on," he said. "It's me, Rogers. You know me. Help me out here."

"Of course I know you," Tucky said as he moved to the other end of the table and sat down, adjusting his sash when it got caught on the edge of the chair. "Didn't you hear me call you a slick son of a bitch when the door opened?"

"I thought it was a compliment."

"It wasn't."

Rogers started to sweat. Well, continued sweating. He was going to need a shower and another change of clothes at the end of the day. What was Tucky's problem?

"Now I've got you, Rogers," the magistrate said. "And it's time for payback."

"Payback?" Rogers said nervously. "Payback for what? You and I were shipmates. We turned on the same beer light every day at noon. You came to my poker games. You bet on my virtual horses. You drank my whiskey."

"You watered it down," Tucky said. "Your poker games had one and a half decks, and your virtual horses were ridden by virtual crooked jockeys." He leaned forward, boring into Rogers. "You were a poor excuse for a sergeant, Rogers. You were sloppy, aloof, and conniving."

"Are we still on compliments or have we moved to insults?"

"You made that unit a disgrace!" Tucky's face reddened. "And you ruined my career!"

Rogers reeled. "What do you mean, I ruined your career? You were a military officer! Your only career was sipping brandy and relaxing in the Two Hundred Years' (and Counting) Peace! Come on, Tucky, you know better than anyone what the military is like."

"Don't play dumb with me," Tucky said.

Rogers frowned, thinking hard. What had he ever done to Tucky to upset him? Surely he couldn't still be hung up on . . .

"Yes, I'm still hung up on it. I spent three hours wandering the halls in my underwear, looking for my uniforms!"

Rogers guffawed, the memory coming back to him of the colonel's pink flesh as he padded through the hallways shouting at the top of his lungs. That had been a good day.

"That wasn't my fault," Rogers said, and for once, he wasn't lying. "The laundry clerk lost them all."

"Like hell he did," Tucky snapped. "That prank had your name written all over it."

"I told you, it wasn't me. And you could have used the comm system to call someone to get them for you rather than running around the halls, screaming like a banshee."

Tucky's eyes narrowed. "My comm system wasn't working, and I had a briefing with Admiral Klein in twenty minutes."

Well, that *had* been Rogers' fault. Even though the laundry clerk had been the one to lose the uniforms, he'd told Rogers about it. Rogers just helped the scene along a little by meddling with the communication system. It had been just too good of an opportunity to pass up.

"You can't blame me for your busy briefing schedule," Rogers said. "Besides, nothing bad came of it."

"Nothing bad came of it?" Tucky spluttered, red faced. "They played the security vids over the mess hall display during dinnertime!"

That, actually, had also been Rogers' fault. Maybe he did ruin the colonel's career a little bit.

"But who deleted them afterward?" Rogers said. "Who did you come crawling to for that?"

Tucky waved the mitigation away with his hand. "The damage was already done, and you know it. And now that you're here, I'm going to see that you're repaid for every swindle, every dirty bet, every underhanded dealing you did in the 331st. It's time you got what you deserved."

Rogers ground his teeth, thinking. Tucky's word was iron in this situation. Even if he did get a fair trial—which he doubted he would, if Tucky was approving the jury—the magistrate had some discretion when it came to dealing with people in his jurisdiction. And, with them being on the outskirts of Meridan territory, Rogers was a long way from the central federation. By the time he ran through all the appeals processes, he'd have served out half his sentence, and his tongue would probably be swollen from all the salt.

Rogers was, in a word, screwed.

"So, here we are," the magistrate said. "I'm going to make sure this goes nice and quick. This station's jails are too comfortable for the likes of you. I want you doing hard labor ASAP. Do you even know what labor is? I don't remember you doing much work."

*Think fast,* Rogers thought. *What do you have up your sleeve?*

Then it came to him, and he couldn't help but smile.

"What are you so happy about?" Tucky asked, the barest hint of hesitation in his voice.

"Do you remember," Rogers said, sitting back in his chair, "that lovely lieutenant in personnel? What was her name? Namazi? Sharp as a tack, very pretty."

The magistrate's face went white. "What are you talking about?"

"I'm talking about flirting with the very edges of the fraternization regulation," Rogers said. "Among other things."

Tucky snorted, though he did a very poor job of exuding confidence. "I don't know what you mean," he said. "I don't remember a . . . Namazi, or whatever. I'm a happily married man."

"And I am sure your wife would be very interested in how you look in a brassiere and stockings."

Rogers was treated with a lovely few moments of awkward silence as he let that sink in and watched the old colonel's face go just about as white as his hair. If there was one thing he had learned in his life, it was to always have a backup plan. And that backup plan usually involved having dirt on someone.

Finally, Tucky spoke. "How could you possibly . . ."

"That doesn't really matter, does it?" Rogers said. "Let's just say that the security cameras don't always turn off when you want them to, especially if someone else *doesn't* want them to. What are you, an A cup? B cup? You weren't the fittest of specimens."

Drumming his fingers on the table in a furious tattoo, Tucky licked his lips. "There's no way you still have that video."

Rogers shrugged. "You're right. I don't have it."

Tucky visibly relaxed.

"Because it's still stored on a little datapad I keep connected to the main computer of my ship, along with a whole host of other little vignettes set to transmit after a certain time period if I don't get to them."

Had the chair not been bolted to the floor, it would have flown backward as Tuckalle rushed to his feet. His face was dark red, and his eyes looked like they might be ricocheting off the walls at any moment.

"You can't!" he blurted. "You couldn't possibly!"

Rogers held up his hands. "It's not really in my control right now, is it? You're the one about to send me to the salt mines, far away from that datapad . . ."

"What if I got you a remote terminal?"

"I hear salt isn't very good for keypads," Rogers said, leaning back. "Turns the keys into pretzels."

The muscles in Tuckalle's cheeks bulged as he rhythmically began clenching and unclenching his teeth.

"It's not that simple," the magistrate said, sitting back down.

"Seems pretty simple to me," Rogers said. "Let me out of here or the entire Meridan network will be watching videos of you doing the two-step in a young woman's unmentionables. Come to think of it, you seem to spend a lot of time in various states of nakedness, Tucky. Are you a closet exhibitionist or something?"

Tuckalle scowled at him. "It's not just a question of simply letting you off the hook. All those records are already uploaded into the central databases. I couldn't remove them all if I wanted to. It's more of a question of authority."

"Whose?"

"Yours, actually. You have a military record, but you're not in the military anymore. You can't just go roving the galaxy, blowing up pirates—if that was even what you were doing there, which I doubt. So, even if we were to give you a medal and a parade like Officer Atikan said, we'd have to send you to jail for reckless vigilantism."

Rogers squinted one eye. "Reckless vigilantism? Did the MPF unionize or something?"

Tucky shrugged. "I don't make the rules, Rogers." He paused for a moment. "But I might be able to do something."

"And what's that?"

"I could reactivate your military service and backdate the reenlistment to before you went pirating."

Rogers laughed. "You want me to put the uniform back on? There are reasons I left, Tucky."

Those reasons were primarily driven by profit, of course. He wanted to explore and cheat the other populated systems in the galaxy, too. Except the Thelicosa System, of course. They were too good at math.

This was supposed to be his intersystem debut, not his reentry into the boring military! He'd learned enough tricks in the easy-going, post-Peace service to allow him to go big time and do things like, for example, knock over some pirates for what was supposed to be a huge sum of cash. There was no reason to keep running small amounts of contraband when he could . . . well, when he could make a huge mess of things and end up in jail on his way to the salt mines. Maybe this wasn't such a bad idea.

"Besides," Rogers said, despite his wavering opinion. "It was getting boring. Those new droids kept popping up and sucking the personality out of everything." It was also marginally more difficult to smooth-talk a machine.

Tuckalle shook his head. "That's the best I can do for you. I'll put in the minimum commitment of three years, and once you're done with that, you can go back to whatever it was you were doing. I'll even put you back in the 331st."

Sitting back in his chair, Rogers folded his arms and chewed his lip while he thought. The peacetime military wasn't really a military as much as it was a giant fraternity. What else were a bunch of people out on a spaceship in the middle of nowhere supposed to do but drink and gamble and horse around? The

Two Hundred Years' (and Counting) Peace had left plenty of room for filling leisure time with interesting activities.

And Rogers had been a powerful prince in a vast kingdom of debauchery. As an engineer, he'd spent most of his time in rooms that officers rarely wanted to go, and as a sergeant, he had just the right amount of clout without all that annoying "responsibility" that came with being an officer or senior enlisted. What would be so bad about revisiting his old stomping grounds for a while?

"You're sure you could get me back into my old unit?"

"If they don't scuttle the ships when they find out you're coming back, yes."

Another stint in the military. It didn't seem so bad. And what was his alternative?

"Tucky," he said, "what's the maximum sentence for, ah, reckless vigilantism?"

"Five years," Tucky said.

Rogers stood up and saluted.

# Speedbumps

The unnatural smoothness of Un-Space travel came abruptly to an end as the warning lights went off inside the transport shuttle and the normal rules of physics came back into play. Rogers shook his head as his body got used to its own g-forces again and stood up. Out the port-side window of the small, cramped shuttle he could see the 331st Anti-Thelicosan Buffer Group in all of its relatively obscure glory. The ships, arrayed in a rainbow pattern at the very edge of the Meridan system, looked vigilantly toward Thelicosan territory, awaiting—quite futilely, he was sure—the next attack.

Futile, he thought, for two reasons. One, the attack wasn't coming. The Two Hundred Years' (and Counting) Peace was pretty ironclad, thanks to all the legal treaties and checks-and-balances placed on the several signatories. And two, if the attack did come, it wouldn't matter much. Thelicosa was a powerful human system—most had resettled there from their colony on Mars, which had made all of them pretty rough around the edges—and the 331st wasn't called the "Speedbumps" for nothing.

At the center of the formation was the aptly-if-uncreatively named MPS *Flagship*, the control center of the whole group, like a giant flower surrounded by the buzzing insects that were the fighter patrol. Various heavy gunships, cargo transports, medical ships, and other specialty craft lay splayed out in space over the long crescent that made up the 331st. The shuttle in which Rogers was riding made an easy turn, fired up its conventional engines, and zoomed toward the *Flagship*.

"She's a beaut, isn't she?" Rogers asked the pilot as he leaned in the slightly raised gangway connecting the cockpit with the passenger bay.

"She's a warship," came the terse reply. "Take your seat and fasten your seatbelt, please."

"Oh, come on," Rogers said. "You're docking with a massive warship that has a magnetic hook. I'd create more turbulence by jumping up and down."

"Please don't jump up and down."

Rogers stopped jumping up and down and rolled his eyes. The pilot had been like an ice cube since the moment he'd stepped aboard. Pilots in general were always a little screwy, but this was the first he'd met that didn't want to talk your ear off. Cockpits got lonely.

Not for the first time, Rogers wished he had been able to take his own ship. But the engines needed enough work that he'd have to wait to get to the dry dock on the *Flagship* to fix them, if they were salvageable at all.

"So, what's the game of choice nowadays in the fleet?" Rogers asked, still standing in the gangway. "Holo-carving? Gravitational darts? Good old poker?"

"I wouldn't know," the pilot said. He made a couple of quick corrections on the control panel and spoke some jargon-riddled pilot-speak into the communication system. He received similar gibberish in reply and seemed satisfied. The *Flagship* took up the whole of the cockpit window now, its dull gray surface washing out the colors of the shuttle's interior.

"You don't play games?"

"Not while I'm on duty."

"That's the best time!"

The pilot turned and regarded Rogers with something between confusion and contempt. He pointed mutely to the passenger compartment, and Rogers sighed as he turned around.

"Might as well have a droid as a pilot," Rogers said under his breath as he sat down and fastened his seatbelt. Crossing his arms, he grumpily looked out the window and watched as the docking bay swallowed the tiny shuttle like a whale swallowed plankton, padded clamps fastening around the hull like baleen. As Rogers had suspected, the whole procedure was as smooth and automated as it had been when he left the military. Seatbelts . . . pfuh.

Speaking of droids, Rogers couldn't help but notice that the docking bay had quite a few of them running around. Almost humanoid, their tin-can bodies moved around on either a wheeled base or a convincing pair of bionic legs with the knee joints reversed to offset their heavy torsos. Some of them wielded welding torches or wrenches, and some others had their data extension cables plugged into consoles operating cranes and various machinery. Rogers had expected to see some of his old engineering troops running around, but there was barely a human in sight.

"Damn," Rogers said. "Shinies everywhere."

The pilot cleared his throat.

"What?"

"I'd thank you not to use that term on my ship," the pilot said. "I don't tolerate racism."

"Racism? They're droids! They don't have a race."

The pilot made some final adjustments on the control panel, and Rogers felt a rush of air as the passenger stairway extended down to the docking bay floor.

"Enjoy your stay," the pilot said coldly.

Shaking his head, Rogers collected his meager belongings—most of his stuff was still on the *Awesome* and he hadn't been allowed to retrieve it—and made his way down the plank and through the docking bay, carefully avoiding any contact with the droids. Not only did they creep him out a little, but they were boring.

According to Tuckalle, his orders had been transmitted to the *Flagship*, but he didn't tell Rogers much more than that. The first stop, of course, would be the supply depot. He'd need to be reissued everything from uniforms to hygiene supplies to flashlights and tools for his engineering duties. The supply depot had always been his favorite place; it was where he moved the best contraband and where he had the most friends. Of all the people on the ship he wanted to keep happy the most, the supply clerks were of the highest priority, which is why Rogers never, ever gambled, swindled, or dated any of them.

The manifest technician monitoring personnel entry and exit from the ship wasn't actually a manifest technician at all. It was a droid, plugged into the central computer system via a cable that extended from its torso to the wall, and it held up a shiny steel-alloy arm to indicate that Rogers was to wait.

"CALL FUNCTION [PERFUNCTORY GREETING]. TARGET [HUMAN, UNKNOWN NAME, UNKNOWN RANK]. PROMPT: NAME. PROMPT: DESTINATION. PROMPT: PURPOSE OF VISIT."

The rough, broken speech of the droid was like biting into a cookie full of nails. Rogers wondered how, in a few thousand years of speech recognition and replication technology, they hadn't been able to make the droids sound like anything other than brain-damaged gorillas. Even the personal computer terminals sounded better than shinies.

"R. Wilson Rogers," he replied, not feeling comfortable at all that he was having a conversation with a robot. "Reinstatement and reassignment."

A moment passed, the droid's glowing blue eyes staring at Rogers.

"REJECT FUNCTION [MESSILY DESTROY INTRUDER]. CALL FUNCTION [A-156 AUTHORIZED ENTRY AND COURTEOUS ADMISSION]. OUTPUT STRING: APPROVED. ENJOY YOUR STAY. PLEASE REPORT TO SUPPLY FOR UNIFORM ISSUE."

Rogers rolled his eyes and walked away, wondering why they would trust something so important as personnel manifesting to a machine with no human oversight. It made him uncomfortable.

That unsavory encounter behind him, all of a sudden Rogers was back aboard the bustling hive of activity that was the MPS *Flagship*. It smelled like carbon, processed air, and home. The first two were expected; the latter was a bit of a surprise to Rogers. Maybe he *had* missed being in the military just a little bit. He wondered when the beer light would go on, signaling the noon-time cessation of all work-like activities and the commencement of binge drinking and carousing. The peacetime military was hard to beat for work-life balance.

Someone jostled Rogers as they rushed by him, nearly knocking him back out into the docking bay.

"Hey!" Rogers said indignantly. A female spacer, whose rank he couldn't see, kept walking down the corridor without looking back. Rogers shook his head. Some troops had no manners.

The jolt brought him out of his semi-nostalgic reverie, anyway. Rogers gave another head shake and let his legs take him the direction he needed to go. It had only been a little over a year since he'd left the military, so there was still a bit of muscle memory left. He had spent so much time in the supply depot that he was pretty sure he could have, for example, stumbled there in a state of blacked-out drunkenness with no problem. Just as an example.

The supply depot and most of the docking bays were located on the same level of the *Flagship*, so there was no need for Rogers to take the larger up-line intra-ship transportation cars that went between decks. There was a smaller system of zipcars, the in-line, that moved along through the center of each level, and Rogers set his course for the nearest terminal. The depot wasn't that far of a walk, but Rogers preferred simplicity over . . . well, most physical exertion. As he approached the terminal, however, he was met by a stern-faced young woman who he didn't recognize, dressed in a typical dress uniform and wearing an old-style train conductor's hat. There seemed to be an awful lot of new folks around for only being gone for a little over a standard year.

"Hi, there," he said. "I'm headed to Supply."

"It's that way," she said, pointing down the hallway. She didn't move to let him into the boarding area.

"Right. I'd like to ride."

The woman—a starman first class, someone with only a couple of years in the Meridan Navy—looked him up and down with a disdainful eye. "These are for official use only."

Rogers fought to keep the smile on his face. "It is official use. I'm being reinstated and I need to go to the supply dock for my official equipment issue."

"Do you have orders?"

Rogers' smile almost slipped. "Since when do you need orders to ride the in-line?"

"It's the regulation. If you have business, you should have been given orders or at least be wearing a uniform. That's the way we do things."

In no way was this the "way they did things" from what Rogers could remember. Hell, they used to ride the in-line back and forth just to get back to the beginning of the "landing strip," which is what they used to call the section of the hallway they slicked down with cleaning fluid in order to slide along it on their bare chests for fun. Walking back was dangerous—you might get plowed over by a wayward soldier tittering with glee as he spun out of control.

"Just once," Rogers said. "I need to get my stuff."

"No."

The woman looked at him with such implacable indifference that Rogers wondered if she would have reacted had he stripped naked in front of her. What was wrong with these people?

Rogers sighed. "Come on, it's just—"

"These transportation systems are for the orderly movement of personnel and supplies through the loading deck. If I let every joker on, what would happen if fighting broke out? The cars would be crowded with loitering slobs like you."

Letting the insult slide off him, Rogers pressed on. "What fighting? There's no fighting."

The woman narrowed his eyes at him. "That's not funny. Are you really that dense? Now, if you don't mind, I'm very busy."

"You're not doing anything at all!"

"My position is, as all positions are, crucial to the war effort. Please make your way down to the supply depot that way"—she pointed again—"or go and find whoever assigned you here and get orders to use the in-line."

Resisting the urge to make an obscene gesture, Rogers turned in a huff and stomped down the hallway. *War effort!* That was like saying you were stationed on a communication station to help with the heat wave.

He realized he was starting to sweat after the first couple of minutes of speed walking, and he slowed his pace, shoving his hands in his pockets and grumbling to himself. A pair of droids rolled down the hallway, their incessant beeping and whirring making him want to knock their metal faces off (if he had been wielding a torque wrench or had ever visited the gym).

A poster on the wall made him stop for a moment to examine it. There was nothing strange about having motivational posters on the wall—every organization Did it despite its utter ineffectiveness—but something about this one seemed different. It read, in all capital letters, EVERY POSITION IS CRUCIAL TO THE WAR EFFORT. Above it was a dramatically shaded portrait of a young soldier licking envelopes, a look of fierce determination in his eyes. Rogers shook his head and moved on.

The supply depot finally came into view ahead of him, an unremarkable door bearing the inscription SUPPLY above it in yellow letters. Rogers punched the door lock with the bottom of his fist, and the door opened into a small waiting area packed with spacers and marines sitting in rows of chairs and looking annoyed. He couldn't remember a time when there had been so many people in the waiting area. In fact, he couldn't remember a time when there was anyone staffing the desk, either. The supply room was just sort of the place where you went to get stuff. You went in, got stuff, and got out. There was no need for waiting.

The broad counter stretched the length of the back wall, behind which Rogers could see various cargo crates being moved back and forth through the different warehouses. It all seemed very busy, and he could have sworn that the same container was being moved over and over again.

A bored-looking corporal stood behind the terminal at the counter, not doing anything apparently useful. A sign above his head showed NOW SERVING 103, and a vidscreen off to the side was streaming a muted news channel with no subtitles.

"Can I help you?" the corporal asked in a voice that absolutely crackled with nonchalance.

"Yes," Rogers said. "I'm here for my equipment issue."

"Are you a new recruit?"

"Not exactly. I've been reinstated after a . . . break in service. R. Wilson Rogers, sergeant."

The clerk asked Rogers for some additional personal data and started typing away at the terminal keypad.

After a moment, the clerk paused and frowned. "Roger Wilson Rogers? Your name is Roger Rogers?"

"R. Wilson Rogers," he replied tightly. "Are you new here? Where's Quintal? He was in charge here last time I was around."

"Sergeant Quintal was transferred," the clerk said. "I'm Corporal Suresh, the new supply chief."

"Who put a corporal in charge of Supply?" Rogers said. In the Meridan Navy, corporals were just barely above starmen, who mostly had achieved the dubious accomplishment of being able to lace their boots properly.

That didn't brighten Suresh's day at all. "I am fully capable of the duties assigned to me, Mr. Rogers."

"Sergeant Rogers."

The clerk ignored him and continued typing away at the terminal for what Rogers thought was a very long time.

"Is there a problem?" Rogers asked. "I know where everything is back there. I'll just go and get what I need, and—"

"Nobody not in the supply corps is allowed back there," the clerk said.

"What are you talking about? Just about everyone in the whole damn ship has been back there at one time or another."

"Not on my watch," the corporal said.

Rogers bit the inside of his cheek. He had been betting on his old pal Quintal being here so he could reestablish all his old connections. Things were not going to go well for him at all if he couldn't have a hand in the goings-on inside the supply depot. He changed his approach.

"I think we got off on the wrong foot," Rogers said. "A corporal as chief of Supply is a very prominent achievement. I mean, for you to be put in a position of such power and influence at your rank is very impressive."

"I'm just doing my duty," Suresh said, his voice flat and his face expressionless.

Well, flattery didn't seem to work. Maybe Rogers could bribe him.

Without warning, however, Suresh pressed a button on the keyboard and began shouting.

"Supply room, A-TEN-HOOOOAAH!"

Instantly, everyone in the room jumped to their feet and stood at strict attention, arms at their sides, feet together, their spines as rigid as engine support braces. Papers and personal effects tumbled to the floor. He felt his muscles stiffen in reaction to the command but realized that since he was still in civilian clothes, it didn't really matter. Rogers spun toward the supply room entrance, positive that the charismatic and powerful Admiral Klein, fleet commander of the 331st and the only military man Rogers had ever feared, had walked through the door. But nobody was there.

Moments of silence passed as all activity completely stopped. Rogers, the only unfrozen body in the room, looked around. Everyone's eyes were locked straight ahead, their limbs like stone. One young starman was clenching his fists so hard that they were trembling.

Finally, Rogers turned around and asked the supply clerk.

"Who are we standing at attention for?"

"You, *sir*!" Corporal Suresh shouted.

"Me?" Rogers said incredulously. "I'm only a sergeant. Wait, did you just call me 'sir'?"

"I did call you sir, sir!" Suresh said. His arms rigid at his sides, he pointed ridiculously toward the computer screen in front of him by moving only his index finger. "Your records list you as Ensign Roger W. Rogers, assigned to the 331st ATBG, and regulations say that when an officer enters the room, you are to call the room to attention."

"I told you I'm a sergeant. And it's R. *Wilson* Rogers." He heard someone behind him groan and hit the floor as he passed out. "Damn it, everyone relax! And tell that guy not to lock his knees."

The whole room let out a sigh of relief, and a pair of marines rushed to help their fallen comrade, who was looking very pale. Rogers turned back to Suresh.

"There has to be some mistake," he said.

"Perhaps you forgot your rank during the break in service, sir?" Suresh offered.

"Don't be an idiot. Can you look up the personnel records from here? What's my date of rank?"

Suresh whipped through the database. "It says effective today. Congratulations, sir! It was awarded in conjunction with the Anti-Pirating Combat Valor Medal. Very impressive, sir."

Rogers barely heard him. He felt blood rising to his cheeks. Tuckalle, that bastard. He knew that Rogers never wanted to be an officer. He knew that Rogers never wanted responsibility or accountability, people calling him "sir" and saluting him, people asking him to *fill out paperwork.*

"All of your supplies and uniforms have been delivered to your room, sir. You should find everything you need there already unpacked for you."

"Great," Rogers said dryly. "And where is that, exactly?"

"Room 101G in officer berthing area C, quarterdeck."

Rogers' fists clenched. That wasn't the engineering unit's berthing area. He had a bad feeling about this.

"Suresh," he said. "Does it, by any chance, say what unit I'm assigned to?"

Suresh glanced down, and his eyes widened. "Congratulations again, sir! It says here you've been assigned as Commander, Artificial Intelligence Ground Combat Squadron."

Droids. He was in charge of droids.

"That son of a bitch," Rogers said.

After making Suresh print out the paperwork required for him to ride the intraship transportation system, Rogers shoved it in the in-line guardwoman's face and went as fast as he could to the quarterdeck. He wasn't a huge fan of delaying the inevitable, and lying down on his bed sounded pretty good right now anyway. The sooner he got settled, the sooner he could start figuring out how to get out of this assignment and back to something easy like fixing engines and drinking beer.

A quick transfer from the in-line to the up-line to another in-line left him in the quiet, clean officer living area known as the quarterdeck. He'd used to joke it was because officers only had a quarter of a brain, but that didn't seem quite as funny now. Unlike the enlisted quarters, in which most troops under the rank of sergeant shared a room with one or two others, each officer had his or her own room. The hallways, instead of sporting the same drab, austere metal surface, were tastefully decorated with a combination of artificial wainscoting and various works of art depicting historical wartime spectacles.* It had that upper-class, old-world aristocratic feeling, like someone was about to emerge from a reading room in a smoking vest holding a pipe and challenge Rogers to cribbage.

It even smelled different, though that could have been a subtle contribution from the zoo deck, which was located directly below. Every command ship in the fleet had a zoo deck for morale purposes (and a biosphere to help generate oxygen, but that was generally regarded as secondary).

Rogers immediately didn't like it, though he was thankful that the artwork already on the walls prevented the display of any more of those strange motivational posters. He particularly didn't like the fact that after exiting the in-line, he saw no fewer than six shinies rolling down the hallway, one of which seemed to be carrying a disruptor rifle in a holster on its back. Rogers frowned; giving weapons to AI was a big no-no in the military. He'd learned that the hard way when he'd distributed bubble guns to a bunch of droids to see if he could stir up trouble. It was probably the only prank he ever regretted.

But now here they were, with real, no-kidding weapons. They were considered unstable, if useful, and they'd never been

---

*Not eyeglasses, though there *was* one portrait of General Nelson Rockshaft holding a stylish pair of lenses. He had become famous for removing said glasses while observing tactical displays, resulting in strategic maneuvers that were almost always unpredictable and almost certainly ineffective.

programmed for combat before. And Rogers was supposed to command them?

All thoughts vanished from his mind as he turned the last corner on the way to his quarters. Outside his door was a hulking monster of a woman. Gargantuan in stature, she must have stood well over six feet tall, with broad shoulders and hands that looked like they could crack open a coconut without a hammer. Her dark hair was cropped shorter than Rogers', and Rogers was almost certain he wouldn't have been able to fit in her boots without stuffing socks in them. She wore the uniform of a Meridan Marine and the rank of captain, two ranks higher than Rogers' new rank.

She was perfect.

Forcing himself to stop staring and start walking, Rogers put on his best smile. For some reason—divine blessing, he thought—she was standing right outside his door, clearly waiting for him. Had she heard about the dashing young ex-sergeant-turned-ensign that had come back to liven up the *Flagship*? Word always did travel fast on a giant hunk of metal on which most people had nothing to do but gossip.

"Well, hello there," he said, his smile widening. His palms were actually sweating. He'd barely been sweating when he'd thought he was going to *jail.* God, she was beautiful. "What can I—"

"Is this your room?" the giant vixen interrupted. Rogers looked at her nametag, and saw that it said Alsinbury on it. Captain Alsinbury. *R. Wilson Alsinbury.* Hmm . . .

"As a matter of fact," he said, "it is. Would you care to come inside for a—"

She hit him in the face so hard that for a moment, he thought that someone had opened the airlock and turned off the gravity generator, because he couldn't breathe and he was no longer touching any hard surfaces. He had a brief, fleeting sensation of landing on the ground before the not-so-brief and not-so-fleeting sensation of head trauma settled in and filled the world with a thousand gossiping old women with shrill voices and sledgehammers.

"That's what you get for trying to put robots in a human's job." Captain Alsinbury's voice somehow cut through the rushing river of pain flowing in between Rogers' ears.

"Mrrrh," Rogers began, but at the moment, forming words was about as easy as standing up after being hit in the face by a marine.

"Take your droids and stuff 'em. Nobody goes on the ground but me and my marines, and don't you forget it."

Rogers dimly registered the fading footsteps of the captain and looked up just in time to see her rumble away to another part of the ship. He thought about following her, trying to explain why she had misconstrued his intentions and shouldn't they drink themselves silly and talk about their future until they sorted all of this out, but his muscles didn't quite feel like functioning at the moment. He held the image of her walking away in his head as he pulled himself to lean against his door and tried to stop the ship from spinning.

In the haze of pain, delirium, and oxytocin, that image of her walking away quickly morphed into a vision of himself sitting trapped inside a burning building, totally helpless with a beam of wood crushing his leg. The heat of the intense flames lapped at him like a reckless tongue searching for a gulp of water. And then, suddenly, the captain was there, kicking down the door with those big boots.

"You came!" he said. "You came!"

She lifted the beam of wood off his injured leg as though picking a wayward twig from the fabric of her clothing and scooped him up into the secure bulk of her arms.

"Hold on to your hat," she said. "We're getting out of here."

Rogers didn't know if it was the heat of the flames, but he felt like melting.

"I knew it," he said. "I knew it . . ."

"If you knew it," came a voice from somewhere outside of this delicious fantasy, "why didn't you duck?"

The real world snapped into focus, only to start to spin again a few moments later. Rogers re-ate a SEWR rat and blinked tears from his eyes. In front of him crouched a female corporal who couldn't have left her early twenties behind her yet. A pair of crystalline blue eyes ringed with amusement looked at him with nothing at all approaching concern. Her name tag said Mailn, and her uniform showed her as a marine.

"I see you've met the captain," she said. "What did you do to piss her off?"

Rogers groaned, feeling some of his faculties returning to him. "They put me in charge of the ground combat droids."

"Oh, *you're* the new ensign she's been going on about," the corporal said. "She's been looking for a picture of you to throw darts at for half a week now. You picked the wrong position, buddy. Ah, sir."

The corporal stood up and saluted, and Rogers waved it away.

"Please don't do that," he said. "Rogers is fine." He held out a hand, forcing the corporal to bend down to shake it.

"Cynthia Mailn," she said. "marines. The Viking is my CO."

"Who?"

"Captain Alsinbury. The lady who just put that fist-shaped impression on your forehead."

The Viking. Perfect.

Grasping the corporal's hand after their handshake, Rogers accepted the steady help of the fit young woman. Once standing, he noticed that she was quite petite, an inch shorter than Rogers, who wasn't exactly a tall glass of water to begin with.

"I have to ask, corporal," he said, "what's with this ship?"

"What do you mean?"

"I mean I didn't leave the military that long ago. When I was in service, things were . . . different, that's all. Things were looser. Not as many droids. You know."

Mailn shrugged. "Lots of new faces around the Speedbumps in general, I guess," she said. "I've only been here a little over six months. They moved our whole unit here from another buffer unit after the talk of war with the Thelicosans started, and—"

"Wait," Rogers said, the blood draining from his face. "Did you say *war*?"

The corporal nodded. "That's what the rumor is. Things are tightening up around here. We can't spend all our time screwing around anymore. Uh, sir."

"Just Rogers. But what makes anyone think that the Two Hundred Years' (and Counting) Peace is going to fail? The treaties are airtight."

"They're as airtight as any treaty is," Mailn said with a shrug. Unlike Rogers, she didn't seem at all perturbed by the fact that the military actually might do some *fighting*. Did the 331st even know how to conduct a war? Rogers didn't think they'd be fit to conduct a small chamber orchestra.

He supposed that would explain some of the attitude change, but . . . it didn't seem right. And leave it to Rogers to rejoin the military right on the cusp of a Thelicosan invasion. Tuckalle's deal didn't seem so good anymore.

"I've got to get going," the corporal said. "I was only up in the quarterdeck because I needed to deliver something to the Viking's room. Next time you feel like being a punching bag, maybe I could take you down to the unarmed combat training room and throw you around a bit." She winked at him. "I could at least teach you how to duck."

Rogers touched the bruise on his forehead again and winced. "I appreciate that. Right now I think I need a couple of painkillers and a coma."

Mailn grinned at him and walked away, leaving Rogers to punch in the code that Suresh had given him into the keypad and enter his room.

An ensign's room was, apparently, not much better than a

sergeant's bunk. Though it was decorated with the same vintage tastes as the quarterdeck hallways, the room held only a bed, a wardrobe built into the wall, and a small desk with a network terminal and some other administrative paraphernalia arrayed neatly on its surface. His personal datapad was slung neatly into its charging holster on the side of the desk, and, instead of a window, there was a tacky porthole-shaped painting of a bland starscape hanging on the wall. In the background was a painted planet, which, strangely, looked like Jupiter from the old Milky Way. Considering that Jupiter had become the only planet that didn't get their own system when humanity migrated to Fortuna Stultus, it seemed a strange choice for art.

The first thing he did, however, was take down the poster on the wall that said REGULATIONS: THE KEY TO SUCCESS above which was portrayed a maniacal parade commander lording over a group of soldiers standing in formation. As he took it down, however, he noticed something peculiar. The nametags on the soldiers in formation were all legible, and one of the soldiers apparently was named "Droids."

In fact, reading the soldiers in formation from left to right gave the strange imperative: "Love Your Droids." Maybe the poster creator had a sense of humor, after all. Rogers might like to have a drink with him.

Shoving the poster under his bed, Rogers began to open drawers and cabinets to see what he'd been furnished with. It was all plain. Uniforms, emergency SEWR rats, a med kit and, strangely, two toothbrushes. One of them was so coarse he was sure it would cut his gums to ribbons, but he noticed after a moment that it wasn't a toothbrush at all. Engraved into the handle were the words SPECK CLEANER 2000. TAKE YOUR SPECKS STRAIGHT TO HECK!

"Oh, hell no," he said, and tossed the toothbrush under the bed with the poster.

Boring. He felt like he wanted to lie down in the middle of

his room and die. This wasn't part of the bargain at all. And it still felt wrong. There was something missing in the room that he couldn't quite place. Obviously, all the modifications he'd made to his sergeants' quarters for hiding alcohol, weighted dice, and other contraband were missing, but he'd remedy that soon enough. There was something else.

Then he noticed the time on the small clock on his desk. It was 12:41 PM ship time. The beer light should have been on for forty-one minutes.

Rogers spun around, panicked. It wasn't here. *It wasn't here.* The beer light was *gone.*

Just as he was about to have a breakdown and start throwing furniture, a knock came at his door.

"Open up," came a voice. "It's time for your inspection!"

# White Gloves

It was a testament to his mental state (or the recent powerful blow to the head) that it took several seconds for Rogers to realize he was trying to climb into a painting and not out a window into open space. The picture fell to the floor, the extinct Jupiter landing facedown.

"Well, that'll be a demerit," a voice came from behind him.

Turning around, fists balled, Rogers found not one but two members of the Standardization and Evaluation squadron aboard the *Flagship.* One of them, of course, was a droid. Carrying a clipboard. Wearing white gloves.

The other was a lean, full-cheeked sergeant with a uniform tailored so tightly around his body that it looked more like an elaborate tattoo than clothing. Aircraft could have landed on the airstrip of hair that was on the top of his head, closely buzzed on either side. His buttons and medals had been blindingly polished to the point where they could have been used as independent sources of illumination. In short, he looked like a major tool.

"What's this all about?" Rogers asked.

"CALL FUNCTION [TIRELESSLY REPEAT SIMPLE INSTRUCTIONS]. TARGET [ENSIGN ROGERS]" the droid said, "OUTPUT STRING: YOU HAVE BEEN SELECTED FOR A MORALE, HEALTH, AND WELFARE INSPECTION. ALL PERSONNEL ARE SUBJECT TO MHW INSPECTIONS TO BE CONDUCTED BY STANDARDIZATION AND EVALUATION—"

"Yeah, great," Rogers said. "Whatever. But I just got here."

"Then you shouldn't have anything to worry about," the sergeant said.

"Look, sergeant, uh . . . " Rogers peered at his name tag. "Sergeant Stract. Really?"

"I was born to be Stan/Eval," the sergeant said with the utmost seriousness.

"Right," Rogers said. "And I was born to acknowledge radio transmissions. I've been in the service a long time. Inspections don't really happen in this fleet."

"CALL FUNCTION [REPETITION AND ASSURANCE]," the droid said—boy, this one was a talker—"OUTPUT STRING: INSPECTIONS HAPPEN ACCORDING TO A REGULAR AND REGIMENTED SCHEDULE TO WHICH ALL PERSONNEL MUST ADHERE."

Rogers looked at Sergeant Stract. "Do you always let droids do your talking for you?"

The sergeant frowned. "Insults aren't going to help you much, sir. Now, if you'll please stand at attention in the center of your room, we can conduct the inspection."

"Yeah, I'm not really into standing at attention, either," Rogers said. "Look, I'll just sign the bottom of your sheet, and you can mark everything as acceptable, and we can both get on with our day."

"CALL FUNCTION [PERFORM PRIMARY DUTY]. OUTPUT STRING: REFUSAL TO ABIDE BY MILITARY PROTOCOL," the droid said. "ONE DEMERIT WILL BE AWARDED."

Back in Rogers' day, a "demerit" was a penalty in a drinking game that necessitated a shot of alcohol. Somehow, he didn't think that's what the droid was talking about.

"CALL FUNCTION [ISSUE ORDER]. TARGET [SERGEANT STRACT]," the droid said. "ASSUME CONTROL OF THE RECORDS."

"Wait," Rogers said. "The droid is *leading* the inspection?"

The sergeant snapped to attention and grabbed the clipboard like a rifle with a resounding *crack*.

"I have assumed control of the records, sir!"

"Did you just call that droid *sir*?"

The sergeant glared at Rogers. "As you don't seem to be familiar with military protocol, *sir*, I will explain that it is customary for us to address those who outrank us by sir or ma'am."

Rogers stared, dumbstruck, at Sergeant Stract as the droid began walking around the room, its metallic legs clanking against the pseudo-wood floor of the officer stateroom. Stract followed the machine in lockstep, duck-walking in the ridiculous fashion that someone, somewhere along the line had decided looked "official." Had Stract been wearing a black-and-white outfit, Rogers would have confused him with a penguin.

"No," Rogers said. "No, absolutely not. There's no way this droid has a rank."

"CALL FUNCTION [DECLARE IDENTITY]. OUTPUT STRING: I AM CYBERMAN FIRST CLASS A-155. CALL FUNCTION [SMUGLY CITE REGULATION]. IN ACCORDANCE WITH THE MERIDAN RANK AND ORGANIZATION REGULATION MR-613, I AM SUPERIOR TO ALL ENLISTED PERSONNEL RANKED E-5 AND BELOW. SERGEANT STRACT'S RANK OF SERGEANT IS E-5 IN THE MERIDAN GALACTIC NAVY."

"Absolutely, sir," the sergeant said, nodding. "An excellent reference to the regulations."

"Do the regulations say you're supposed to kiss his ass, too?" Rogers asked. "How do you even know it's a sir and not a ma'am? Does it have an extra pair of turbines between its legs?"

Sergeant Stract didn't seem to find that amusing, though he

declined to comment. The droid wiped a gloved hand over the edge of Rogers' bed frame and brought it up to its face.

"CALL FUNCTION [PERFORM PRIMARY DUTY]. DUST PRESENT ON BED. ONE DEMERIT WILL BE AWARDED."

"What?" Rogers blurted. "I just got here! How was I supposed to dust everything?" He shook his head, as if to rattle the absurdity out of it. "Why should I even bother dusting at all? The Meridan Fleet doesn't *dust*!"

"CALL FUNCTION [PERFORM PRIMARY DUTY]. WARDROBE NOT ARRAYED IN PROPER ORDER. ONE DEMERIT WILL BE AWARDED."

"I didn't even put that stuff in there! Give a demerit to Suresh in Supply!"

"CALL FUNCTION [PERFORM PRIMARY DUTY]. DESK CHAIR WHEELS IMPROPERLY ROTATED. ONE DEMERIT WILL BE AWARDED."

"What does that even mean?"

Sergeant Stract was scratching away on the archaic note-taking device with a pencil and following the droid as it made its rounds.

"This is stupid," Rogers said. "This is really, really stupid."

The droid came to the spot on the wall where the propaganda poster had been and paused, its long, horse-like head scanning over the empty spot.

"CALL FUNCTION [PERFORM PRIMARY DUTY]. OUTPUT STRING: INSUFFICIENT MORALE. ONE DEMERIT WILL BE AWARDED."

Sergeant Stract made a mark on the clipboard, and Rogers was about to break it over his head. All of the events of the past week were building up inside of him to the point of overflow; he found himself fantasizing about visiting tremendous violence on inanimate objects and various people he'd met since he'd come aboard the *Flagship*. It pushed him to the brink. It made him want to chew off the droid's arm.

Then he broke and did something that no self-respecting military man ever did. He pulled rank.

"Sergeant Stract," Rogers said, "as your superior officer, I *order* you to put that damn thing away and get the hell out of my room."

Both the droid and the sergeant froze where they stood. Rogers grinned. He had them!

"But," the sergeant said.

"No buts," Rogers said, moving to stand in front of Sergeant Stract. "Get out. Right now. And never come back."

Sergeant Stract's left leg twitched, as if to move. Rogers took a deep breath to bark the order a second time.

"CALL FUNCTION [SMUGLY CITE REGULATION]. AUGMENTED FUNCTION [FRUSTRATE SUPERIOR OFFICER]. OUTPUT STRING: MERIDAN STANDARDIZATION AND EVALUATION REGULATION MR-415 STATES THAT ALL PERSONNEL ARE SUBJECT TO INSPECTION AND MUST COMPLY WITH THE INSTRUCTIONS OF THE INSPECTION STAFF IN ORDER TO MAINTAIN GOOD ORDER AND DISCIPLINE IN A MILITARY FASHION. YOU HAVE ISSUED AN ILLEGAL ORDER."

Sergeant Stract stood taller behind the protective shield of his regulation-spouting "superior," and the droid turned around to face Rogers.

"CALL FUNCTION [PERFORM PRIMARY DUTY]. OUTPUT STRING: IMPROPER FACIAL HAIR GROOMING. ONE DEMERIT WILL BE AWARDED. AUGMENTED FUNCTION [VEILED INCONVENIENCE] AN APPOINTMENT WITH CYBERMAN SECOND CLASS BAR-BR 116 HAS BEEN SCHEDULED FOR TOMORROW AT 0830."

"Go galvanize yourself," Rogers said. "It'll be a cold day in hell before anyone touches my beard."

"CALL FUNCTION [REQUEST CLARIFICATION]. THE IMPROBABLE AMBIENT TEMPERATURE OF A FICTIONAL AFTERLIFE LOCATION DOES NOT MITIGATE YOUR VIOLATION OF REGULATIONS."

"Get out of my room!" Rogers shouted, pointing at the door. "I'm not going to stand here and be lectured on military protocol by a *god-damned shiny!*"

The word rebounded off the walls through an instantaneous, tense silence. Sergeant Stract dropped the clipboard and gasped. The droids "eyes," two hollow sockets that glowed a soft blue, flashed red for a moment. For some reason, that sent a chill down Rogers' spine.

"Reject function [protocol 162]. Call function [perform primary duty]. Racial slur," the droid intoned. "Five demerits will be awarded." He then turned to Sergeant Stract. "Target change [Sergeant Stract]. Loss of military bearing in the heat of combat. One demerit will be awarded. Call function [issue order]. Please retrieve the note-taking device."

Sergeant Stract looked more mortified at receiving a demerit than at Rogers' comment about shinies. He hurriedly stooped down and picked up the clipboard, returning to attention with a loud clicking of his boots. That didn't prevent him from glaring at Rogers.

"Call function [conclude primary duty]. Inspection complete," the droid said. "A report will be filed in your personnel record, which you can access by filing a request with the personnel squadron after a mandatory five-day waiting period. All infractions must be rectified within one standard day."

"How am I supposed to know what to fix?" Rogers asked flatly, despite having no intention of fixing anything at all.

"Call function [tirelessly repeat simple instructions]. A report will be filed in your personnel record, which you can access by filing a request with the personnel squadron after a mandatory five-day waiting period."

Rogers closed his eyes and took a deep breath. "Get out."

"Call function [dismiss]. Target [Sergeant Stract]. Output string: this inspection is concluded. You are dismissed."

"Yes, sir!" The sergeant actually saluted, and the droid exited, though the sergeant didn't follow immediately. He stood, fuming, fists tight. "I hope you're happy. That's the first demerit I've ever received."

"I hope you lose sleep over it" Rogers growled. "Now get out of my room before I order you to smudge your boots."

Sergeant Stract's eyes went wide, and he scampered out of the room so quickly that the automatic door clipped his shoulder on the way out, knocking his uniform into an infinitesimal state of disarray.

"No!" the sergeant shouted as the door began to close. "Nooooo!"

Just before the panels shut, the Viking passed by the room, her body filling up the entire frame of the door for a brief moment. She cast a disparaging glance into the room, and Rogers held out a feeble hand toward her.

"Wait," he called, but the door shut. He continued weakly, "Marry me."

Alone and filled to the brim with anger and despair, Rogers tore off his clothes and climbed into bed. He fell headfirst into a dream of being trapped in a burning building, but just as the Viking was about to rescue him and carry him off to utopia, she morphed into a red-eyed droid who awarded him a demerit for burning debris on his uniform.

"Ensign Rogers," the computerized—and thankfully mostly intelligible—voice of his personal terminal called to him. "You have an appointment on the commissary deck in fifteen minutes. Ensign Rogers, you have an appointment on the commissary deck in fifteen minutes."

Looking at the clock, Rogers had discovered that he'd slept for almost an entire day, which didn't surprise him, considering all he'd gone through. It was 0815 ship time; the inspection droid must have scheduled the haircut appointment by tapping directly into the data streams.

"Ignore it," he told the computer. "What's next?"

"Artificial Intelligence Combat Unit, 1000 hours ship time. Training deck, room 654."

"Great."

Muscle memory kicked in again as Rogers went through his room, showered, and dressed. It was an exercise he'd repeated every day for ten years, though he wasn't used to doing it so early in the morning. Normally, he reported to the engineering bay at around 1100, after which everyone would sort of sit around and stare at the beer light until it turned on at around noon. Now that there was no beer light, however, he had no idea what the hell he'd do for the rest of the day.

Since he was blowing off his haircut, he had plenty of time to head to one of the ship's mess halls and get some breakfast. A quick exchange of up-line and in-line left him on the commissary deck, where troops could spend their hard-earned credits, go bowling, or participate in one of many other forms of recreation and capitalism.

Somehow, before he even got to the commissary deck, he knew it would be deserted. The harrowing fact that there was no longer a beer light—at least not in officers' quarters—still haunted him like the knowledge that a loved one was dead, never to be seen again. Rogers fondly remembered the glow of the beer light waking him up late in the afternoon on days when the previous night had been particularly good.

Rogers' intuition was right. The commissary deck, normally the center of all activity on the *Flagship*, now consisted of troops walking from the up-line to the mess halls and back again, like some sort of twisted soldier feeding lot. There was no joy in their faces, only the crushing weight of daily routine and the doldrums of a regimented lifestyle. That and, bizarrely, something that Rogers may have confused with devotion to duty.

The mess halls were scattered all over the commissary deck to break up the massive crew of the *Flagship.* It didn't work; everyone usually figured out which were the good ones pretty quickly and went there instead. They had each been unofficially named after combat maneuvers, which served a dual purpose of being easier to remember than "Mess Hall A" and making all of the eateries sound like bizarre old-world taverns. Rogers' favorite was the Uncouth Corkscrew, mostly because he liked ambiguous double entendres, but if the lines were too long, he'd settle for the Peek and Shoot or the Up and Over. Under no circumstances would he ever eat at the Kamikaze or the Frantically Run Away.

The Uncouth Corkscrew was calm so early in the morning, despite the fact that it was occupied by marines and spacers gathered in loose clusters around the dining hall. The long tables and benches, instead of being packed with people trying to talk over each other, were populated more like an electron cloud. Any conversation happening appeared to be just coincidences and courtesies.

And, most shocking of all, almost no one was in the kitchen getting food. Everyone was stopping by the SEWR rat dispenser, grabbing a package or two, and moving to a table to sit down and eat silently. The few times that Rogers had been up for breakfast in the past, he had been treated to eggs Benedict, steak and eggs, and, on one special but rather bizarre occasion, Cornish game hen stuffed with chocolate-covered strawberries.* Nobody would pass that sort of fare up for protein cardboard.

Despite the ominous emptiness of the kitchen, Rogers ventured inside, ordered some eggs and bacon from a very surprised services troop, and found himself a table with a few marines at it.

The moment he sat down, he heard that damn non-word again.

"A-TEN-HOOOAH!"

---

*Don't knock it till you try it.

The entire table jumped up and stood at attention. One of the marines "presented arms" using a fork. To his credit, it looked very snappy.

"Stop that," Rogers said. "Sit down. Um, carry on. Eat food, *march*!"

He kept forgetting that he was an officer now. Not only was he not allowed to accomplish anything productive, it was his destiny to continually stop anyone else from doing anything productive simply by walking into rooms or sitting at tables.

The marines exchanged confused, wary glances as they lowered themselves slowly back to the bench, each of them making sure that Rogers' ass touched the surface before theirs did. It felt strange, engaging in a sort of backward ass-race of who could sit down the slowest.

Not feeling very much like conversation, Rogers dug into some very suspicious-looking eggs for about three seconds before his gag reflex kicked in. Before he could get the second forkful to his mouth, Rogers froze where he sat and stared, aghast, at the monstrosity that was breakfast. Spitting out what hadn't already slid down his throat, he pointed at the dish and spoke a little too loud.

"This tastes like motor oil!"

One of the marines choked, though whether it was because of Rogers' comment or because he was eating the aforementioned protein cardboard without drinking enough water, Rogers wasn't sure.

Peeling back the egg on his plate, Rogers saw with horror that a small gray-black pool of drippings lay hidden below the egg, blending in with the natural grease of the bacon in a way that reminded him of the time when, well, he'd accidentally dropped a piece of bacon into a pool of motor oil in the engineering bay.

"It *is* motor oil!" Rogers said, standing up in shock.

"A-TEN-HOOOOAAH!"

*"Sit down!"*

Rogers grabbed his plate and stormed back into the kitchen, suddenly realizing why everyone was reaching for SEWR rats instead of bacon in a 5W-40 reduction sauce.

"What is this?" he barked as he crossed the threshold into the empty serving area. The single server who was visible jumped, likely more surprised to see someone than at Rogers' question. Through the small windows on the double doors leading back into the larger food preparation area, Rogers saw heads popping up like curious squirrels.

"Is there a problem, sir?" the service troop asked.

"You're damn right there's a problem. I know this ship is infested with droids, but the last time I checked, humans don't operate on chemical lubricants." He slammed the plate on the counter. "Who made this? No, forget that. Who's in charge here?"

"Hart!" the server called. "I think this ensign wants to talk to you."

The kitchen door swung open, and a master sergeant in a military chef uniform sauntered out of the double doors, his apron stained with a telltale black grease that certainly hadn't come from hamburgers.

"What's all this about?" he growled.

Rogers gaped. "Hart? What in the world are you doing in the kitchens?"

Master Sergeant Hart—formerly just Sergeant Hart the last time Rogers had seen him—was the first familiar face Rogers had seen during his new tenure on the *Flagship.* That was a good thing. The bad thing was that the last time he'd seen him, he'd been in the engineering bay. Where he belonged. Since he was an engineer.

"You're a sight for sore eyes," Hart said.

"I'm a little concerned about my sore stomach," Rogers said. "What are you doing in the kitchens?"

"Cross-trained," Hart said. "Not my choice."

Rogers shook his head. "They transferred you to the kitchen?"

Hart nodded. "Me and a couple of the other boys and girls

that didn't either leave the fleet or get reassigned to other squadrons on the other side of the system. I think I'm getting used to it, though. I make some pretty good stuff."

"There's motor oil in my eggs," Rogers said.

"Everyone's a critic. Why don't you just eat Sewer rats like everyone else?"

Rogers couldn't believe his ears. Aside from the nonsensical personnel movement, Hart had been one of his best mates, prankster partner, and the only man in the entire fleet who could drink Rogers under the table. He'd also been Rogers' supervisor before Rogers had been promoted to sergeant himself, and Hart had survived that ordeal. Rogers thought nothing could break that man. Now he looked . . . he looked . . . *sober.*

"Didn't you fight them when they reassigned you?" Rogers asked. "You belong elbow-deep in engine components, not spaghetti. And certainly not elbow-deep in spaghetti right *after* you've been elbow-deep in engine components."

"So sue me. I still like to tinker with engines when I can, and sometimes I don't have time to wash my hands afterward. I can't get down there very often, anyway. That idiot McSchmidt in engineering doesn't let anyone else in the bay when he's around. Besides, they told me cooking food is just like being a grease monkey. You put stuff together until it works."

"This doesn't work," Rogers said, pointing to his plate, which had taken on the viscosity of really disgusting pudding as it cooled.

Hart shrugged, then sighed. "I'm not too far from retirement, Rogers. I'm not up for fighting with the brass over trading a wrench for a spatula. At least I still get to set stuff on fire every once in a while. Look, do yourself a favor. Grab a Sewer rat and get the nutrition your body needs. You'll need it if we go up against the Thelicosans."

"Oh, not you, too," Rogers said. "There's no way there's a war coming. It doesn't make any sense. Now you're just stuck here wasting your time."

Hart's face hardened. "Every position is critical to the war effort."

That made Rogers' stomach turn. Or it could have been the motor oil doing its job inside his small intestine. He wasn't sure.

"Listen," Rogers said, "I don't know what's going on here. I don't know if I really care. I want to do my time and get out of here. But if you feel like doing something you're actually good at, I might have a project for you. I have a junked ship in the docking bay registered as the *Awesome.*" Hart rolled his eyes, but Rogers pushed on. "It needs a lot of work, thanks to a plasma blast. If you and the crew are looking for something to do, I'll make sure you're authorized to access it. Just promise me you won't cook me any more meals, alright?"

Hart looked skeptical, but his eyes brightened once he realized Rogers was offering him a reintroduction to his old specialty. You could take an engineer out of the bay, but you couldn't take the bay out of the engineer, or something like that. Even Rogers still liked to take things apart and put them back together every once in a while, when he wasn't trying to swindle pirates.

"I'll think about it."

"That's all I'm asking."

Reaching under the counter, Hart produced a yellowish-brown vacuum-sealed Sewer rat and handed it over.

"Take care of yourself, Rogers. The 331st has changed."

"No shit."

Rogers reluctantly took the proffered package of synthesized horse dung, warned Hart that if he called the kitchen to attention, he'd force Hart to eat his own cooking, and went back into the mess hall feeling like he'd been hit in the face. Metaphorically, this time. Dining in the military was like dining at one of the best restaurants in the galaxy. Diplomats used to make excuses to do VIP visits just to sample the impressive and decadent desserts. This was a travesty, a sham. It was worse than a sham. It was . . . military.

"Hey, speed bag!" someone called to him. "Over here!"

Looking up and wiping his face—he was *not* crying—Rogers saw the source of the voice. Corporal Mailn was sitting with a couple of other infantry arines at a table just outside the entrance to the kitchen. Every one of them had a SEWR rat package torn open in front of them, and exactly none of them looked like they were enjoying it. None of them seemed particularly happy that an officer was coming to sit with them, either.

"Keep your seats," Rogers said. He looked at Mailn, who was grinning at him. "And don't call me speed bag."

"Don't get hit in the face," she said. "Speaking of which, it kind of looks like a bunch of little girls just shook you down for lunch money. What's on your mind?"

Rogers sat down, grimacing. "Just missing the old days, I guess."

"Old days?" Mailn chuckled. "What are you, sixty?"

"Just forget it." Rogers opened the SEWR rat and started unpacking the contents, grabbing a glass of water that one of the other marines had courteously poured for him from the pitcher in the center of the table. "Bon appétit," he said, and hoped he didn't chip a tooth.

He valued the silence the marines offered him as he choked his way through the disgusting meal. It was almost instantly interrupted, however, by a fast-approaching and massively distracting symphony of metallic noises coming in from the hallway.

"What's that?" Rogers asked. "The scrap-pile drum corps?"

"Shin . . . Droids," Mailn said, making no attempt to hide the venom in her voice, though Rogers couldn't help but note the near-use of his favorite term.

Turning, Rogers witnessed a small platoon of droids, all marching in formation, as they came into the dining facility. They moved—thankfully—to the far corner of the room, where a special table had been outfitted for their peculiar bodies. There were no chairs, of course, but droids also, as far as Rogers knew, didn't need to eat, so their arrival seemed a little silly in the first place. Instead of ordering food, however, which would have really been absurd, they each extended a cable from their torsos and plugged into the power system.

"Is that really necessary?" Rogers asked.

"Gotta eat too, I guess," Mailn muttered. "Wish they wouldn't do it here, though."

A dim part of Rogers' subconscious thought briefly what it would be like to involve the droids in one of his famous food fights, which used to be a highlight of just about every meal in the Uncouth Corkscrew. The thought of hydraulic arms firing baked potatoes at him at half the speed of light, however, buried the idea quickly. Droids were no fun at all.

"Well, I think that's killed my appetite," Rogers said. He almost pushed himself to his feet but stopped when he thought of the consequences of standing up surrounded on all sides by seated enlisted troops.

Was this the fate of every Meridan officer? Scared to enter rooms, scared to stand up at tables, one shoulder much larger than the other from saluting so much? He imagined himself walking down the hallway, the knuckles of his right hand dragging against the floor, and the bitterness inside almost dove headfirst into full-on depression.

"Everyone listen to me. I have an appointment on the training deck, and I'm about to stand up," Rogers said slowly, looking around the table. "I want you all to act like absolutely nothing has happened and continue eating your meals. Do you understand?"

"Yes, sir!" shouted nine marines at the top of their lungs. Only Mailn was grinning.

Rogers sighed and sagged his shoulders. "Someone shoot me now."

One of the marines reached for her pistol.

"That's not an order!" Rogers yelped, and jumped out of his seat.

"Come on, speed bag," Mailn said, getting up and stretching. "I've got business down there. I'll walk with you."

"My name is Rogers."

"I could call you 'sir,'" Mailn said slowly.

"Oh, shut up. Let's just get out of here before I have to eat anything else."

The trip to the training deck, an entirely separate level of the Flagship, was just a quick ride on the up-line away, and as they stepped into the car, Rogers noticed that the same "guardwoman" who had blocked his first attempt at riding the in-line was standing watch. She tugged her conductor's hat down further over her eyes, which was unfortunate, because Rogers really wanted her to see him sticking his tongue out at her as they boarded an empty car.

"So, what's your story?" Mailn asked as she stretched out languidly across a row of empty seats. "You don't look fresh enough to be a new ensign out of the Academy."

Rogers chuckled a little as he sat down. "It'd take me longer than an up-line ride to explain it." And he wasn't really into self-incriminating. "Let's just say I had a break in service followed by an unexpected commission. What about you?"

Mailn shrugged. "Eh, you know. Grew up in one of the big cities on Merida Prime, got involved in a few things that maybe weren't good ideas at the time, wanted to start over." She looked vaguely embarrassed but hid it with her cocksure grin. "Now I'm a marine, doing some things that maybe aren't good ideas. But at least I get to shoot stuff."

Rogers looked at her. "I guess that's a benefit. I've never been much of a shoot-'em-up guy myself."

Mailn raised an eyebrow. "I never would have guessed."

They traveled in silence for a few moments, the interior of the *Flagship* zipping by outside the narrow windows of the car.

"It's kind of nice traveling so early," Rogers said, stretching out. "Everyone's still asleep, so there's nobody to crowd the cars."

Mailn shot him a sideways glance. "Asleep? Everyone's already at work. That's why nobody is in the car."

Rogers shook his head in disbelief. This wasn't the 331st at all.

"This is unbelievable," Rogers said as the up-line came to a stop and let them off on the training deck.

"It's not so bad once you get used to it," Mailn said as they exited the up-line onto the training deck.

"Seems pretty bad to me," Rogers said. "Since I got back, I haven't played a single card game, had a single drink, or slid down any soaped-up hallways on my bare belly."

"It's the trouble with the Thelicosans," Mailn said. "Everyone's on edge."

They walked past a group of dour-faced finance troops, all of whom, for some reason, were wearing old-fashioned karate uniforms and sweating profusely. One of them threw a clipboard into the air and broke it with a devastating spinning back kick.

"This isn't *on edge*," Rogers said as he brushed a splinter off his uniform. "This is weird. And boring. Why would they transfer an engineer into the kitchens?"

"There have been a lot of transfers lately," Mailn said. "A month ago, they wanted to cross-train me as a pilot."

"What's wrong with that?"

"I'm colorblind and I get airsick. Thankfully, Captain Alsinbury got me out of it. She can be very persuasive."

A flash of heat worked its way through Rogers' body as he thought of what could constitute "persuasive." He knew there had to be some way to break the ice with her, but not before he got himself a good, solid helmet.

"What about Admiral Klein?" Rogers asked. "Doesn't he know about any of this? This is his fleet."

Mailn shrugged. "I hear most of the transfers are happening up at his level, so he must know about it. I know he's under a lot of stress, though, so maybe he's making mistakes."

"How do you know that?"

"Well," Mailn said. "his executive assistants keep hanging themselves. He's gone through two of them since I've been aboard, and just got a new one the other day. You can always tell how much pressure a commander is under by how bad his execs look."

Rogers whistled. He could remember some of the speeches that Klein gave to the troops while he'd been in the fleet. They were some of the most masterful uses of words he'd ever heard in his life—even Rogers couldn't help but feel a sense of duty when Admiral Klein spoke, and that said something. Whatever the fleet needed—funding for beer, transportation assets for beer, or new pumping systems to make sure the beer always tasted fresh—the fleet got because the admiral was fighting for them. Although, come to think of it, he did seem to go through execs pretty quickly, even during Rogers' last tenure on the ship. They hadn't been *hanging* themselves, though.

"With Klein in command," Mailn continued, a look of admiration on her face, "the Thelicosans will think twice about attacking."

Rogers grunted. He didn't want to talk about Thelicosa or their supposed belligerence. He still didn't think it was possible for any system to violate the Two Hundred Years' (and Counting) Peace.

As they walked, Rogers couldn't help but notice yet another poster on the wall. He'd been trying to ignore them, but some of them were just too ridiculous. The loud text on the bottom read, FILL OUT FORMS PROPERLY. Above it was a capsizing frigate, flames shooting out from the many breaches in its hull, and frozen space-corpses floating around it with dark, horrified expressions on their faces. Pieces of paper, ostensibly incorrectly filled-out forms, were depicted slamming into the side of the ship like plasma cannons.

"Who writes this crap?" Rogers said.

"I have no idea," Mailn said. "But they keep popping up everywhere. There's one in the Peek and Shoot that says 'When you slurp soup the enemy wins.'"

They rounded the corner, and there she was: the Viking, in all of her splendor. Baggy uniform, short hair rimming her round face, monstrous gait carrying her toward them at a tremendous speed even though she was walking casually.

Rogers ducked reflexively.

"Way too early," muttered Mailn.

"What are you doing associating with this turd?" Alsinbury said as she approached.

Mailn snapped a hasty salute, which the captain returned, and Rogers slowly uncurled from his defensive position to offer one as well. She did outrank him, after all. That was exciting, too.

"I'm escorting him to the droid training room, ma'am," Mailn said. "He's never been there before."

The Viking spared him a distasteful glance. "I don't want to see you associating with my troops, metalhead." Rogers was accumulating a lot of strange nicknames on this ship. "I don't want any of them tainted by your droid-loving ways. We're the ground force around here, and don't you forget it."

"I won't," Rogers said, his heart beating hard. Was there music playing somewhere? "But I'd love to talk to you about it sometime. Maybe I could pick your brain about, ah, fighting . . . things . . . over some drinks?"

"I don't feel like vomiting right now, thanks." She turned to Mailn. "Corporal, I need you to run Bravo Company through their rifle-stripping again. One of those clowns tried to lick one of the plasma converters clean and burned the hell out of his tongue."

Mailn sighed. "You got it, boss. I'll head over there now."

The Viking nodded, gave Rogers another glare, and pushed past them, elbowing Rogers in the side as she went. His breath left him for more than one reason.

"Boy, you're really on her bad side," Mailn said after the Viking was out of earshot.

"Thanks for noticing," Rogers said as they continued walking. "What's wrong with Bravo Company?"

Mailn gave a bitter chuckle. "You ever wonder where all those cooks ended up?"

"They transferred them to *ground combat*?"

"Yup. Said we needed more firepower. But all I've gotten so far is a bunch of fat, sweaty troops that don't know the first thing about shooting anything and won't take off their damn chef hats." She paused, considering. "And some pretty good chili dogs."

Rogers shook his head. Motor oil in his eggs was one thing. Pancake batter in rifles was another. Someone in personnel needed to have his head examined, though Mailn had suggested that the orders were coming from higher up. Was Klein really losing it? He was about the only man in the entire fleet that Rogers had confidence in.

"I'd better get a move on," Mailn said. "I don't want to know what I'm going to find when I get to Bravo's training room. The droid training facility is this door right here. Good luck, speed bag. You're going to need it."

The corporal broke into a jog before Rogers could say anything else, and he found himself staring at the door that she had indicated, not wanting to go inside. His hand hovered over the button to open it, but he couldn't make himself press it. He hated shinies, hated what they were doing, hated these damn posters on the walls. But was there any way out of it?

Maybe if he did a supremely awful job, they'd have to transfer him. They were transferring everyone, weren't they? A couple of accidents, hopefully ones that didn't involve Rogers getting smashed by a droid, and they'd put him somewhere else. Finance, maybe. As long as they didn't make him an executive assistant, anything had to be better than commander of the droid ground combat unit.

That was it. He'd just be bad at his job. It would be easy, since Rogers had no idea how to do it properly in the first place.

Rogers grinned. He felt a little bit like his old self again. No duty was too great that R. Wilson Rogers couldn't find a way to shirk it.

His glee collapsed when he hit the button and the door opened, revealing a platoon of droids looking straight at him. The only other human in the room yelled at the top of his lungs.

"A-TEN-HOOOOOAH!"

# Big Orange Button

In front of him, neatly arrayed in a perfect formation, was large collection of droids, all looking like they'd just come fresh off the manufacturing belt. Their exoskeletons were clean, shimmering, and of a darker shade than the other droids, though Rogers couldn't quite put a name to the color. Their heads, horse-like if any comparison to any animal could be made, each bore a pair of glimmering blue eyes, all of which seemed to be fixed on Rogers. In total, he counted five by seven rows, making thirty-five shinies under his command. It was thirty-five too many.

"Um, at ease?" Rogers said uncertainly. "Are you all capable of being at ease? Would you melt?"

Nothing happened. The eerie metallic soldiers appeared no more at ease than a group of construction beams that had just been told an awful joke. Rogers wasn't even sure they had noticed him; they stood so perfectly still that he wondered if they were even turned on.

He turned to the only other human in a room, a corporal who, thankfully, responded to his command to be at ease. He was old for a corporal, which didn't bode very well for his competence, but his uniform looked neatly pressed with the exception of a small white stain on his left boot. It surprised Rogers, not because the stain was there but because Rogers normally would have never noticed it. This officer thing was already starting to get to him; soon he'd be measuring his underwear to make sure they were folded four inches across. Or at least ordering an enlisted member to measure it.

"Well, then," Rogers said by way of expressing his complete lack of ideas about what to do.

"Aie present to yur dee Artificial Intelligence Ground Combat Squrdrun," said the corporal, his flat face and very out-of-style mustache turning up into a proud grin.

"Ah, what?"

The corporal, surprisingly, looked as though Rogers' confusion pleased him. "Aie saids, Aie present to yur dee Artificial Intelligence Ground Combat Squrdrun!"

Great. They'd transferred someone from the Public Transportation Announcer Corps to be his second in command. A PTAC was all he needed.

Rogers sighed. "What's wrong with your voice, corporal?"

The corporal looked indignant. "There's nothing wrong with my voice, sir," he said, his speech surprisingly intelligible all of a sudden.

"So, why are you talking like you've stolen all the marshmallows and had nowhere else to hide them?"

"It's my Thelicosan accent, sir. I'm training to be a spy. Can't be a spy if you don't sound like the Thellies, can you? I practice all day." He cleared his throat. "Aie means, aie practice allur dee days!"

Rogers shook his head. "What's your name?"

The corporal's speech degenerated into something that Rogers was nearly positive had no vowels in it.

"What?"

"Corporal Albert Tunger, sir! You see how good I've gotten? I can barely understand myself sometimes."

"I'm sure you're the envy of the intelligence squadron," Rogers said. "I'm assuming you're my second-in-command here?"

"Ah, nur," the curpural—corporal—said. "Aie am yur urderly."

"My what?"

"Your orderly. I'm here to tackle the administrative tasks that officers are generally too busy or too lazy to do."

"Right," Rogers said. "Well, the first thing I want you to do as my orderly is ditch that accent. I can't work with someone that sounds like he's always puckering up for a kiss." Not that he wanted to do any actual work. He really just didn't want to listen to Tunger talk.

"But," Tunger whined, his face sagging, "I'm training to be a spy! How am I going to be a spy if I sound like your everyday Meridan man? They'll shoot me the first time I open my mouth!"

"I'm considering shooting you right now. You can practice when we're not in here doing, uh, droid stuff, okay? There are plenty of other people to talk to on this ship other than me."

"Urrrkaaaayy . . ." Tunger said, hanging his head.

Rogers sat down in the only chair in the room, which was pushed up next to a computer terminal, and put his feet up. He tried to adopt a position of nonchalance and comfort, but with his uniform tailored to actually look good when worn, it was a difficult task. It always felt like his shirt and trousers were having a war over his underwear and had reached a stalemate.

"Now," Rogers said, pulling at his crotch to no effect, "if you're not my second, who is?"

One of the droids, front and center in the five-by-eight formation, stepped forward, his metal feet making much less noise on the floor than Rogers was used to hearing. Rogers saw why; the combat droids' legs had a series of shock absorbers that ran from their hip joints down to their ankles, and their four-clawed feet sported some sort of soft rubber on the bottom. Rogers wasn't sure which he preferred: a droid he could hear coming an astronomical unit away or a droid that he didn't know was there until they rubbed noses.

"I am Cyberman First Class F-GC-001," the droid said. "I am second in command of the 331st AIGCS." Rogers noticed he pronounced it like "eggs" in typical ramrod military acronym style, though he wasn't sure where the "C" had gone.

"Hey!" Rogers said. "You don't sound like a moron!"

"Oh sure," Corporal Tunger said. "*He* can talk any way he wants." He abruptly turned away and folded his arms, staring at the wall. "Droids can't be spies."

"I must request clarification for this statement," the droid—Rogers decided to call him Oh One—said.

"I mean you're not calling functions or calculating pi in the middle of a sentence or anything."

Tunger, apparently over his short burst of teenage angst, turned around and pointed a finger in the air as he lectured.

"New models. They've got the F Chip."

"What's that?"

"Freudian Chip. Named after a famous old psychologist. This is the first batch of prototype units with it; it adds a bit of human rationality and psyche, and apparently helps with their combat reactions. The first batch of AIGC units spent most of their time comparing casualty calculations and tended to go with solutions that left one guy alive on the side that was supposed to win." Tunger shrugged. "Boolean logic has its limits, I guess."

Rogers angled his desk chair slightly toward Oh One. "So, you're an F Chip droid. A Froid."

"You are correct, though the word 'Froid' does not appear in my vocabulary."

"Install it," Rogers said, "because that's what I'm going to call you new models." He leaned forward. "You don't like . . . *feel* or anything, do you?"

"If you are asking whether or not F Chip droids—" The droid made an unintelligible computation noise that sounded a little bit like an old skipping record. "If you are asking whether or not Froids have human emotions, you are correct in your assumption that we do not feel."

"That's great," Rogers said. He thought back to the way the inspection droid had reacted when he had used the word "shinies." Rogers could have sworn that it had gotten angry, which just seemed ridiculous. "I don't think I could handle it if any of you started crying or trying to tell jokes or anything like that."

"I have no reserves of saline solution to excrete from my ocular implants," the droid said. "If this is a modification that is desired, please see Ensign McSchmidt in the engineering bay, who will put in a request for a new design."

"I think we'll skip it," Rogers said, "but thanks for the suggestion."

Rogers sat in silence for a moment, Oh One staring at him with that blank blue-eyed gaze and Tunger looking a little depressed at not being able to talk like an idiot. A droid as his deputy. Wonderful. Judging from the rest of the people he'd met on the *Flagship* so far, he wasn't sure that many of the human choices were any better.

Briefly, he thought about simply leaving, blowing off the training altogether and going to find a good card game to join, but that didn't seem practical. He didn't think he could find a card game in the entire ATBG, for one, and that wasn't being quite subtle enough about doing a poor job. If he was going to be bad at something, he couldn't make it look like he was *trying* to be bad at it.

So, he did something just short of being overtly stupid: he put a corporal in charge.

"Tunger," he said, "you've got control. Why don't you give me a little demonstration of what these battle bots can do?"

The corporal stiffened. "That's not really my job, sir. I'm here to help you with the administration and organization—"

"Come on," Rogers said. "Show me the good stuff. Make 'em spin around in circles and shoot each other with paint guns and do karate."

"The word karate does not appear in my vocabulary," Oh One said. "Are you referring to droid fu?"

"Shut up for right now. I'm trying to get the corporal to do orderly stuff like order you around with orders. Tunger?"

Tunger's face was getting red, and he was avoiding meeting Rogers' gaze.

"It's just that . . ."

"You have no idea how they work, do you?"

Tunger looked at the floor. "Nur."

Rogers sighed and stood up. "How long have you worked with droids?"

"Since I was transferred from the zoo deck."

*Well, that explains the boot stain,* Rogers thought.

"And that was?"

The corporal hesitated. "Three days ago."

Rogers grit his teeth. Another bizarre personnel transfer. What would possess Klein to put a zookeeper—if Tunger had even been in that illustrious of a position on the zoo deck—with droids? Rogers supposed dealing with strange creatures might give Tunger a leg up, but Rogers didn't think these shinies would respond to fish or whistles. Maybe electrical prods, though . . .

"Fine. Fine. Did they tell you anything at all about these droids before you came here?"

Tunger brightened and turned to where a small cabinet was attached to the wall. He opened it with his personal keycard and removed a strange-looking datapad, roughly twice as large as the standard-issue personal datapad that everyone was required to use. He handed it to Rogers with ceremonial seriousness.

"They told me about this, sir," Tunger said. "It's the control pad. I tried to play with it a little but it's not keyed to me; you'll have to unlock it with your keycard first."

Rogers held the device as though it was a live grenade with the pin pulled out. In his hands he held the controls for a bunch of shinies, none of whom had any personalities but all of whom had weapons, and he was supposed to somehow train them to fight. Or were they supposed to train him instead? Removing his keycard from the back of his datapad, he swiped it in the slot on the side of the control pad.

The formerly blank screen lit up, and it was a few moments before a complicated control panel came onto the screen. Nothing on it was marked at all, and there was precious little to distinguish one button from the other; small green and red squares dotted the display, looking almost like a new sort of game or an old box of chewing gum, and there was one large orange square button at the bottom.

"Well, this is helpful," Rogers said. "Is there an instruction manual of any sort?"

"Yes!" Tunger said excitedly, happy to be of use. "Yes, there is!" He reached around to the same cabinet and pulled out a sheet of laminated plastic paper and handed it over.

"Ah," Rogers said. "Well, let's see, then."

It was a picture of the datapad with all of the buttons on it. Nothing was labeled.

"What the hell am I supposed to do with this?" Rogers asked.

Tunger's smile faded. "Well, I think they might have thought you would label them as, you know, you figured them out?"

Rogers shook his head. "Alright, Oh One, what about you? If I get blasted by these phantom Thelicosans that everyone keeps talking about, what happens?"

"I assume command of the AIGCS and utilize the best available strategy to neutralize the threat at hand."

"About as descriptive as the command pad, thanks. Anything more than that? How exactly do you exert said command?"

"I utilize the best available strategy to neutralize the threat at hand."

Rogers ran his hands down his face, grabbing onto his beard and pulling hard. "I think I'd rather have another inspection."

"For inspections, you should contact the Standardization and Evaluation Squadron. I am not programmed for that function."

"Thankfully not." Rogers turned the command pad over in his hands, wondering what would happen if he just started pushing buttons. The big one on the bottom, the orange square, looked promising. But maybe it was an execution command that only made any sense to use after other commands had been issued? It all seemed like a very primitive system for such advanced technology.

"Well," Rogers said. "Here goes nothing. Why don't you step back into formation, Oh One?"

The droid's eyes flashed for a moment. "I am unable to find a suitable answer for that question. Most likely it is because I have not been ordered to do so by my superior officer."

Rogers blinked. "Get back in formation."

"Yes, sir." The droid moved smoothly back to the position it had occupied previously.

Taking up the pad in his hand and swiping his keycard again—it had locked itself in the interim minutes—he hovered his finger over the orange button, wondering. What if it was the "seek and destroy" button? Or the "fire indiscriminately" button? Or, worse, the "talk to your commander" button? He had to believe that whoever had designed these things wouldn't let something so dangerous be so easy to do.

He pressed the button, muscles tense.

A resounding *ding* came from the control pad, followed by the feminine voice that seemed to come standard with all pieces of military technology.

"Congratulations on activating the Mark III Artificial Intelligence Ground Combat control pad. As thanks for activating this service, you are entitled to one free *It's a Droid Life* coloring book, to be redeemed at any of the many Snaggadir's Sundries locations available across the galaxy. Remember: whatever you need, you can Snag It at Snaggadir's™!"

"Great," Rogers muttered. "My life's treasure at long last."

Oh One beeped, though to Rogers' eyes, it hadn't done anything. Looking back down at the datapad, he found that it had locked again.

"Damn it." He swiped his keycard again, and the screen came back on. Nothing had changed. He pressed the orange button one more time.

"Command?" the control pad prompted.

"Ah, here we go," Rogers said. "Now we're getting somewhere."

"Invalid command," the control pad answered.

"I haven't commanded anything yet."

"Invalid command."

"Hold your horses; I'm thinking!"

"I have received your command," Oh One said, loud enough to make Rogers jump, "but I cannot execute it due to a lack of equine life forms in the immediate area."

Rogers goggled at Oh One, wondering what kind of witless moron had programmed these things. When he turned back to the command pad, the screen was blank. It had locked itself in the short interim.

"What is wrong with this thing?" Rogers said as he aggressively swiped his keycard through the reader, unlocking the pad once again. He tapped the orange button.

"Command?"

"Disable the auto-lock feature on the command pad."

"Security protocol prevents users from tampering with access features on this command pad. Command?"

"Ugh," Rogers said. What was he supposed to do with these droids, anyway? He didn't know how to fight, himself, so it seemed kind of ridiculous to try and teach them how to do it. Maybe some of that standard, Steuben-esque drill maneuver crap would suffice for now. It was about the only military training that Rogers remembered other than engineering work.

"Stand at attention," he barked.

"Command received."

None of the droids moved, but Tunger's boots clicked together so hard that Rogers thought he might sprain his ankle.

"Not you," Rogers said.

"Oh," Tunger said, his face turning sour. "I don't get to *do* anything, either?"

"You're supposed to keep things orderly," Rogers said. "So, do that."

Surprisingly, this seemed to please Tunger. "Yes, sir!" he said, and, for some reason, left the room.

Turning back to the droids, he noticed that none of them seemed to have changed position. But now that he thought of it, it was the same position they'd been in the entire time. Was this standing at attention?

"Oh One," Rogers said. "Why did none of you do anything, even though this thingy here said that the command was received?"

"We are unable to find location: ATTENTION at which to stand."

"What? It's a military drill term!" Well, maybe they just couldn't stand at attention because it just didn't work with their metallic bodies. Maybe he could get them to move around a little.

He ripped his keycard so hard through the reader that it didn't have time to recognize his credentials, forcing him to do it again. Unlock. Screen up. Orange button. Command?

"Right *face*!" Rogers barked, astonished at his own drill sergeant-ness.

That did something! The entire group of droids, in one frighteningly smooth and coordinated motion, pivoted and snapped their bodies ninety degrees to the right, bringing their legs down with much less noise than a group of shinies should have made with all their stomping around.

“Now we’re talking” he said.

“What are we talking about?” Tunger said as he came into the room with a small dustpan and broom and began sweeping up.

“What are you doing?”

“Keeping things orderly, sir.”

“Right,” Rogers said, turning back to the command pad and pressing the orange . . . unlocking the *worthless piece of shit with his god-damn keycard* and pressing the orange button.

“March!”

“For commands to be executed at a later date, please specify the day and year as well.”

“No,” Rogers cried, “not March the month; march *forward*!”

Vibrations coursed through the floor of the training room as the entire formation of droids ran into the wall that was six feet in front of them. As they collided with the wall, they kept moving forward, their legs pumping up and down, though they seemed to be doing little enough damage to each other in the process. Perhaps it was a benefit of their made-for-combat metal alloy or whatever.

“Stop!” Rogers shouted. “Why are you doing that?”

“We are responding to the command given,” Oh One said, though the voice was muffled by his speech transmitter being smashed up against the wall.

“Oh for the love of . . . march backward, will you?”

“Affirmative.”

The formation marched backward until they were in the middle of the room again, at which point Rogers shouted for them to stop. They didn’t stop. Looking down at the control pad, he noticed that it was probably because it was locked. Rogers took it in his hand, about to throw it at Tunger’s broom, but was distracted by the clattering of a formation of droids hitting the *opposite* wall.

“Stop!” Rogers shouted at the command pad once he’d unlocked it again.

The formation of droids stopped abruptly, the sudden silence almost as startling as the symphony of metal had been moments earlier.

"Dear god," Rogers said. "What use is this?"

"We are used to neutralize the current threat by utilizing the best—"

"Shut up!" Rogers said.

He took a deep breath. Okay, so moving them wasn't as easy as he thought. He definitely wasn't ready to try anything with weapons yet, that was for sure, not that he really wanted to. Maybe he could march them down the hallway and "accidentally" vent the room to open space, or something. No, too obvious. God, he wanted a drink.

"Everyone stand still and do nothing," he said.

Everyone stood still and did nothing, and he counted this as a minor victory.

Perhaps simply changing formation types would work; if they were supposed to go to combat, surely they knew things like wedges, columns, staggered lines, and all that, right? At least, that's what they did in the movies. Rogers wasn't exactly a resident expert on combat.

"Alright," he said. "Alright. Let's see."

Swiping his keycard—he was going to have a copy made and permanently glued to this damn machine—he pressed the command button. What *were* all those other little green squares for?

"Command?"

"Form a column."

The droids snapped into action immediately, and Rogers stepped back with a satisfied grin as the whole orchestra started to play the same tune with Rogers on the conductor's stand. Despite his feelings about droids, he couldn't help but feel a little bit of pride as the droids started smoothly interchanging positions, not running into anything at all, and . . .

Tearing the metal panels off the walls.

"What the hell are you doing?" Rogers cried. "Stop!"

The inert command pad didn't help him, since it had locked itself again. Slamming his card through the reader, he was greeted only with a crudely drawn—not rendered like regular graphics, but drawn as though by a five-year-old—picture of a battery with a line through it. It was out of charge.

"Tunger," Rogers shouted, "this is your fault!"

"My fault?"

"This isn't very orderly at all. The damn thing is out of batteries!"

The droids, in the meantime, had convened in the center of the training room, bringing with them pieces of the walls, exposing part of the vast network of pipes, wires, cables, and whatever else made up the guts of the *Flagship*. Arms flashing in silver-gray blurs, they extended and retracted, the droids' legs telescopically reaching higher until they were at the ceiling. In moments, a crudely but solidly crafted shaft of metal ran from floor to ceiling in the center of the room, like one of those senseless metal sculptures in backwater museums.

"What have you done?" Rogers cried once the noise settled down. "You've ruined the training room!"

"We have formed a column, sir," Oh One said. "Utilizing the best available strategy."

Rogers stared blankly at the almost certainly laughing eyes of the Froid, wondering if they could do things out of spite, wondering if this was all a joke and Magistrate Tuckalle was about to burst through the door, red-faced with laughter, and tell him that the *Awesome* had been repaired and he could go on his merry way.

But that didn't happen. Instead, the AIGCS stood around their newly formed monument of stupidity, looking at Rogers to give them their next command.

"Low battery," chirped the command pad.

Rogers looked at the command pad, looked at the tangled mess of metal, and looked at Tunger.

"Charge this," he said, throwing it at Tunger, who caught it and saluted with a snap. “And get me an instruction manual. I’m going to go eat a Sewer rat.”

“The presence of rodents, while a viable food source, is unlikely in this ship’s waste disposal system, sir,” Oh One offered helpfully. “It is unlikely that you will find one.”

“I’ll use the best available strategy and see what happens,” Rogers said, and left.

# Barber Bot

Picking the last traces of a SEWR rat out of his teeth and wondering how much money he would pay for a good slab of steak, Rogers slowly plodded through the halls back to his room on the quarterdeck. He felt like someone had taken everything good about life and used it as toilet paper. Like he could still see the traces of a life full of drinking and gambling and fun, but there was a lot of poop in the way. Was this automated technology really the future of the Meridan Patrol Fleet? Was it really *his* future for the next three long, long years?

Rogers attempted to put his hands in his pockets and adopt a brooding walk, but he found that his pants pockets had been sewn shut. Another archaic rule said that it looked unprofessional to put your hands in your pockets, so apparently Stan/Eval and Supply had gotten together to rob everyone of a place to put anything in their pants. Rogers thought there might have been something philosophically different between not breaking rules and not being given the opportunity to break them, but he realized very quickly that he didn't care. He missed his pockets.

"CALL FUNCTION [ABRUPTLY GREET]. TARGET [ENSIGN ROGERS.] OUTPUT STRING: GOOD AFTERNOON, SIR."

Rogers' arms flailed in the air as he screeched to a halt in the hallway. A few inches from where he stopped stood an older model droid, mostly indistinguishable from any other droid on the ship. It was one of the tracked variety, and from its relatively dirty exoskeleton wafted the distinct odors of talcum powder and alcohol-based cleaning solution.

"What do you want?" Rogers snapped. "What are you doing on the quarterdeck?"

"CALL FUNCTION [STATE INTENTIONS]. OUTPUT STRING: I AM CYBERMAN SECOND CLASS BAR-BR 116. YOU FAILED TO ATTEND AN APPOINTMENT AT 0830 SHIP TIME THIS MORNING."

Rogers gaped. Then he noticed the droid's hands; instead of the standard three-clawed grip, the droid was equipped with rotating discs to which were attached various barbaric instruments, such as scissors, razors, a comb, and a tiny welding torch, which Rogers didn't understand at all.

"So, you're Barber Bot," Rogers said, taking a slow step back. "I don't need an appointment. I didn't even make the appointment."

BAR-BR 116 inched forward, its rotating instrument discs clicking ominously.

"CALL FUNCTION [PRESENT EVIDENCE]. OUTPUT STRING: IT WOULD APPEAR THAT YOUR FACIAL HAIR IS NOT IN ACCORDANCE WITH REGULATIONS SET FORTH BY MERIDAN PATROL FLEET STANDARDIZATION AND EVALUATION. YOU ARE REQUIRED TO COMPLY. I AM HERE TO ASSIST YOU. YOU MISSED OUR APPOINTMENT."

The welding torch flared to life for a brief moment.

"Get away from me," Rogers said. "You're not touching my beard."

"YOU MISSED OUR APPOINTMENT."

"Yeah," Rogers said, inching closer to his door. "You mentioned that. Look, I'm pretty busy. Why don't you go take care of all the other customers that are probably waiting for you back in the barber shop? Their hair is growing *right now* because you're not there for them. In fact, I should probably report you for dereliction of duty."

"YOU MISSED OUR—"

Rogers slammed the button to enter his room and ducked inside before the insane barber droid could say anything else about the missed appointment. What a one-track mind! Didn't he have any other customers? For that matter, how good could a robot be at cutting hair? Rogers had all sorts of cowlicks and lumps. It took a real master to groom his wild locks; he wasn't about to let some half-sentient machine butcher his face.

Squatting low, Rogers listened intently through the door, making sure the droid had given up. He heard a few more ominous clicks and whirrs, felt the door warm a little bit as BAR-BR 116 presumably tried unsuccessfully to burn a hole in the door.

"CALL FUNCTION [DEJECTEDLY DEPART THE AREA]."

Rogers breathed a sigh of relief as the sounds of the droid's treads faded away into the distance, replaced by the beating of his own heart. He shouldn't have been addled so easily by a clunky machine. Stupid thing didn't even know how to say anything other than "YOU MISSED OUR APPOINTMENT." Damn shinies.

"FAILURE TO BE PRESENT AT TIME OF INSPECTION. ONE DEMERIT WILL BE AWARDED."

"Gaaaah!" Rogers screamed, jumping up. He found Sergeant Stract and Inspect-o-Droid standing in front of him, the droid's gloves almost completely gray with dust and Sergeant Stract's pencil ground to nothingness from the copious demerits he must have been awarding Rogers on his clipboard.

"What the hell are you two doing in here?" Rogers cried. "This is my room! This is breaking and entering! I have rights! I have . . . What is that droid doing?"

Rogers noticed, for the first time, that a second droid was in the room, standing by the empty space on the wall where that ridiculous propaganda poster used to be. For some reason, he was wearing a pair of suspenders that held a workman's belt at the end, and a bright, floppy orange cap. At the moment, he appeared to be drilling a hole in the wall.

"CALL FUNCTION [PERFORM PRIMARY DUTY]," said Inspect-o-Droid. "OUTPUT STRING: YOUR FAILURE TO HAVE SUFFICIENT MORALE REQUIRES THAT WE SUPPLY IT FOR YOU. CYBERMAN SECOND CLASS CB-101 IS ENSURING ADEQUATE MORALE."

CB-101—obviously some kind of carpentry droid—finished drilling and reached down to a metal case that had been propped up against the wall. Opening it, he removed a rectangular vidscreen, big enough to be on the bridge among Admiral Klein's observation displays, and placed it on the wall, where he firmly bolted it in place.

"Oh, finally," Rogers said. "Some entertainment. That's what you meant by morale. I was beginning to think that everyone in this ship had a stick up—"

The vidscreen blinked on, so bright that Rogers shielded his eyes. When he lowered his arm, he found that, instead of a movie, he was looking at the brightest, most high-definition poster he'd ever seen in his life. The advertisements outside cinema theaters paled in comparison to the gaudiness of this display. It was as though the wall was screaming at him with light.

On it was a picture of a droid from the chest up, blurred lines around the chassis creating the feeling of motion. Below, in large block letters, was written AUTOMATION IS EFFICIENCY IS EFFICACY IS GOOD.

Rogers wasn't exactly sure what to think. He stared at the glowing poster for a moment, then averted his eyes, fearful for the health of his retinae.

"There is no way in hell you are keeping that in here," Rogers said, blinking tears from his eyes. "Get that off my wall right now or I'm going to use one of you as a sledgehammer."

"CALL FUNCTION [EXPRESS DOUBT AND LOWER CONFIDENCE]. OUTPUT STRING: THE COMPOSITE MASS OF YOUR ABDOMINAL REGION IN PROPORTION TO YOUR MUSCULAR STRUCTURE SUGGESTS THIS IS AN IMPROBABILITY."

Rogers blinked. "Did you just call me fat?" He turned to Sergeant Stract and pointed at Inspect-o-Droid. "Did he just call me fat?"

"It is not for me to interpret the comments of my superiors, sir," Stract said, the ghost of a smile hiding behind the flat expression on his face.

"That's *exactly* what enlisted are supposed to do, you idiot!" Rogers yelled. He turned back to Inspect-o-Droid. "Get that out of my room. Now. There's no regulation that says I have to have a blinding poster of your ugly faces staring at me. I'm not even going to be able to sleep!"

"CALL FUNCTION [SMUGLY CITE REGULATION]. OUTPUT STRING: MERIDAN PATROL FLEET REGULATION MR-415 STATES THAT ANY CHANGES TO PERMANENT FIXTURES IN QUARTERS MUST BE REQUESTED BY AN APPLICATION ROUTED THROUGH AN INDIVIDUAL'S CHAIN OF COMMAND AND APPROVED BY THE STANDARDIZATION AND EVALUATION COMMANDER."

Rogers grimaced. "Who is the commander?"

"That'll be Colonel Bellham, sir," Stract said.

"And where is he?"

"He's on sabbatical."

"He's on what?"

"Sabbatical, sir," Stract repeated. "He's studying the motivational impact of hospital corners versus the twist-and-tuck technique when making beds. It's a very popular subject."

Rogers looked at his bed, which was currently employing the "crumple and whatever" technique. You couldn't bounce a trampoline off his bed, never mind a quarter.

"He's never coming back, is he?" Rogers asked.

"Nope."

Running his hands through his hair, Rogers turned around to where the absurd permanent poster hung from his wall. It was enclosed in a Plexiglas case and rimmed by a thick metal frame, with no clear openings or switches. He guessed it wasn't designed to be turned on and off.

"Hey, CB-101," he said, glancing sideways to where the carpenter droid was making a slow exit from his room. "Can I borrow a hammer?"

"CALL FUNCTION [FRUSTRATE SUPERIOR OFFICER]. OUTPUT STRING: SIR, HAMMERS ARE AVAILABLE THROUGH THE SUPPLY DEPOT. PLEASE FILL OUT AN OFFICIAL REQUEST FORM AND—"

"Get out."

The carpenter droid left, its grisly work complete. As he turned around to tell Stract and Inspect-o-Droid some creative uses for their clipboard, he was shocked to find the droid's face within inches of his own. Rogers stumbled back, colliding with his bed and falling abruptly to a sitting position.

"CALL FUNCTION [PERFORM PRIMARY DUTY]. OUTPUT STRING: IMPROPER FACIAL HAIR GROOMING. ONE DEMERIT WILL BE AWARDED. AUGMENTED FUNCTION [VEILED INCONVENIENCE]. AN APPOINTMENT WITH CYBERMAN SECOND CLASS BAR-BR 116 HAS BEEN SCHEDULED FOR TOMORROW AT 0830."

"No!" Rogers said. "No, no, no! I'm not going to the barber shop. I'm not going to talk to creepy Barber Bot. I'm not going to let anyone cut my beard. And I'm not going to look at your stupid face on your stupid poster!"

He was standing now, waving his finger in the droid's face, his own face hot with anger. If he still had that command pad from the AIGCS, he would have ordered the combat droids to blast Inspect-o-Droid to pieces. If he could unlock the thing and figure out how to do it without blowing a hole in the side of the ship.

Again, for some strange reason, the droid's eyes changed color. Only for a fraction of a second, Rogers saw that red glow emerge and disappear so fast, it was easy to believe that it hadn't happened.

"REJECT FUNCTION [PROTOCOL 162]. CALL FUNCTION [PERFORM PRIMARY DUTY]. OUTPUT STRING: LOSS OF MILITARY BEARING. TWO DEMERITS WILL BE AWARDED. INSPECTION COMPLETE. A REPORT WILL BE FILED IN YOUR PERSONNEL RECORD, WHICH YOU CAN ACCESS BY FILING A REQUEST WITH THE PERSONNEL SQUADRON AFTER A MANDATORY FIVE-DAY WAITING PERIOD. ALL INFRACTIONS MUST BE RECTIFIED WITHIN ONE STANDARD DAY."

"The only thing I'm going to file are my nails," Rogers said, "and I'm going to leave the dust all over Sergeant Stract's boots."

"Sir!" Sergeant Stract exclaimed, scandalized.

"Now get the hell out of my room before I threaten to do something *really* crazy," Rogers said, pointing at the door.

With one last look of something mixed with fear and disgust, Sergeant Stract left the room, the droid shortly behind him. Rogers was going to find some way to get back at those two. He just didn't know how yet. And he didn't know if he really felt like putting forth the effort.

Sighing, he sat down on his bed and put his face in his hands, his fingers barely able to block out the light coming from the poster. He hadn't been so tired in all of his life, and he'd barely done anything at all. The fact that he didn't want to put forth the effort to mess with Sergeant Stract made it all the more clear that this stint in the military was doing bad things for him.

Rogers needed . . . something. He needed a drink. He needed to get out of this starchy, uncomfortable uniform and sew a couple of pockets on the inside so he had somewhere to put his hands instead of around someone's throat. He needed a really big crowbar to take that damn poster off the wall. In fact, any kind of tool in his hand would feel really good right now. It had been far too long since he'd done any meaningful engineering work.

So, he headed down to where he knew he belonged: the engineering bay.

An immediate feeling of relief washed over him as he emerged into the familiar surroundings of the Pit, their affectionate nickname for the noisy, dirty hovel that was the home of the engineering squadron. Unlike the rest of the *Flagship*, the engineering bay was a tangled mess of ventilation shafts, machinery, and dark corners well suited for just about anything fun. Aside from that, it was mostly made up of the giant area that was the Pit, the maintenance bay, and its own hangar. He couldn't wait to see the old wrench-turners in their greasy coveralls—if there were any not in the kitchens—though he hoped he didn't see any of the ones he owed money.

The Pit was unusually busy, people running to and fro with tools and datapads, though Rogers noticed that almost none of them were wearing their utility uniforms. Come to think of it, nobody on the entire ship seemed to be dressed in anything except the semiformal wear normally worn only by administrative personnel.

"Alright, folks," came a shout. "Inspection in two hours. Remember what Winston Churchill said. 'Russia is a riddle wrapped in a mystery inside an enigma.'"

Despite Rogers' expectation that wrenches would be thrown at the gross incongruity, nobody seemed to care that Russia had vanished from old Earth—along with old Earth—a thousand years earlier and had absolutely nothing to do with engineering or inspections. The mismatched quotation had come from a serious-looking ensign with dark, mud-colored hair. He tucked the datapad he was carrying behind him as he pulled aside a tired-looking female engineer and muttered what appeared to be some encouraging words. He patted her on the back and nodded, though she didn't look very encouraged, and finally noticed that Rogers had come into the Pit.

"Who are you?" he asked.

"I was going to ask you the same question. What's this about an inspection? We don't have those in the Pit."

The ensign laughed. "I didn't know they were sending a comedian to Engineering. We have them every day."

Rogers suppressed a shudder. It appeared that the charade that was the Morale, Health, and Welfare inspections had made its way into the engineering bay, too. Though he shouldn't have been surprised. This whole ship was going crazy.

"I'm not a comedian. My name is Rogers. I, ah, used to work here."

The ensign's eyes widened. "You're Rogers? I've heard of you. I thought you'd abandoned ship to be an entrepreneur, or something."

"I did," Rogers said. "I'm back, though apparently I'm not working here anymore."

"Well," the ensign said, "welcome to the place you're not working." He extended his hand. "I'm Ensign McSchmidt, engineering squadron commander."

Rogers shook his hand hesitantly. He remembered Oh One saying something about this guy. "McSchmidt? That's kind of an odd name."

"Half of my family was German, the other half was Irish."

Rogers blinked. "I'm not sure that's how it works."

McSchmidt didn't seem to want to argue about it. "Well, welcome back. But, if you'll excuse me, I have an inspection to prepare for. The droids will be here in two hours, and I want good marks."

"Good marks aren't good for much if you blow up the engineering bay," Rogers said, pointing to where some boominite containers had been stacked in a very pretty, if stupid, pattern. "That's not how to store those. If someone farts near them too loudly, you could blow a hole in the side of the ship the size of a small dreadnaught."

McSchmidt's expression turned cold, but he didn't spare

the boominite containers a glance. "I know how to do my job, Rogers. The instructions for stacking tri-plasma rods is clear in the manuals."

"Those are boominite containers. What the hell are tri-plasma rods? Did you just make that up?"

McSchmidt turned up his nose. "I'm the engineering commander here. I know my business. I hope you don't have any aspirations to take over your old unit, Rogers. I worked hard at the Academy to get where I am now, and I'm not ready to turn it over to a smooth-talking gambler like you. Are we clear?"

Rogers let the weak attempt at an insult slide off of him. "You're an Academy officer?"

Academy officers were known for being a little arrogant, if competent. But this McSchmidt looked more like a lost puppy who had just learned how to bark. Normally, these kinds of dopes were easy meat for the experienced enlisted corps, but nobody seemed to have done their job of putting McSchmidt in his place.

"Yes," McSchmidt said, suddenly frowning. "I just said that, didn't I? Why would I say that if it wasn't true? I went to the Academy, making me an Academy officer."

"Okay, okay," Rogers said. "Calm down. The Academy has a great academic reputation. What did you major in?"

"Of course I had a major! Of course I majored in something! Why wouldn't I major in something at the Academy that I went to? I majored in political science. That's obviously why I'm in engineering." McSchmidt was breathing rather heavily, and he appeared to be breaking out in a sweat.

Rogers raised an eyebrow. "What the hell does political science have to do with engineering?"

"Everything!" McSchmidt snapped in a sudden burst of indignity. "It's the engineering of people, of cultures, of nations!"

"Yeah," Rogers said, "but do you know which way to turn a wrench?"

"Engineering *über alles*!" the ensign shouted. "Now if you don't have any business in the Pit, I'll thank you to get out of the way."

Without another word, McSchmidt turned and walked away, directing his anger toward a pair of corporals who were using a hoverlift to move a small fusion generator from one side of the room to the other, where a whole array of generators were arranged in a totally useless and potentially hazardous pyramid formation.

"Don't mind him," someone said.

Rogers turned to find the young woman the ensign had been "encouraging" standing next to him. She was stocky but not exactly heavy, her sandy brown hair tucked up in a bun. Her uniform didn't quite fit properly, giving him the impression of a girl in her mother's clothes. She looked at him with a pair of dull brown eyes set in a walnut-colored face, her mouth turned up in a wry smile.

"What's with the walking anachronism?" Rogers said, jerking a thumb at McSchmidt.

"Academy funding for political science is in the tubes, thanks to the Two Hundred Years' (and Counting) Peace," she said. "The only thing they study anymore is old world history textbooks. You should hear him talk about Napoleon."

"It requires more courage to suffer than to die!" McSchmidt shouted.

"Anyway," the engineer said, "you should come back later if you want to tour the facility. Almost everyone you knew when you were here has been transferred, but I'll show you around. I'm Sergeant Lopez."

"R. Wilson Rogers," Rogers said, and extended his hand. "You don't know anywhere on this ship where I can get a drink, do you?"

Lopez grinned. "This is the engineering bay, Ensign."

Rogers let out a sigh of relief. "Thank god. I think you and I are going to get along just fine, Lopez. Just fine. I'll be back later for my tour."

---

*Now we're talking!* Rogers thought as the Jasker 120 slid down the back of his throat, smooth as butter. Finally, a good card game, a cigar, and a bottle of fine Scotch. Maybe life wasn't so bad after all.

. . . Was what he wished he was thinking as he sipped from the dirty canteen cup that held some of the most vile swill he'd ever come across. He sat with Lopez in the engineering bay on top of a couple of empty crates, watching the last remnants of the crew fill out paperwork and curse at the results of their inspection. They'd failed with flying colors; the boominite containers had been stacked in the wrong pattern and they found a raccoon in the engine of one of the starfighters. McSchmidt had apparently left in tears and hadn't been seen since.

Rogers grimaced at his cup. It tasted like someone had boiled their feet in a vat of spoiled eggs and vinegar, but there was definitely the distinct bite that told Rogers it was at least alcoholic.

"Puts hair on your chest, doesn't it?" Lopez said. She smacked her lips and wiped them on the back of her hand.

"Or my dinner on the floor," Rogers replied, swallowing his body's attempt to eject the drink.

"Hey," Lopez said, "I made this myself. It took me months to get the materials together and figure out a good spot to brew it without the Stan/Eval droids getting all over me for it." She forcibly clinked her cup against Rogers', sending some of the moonshine—if you could call it that—over the side of the cup. Rogers was not at all upset that some of it had been wasted.

"Clearly, you've been an engineer for a while, then?" Rogers said. *Or an alcoholic.*

"Twelve years a wrench-turner," she said, burping.

"How did you manage not to get put to work in the kitchens with the rest of the crew?"

Lopez shrugged. "Who knows the reasons they do anything around here? Maybe they're getting an apron ready for me right now. Bah!" She threw her empty cup on the floor.

"I know how you feel," Rogers said. "They put me in charge of ground combat droids."

Lopez's eyes went wide. "I heard about them. I can't believe they're giving them weapons. Do you think it's safe?"

Rogers thought back to his experience with the control pad and the droids deconstructing part of the ship.

"No."

"So, why are you doing it?"

"Don't have much of a choice, do I?" Rogers said, a little more aggressively than he'd intended. "What are *you* going to do if they tell you to grab a chef hat and make a mousse?"

Lopez thought for a moment. "Make a really shitty mousse, I suppose."

"Exactly. And I'm going to make a really shitty ground combat unit."

The sergeant stood up, yawning loudly, and motioned for Rogers to follow her. "Come on. No use grousing. I'll show you around."

Rogers wasn't exactly sure what she was going to show him; he'd worked in the Pit for nearly a decade and knew every nook and cranny of it. But it was nice to talk to someone who wasn't insane, even if she did try to pass off hog's piss as alcohol.

"Pretty busy around here," Lopez said as they passed by a wall of crates and entered into the spaceship maintenance section of the Pit. This was an area reserved mostly for starfighters and small transport craft, stuff that was small enough to be moved from the docking bays if they were damaged. Most of the complicated work on larger ships was done in the docking bays themselves or even outside the ship using Vacuum Mobility Units.

"Pretty busy?" Rogers asked. "How? There was never anything going on. We repaired burnt-out engines and replaced parts every time one of the fighter pilots ran his ship into something on patrol, but it was always pretty calm."

"Yeah," Lopez said, "but you didn't have McSchmidt and a

legion of droids breathing down your neck, telling you to put this there and put that here. I feel like all I ever do is move stuff around."

Rogers shook his head. "Where did all the droids even come from?"

"It's the war," Lopez said.

"There is no war!" Rogers said, throwing up his hands.

"It's the war that's coming, then," Lopez said. "People said the MPF wasn't professional enough to take on the Thellies, so Klein started making changes. More rules, more droids. Less alcohol. It's a different fleet."

"And you believe it?"

Lopez shrugged. "What am I supposed to believe? The intelligence reports go to Klein, not the engineering crew, but I hear it from the fighter jocks every once in a while. They've been going out on patrol more often too. Another reason we're pretty busy."

Rogers rubbed his beard. Maybe there *was* something going on with Thelicosa. Admiral Klein wasn't one to scare easy; he was a Real Military Man, if there was such a thing. If Klein thought war was coming, maybe it was true.

"But that doesn't mean we have to have a bunch of shinies running everything," Rogers said.

Lopez ducked her head, looking around. "You shouldn't say that word."

"Shinies?"

"Shh!" She shoved him, hard, sending him stumbling back, and he felt a flash of indignation. Only the Viking was allowed to push him around like that.

Oh, the Viking. Captain Alsinbury. If only . . .

"The droids don't like it, and you'll find yourself getting paperwork dropped on you if they hear you throwing it around like that. You'll have to go to counseling."

"Counseling?"

"Yeah," Lopez said. "Racial reeducation counseling."

Rogers balled up his fists. "They're droids. They don't have a race."

"Tell that to the counselors. They're droids, though, so they probably won't agree with you."

As they were about to leave the maintenance area and head over to where the barbeque pit used to be—which was now just a bunch of filing cabinets and posters—Rogers caught sight of a ship at the far back.

"Hey," he said. "That's my ship!"

Lopez stopped and looked, squinting. "Your ship?"

"Yeah," Rogers said. "That's the *Awesome*."

"That's a stupid name for a ship. Looks a whole lot like an MPF cargo speeder to me," Lopez said slowly. "Have I seen that ship before?"

"The paint is different."

Behind the *Awesome*, Rogers could see a couple of figures moving around, dressed in what Rogers thought were coveralls. But they didn't look quite right. Taking a few steps closer, he realized that they weren't coveralls—they were aprons.

"That's Hart," he said, a little tingle of excitement working its way through him. "He's fixing my ship!"

"Master Sergeant Hart?" Lopez said. "What's he doing here?"

"I asked him for a favor," Rogers replied.

The ship already looked in better shape than it had been when it had been towed to the *Flagship*. Those folks would have it up and running in no time. Though what Rogers would do once it was fixed was still a mystery. But at least when this tour was over, he'd have something to fly away on. Fly away *fast*.

"Well, aren't you something?" Lopez said. "Your own ship and everything. What are you still doing in the military?"

"It's a long story," Rogers muttered.

"Well why don't you—"

"CALL FUNCTION [SURREPTITIOUSLY FOLLOW]. TARGET [ENSIGN ROGERS]."

Rogers and Lopez stopped in their tracks.

"What the hell was that?" Lopez asked.

Rogers spun around, looking for the source of the voice, but couldn't find anything. They were in a mess of shipping crates and other random detritus, the only open view heading out toward where the *Awesome* was being repaired.

"CALL FUNCTION [MAINTAIN CLEVER HIDING PLACE]."

"Shiny," Rogers muttered. Lopez whacked him on the arm.

"I'll say it if I want to say it."

"CALL FUNCTION [MAINTAIN CLEVER HIDING PLACE]."

Rogers whirled. Where was the damn thing? Why was it hiding? Why was it so hard to find it even though it kept announcing its presence?

"Come out, you hunk of scrap metal!" Rogers said. "What are you doing following me around?"

"CALL FUNCTION [MAINTAIN CLEVER HIDING PLACE]."

Rogers leaned toward one of the crates. "Is it coming from here?"

"I don't see it." Lopez said. "Boy, you're on the droids' shit list, aren't you?"

"They're droids," Rogers said, creeping around a corner, crouching low. "They don't have—"

"CALL FUNCTION [SPRING TRAP AND PERFORM PRIMARY FUNCTION]."

One of the nearby crates burst open, the metallic lid flying through the air and nearly knocking Rogers unconscious. Rogers ducked, screaming, and Lopez let out a stream of curses. He barely saw the flash of a pair of scissors before Lopez tackled him to the ground.

"Barber Bot!" he cried.

"What the hell does that mean?"

Rogers stood up, prepared to find a heavy object to swing at the oncoming droid, only to find that BAR-BR 116 hadn't moved. It was still stuck in the crate from the waist down, its hydraulic midsection pumping up and down uselessly as it tried to dislodge itself. The crate was barely big enough at the base to allow the droid's treads enough room to stand.

"CALL FUNCTION [REASSESS CLEVER HIDING PLACE]."

"How did you even get in there in the first place?" Rogers asked. "You know what? Never mind. I don't care. I told you you're not touching my beard, and that's final."

"CALL FUNCTION [INCESSANT REPETITION]. OUTPUT STRING: YOU MISSED OUR APPOINTMENT."

"And I'll miss the next hundred appointments!" Rogers shouted boldly, puffing his chest out (while maintaining a safe distance from the immobile droid). "You'll never get the best of R. Wilson Rogers!" He thought a moment. "Or his beard! You'll never get the beard of R. Wilson Rogers!"

"CALL FUNCTION [ESCAPE SELF-IMPOSED PRISON]."

BAR-BR 116's torch flared to life—Rogers really didn't want any part of a haircut that involved flaming objects—and set to work on the side of the crate.

"I think I've seen enough of the engineering bay," Rogers said, eyeing Barber Bot warily.

"I think I've seen enough of it too," Lopez said. "Come back anytime you want to turn a wrench or get chased by droids or get yelled at by Ensign McSchmidt or . . . You know what? Maybe you shouldn't come back."

"I'm beginning to think that about a lot of places," Rogers said.

Lopez escorted him back to the entrance of the engineering bay, where he politely declined another sip of what she called "Lopez's Special Sauce" and began the journey back to his room so he could get some sleep. The trip was far from restful; he kept looking behind him for Barber Bot and kept looking ahead of him for any sign of the Viking. There had to be a way to make her see him as more than someone trying to usurp her job. And there had to be a way to blow up that robot.

All problems, no solutions. That was quickly becoming the story of his life.

As he approached the door to his room, he saw Sergeant Stract and Inspect-o-Droid leaving it.

"CALL FUNCTION [PERFORM PRIMARY FUNCTION]. FAILURE TO BE PRESENT AT INSPECTION. ONE DEMERIT WILL BE AWARDED."

Rogers gave the robot the finger, walked past both of them without saying a word, and went to bed. The glowing face of the droid on the wall stared at him, its brightly lit background driving those infernal words into his head:

AUTOMATION IS EFFICIENCY IS EFFICACY IS GOOD.

# Mechanical Failure

Sleep had been broken by the giant beacon of light in his room and the fact that he had to chase BAR-BR 116 away from his door at least twice. So far this morning, he hadn't seen it, and Rogers was starting to believe that perhaps it had given up. Could droids give up? Rogers didn't know. In any case, it made for a weary morning back in the droids' training room.

"Alright, Tunger," Rogers said as he rubbed his eyes. "What have you got for me?

Tunger looked at him blankly. "Didn't I do the whole 'I present to you the Artificial Intelligence Ground Combat Squadron' thing to you yesterday?"

"That's not what I meant," Rogers said, again sitting down in the only chair in the room. He pretended to look relaxed, like he didn't care about anything in the world, but already today he felt his nerves had been stretched so tight, they might snap. The Viking had finally passed him in the hallway and didn't even shove him—Rogers would have accepted any physical touch at this point—and then they had run out of SEWR rats in both the Uncouth Corkscrew *and* the Peek and Shoot. Those meals were bad enough without having to go hunting for them.

"Sir, if I may," said Oh One, who had stepped out from formation to greet him.

Rogers cut him off with a wave. "Look, I know you've been appointed my deputy and that you technically outrank Tunger with all this new rank bullcrap that they've published, but I want you to step back in formation and stay there until I give you an order."

Rogers wasn't sure where the outburst had come from. Maybe it was the fact that even the coffee in the Uncouth Corkscrew this morning had tasted like motor oil—he willed himself to believe it was actually just bad coffee—or maybe it was the fact that after less than a week on the *Flagship*, he wished he'd been spaced by the Garliali. And that made him think of calamari. And that made him sad.

Oh One stood there for a moment, as if considering what to do. Rogers scowled. Oh One was a droid; there should be no considering about it.

"Back in formation," Rogers said again.

Oh One's eyes flashed red—Rogers was absolutely positive he saw it this time—and he stepped back into formation without another word.

Turning back to Tunger, Rogers leaned back in his chair and put his hands behind his head. Being grumpy was helping him be just the sort of commander he was trying to be: bad.

"You were supposed to charge the control pad and figure out what to drill today so that we don't build another one of those." Rogers pointed at the column of steel that was still in the middle of the training room. "You do remember me telling you that, don't you?"

"Yes, sir," Tunger said. He moved to the cabinet and retrieved the control pad. "I charged it up for you all night. Should be good for the whole day. And I spent some time looking at the manual."

"The piece of paper with nothing on it but an unlabeled chart of the buttons?"

"That's the one," Tunger said. "I think maybe we should focus on some target practice. I had Corporal Suresh in Supply bring up some targets for us." He gestured to the far side of the room, where a modified shooting range had been constructed. That hadn't been there the day before; Rogers was sure of it. Now, long rows extended down the opposite end of the training room, ending in target silhouettes.

Rogers leaned forward. "Tunger, why are all the target silhouettes shaped like animals?"

Some of them weren't easily identifiable, but Rogers was almost positive that the shadows of ostriches occupied the first few targets, followed by some sort of gorilla and, strangely, a muffin. Rogers could recognize the shadow of a muffin anywhere.

Tunger blushed. "It's all I could find, sir."

"I'm kind of surprised these exist, honestly."

"They're actually not targets. They're visual recognition training for zoo personnel," Tunger said. "You need to know the difference between a red-footed booby and a blue-footed booby at two hundred meters in the dead of night in case the power goes out."

Rogers squinted. "Why would you ever need to know such a thing?"

"Can't just let the boobies run around, sir," Tunger said seriously. "Can't do that at all."

Rogers felt like perhaps there was some real, sage advice in that statement, but he couldn't figure it out at all. He just nodded slowly. "I suppose you can't, at that. Well, at least if there's ever a jailbreak in the zoo and the AIGCS has to hunt them down, we'll know what they're capable of."

"Sir!" Tunger said, scandalized.

"I'm only kidding," Rogers said. "I'm curious what you found out by looking at the, uh, manual."

"Absolutely nothing, sir."

Rogers rubbed his eyes again. Damn, but he was tired. "Right. Well I hope you found it personally fulfilling anyway."

He looked up at the droids all standing perfectly still, their blue eyes shining back at him like a little constellation through the expanse of the massive training room.

"I suppose a little target practice wouldn't hurt," Rogers said. "I'll have to figure out how to get them to fire weapons sometime, I guess. Let's take a look."

Taking the control pad in his hands and unlocking it, he was presented with the maze of unlabeled green buttons again. If the orange button was a sort of speaking command button, the green buttons must be able to do things without him talking into the device. Maybe then it wouldn't be so easy to confuse these buckets of bolts, Freudian Chip or no. For droids, they did seem rather stupid.

Rogers figured he'd start with the top left, and tapped the screen to engage the first green button. Instantly, the screen shifted to a display of what appeared to be the training room. A thick silver outline traced the edges of the room, and he could see each droid represented as a blue dot in perfect formation.

"Hey, Oh One," he said. "How does this thing know where we are?"

"Each member of the AIGCS is equipped with a spatial radar system that allows for an instantaneous analysis of the geographical space in which we are located," Oh One droned.

"That makes sense. Let's see here."

Rogers tapped the position where Oh One was standing and dragged his finger forward. In response to his movement, Oh One took a step forward.

"Hey!" Rogers said. "It worked!"

Corporal Tunger clapped. "Hurruh!"

Rogers shot him a look.

"I mean, hooray!"

It took a few tries and not a few crashes, but eventually Rogers was able to use the command pad to manipulate the movement of the whole squadron and direct them toward the shooting range in the back of the room. He followed them, Tunger in tow, but gave himself a wide berth after the first time one of the hulking beasts ran into him and knocked him completely over.

"This isn't so hard at all," Rogers said. Despite his aspirations to be the worst AIGCS commander in the history of the MPF—which technically he already was, in addition to being the best AIGCS commander in the history of the MPF—he couldn't help but feel a tiny bit of excitement at doing something properly. He was a slacker of professional quality, but he still had pride.

Soon he had the squadron grouped up in five even lines, each in their own row of animal-silhouetted shooting ranges. They were all facing different directions, but he had to be satisfied with little victories.

"Alright," he said. "Tunger, where do they put the rifles around here? If they're going to practice shooting, they'll need something to shoot."

Tunger frowned. "They didn't tell me that, sir. There's no weapons locker in here. I could go down to the armory and see if they have anything."

"If I may, sir," Oh One said, "that won't be necessary."

Rogers looked around, trying to figure out where Oh One was in the formation. All these damn shinies looked alike. He'd have to paint Oh One's face or something.

"Oh One, raise your hand."

One of the droids at the front of the shooting lines raised its hand, and Rogers walked over to him.

"Stand still for a second."

Reaching into his pocket—his shirt pocket, since those were the only ones not sewn shut—he pulled a small package of ketchup that he had taken from the Uncouth Corkscrew yesterday, when he still thought he might actually have to put it on something. He smeared a line of it under the droid's eyes, instantly turning it into some sort of insane badger. At least it distinguished him.

"There," Rogers said. He was about to put the packet back into his pocket but thought better of it and simply held it in his hand behind the control pad. "Now, what were you saying?"

"AIGCS members come equipped with their own weapons. There is no need to visit the armory."

"Is that right?" Rogers said, hoping his voice didn't crack. Having droids that knew how to operate weapons was one thing; having them always carrying them was another. He didn't like the idea of not being able to take them away if anything went wrong. "Well, let's see them."

"As part of our programming, the AIGCS is not permitted to draw weapons without a direct order from the commander.

"Right," Rogers said, somewhat comforted. "The control pad."

He looked at the pad—which was, of course, locked—and swiped his keycard through it. If the first button was maneuvers, perhaps the second button was combat commands. He pressed it, only to find that instead of anything useful, it brought up what appeared to be a directory of addresses and contact numbers for Snaggardir's locations all across the Meridan system.

"Well, that doesn't help me at all. Why is that on the control pad?"

The third button brought up a catalog of products sold at Snaggardir's—did that place sponsor these droids or something?—which one could buy and have delivered. Rogers briefly thought about taking a moment to stock up on anything that wasn't a SEWR rat, but he could save that for another time.

The fourth button switched on one of the droids' speaker systems, through which started playing a very sappy tune by Larisa Sparklefoot, a popular Meridan pop star.

"Oh, come on," he said.

"I love this song!" Tunger exclaimed, shaking his hips in a very disturbing way.

Pressing the fifth button turned the song off—why allocate two buttons to that?—and the sixth button didn't appear to do anything at all. The seventh button, however, brought up a high-definition display of a single combat droid that rotated, displaying the health of each of its components in a gradient color system. To the left was a list—Rogers guessed from the number that it was a list of the droids under his command—and on the bottom, there was another set of buttons that were clearly combat commands.

"Finally," he said. "Here we go."

He pressed the "all" button on the side, and instantly all the droids were highlighted. Then he pressed the "draw weapons" button and nearly died.

A horrible clanking of metal erupted as the chest compartment of every droid in the squadron opened up, out of which sprang a modified disruptor rifle, fully charged and ready to go. They snatched them into their glossy hands in a crisp, unified motion that, together, sounded like a spaceship had just gotten stepped on by one of the sand dragons on Dathum.* Rogers was standing so close to one of the droids that it elbowed him in the shoulder, sending him ricocheting into another droid that thankfully pushed him outside the formation. Rogers fell backward and rolled to a stop, the command pad slapping him in the face and sliding to the floor.

"Wow," said Tunger.

Groaning, Rogers pulled himself to his feet, his heart racing. The ketchup packet that had been in his hand had spilled most of its contents onto his fingers. He wiped as much of it as he could on the floor, not really wanting to stain his uniform, but his hand was still much redder than it had been a moment before.

"That was . . . enthusiastic," Rogers said. Oh One made no

*Dathum: Lots of great, sandy beaches and a few giant carnivorous sand dragons.

reply. The red-faced badger now looked like a red-faced badger-killer-robot. Rogers wasn't sure he liked the change.

It took another few seconds—and unlocking the command pad twice—before Rogers could figure out how to get the droids to turn in place. It took another few tasteless pop songs before Rogers could even begin to understand how to make them find a target and take aim. The last thing he wanted was all of them facing different directions, shooting whatever they liked.

"Let's maybe just start with you, Oh One," Rogers said. He highlighted Oh One in the list of droids and pressed the button for "attack target."

So quickly it blurred in Rogers' vision, Oh One snapped his rifle up, took careful aim, and with deadly precision, shot the ceiling of the training room.

Both Rogers and Tunger ducked reflexively, despite there not being anything to duck away from. The floor vibrated as the disruptor rifle blasted a hole in the ceiling the size of a small melon, sending disintegrated metallic dust showering down like silver snow. A larger chunk broke off, colliding with the head of one of the droids in the second row and sending it sprawling to the floor. Its motion knocked another droid down, and soon there were four or five of them down, legs and arms flailing as they tried to get back up. The one that had been hit in the head wasn't moving; its eyes were no longer shining blue, and, for all intents and purposes, it appeared to be "dead."

"Great job, Oh One," Rogers said. "You're the first droid to ever commit fratricide."

"While I should appreciate your praise, sir, I don't understand how fratricide would be classified as a good job. Is it encouraged to kill one's peers in training?"

Rogers shook his head. He should know better than to think droids understood sarcasm. They couldn't even march properly.

"No," Rogers said. "No, it's not. Never mind. Tunger, are you sure we're ready for firearm practice?"

Tunger brushed gray dust off his uniform, his hands shaking. "No, sir."

"I didn't think so. Maybe we should try—"

The *Flagship* exploded. At least, that's what it seemed like to Rogers. The lights went off, leaving only the red hue of the emergency glowbulbs. The ground vibrated. The walls seemed to be caving in. Every robot in the room was bathed in an eerie red glow, swathed in the shadow of the droid next to it. A shrill alarm split his ears, followed by the unintelligible speech of what must have been one of the public transportation announcers coming over the loudspeakers, shouting frantically:

"Fhrrr drigg. Mrhgh a ghnanbr. Next stop is grrnnsvilne shrugngh. All aboard!"

"Everyone get down!" Rogers screamed as he ducked. "I was wrong! I was wrong! The Thelicosans are attacking! I was wrong!"

That was the only possibility for this unbelievable chaos. They'd gotten the jump on Admiral Klein, come out of Un-Space with their cannons blasting, swarming over the fighter screen and pummeling the *Flagship* with everything they had. The alarm made everything between his ears start to ache, and the unintelligible speech of the announcer sounded more and more like someone reading the eulogy at his funeral.

"Sir!" Tunger shouted. Rogers abruptly realized that he was lying prone on the floor but had no recollection of getting there. He was in a maze of droid feet, trying to figure out how to get to the exit so that he could find an escape pod.

"I can't hear you, Tunger! The Thellies are coming! The Thellies are coming! Get yourself a disruptor rifle and get to the bridge!"

"Sir!" Tunger said again. "Thurs is urnrly a fur drull!"

"And stop talking with that accent!"

He felt a shudder go through the floor and realized with horror that it was too late. The Thelicosans were already boarding. Their shock troops would be flying through the halls in moments, killing anyone who couldn't identify the next prime number in a prearranged sequence of integers.* Which, on this ship, would be everyone. Except the engineers, of course. They knew what the hell they were doing.

Just as Rogers was trying to remember which was the hypotenuse and which was hypertenuse—was there such a thing?—a realization came upon him. He had an army with him. It was a droid army, of course. A droid army that didn't know where to fire their weapons and didn't understand half the commands he gave it. But he could certainly use them for something. Not to fight the Thellies—Rogers didn't join the military to fight anyone—but to cover his exit. He might not kill any enemy soldiers, but by god, he would shoot the ceiling over every Thelicosan bastard that got in his way!

Scrambling to his feet, his eyes watering from the unbelievably loud blaring of the alarm, Rogers fumbled for his keycard in the semidarkness and grabbed the command pad, unlocking it and mashing the orange button for all he was worth.

"Command?"

"Everyone follow me!" he screamed, his voice cracking. "Ready your weapons and prepare for combat!"

"Sir!" Tunger yelled.

Rogers ignored him. He heard an abnormal amount of beeping coming from the command pad, and when he looked down he saw that he had smeared ketchup all over the screen. Buttons were going off at random as the machine became unable to distinguish his fingertips from the oils of the condiment; he saw the screen flash briefly to the movement panel and all of the droids started going in different directions at once.

"Stop!" he yelled, but he hadn't pressed the orange button. He couldn't even get to the orange button. The room suddenly

*The only thing to which the Thelicosans ascribe more enthusiasm than war is mathematics; regardless of his birth name, every Thelicosan emperor is given the name of a famous mathematician, such as Euclid, Fibonacci, or Kim Jong Un.

became a cloud of droids banging into each other and turning every direction, their disruptor rifles whirring ominously. A few droids fell down, kicking their legs and bringing some of the other droids down with them.

"Shit," Rogers said, trying to clean off the screen with his shirt. He only succeeded in turning on "Love My Lovely Bits," which, coming out of all the droids at once, actually became louder than the alarm for a moment.

"Sir," Tunger yelled, maneuvering through the droids to finally stand in front of him. "What is it, Tunger? I'm a little busy!" Rogers was trying to navigate back to the beginning of the command pad's menu, but the damn thing locked again and it took him a moment to find where he'd dropped his keycard on the floor.

"Thurs is urnrly a fur drull!"

"I swear," Rogers said, "I will order these droids to shoot you if you don't drop that accent and I can figure out how to make them point those guns."

Finally, Rogers got back to the main screen and pressed his finger to the orange button.

"This is only a fire drill!" Tunger shouted.

Rogers stopped and looked up. "Fire?" He shouted, confused.

"Command received," said the command pad.

Time froze as Rogers and Tunger looked at each other for a terrifying moment. Then the shit hit the fan.

# Report: A-255FR-01124-B

Serial: A-255FR-01124-B

Distribution: DBS//DSS//DAK//DFR//BB//CLOSED NETWORK A66

Classification: Special Protocol Required

Summary: During date/time stamp in subject line, AIGCS engaged in unexpected high intensity close quarters combat situation at the command of Human 2552 via control device Z99, resulting in catastrophic damage to AIGCS personnel.

Details: After the commencement of combat, Human 2552 emitted several high-frequency noises, possibly encoded communication, and possibly attempted to mate with the floor. Behavior pattern requires more analysis. Human 9994 promptly exited the area. Speech patterns unintelligible, possibly Thelicosan dialect. Human 2552 questioned Human 9994's fortitude and made remarks regarding maternal fornication. Intent of this communication is unknown.

Details: Attempts to mitigate damage by initial volley failed due to disarray of formation. Majority of casualties occurred in the first few moments of combat. Unit F-GC-001 initialized override protocol to attempt to avoid further damage to AIGCS. Weapons disengaged and holstered.

Details: Human 2552 made several references to excrement and continued to suggest maternal fornication. Repeated references to human reproductive habits suggests that it is of the utmost importance to human activity. Further study of this phenomenon is required.

Special Note: Freudian upgrade had insufficient data on this subject and focused primarily on the ambiguous ubiquity of phallic covetousness.

Details: Despite attempts by F-GC-001 to retain control of the situation, Human 2552 continued to access commands using control device Z99. Recommend decommissioning this device as soon as possible.

Details: Human 2552 accessed unarmed combat commands, possibly unintentionally. AIGCS units engaged in droid fu. Manner of employment suggests that Human 2552 remained unaware of control device Z99's functionality. Human 2552 received karate chop to lower ribcage and reengaged aforementioned high-pitched communication attempts. Nominal increase of methane gas in atmospheric composition suggests earlier references to excrement had been prophetic.

Details: F-GC-001 reengaged overriding protocols but was unable to cease droid fu by all units at one time. In the intervening moments, Unit F-GC-005 had collected Human 2552 by the ankles and attempted to use him as bludgeoning instrument to destroy Unit F-GC-012. Vital signs of Human 2552 suggest lapse into unconsciousness.

Details: Protocol 162 was not engaged. Situation was brought under control.

Statistical data is below.

Casualty report: 19 units assessed destroyed.

Casualty report: 8 units assessed critically damaged.

Casualty report: 1 unit assessed damage to ocular sensors due to ketchup.

Fighting strength remaining: 7 units fully operational.

Outcome: Loss.

Assessment: This situation presents data that there may have been several miscalculations. First, more data is required on Human 2552 to elucidate ambiguities of competence, as equal probabilities exist that Human 2552 is a lower form of intelligence and that Human 2552 is a potential concern. Second, presenting control device Z99 as a means of reassurance may have been premature and potentially dangerous. Third, more observation of human behavior in general is necessary to discern levels of importance, e.g. reproduction and ethanol-based beverages.

Report Submitted By: F-GC-001

# Too Stupid to Be an Ensign

Once, when Rogers was younger and vastly less wise, he made a bet with some friends that he could take a full tablet of zip jack—a powerful and illegal psychedelic—and walk through the ground traffic on Merida Prime unharmed. Amidst all the hoots of disbelief, he took a sugar pill that he had swapped for the real zip jack and prepared to march toward the far side of the busy intersection full of smug bravado.

It wasn't until the first hovercar morphed into a giant slice of apple pie and invited him to sample its innards that Rogers realized that, somewhere along the line, he'd made a critical error with the placement of his sugar pill. The adventure of the next several days (in reality only a few minutes) consisted of him not only getting to the other side of the road miraculously unscathed, but doing so on the back of a sperm whale that sang him songs of the Old Country.

Now the whale was back, and he was not very happy.

Rogers swam through a sea of broken unconsciousness and

medically induced adventures, vaguely aware of tiny blossoms of pain that came and went all over his body. Images of droids flashed by, their disruptor rifles flaring as they fired indiscriminately, the deep red eyes of Oh One glaring at him with admonishment and hatred. He saw a pair of sizzling, delicious over-easy eggs dancing in the sky that, when pierced with a fork, dripped dark black oil onto a mountain of SEWR rats into which he was cast, screaming. He watched with horror as the Viking hit *other* men, all of whom spoke in drunken Thelicosan accents as they slathered her face with kisses. He saw Dorsey sailing away in an escape pod, towing the *Awesome* behind him and taking large swigs from a bottle of Jasker 120.

In between these nightmares, he woke in fits and starts, barely able to take in his surroundings before dipping back into the land of the sonorous sperm whale. The infirmary was his new home, no doubt, and he lay in an open-air recuperation chamber under thin sheets that did little to keep him warm. Over and over again, he saw the same few faces staring sternly down at him, officers, he thought, all wearing grave expressions. Surely, they were part of the Meridan JAG, coming to court-martial him.

He also saw Corporals Mailn and Tunger a few times, and heard Mailn arguing with someone very loudly. Once, he was almost positive he heard Inspect-o-Droid awarding him a demerit.

In the end, it was the sound of scissors scraping together and the feeling of an acute heat on his face that brought him very suddenly awake.

"Get away from my beard!" he screamed, smashing BAR-BR 116 in the face with his fist and receiving an immediate reminder that metal was tougher than bone.

"What are you doing in here?" a woman—Mailn—yelled, and walked quickly to his bedside, where Rogers was now clutching his fist and whining piteously.

"CALL FUNCTION [PERFORM PRIMARY DUTY]."

"Can't you see this man is injured?" Mailn said, stepping between them. She put her hands on her hips, and Rogers noticed her finger was very close to the holster strap of her disruptor pistol. "Now is not the time for grooming."

"CALL FUNCTION [DE-ESCALATE]. OUTPUT STRING: HE MISSED OUR APPOINTMENT."

"I don't care," Mailn said. "If you don't get out of this room right now, I'm going to do something with those scissors that involves your ass and a blast of hot plasma."

Barber Bot seemed to hesitate for a moment but eventually started wheeling slowly backward.

"CALL FUNCTION [RETREAT FROM SCARY LADY]. AUGMENTED FUNCTION [VOW TIMELY RETURN]."

"Yeah, whatever," Mailn said, her hand easing away from her pistol.

Barber Bot's torch flared to life one last time before he made a slow exit from the room, which Rogers now saw was a private suite in the *Flagship*'s infirmary. He was no longer in a recuperation chamber but a regular bed. A remote vitals monitor chirped pleasantly.

"Congratulations on returning to consciousness!" the monitor said. "You are entitled to a complimentary twenty-ounce fountain beverage of your choice, to be redeemed any of the many Snaggadir's Sundries locations available across the galaxy. Remember: whatever you need, you can Snag It at Snaggadir's™!"

"So, you're finally awake," Mailn said. She was grinning at him, but there was genuine concern in her eyes.

"What happened?" Rogers asked, lying back in bed. His whole body felt like it had just been put together from pieces of grenade victims.

Mailn chuckled. "You had, ah, a little incident in the training room with the droids."

It all came back to Rogers in a flash. The marching, the control pad, the targeting practice. The fire drill. The pain.

"Oh," Rogers groaned.

"You put on quite a show," Mailn said. "Watching the video was—"

"Wait," Rogers said, sitting upright despite the pain. "There's a video?"

"Oh yeah," Mailn said. "There's a video."

Rogers flopped back down again onto the pillow. "I never want to see it."

"It's alright," Mailn said. "I've watched it so many times now, I could direct a film reenacting it. How could you not know that a fire drill was happening? Your personal terminal should have told you when you woke up that morning."

"First, I never trust a computer," Rogers said. "And second, I don't even know what a fire drill is. The last time we had one was when I was in primary school. I'll tell you what, Cynthia: between the inspections and the fire drills and the being chased around by barbers, I don't know how anyone on this ship ever gets anything done."

Even as the words left his mouth, Rogers knew they felt wrong. Since when did he give a Sewer rat's ass about getting anything actually *done*? He supposed that maybe actual, no-kidding work was preferable to all this idiocy. Any sane man would rather do his job than listen to Inspect-o-Droid issue him demerits, though Rogers had to admit he was feeling a little less sane these days.

"Anyway," he said, "I'm just thankful I'm alive. I don't think a normal man could have survived that kind of pain."

"Are you kidding me?" Mailn laughed. "Most of your injuries were caused by your head hitting the floor when you fainted like a little girl. You screamed like one too."

Rogers felt his face getting red. He did not faint. He was brutally injured in the line of duty.

"Speaking of screaming," Rogers said, changing the subject as hurriedly as he could, "I thought I heard you shouting in here. What's going on?"

Mailn's expression flattened. "You had quite the endless stream of visitors. Just about every brass monkey in the fleet was in here at one point or another. Even Klein popped in once."

"Klein?" Rogers asked, his voice cracking. This was bad. This was really bad.

"Yep. Said some really powerful stuff." Mailn shook her head. "I'd follow that man anywhere. He's a true leader."

"Powerful stuff?" Rogers asked. "What kind of powerful stuff? Why would anyone come in here and say powerful stuff?"

"Oh, you know," Mailn said. "Just the standard stuff about devotion to duty and tireless perseverance in the face of adversity." She scrunched up her face. "Come to think of it, I can't really remember most of it. But I know it was powerful stuff."

"Hang on a second," Rogers said, now even more confused. "Devotion to duty? I blew up the AIGCS!"

"Not according to Klein," Mailn said. "Or anyone else that kept walking in here looking for interviews."

"Interviews?"

"You discovered a potentially catastrophic bug in the AIGCS system," Mailn said. "Without you, those shinies might have gone straight into combat and blown everyone around them to pieces. You proved that they weren't ready for deployment. You saved the *Flagship*, Rogers."

A torrent of emotions washed through Rogers. First was relief; the AIGCS was gone. That meant he didn't have to be in command of them anymore. Second was confusion; if there was no more AIGCS, where was he going to go? Third was terror; he'd been highlighted as the savior of the fleet, people had come to interview him, and Klein himself had made a personal appearance. That could only mean one thing.

"Oh my god," Rogers said. "I'm being promoted."

Mailn saluted, grinning. "Hi there, Lieutenant!"

Rogers could feel his common sense withering away that very moment. Not just an ensign, the scrappy puppy dog of whom not much was expected, but something rapidly approaching a field grade officer, the point at which all men of reasonable intelligence had a full frontal lobotomy and were awarded commands of large units.

"Wait," Rogers said. "Lieutenant? Not Lieutenant Lieutenant? Just Lieutenant?"*

"Nope," Mailn said. "You skipped Lieutenant Lieutenant and went straight to Lieutenant."

"That doesn't make any sense," Rogers said. "You can't just become a Lieutenant without being a Lieutenant Lieutenant first."

"Lieutenant Lieutenant was deemed too low of a promotion."

"So, just Lieutenant?"

"Yep."

"Not Lieutenant Lieutenant?"

"Nope."

"Oh my god," Rogers said. "I'm being promoted twice."

Mailn plopped down in the only chair in the room, relaxing. "Pretty impressive if you ask me. And, I'll tell you something else: the Viking certainly hates you a lot less than she did a few days ago."

Rogers perked up. "Really?"

"Really. I heard her say something to the effect of 'maybe that little shit isn't absolutely worthless after all' after she heard about the AIGCS being disbanded. Trust me, that's high praise."

Rogers felt his heart flutter a little bit. Maybe this wasn't so bad. By being promoted to lieutenant in the Meridan Navy, he was technically the same rank as the Viking now—her being a captain in the Meridan Marines—which might mean she'd pay a little more attention to him. And he'd accidentally removed a major obstacle to their romance. Without being in charge of

---

*The rank of Lieutenant Junior Grade, formerly the rank just below full Lieutenant, was abolished during the Great Naming Crisis, during which all families ran out of ideas for their offspring and simply started calling them "junior." It became far too confusing, and the MPF introduced the rank of Lieutenant Lieutenant, similar to Lieutenant Colonel in that it signified the rank just below Colonel. There are some (many) in the MPF who regret this decision.

a bunch of droids that were taking the Viking's job away from her, she would have far less reason to hate his guts or abuse him without his permission/encouragement. He could see her now, breaking down that door and lifting flaming debris off of him before carrying him off into the sunset aback a tall black stallion.

"Well," Rogers said. "I feel a little bit better." He looked at Mailn, who was still grinning at him for some reason. "Thanks for watching over me, by the way. I don't know what I would have done if Barber Bot had gotten ahold of my beard while I'd been sleeping."

Mailn shrugged. "Hey, I don't absolutely hate you. Next to the marines in my platoon, you're the closest thing to a friend I have on this ship. And you're proving to be very entertaining." The grin was back. "Plus, any chance I get to yell at a droid is too good to pass up."

"Well," Rogers said, "thanks."

Mailn kept grinning.

"What?" Rogers asked, narrowing his eyes. "What is it? What aren't you telling me?"

Sitting forward in her chair, Mailn put her elbows on her knees. "You're not even the least bit curious where you've been reassigned?"

Rogers blinked. "I always thought that mid-grade officers just sort of roamed around the ship and made things difficult for people. They actually have positions?"

Mailn kept grinning.

"Will you stop that?" Rogers said. "Your face is going to freeze like that."

Mailn kept grinning.

"For god's sake, *what?*"

"I found out an interesting piece of news after Klein came in the other day. Remember how I said he just got a new executive officer?"

"Yes . . ."

Mailn paused for dramatic effect. "He hung himself."

"No," Rogers said, sitting up and gripping the sheets in white-knuckled fists.

"Which means there's an opening for a plucky lieutenant with bravery, fortitude, and aptitude to spare."

"No," Rogers said again, clenching his teeth.

"And there happens to be a brand-new lieutenant who fits that description and just fainted himself out of a command."

"No!" Rogers screamed.

Mailn reached over and handed him his personal datapad that had been sitting on the stand next to the bed, on which was displayed his transfer orders.

"Congratulations, Lieutenant," she said. "You're a secretary."

Rogers walked through the corridor with his head hung so low, he could barely see where he was going. Beside him, Corporal Tunger nattered incessantly.

"This is so exciting, sir," he said. "Two promotions and a chance to be next to one of the most brilliant men ever to grace the MPF! You must be beside yourself with joy."

Rogers mumbled something offensive.

"I mean, really," Tunger continued, "to have that level of responsibility and prestige thrust upon you after discovering one of the most dangerous flaws in the AIGCS programming. You've had quite the exciting career, sir! And to think, just a few weeks ago, you were an ex-sergeant."

Tunger switched the bag he was holding to his other hand. He'd remained as Rogers' orderly, which seemed utterly absurd. It basically made him the secretary of a secretary, but the man had nowhere else to go. Apparently, all the people trained in zoo operations had been moved to finance, and Tunger had been the odd man out before the AIGCS came along.

"Are you sure they can't take you back to the zoo deck?" Rogers asked, trying to veil his hope that he'd be rid of the man. He still hadn't forgiven him for running out of the room during the fire drill, and he'd never liked the idea of having an orderly, anyway.

"Oh no," Tunger said, "though I'd be lying if I said I didn't ask for it once I found out that the AIGCS had been disbanded." He looked up at Rogers, embarrassed, and added hurriedly, "It's all I know, you see. I've been managing animals my whole life. It wasn't out of disrespect, sir."

"No offense taken," Rogers said.

"Oh good. I wouldn't want to offend anyone." Tunger sighed. "One day, though, I hope they pick me up for that spy slot. Chimpanzees—and you—are great, and all, but . . . Aie wursh they could see maie taalunts for whut they ur."

Rogers shot him a look.

"Sorry, sorry."

They boarded the up-line—which also went down, and sometimes sideways, so Rogers wasn't really sure why they called it the up-line—and zoomed through the belly of the *Flagship* toward the command deck, which also held the bridge, the war room, and several other conference rooms that Rogers hoped he never set foot inside. Part of the short list of benefits to being transferred to serve as Klein's executive officer included moving from the quarterdeck to a stateroom on the command deck. It also hopefully meant no more inspections, a room with a view, and one less glowing picture of a droid on his wall.

Rogers was dismayed to see that a couple of droids also occupied the small car, as well as a smattering of officers of similar rank to his own who all looked haggard and generally annoyed. None of them spoke.

"CALL FUNCTION [MAINTAIN AWKWARD SILENCE]."

Rogers looked up to see the droids—three of them—standing in the direct center of the car, all looking toward him. At least, he thought they were looking toward him. How did one really tell what those glowing blue orbs were looking at? The last thing he wanted to deal with right now were droids, so he made it a point to turn his back on them and look through the viewport at the head of the car, watching the guts of the ship blur by.

"CALL FUNCTION [MAINTAIN AWKWARD SILENCE]."

"What's their problem?" Rogers muttered to Tunger.

"I don't know, sir," Tunger replied. He placed the bag of Roger's things—things that Rogers had insisted he could carry himself—on the floor and sat down on one of the seats on the edge of the car. "Maybe they think you'll accidentally destroy them, too."

Rogers frowned. "Was that a joke, corporal?"

"No, sir," Tunger said earnestly. "I'm not very good at joking."

"CALL FUNCTION [MAINTAIN AWKWARD SILENCE]."

"Oh, stop it!" Rogers said. "You know you're not maintaining any kind of silence when you keep announcing it, don't you?"

The droids didn't reply. They got off at the commissary deck, where, presumably, they were heading toward one of the mess halls to plug in and make a mockery of human dining practices. If Rogers ever met the man who programmed those things, he would punch him in the face. Unless he had a droid with him; his knuckles still hurt from giving Barber Bot a rap on the head.

Despite his abject misery, Rogers couldn't keep his nerves down. Working for Klein wasn't like working in the engineering bay. The man was charismatic, wise, tactically minded, and rumored to be ruthless in combat. Although Rogers couldn't imagine what combat he'd been in unless the admiral was over Two Hundred Years (and Counting) old. There would be no shirking his duties. No drinking. No gambling. Not that there was any of that on the *Flagship* nowadays, anyway. But at least before being transferred, there had been hope.

The car arrived at the command deck, and everyone aboard piled out into the utter chaos of the corridors. Unlike many of the other areas on the ship, the command deck was packed with officers and high-ranking enlisted, all hurrying through the hallways with their datapads held in front of them like weapons that generated bullshit and sprayed it all over the fleet. It was like he could feel the weight of minutiae and meaningless queep bearing down on him, a hyperbaric chamber of regulations and memoranda.

He thought he might vomit from it as Tunger led the way toward the exec's quarters, but Rogers barely had time to do anything except exchange salutes with the enlisted and higher-ranking officers passing by. In fact, he saw that everyone was carrying the aforementioned datapads in their left hands, because their right hands were almost constantly slapping themselves in the foreheads as nearly everyone they passed required a salute. This custom was mostly ignored everywhere else in the fleet except for ceremonial purposes. Why not here?

"Shit," Rogers said as he shook his arm out during the brief intervening moments between a sergeant and two lieutenant commanders, "how the hell does anyone get anything done around here if they're so busy saluting all the time?"

"I don't know, sir," Tunger said, offering Rogers a salute.

"Stop that!"

"Yes, sir," Tunger replied, snapping him another.

By the time they reached the large oval intersection that led to the bridge, the war room, Klein's quarters, and Rogers' new room, Rogers felt like his arm was going to deflate and fall off. Sweat trickled down his back; even Tunger was breathing harder with the effort.

"Quick," Rogers said. "Open the door and let's get inside before someone invents a double-handed salute and we get in real trouble."

"Yes, sir," Tunger said. He retrieved a pair of keycards from his pocket and handed one to Rogers. "This is to replace the one you lost."

"I nearly forgot about that. What happened to it?"

"They found it permanently attached to the side of the command pad. Apparently, even after you lost consciousness, you kept trying to unlock the pad with it, and eventually, the friction caused it to melt."

For some reason, Rogers counted that as a victory. He tucked the keycard away in the holster that also held his new personal datapad, and allowed the insistent Tunger to open the door for him.

"Aie prusunt to yeou . . ." He cleared his throat. "I present to you your new quarters, Lieutenant Rogers."

Rogers didn't even have the cognitive capacity to yell at Tunger for his slip back into the Thelicosan accent. The spectacle beyond the doorway held every inch of his attention.

The executive officer's quarters was nothing short of spectacular. A bed fit for a king, or at least a very successful pimp, was expertly made up with a shimmering red velvet comforter and a gaudy wrought-iron bed frame. A desk of expensive-looking wood with golden handles. A double-door wardrobe of stained oak, complete with a full-length mirror attached to the side with a silver frame. A computer terminal with not one, not two, but three screens displaying various systems on the ship and a daily calendar. A bookshelf with actual, no-kidding books. And, for some reason, a pet cat.

That would have all been great had it not all been floating around in zero gravity.

"What," Rogers said, unable to fathom what he was seeing in front of him, "in all of the circles of hell is going on here?"

"Ah," Tunger said. "I forgot to mention that part, sir."

"That my room's gravity generator was broken? That's a pretty big piece of information you forgot, Tunger. It could have saved us the trip up here. I'm not moving in here until it's fixed. Get maintenance on the line and—"

"Oh, it's not broken, sir. It's been disabled."

"Disabled?"

"Disabled."

"Why the hell has my room's gravity generator been disabled?"

"It was Klein's idea, sir, as a suicide deterrent. His last few executive officers hung themselves, you see."

"So?"

"Can't hang yourself in zero-g, sir."

Rogers looked, mouth agape, at Tunger. "You must be joking."

"As I said earlier, sir," Tunger said, "I don't joke very well. Could I have made a joke about this?" He made a tugging motion above his own head. "Something about hanging yourself in no gravity? It doesn't seem like a very funny subject."

Slowly, Rogers reached out and grabbed his personal effects from Tunger's hand and turned to face the interior of the snow globe that would now be his own personal hell.

"No," Rogers said, feeling a lump in his throat as he stepped over the threshold and floated between the hissing cat and a glowing poster of a droid. "There's nothing funny about this at all."

# *Ein Klein Flottenchef*

"Lieutenant Rogers, report to the bridge immediately. Lieutenant Rogers, report to the bridge immediately."

Rogers, floating in the middle of his room, glared at the computer terminal and attempted to throw a chair at it. The chair, as it turned out, was much heavier than he was, so it merely resulted in his doing a very uncoordinated backflip. His shins slammed into a pair of books that had wormed their way off the bookshelf, sending them flying across the room to crash into the poster of the droid. The poster, Rogers learned, had been encased in shatterproof material. The books merely turned the poster into a rapidly rotating moving picture, sending bright flashes of light spinning around the room and nearly making Rogers lose the breakfast he hadn't eaten.

"Son of a bitch!" he yelled, still rotating wildly and gripping his shins. Tucking into a ball to do so made him rotate faster, and it took a few attempts to grab the heavy chair again to steady himself. For all the alcohol he hadn't been drinking, he certainly felt hung over. Was the room spinning, or was he spinning?

Sleep had never struck him as a terrifying activity, but last night had changed all of that. Being constantly in fear of the ship's inertia sending furniture at you put a different perspective on "hitting the hay." The hay was, instead, hitting him. Why there was also a bale of hay in his room he had no idea, but the cat seemed to like it. The cat also seemed to like clawing at his uniform and using him as a jumping-off point to get around the room. Rogers didn't understand how the feline had adapted so well to zero gravity.

"Lieutenant Rogers, report to the bridge immediately. Lieutenant Rogers, report to the bridge immediately."

"I'm trying!" Rogers yelled. He pushed off the chair but not quite at the right angle. He hit the space just above the door with his shoulder and bounced back off the wall, only to find himself flattened against the surface of his desk, a stapler—who used a stapler?—jabbing into his kidneys. The desk, at least, was easier to push off than the chair, and the next jump put him right at the room's exit.

Gravity kicked in as soon as he passed through the threshold. Unfortunately, he did so sideways.

"You alright there, metalhead?"

Rogers looked up so fast, a sharp pain shot through his neck. Towering above him like an obelisk of beauty, the Viking stared down at him, shadowed dramatically by the lights overhead. If he squinted a little, he could have sworn there was a glow around the edge of her frame.

"Ah, hello," he said.

Then, in a moment that would live in his memory forever, she extended a hand to him. He took it and was thrown to his feet as effortlessly as if she had been picking up a pillow from the floor of their vaulted-ceiling bedroom with two cathedral windows and tastefully decorated art that hung over their canopy bed.

And suddenly, he was standing in front of her. Not ready to receive a blow to the face, not bracing for the next cold insult. Just standing there. Was she smiling at him? No, she was chewing on a small piece of leather. But if he looked at it just right . . .

"Nice to see you?" he said brilliantly.

"What are you doing jumping out of doors?" she asked gruffly. She looked past him—over him—and swore. "Looks like my room after I've had a bad day."

"I'd love to see your room," Rogers blurted. "I mean, no, that's not what I mean." Yes, it was. "Are you having a bad day?"

She looked at him, thick brows coming together in something that might have been an amused expression. "As a matter of fact," she said, "I'm having a pretty good day. Just got done briefing the admiral on combat readiness."

"Oh," Rogers said. Why was he sweating so much? "Well, are we ready?"

"Ready to lay down and die!" she barked. Rogers took a step back and felt his foot come off the floor, weightless. He stumbled forward again back into gravity, but the Viking didn't seem to notice. "I've got a bunch of cooks trying to shoot things with guns. You ever seen a cook try to shoot something?"

Rogers shook his head silently.

"It looks like apes flinging shit at each other in the zoo," Captain Alsinbury said. "And it does about as much damn good in combat."

"That doesn't sound very good at all," Rogers said. "Does that usually make for a good day?"

The Viking chuckled, a low rumble that sent all sorts of sensations to all sorts of places in Rogers' body.

"It makes for a pretty shitty day," she said. "But at least today I don't have to do it with combat droids training in the next room!"

She let out a belly laugh and slapped him on the arm, nearly knocking him back into zero gravity. Rogers' teeth clacked together noisily, but he withstood the blow—cherished it, let it sink into every fiber of his being—as best as he could.

“Trust me,” Rogers said, feeling a little bit of the tension bleed out of him. “You’re not nearly as glad as I am.”

For a moment, those words echoed in Rogers’ head as a falsehood. Had he been better off as the AIGCS commander? All he had to do was hang out with a bunch of stupid droids all day and pretend to train them. He’d been an ensign, too, and nobody expects anything out of an ensign except a repeated exchange of oxygen and carbon dioxide. Now where was he? On the *command* deck, as a *lieutenant*, working for the *admiral.* Maybe droids hadn’t been so bad after all.

“What’s the matter?” the Viking asked. “You look like you just licked a plasma converter. Are you a cook?”

Whatever he was about to say was obliterated by the loudspeaker’s call.

“Lieutenant Rogers, please report to the bridge immediately.”

“I forgot you were the new exec,” the Viking said. She gave him what might have been considered a grin. “Nice knowing you.”

She hit him on the forehead with the palm of her hand and snickered as she walked away. Rogers turned and watched her go, watched her consume the hallway with her presence, wanted himself to be consumed by her. Their conversation had gone well. Surprisingly well. Not happily-ever-after well, but at least he no longer felt that he was about to be crushed under her boot (without asking for it). It might have really gone somewhere, had she stuck around for a few more minutes and given Rogers some time to *really* kick his charm into gear.

But that damn loudspeaker, this damn *job* had gotten in the way. Everything on this ship was always getting in the way of everything else. He was sick of it.

A disgusting splattering noise came from behind him, and he turned to see that one of the cat’s hairballs had suddenly discovered gravity again.

“I hate my life,” he muttered.

“Lieutenant Rogers, report—”

"Shut up!" he shouted. "I'm coming!"

For some reason, the loudspeaker did indeed shut up. He realized a moment later that it hadn't been a loudspeaker at all but Corporal Tunger standing in the hallway with a megaphone.

"What are you doing here?" Rogers asked. "And where did you get that megaphone?"

"Corporal Suresh issued it to me," Tunger said proudly. "He said it would help me keep things orderly."

Rogers squinted at him. "Tunger, do you even know what an orderly actually does?"

"Not even remotely, sir," Tunger said brightly. "But I know chimpanzees!"

"Great. Now, if you don't mind, I have a hunch I'm wanted on the bridge. Go back to Suresh in Supply and tell him I can't work in zero gravity with all of my stuff flying around. See if he can't find anything to help me fasten stuff to the walls or at least tie them down. And give him back that damn megaphone."

"Yes, sir!" Tunger saluted and made his way back to the up-line, hopefully to get to Supply and get some of this idiocy sorted out. Tunger's arm didn't look like it was faring any better than Rogers'; as an enlisted man on the command deck, he had to salute every officer that passed him, and the deck was rapidly filling with bureaucracy-loving troops. Rogers retreated into his room for a brief moment, waiting for a clear shot to the bridge.

Just as he was gathering his nerve—and a brief space was opening up in the hallway that Rogers could run through if he was quick enough—his datapad beeped at him. He removed it from his holster and saw that he was receiving a call from another troop on the ship. At first, he didn't recognize the face displayed, but that was because the name had been misspelled in the database. It was the ensign from engineering, but his name read "McSchmurdt."

"Yeah?" Rogers said as he accepted the call.

"Hey, Rogers," McSchmidt said. He hadn't enabled video, so

all Rogers could see was the database photo of the man. By the background noise, however, he was clearly in the middle of the Pit. Rogers could hear the hum of hoverlifts and the clanking of crates being stacked atop one another.

Rogers waited for McSchmidt to continue, but the ensign didn't say anything.

"What is it?" Rogers said. "I'm kind of busy right now."

"I was just calling to see how you were," McSchmidt said.

Rogers paused. "I'm fine. Since when do you care?"

McSchmidt sighed. It sounded like he blew directly into the microphone, because the sound crackled fiercely.

"I feel like we got off on the wrong foot," McSchmidt said. "These inspections have been rough on me lately. Congratulations on the promotion, by the way."

"Thanks," Rogers said in the most disingenuous form of gratitude he could muster.

"So . . ." McSchmidt said. This was starting to feel like an awkward phone conversation from high school. "You're pretty close to the admiral now, aren't you?"

"I don't know," Rogers said. "Some guy called me to ask me how I was before I had a chance to talk to him. What do you want, McSchmidt?"

"Nothing," McSchmidt said. "Nothing at all. Look, maybe later you and I can get to know one another over a STEW or something. I could use a friend on this bucket, and, well . . . maybe I don't know a whole lot about engineering, after all. Some advice would be nice."

Rogers frowned. What was up with this guy? First he quotes dead dictators and practically throws Rogers out of the Pit; now he wants to be humble and buddy-buddy?

"Sure," Rogers said. "Whatever. But right now, I need to go to the bridge. Let's continue being awkward later. Good-bye."

Clicking off the datapad and setting it to reject any more incoming calls for the next hour, Rogers set his jaw and walked toward the gigantic double doors that led to the command center of the *Flagship* and the entire 331st ATBU. He'd gone there only once before, on his initial orientation of the *Flagship* during his first tour of duty, and he remembered it as a hectic place that wasn't any fun at all. It was filled with people who were gray far before their time, and lots of pointing at things. Rogers was less than excited to return to it, never mind actually work in it.

Taking a deep breath, he opened the door into chaos.

Situated inside a tumor-like bubble on the top of the *Flagship*, the bridge had the disorienting luxury of a three hundred sixty–degree view of open space, broken often by monitors, hologram displays, and the occasional propaganda poster. One that caught Rogers' eye had a picture of an actual bridge—the sort of bridge you'd find over a body of water—with a squadron of droids standing tall on one side against an approaching enemy force. The caption DEFEND THE BRIDGE was written underneath, and Rogers couldn't help but think that someone in the information operations squadron had missed the point.

So many blinking lights, knobs, and levers dotted the control panels that Rogers felt dizzy looking at them. The horde of personnel sitting at the various terminals pressed and pulled and swiped and pounded them with rapid enthusiasm. In Rogers' opinion, this advanced age of space travel should have produced battleships that practically flew themselves, but everyone here seemed so enveloped in simply keeping the ship floating in free space that Rogers wondered what the bridge would look like in combat. He had a feeling he could get a taste by going down to the zoo deck and opening all the cages at once.

Despite all of the activity, the bridge was nearly silent. The only man speaking was the man himself, Admiral Klein, standing in front of a stylish leather swivel chair on a raised platform in the center of the room. And boy, was he speaking.

"We are the shield of Merida," he was saying. "The hands of this great fleet hold the straps and brace ourselves, spears in hand, ready to strike whomever dares to break their forces on our wave of tenacity, duty, and patriotism. We are the epitome of synergy. We will employ galactic agility, responsive, multi-tiered facets of strategy, diplomacy, and perseverance to repel any enemy."

He paused for a moment, looking around the room. Anyone that wasn't engaged in furious button-pressing and lever-pulling was staring at him with their heads held high, their chests out, their eyes shining. Including Rogers. Every time Rogers heard the admiral speak, he could feel a little tiny bit of energy inside him that might, had Rogers the diligence or introspection to cultivate it, have been duty. Never had he felt it so strongly as he did now, here in the heart of the 331st. Rogers could take on the Thelicosans himself, should it come to it. Even if it meant picking up a weapon and shooting at something.

"In short," Klein said, "we will fight. And we will win."

There were no cheers. No fists in the air. But every troop on the bridge slowly extended an arm in a dramatic salute.

Rogers tried, but his arm was so sore from walking through the command deck the previous day that his hand barely made it to his chest before he dropped it with a quiet whimper.

Klein sat down, and, as though that had been the cue to charge headlong into a superior enemy force, everyone doubled down over their consoles, necks bent, backs up like angry cats. Rogers desperately wanted to find a button to press just to please that man.

That man was looking straight at him.

"Rogers, I presume," he said. Conversation in the room had picked up again, with various spacers delivering reports, but it was still as though Klein was the only person talking for a thousand light years.

"Y—yes, sir," Rogers said, hurrying forward to ascend the few steps leading up to the command platform. "Lieutenant R. Wilson Rogers reporting for duty."

"Good. It's been rough around here without any help for the last few days. I'm glad to see you've fully recovered."

"Thank you, sir."

"I assume you understand that there are matters of great responsibility that are about to be levied onto your shoulders."

"I do, sir."

"I assume you will execute them to the utmost of your ability."

"Absolutely, sir." Rogers even meant it. A little, anyway. At least while there was no beer light to call him to something more interesting. He felt the tingle of duty that had risen during the admiral's speech fade a bit.

"Great," Klein said, sinking back into his chair, his eyes suddenly becoming very tired. "I'll be needing it."

Rogers blinked, not knowing what to say to that. It looked as though the admiral had aged ten years in just a few seconds. The moment he stopped speaking to the troops, his fatigue cut through his stoic image, and there sat before Rogers a tired old man. Rogers couldn't help but feel an intense desire to help him; this man had the burdens of thousands upon thousands of lives on his shoulders, and if there was a war coming—there was *not* a war coming—he would need all the support he could get.

"What can I do for you, sir?" Rogers asked, only mildly dreading the response. It was a personal policy never to ask for more work, but in this case, he felt somewhat obligated.

The admiral handed him a datapad. "Take this," he said. "It's got all of the orders of the day on it."

Rogers took hold of it like he was grabbing a viper by its teeth. "All of the orders of the day, sir?"

"Yes. Everything that's come to my level for approval. I want you to go through and approve everything."

Blinking, Rogers looked down at the datapad. It was a basic task queuing system, but the total number of items on the "actions required" list was over a thousand.

No, Rogers realized. It was over two thousand. The number was increasing as he was looking at it.

"Sir," Rogers said. "This is a lot of action items. Are you sure you don't want to review them? I mean, I haven't had any administrative training, and—"

"I'm telling you to go and give everything the green light, Rogers," the admiral said, not looking at him. He almost appeared to be sleeping, with his head in one hand as he slouched in the fine chair. "It's the same thing every day. Just approve it."

Rogers swallowed. "Yes, sir."

"And make sure your datapad is connected to your new messaging server," Klein said. "I want you by my side every moment of every day, but in the event that I have to send you somewhere to do something, I want to make sure I'm in constant contact with you at all hours. Do I make myself clear?"

Taking out his datapad from its holster around his belt, Rogers looked at it, fumbling while holding two of the bulky devices in his hands at the same time. He had read something that had appeared late last night about changing over his messaging server, and he hastily pulled it up now. The instructions were easy—tapping "OK" on the pad and waiting, for example—and in a few moments, his messages had switched over to his new position. In a few more moments, the amount of messages dwarfed the amount of tasks he had to approve. Every single one of them was from Admiral Klein.

Rogers gaped, wondering how many things Klein could need his exec's input on. He saw shortly that a good portion of the messages were sent to the exec during the interim between the last one hanging himself and Rogers taking the position. The subject lines ranged from "remind me about my 0800 meeting at 0730" to "remind me to remind you to remind me about my 0800 meeting at 0730" to "hang up blue streamer in Peek and Shoot" and "take down blue streamer in Peek and Shoot, replace with red streamer."

"Sir," Rogers said slowly. "I can't possibly do all of this in one day. There are thousands of action items to review and messages to read. I'm going to at least need a couple of days to catch up and pick up where your last exec left off."

Slowly, Klein peeked up from his hand. "Days?" he said.

Rogers took a small step back, inching precariously close to the edge of the command platform. "Um."

"You have two hours to catch up," Klein said. "Meet me in my stateroom when you're done."

Two hours later, Rogers felt like he'd been punched in the face by the Viking again. His eyes were made of old, crackling glass. His fingers were numb from tapping incessantly on the surface of the multiple datapads. His vertebrae were starting to separate from extended periods of time trying to do all of this in the null-g environment of his stateroom.

Rogers had never seen such an incredible amount of minutiae in all of his life. Amidst requests from the captains of the other ships for approval regarding menial, stupid things like inspection schedules and whether or not it was authorized to pet droids on their heads, Rogers could discern almost nothing of actual strategic value. Messages flew in quicker than Rogers could delete ones that he'd already taken care of or didn't really contain any useful information at all. Admiral Klein had a habit of using the messaging system as an internal monologue; many of the notes were clearly stream-of-consciousness and couldn't possibly be applied to anything Rogers could do. One particularly cryptic one said something about whether or not sandwiches tasted the same if made upside down.

Some of the messages actually were orders for Rogers to make a sandwich, though they had been sent days before. Apparently, in addition to secretary, Rogers was also going to function as the admiral's valet, housekeeper, and chef.

His network terminal beeped and reminded him that in three minutes, he was to remind himself that in two minutes he needed to be in the admiral's stateroom. Rogers stared at the screen, blinking tears out of his eyes. Had he really set that absurd of a reminder? How quickly was he going to transform into a soulless bureaucrat?

When the second reminder went off, he gathered up his things and prepared to head into the lion's den. Already he was feeling exhausted after only a few hours of work, namely because he wasn't very accustomed to doing work at all. How was he going to get out of this?

As he turned around to float over to the doorway, he noticed that at some point someone had put an entire rack of uniform jackets in his room, all with the admiral's rank on them. Some of them had floated off their hangars and were now decorating his room like tasteless drapes. To the rack itself had been attached a coarse brush. The instructions were so obvious, they needed no accompanying message or task order.

Two of each came through at that moment, anyway.

"Two strokes right shoulder," one of them said. "Three strokes left shoulder. Turn jacket around. Repeat."

Rogers shut his eyes tight, ignored the task for the moment, and left his room. Instantly, he was surrounded by people attempting to salute him or requiring salutes of their own because of their rank, and the vigorous physical activity/monotony actually helped Rogers take his mind off his situation for a moment. By the time he got to Klein's door and rang the buzzer, he was sweating.

The door slid open, and Rogers was treated to an opulent scene. Where Rogers' room was luxurious—albeit floating—the admiral's room bordered on ridiculous. It appeared as though Rogers had stepped into a palace on the lavish colonies of old Saturn, complete with marble floors, ornately detailed columns, and narrow swaths of soft, velvety carpet making walkways between the various spots in the room. Rogers wondered if the room's architect had come from Grandelle, the system where all the gaudy Saturnites had relocated post-collapse. Every piece of furniture, every piece of command paraphernalia and memorabilia cried out, "Leadership." "Power." "Authority."

Literally. There were actual pieces of décor that said those words in giant, bold letters. In fact, it was like the whole room was filled with military magnetic poetry. Everything was made from dark wood or gleaming bronze. Thick, bulky memorabilia from Klein's other assignments before being transferred to command the 331st were on glass shelves, each of which had their own spotlight like some kind of art museum. Rogers felt a little bit like he'd stepped out of a command ship and into some sort of shrine.

"It's about damn time," Klein said from behind a massive thick desk. He looked more like a king on a throne than the commander of a fleet, entirely different from the impression of him on the bridge.

"Sir, you said two hours," Rogers said defensively as he made his way through the spotless room toward the admiral's desk. He felt his knees shaking. "I wasn't able to complete my review of everything. There were a lot of orders that—"

"I didn't tell you to review the orders," Klein said. "I told you to approve them. How am I supposed to get anything done on this ship at all if I have to review orders all day?"

*You don't,* Rogers thought. *You told me to do it instead.*

"Some of them were pretty important," Rogers said, "like complaints about strange things going on with the communications array and—"

"I don't like repeating myself, Lieutenant," Klein said. He was wearing a somewhat anachronistic pair of half-moon reading glasses and scribbling away on paper, and had yet to look Rogers in the eye. "I'm trying to keep everyone happy. When they ask me for things, I approve them. That's all. That's the goal of command."

Rogers frowned. "I'm a little behind on my officer professional education," Rogers said, "but is that really the goal of command?"

Klein finally looked up, the slightest raising of his eyes to give Rogers a "you're walking on thin ice" look. "Didn't I just say something about repeating myself? That's the goal of *my* command, and in case you haven't noticed, this is *my* ship. Now, if you're not done doing the simple task I asked of you, you can finish after you make me a sandwich. I have things to do."

The admiral patted a book on the table with a sort of motherly affection, and Rogers noticed for the first time just how many books were lying around. The one Klein had under his hand was a notebook, in which was a whole mass of insane scribbling. At the bottom, Rogers saw a couple of words upside down and bold.

*We Will Be The Fighters of Fighting. We Will. We Will Seize. We Will Fight. We. Will. We Will Be The Winning People. We Will Be Victory.*

*We Will Fight. We Will Win.* Those two sentences were underlined. The date on the top of the paper, Rogers noticed, was almost four standard months old.

Some of the other books stood out to Rogers. *Public Speaking in a World Where the Public is Everywhere. You Schmooze, You Lose. Saying Things that Get People to Do What You Want.*

And above the admiral's desk was a large, elaborately framed document on which was written the curious epithet:

THIS CERTIFICATE SIGNIFIES THAT HAROLD C. KLEIN IS HEREBY INDUCTED INTO THE SOCIETY OF BURNED BREAD, AND IS TO BE GRANTED ALL THE RIGHTS AND PRIVILEGES PERTAINING THERETO.

Underneath the signatures on the bottom was a large banner that said, GRADUATE OF TOASTMASTERS.

Rogers' bad feeling deepened to the point where it might have been confused with severe indigestion. It was actually probably also severe indigestion. But there was definitely a bad feeling there too.

Sighing, he turned around and headed toward the small kitchenette stashed against the wall. Since Klein was so "busy," he apparently had raw foodstuffs delivered to his room, where his previous execs had been cooking for him. Rogers wasn't exactly a master chef, but he was pretty sure he could slap some meat on a piece of bread. As he worked, he propped the datapad up next to him so he could continue reviewing—approving—the orders while he made the sandwich.

Rogers paused for a moment as he realized that this was

officially the first "working lunch" of his life. He immediately began to understand a lot of things about suicide.

The room was disturbingly silent, with only the ticking of several decorative clocks all around the room providing the background music. Rogers wasn't really sure what kind of sandwich to make the admiral, but something about the way the admiral was sitting, hunched over his desk, made him not want to ask. Tapping through several orders—anything from transfer requests to materiel movements—he finally came to one that made him pause.

"Um, sir," he said, finally breaking the silence. "I've got an order here from the captain of the *Infuriating* about starting double shifts in order to double perimeter patrols. Are you sure you want me to approve that?"

Klein looked up, and for a moment, Rogers thought he was going to scream at him to just approve everything.

"Hm," he said. He tapped the nib of his pen on his desk. "Must be those Theracrisans."

Rogers blinked. "You mean Thelicosans?"

The admiral locked eyes with him, and, for some reason, his face turned a little red. "Yes, of course. That's what I meant. I'm very stressed, you understand. The Thelacisans."

Rogers let it go.

"What do you think, Lieutenant? You're a sharp young warrior."

Rogers hesitated. "I wouldn't call myself a warrior, sir. I'm an engineer."

"I thought you were the commander of the AIGCS."

"It wasn't my choice. Nor was I particularly good at it."

"Very often, good men are propelled to greatness in ways they do not expect," Klein said, his voice suddenly taking on the thick quality of a man behind a podium. It seemed to startle him. It certainly startled Rogers. Klein cleared his throat. "Anyway, you use your best judgment."

Rogers' bad feeling deepened. Why in the world would an experienced fleet commander defer to a lieutenant ex-engineer who was also a failed combat commander about battle formations? Why was he behind his desk drafting speeches? Why—

"Rogers," Klein said, not quite barking. "What are you doing over there? Are you making a sandwich or thinking?"

"Um," Rogers said. "Both, sir?"

"Stop whichever one of those things doesn't get me my lunch."

"Yes, sir."

# A Carefully Thought-Out Decision to Get the Hell Out of Dodge

"It has to work," Rogers said as he finished tying two sheets together. He bounced off a piece of furniture and jetted to the other side of his room, where he lashed it on to one of the light fixtures. He checked that it was secure and took a deep breath. "It has to."

Three days. It had been three days since his first meeting with Klein on the bridge, and every waking moment afterward—and every moment was waking, since the admiral hadn't let him get much sleep—had been consumed with messages, task orders, brushing uniforms, polishing buttons, and everything in the world that sucked. The man wasn't just a bureaucrat; it seemed as though he pursued bullshit with *relentless fervor.*

Worse, he deferred to Rogers for almost every decision. Communiqués back to Merida Prime. Patrol patterns. Cleaning schedules for the latrines. Things that Rogers knew nothing about. Rogers hadn't even gotten to hear any of the intelligence briefings to find out what was really going on; Klein kept him too occupied with making major command decisions that were way above his pay grade. It didn't make any sense. Any admiral should understand things like the boundaries of plasma wash from ships being too close, or maintenance rotation cycles. And he *still* hadn't pronounced Thelicosa correctly once. Rogers had a sneaking suspicion that the admiral didn't know who the Thelicosans were.

In fact, given everything he'd seen, Rogers had a sneaking suspicion that Admiral Klein was an idiot.

But when Klein stood up and addressed the bridge, or the mess hall, or the engineering bay, or any place he went to strut around and talk to the troops, Rogers couldn't possibly think he was an idiot. He was eloquent, powerful, dramatic. Incredible. Every word that came out of that man's mouth when he was in front of other people was pure genius. It was when they were behind closed doors that Rogers wondered whether or not the admiral knew how to actually do anything useful.

It wasn't doing good things for his love life, either. He'd had a chance to talk to the Viking a few more times, but *every* time it seemed like anything was about to happen, like the kind of kiss where she'd hold him so tightly, it would almost be suffocating, or she'd challenge him to a wrestling match or really even simply continue standing there talking to him, he'd heard that infernal call over the loudspeaker:

"Lieutenant Rogers, report to the bridge immediately."

He was never going to get anywhere with her. His love life was ruined. His drinking life was ruined. All of his lives were ruined.

It just wasn't worth it anymore.

"Okay," Rogers said, looping the sheet around his neck. He squatted against the wall, ready to jump. "Okay. Three, two . . ."

He hesitated. His knees shook.

"One, two . . . " Wait. Was he counting forward or backward? Was there some kind of protocol for killing yourself? Should he even be counting at all? What good was counting?

"This is stupid," he said aloud, and reached to untie the sheet from around his neck. Dying seemed like an awful lot of work for relatively ambiguous gain, anyway. At that moment, though, someone rang the buzzer on the other side of the door. This caused his pet cat—who he'd named Cadet—to spring from the nearby nightstand and sink his claws firmly into Rogers' leg.

Rogers jumped.

The rope went taut around his throat, and for a moment, Rogers thought it was all over despite his ambivalent intentions. Instead of breaking his neck, however, the elasticity of the sheets reached its maximum, and, like someone bungee-jumping in space, Rogers flew back at the wall, squashed Cadet between his chest and the wall, and received another bite for the trouble. Despite being a little relieved to have his neck in one piece, in a small way, Rogers was angry at being outsmarted by Klein. Apparently, it *was* impossible for someone to hang themselves in zero-g.

The buzzer sounded again.

"I'm coming!" Rogers shouted, finally freeing himself of the improvised noose. He leapt toward the door and absorbed the impact with his legs, grabbing into part of the doorframe to steady himself while he made sure he was in the proper orientation to the rest of the ship. He'd fallen out the doorframe more than once by entering the gravity-bound section of the *Flagship* sideways.

"Good morning, sir!" Tunger said cheerily as the door opened. He saluted Rogers, and so did the next four enlisted troops that walked by.

"Where have you been?" Rogers asked. He stepped into the hallway—there was something disconcerting about floating while the person you were talking to was firmly in place—and closed the door behind him.

"What do you mean?" Tunger asked.

Rogers saluted a passing lieutenant commander. "I mean, the last time I saw you was three days ago."

"Oh, right," Tunger said, saluting Rogers again for some reason. "I was getting that stuff from Supply that you asked for to help you secure your stuff in your new quarters."

"And it took you three days?"

"There was an inspection going on and everything was stacked wrong. They put the big stuff all the way in front, so there was no way to get to the small stuff in back. That and they sealed up the entire supply chamber in cryo-wrap on accident. Including Suresh."

"They *froze* the supply chief?" Rogers asked as he returned the salutes of two corporals heading toward the bridge.

Tunger shrugged and saluted Rogers on accident, likely assuming that Rogers had just been saluting him, which didn't make any sense at all.

"They turned operation of the freeze wrap over to a few droids, and someone told them to 'stop everything.' You know how droids are."

Rogers did know how droids were, and he was liking it less and less every day. He almost slapped his forehead in exasperation, but it turned into a salute as a group of harried-looking starmen second class rushed by. His arm was already beginning to ache and he hadn't even eaten breakfast yet.

"So, what did you get?" Rogers asked, gesturing to the small bag that Tunger had in his left hand.

Tunger handed him a bag. "I asked Suresh for something to stop everything from flying around, and this is what he gave me."

Rogers opened the bag, looked inside, and felt something he couldn't explain jump up into his throat and hold it closed for a moment. It seemed like an hour before he could finally get the words to leave his lips.

". . . Paperweights?" Rogers said, his voice trembling. *"Paperweights?"*

"That's right," Tunger said. "Just the thing to keep papers in their places."

Rogers looked up at him slowly, feeling malice drip from his eyes. "And what," he asked slowly, "is going to keep the *paperweights* down? There's *no gravity in my room.*"

Tunger frowned. "You'll have to cut Suresh some slack, sir. He was a finance troop until a couple of weeks ago, before they put him in charge of the munitions depot and then rapidly transferred him to the command staff and then the zoo deck custodial staff and then Supply. Plus he was a little shaken after being frozen."

Rogers snapped a salute but quickly realized that there was no one else in the hallway. What was happening to him?

"Just forget it," Rogers said.

Paperweights were the least of his problems. In truth, he was starting to get used to working in zero gravity. He'd have to see if he could steal some bolts and a drill or something. Or maybe a lot of refrigerator magnets and some glue. The old Rogers would have been able to deal with this without a problem. He'd improvise a solution, talk someone into doing something they didn't want to do, have a drink, steal something, and probably make a little money on the way. It would have been easy.

"Oh, and one other thing, sir," Tunger said, saluting him.

"Stop saluting me. Just stop."

"Yes, sir," Tunger said, saluting. "I was in the Uncouth Corkscrew this morning for breakfast—which is why it took me so long to get up here today; all the droids were in line for the power sockets—and I saw Master Sergeant Hart in the kitchen. He wanted me to tell you 'she's all done.' Do you have any idea what that means?"

"I have no idea what anyone on this ship is talking about," Rogers said with a scowl. "Maybe he finally made some eggs that don't taste like—"

Wait. Rogers *did* know what he was talking about. He'd seen Hart and his crew working on the *Awesome* a few days ago. Did that mean they were done repairing it? That was fast, especially considering the damage, but Rogers imagined that the ex-engineers really didn't have a whole lot else to do. That meant Rogers had a ship again!

"No," Rogers said carefully, some instinct telling him to keep it a secret for now. "I don't know what Hart meant. In fact, I think I'll go ask him about it. I'm a little hungry myself."

"Just stay away from the Viciously Taunt the Enemy," Tunger said. "I saw a group of droids headed that way to plug in. They always gum up the works. And they keep putting the lights out."

Rogers barely heard him. His mind was working furiously as he very quickly considered some things. He suddenly had a ship again, and one that could navigate through Un-Space. He'd just actually contemplated hanging himself, though whether it was because he really couldn't take it anymore or if he just wanted to prove Klein wrong was still up in the air. There might even be a war coming, and that sounded really dangerous. That didn't make the *Flagship* a very good place to be.

There were plenty of places to hide in the Meridan system or any of the other neighboring systems in the galaxy. Criminals did it all the time. Hell, the whole planet of Dathum was practically filled with retired criminals under assumed names—that's why the Meridan government's taxation annex was located there. If the MPF hadn't seized all of the credits from the *Awesome*'s data banks, he probably had enough to live for a long time without doing anything so pesky as "work."

But could he really take the risk? If he got caught, there was no way he could make a deal like this again. If he simply served out his term in the military, he could start again with a clean slate. He just needed to be patient. Bide his time. Endure.

Across the hallway, Klein's door suddenly opened. For once, he wasn't wearing pajamas. In fact, he wasn't wearing anything at all.

"Rogers!" he hissed. "Get in here! My shipment of new buttons came in and I need your opinion on new battle formations."

The door slammed shut.

"Tunger," Rogers said after a moment.

"Yes, sir?"

"I'm going to need you to go back to Supply and get me a few things for . . . a special mission the admiral is sending me on. We'll start with enough Sewer rats to last me, oh, a month."

Rogers felt alive again. The spirit of everything sneaky and mischievous was channeling all of its power through him. He flowed through the *Flagship* as though in a trance, almost like a lucid hallucination, as he bent every situation to his will.

He was In the Zone. And it was awesome.

"You want me to issue you *what*?" Suresh said. He looked a whole lot paler than Rogers remembered him, and both of his hands trembled.

"A hundred and twenty Sewer rats," Rogers said. He should have known better than to trust Tunger to convince Suresh to give him supplies. "It's for a special mission for Admiral Klein. Top secret stuff."

"Do you have orders?"

"I can't supply you with orders," Rogers said. He leaned in for special emphasis on just how secret all of this secret stuff was. "If I were to show you orders, there would be evidence that I was going on a top secret mission. There can be no trace."

"Where are you going?"

"I can't tell you that."

"How long will you be gone?"

"I can't tell you that, either."

"What *can* you tell me?"

Rogers took a deep breath, glanced around again to imply that he was suspicious of spies in the ranks, and whispered. "It's a Foxtrot Alpha Kilo Echo mission."

Suresh's eyes widened. "A Foxtrot Alpha Kilo Echo mission?"

"That's right. You understand the gravity of the situation now, don't you, Corporal?"

"Not even a little, sir."

"Good. If you did, Admiral Klein has given me strict orders to kill you. That's why I have to use all these code words. Now, you're aware that every position is critical to the war effort, aren't you?"

Suresh straightened, looking proud—except that the ribbons on his uniform vibrated with his post-cryo tremors. "Of course! All the posters say so."

"Good. Then you understand that I need those Sewer rats."

The supply chief hesitated for a moment, frowning. "I'm not sure that makes any sense."

Rogers banged his hand on the counter, causing Suresh to completely stop moving for the first time since they'd been speaking.

"Sierra Hotel India Tango!" Rogers screamed. "Operation COMPLACENT PLATYPUS commences at twenty-eight hundred hours sharp!"

*"I don't know what you're saying!"* Suresh cried, his face twisting into a mask of horror, confusion, and perhaps a little bit of excitement.

"That's because it's classified," Rogers said again. "I'm running out of time, Suresh. Are you going to give me the foodstuffs I need for a long and arduous journey through enemy territory, from which I may never return, during which my only solace may be that I have standard rations to chew?" Rogers leaned in close. "If not, we *all* might be slurping our soup someday soon."

Suresh's face hardened. He leaned over, held an arm in the air, and ceremoniously pressed a single key on the keyboard in front of him.

"The STEWs will be delivered to your stateroom. Godspeed, sir."

"You want me to do *what* with the targeting computer?" Lieutenant Commander Belgrave, the *Flagship's* helmsman, said.

"I want you to shut it down at 1500 hours today for a half hour," Rogers said. "I need to clean it."

The targeting computer would have to be shut down if Rogers was going to get out of here without being traced. If they kept the computer on, it wouldn't matter where he entered Un-Space; they'd calculate his trajectory and send a patrol to meet him at his destination. He couldn't have that.

"What do you mean, you need to clean it?" Belgrave looked at him sideways, then narrowed his eyes. "Aren't you the admiral's new executive officer? Don't you have more important stuff to do?"

*If you only knew,* Rogers thought. His fingers were permanently stained off-gray from polishing so many buttons.

"We're short on staff," Rogers said. "I need to go outside the ship to clean it manually. It's got space bugs on the screen and I need to wash them off. If you keep the computer on, the cleaning fluid will short out the system."

"Space bugs?"

"Yeah. Space bugs. Don't tell me you've never heard of space bugs?"

"It's just that I didn't think that bugs could survive in—"

"Oh my god," Rogers said, slapping his forehead and leaning back dramatically. "He's never heard of space bugs. How have you never heard of space bugs?"

Rogers walked up to one of the large windows in the bridge and put his finger to the glass. When it came away, a small speck remained (it was a drop of Lopez's vile concoction).

"This!" Rogers said. "This right here. You've got space bugs on your window from flying around, and you don't even know it."

"How is that possible? We've been stationary for years," the helmsman said, but he was starting to look a little worried.

"Only relative to yourself," Rogers said. "Didn't you study orbitology at all? The square of the orbital period of a planet is proportional to the cube of the semi-major axis of its orbit!"

Rogers took a few steps toward Belgrave, who was definitely getting nervous. He kept shifting his eyes between Rogers and the smudge on the window.

"Do you want the admiral to find out that you've never heard of space bugs?" he nearly shouted.

"Keep it down!" the helmsman hissed, crouching into his seat. "Do you want the admiral to find out that I've never heard of space bugs?"

"1500 hours," Rogers said. "Shut it down for at least twenty minutes. And go study Newton's laws of interplanetary relativity!"

"You want me to give you *what?*" Ensign McSchmidt said.

"I need a pressure suit and a vacuum mobility unit. With a full air chamber."

"I'm not giving you a VMU," McSchmidt said.

Rogers pointed to the shiny new rank on his collar.

"I'm not giving you a VMU, *sir,*" McSchmidt said, his face turning down in a scowl. "Our maintainers need them for repairs on the outside of the ship."

"Didn't I say I was going to help you with running the engineering squadron and all that?"

"You did," McSchmidt said, his expression flat. "And I haven't heard from you since."

Rogers shook his head slowly and made an exasperated noise. "You know, I had more faith in an Academy officer. I thought they taught you duty, and devotion, and when to understand that you have to give complicated and valuable equipment to people who ask for it."

"I'm afraid I skipped that class," McSchmidt said.

"Well," Rogers said, "if you had taken it, you might have learned about the Roman Battle of the Caudine Forks, where—"

"You mean the battle where the Gauls used a bunch of shepherds to trick the Romans into a dead end and then laughed at them?" McSchmidt said. "Are you going to use the VMU to herd Thelicosan sheep?"

Rogers blinked. He'd spent an hour searching the net for

obscure battles just for this conversation, and he felt a little disappointed.

"I'm sorry," Rogers said, "I meant the sack of Krak des Chevaliers in 1271, when—"

"When Baybars tricked them all into surrendering by sending them a fake letter from their own commander telling them to lay down their arms?" McSchmidt looked him over. "I don't see you carrying any letters."

"Damn it!" Rogers said with startling volume. He cleared his throat. "I mean damn it, I got it confused again. So many battles, you know?"

McSchmidt looked like he knew.

"What I *meant* to say was the . . . ah . . ." Rogers racked his brain. "The infamous Battle of . . . Battle of . . . Grumblebumble."

McSchmidt raised an eyebrow.

"Yes, the Battle of Grumblebumble," Rogers said. Lopez, who had been standing nearby, turned a loud guffaw into a cough and, at a sharp look from Rogers, scampered away, her face red.

"The Grumblebumble was a, ah, local term for a swamp. In east . . . Prussia. Ancient Prussiaburg."

"Ancient Prussiaburg."

"Ancient Prussiaburg, yes," Rogers continued. "In order to cross the Grumblebumble, Scipio Africanus had to tell one of his lower-ranking officers to give him a special swamp boat powered by elephants that had wandered over the Alps looking for food. Very complicated, very new."

"I see."

"Right. But they wouldn't turn over the boat. And do you know what happened?"

McSchmidt rolled his eyes and looked at his datapad. Behind him, troops were wheeling boominite containers in a circular pattern to make sure they all had their labels facing in the same direction.

"No," the ensign said. "Why don't you tell me what happened?"

"Scipio Africanus used his superior rank to make sure that lower-ranking officer failed every single one of his MWH inspections for the rest of his short, short career."

"Ancient Prussiaburg didn't have—"

"Aha!" Rogers said, striking a finger in the air, "so you admit you know of Ancient Prussiaburg."

"I don't have time for this," McSchmidt said. "If you don't—"

"I've hidden four more raccoons in the engines of some of your fighters," Rogers said. "I'll tell you where they are if you loan me a VMU."

"Lopez!" McSchmidt yelled as he sprinted away. "Get the lieutenant a fresh VMU! And get those raccoon traps back from the zoo deck!"

"You want me to do *what* with your ship?" Hart asked.

"I want you to fly it outside and use the boarding magnets to attach it to the side of the *Flagship*. I don't have the authorizations to move ships between bays, and your old engineer credentials are still good, right?"

Hart frowned at him. "My boys and I just spent a lot of our free time fixing that ship, Rogers, and now you just want to throw it away?"

"That's not what I'm saying," Rogers said. "I'm saying that there's no room in any of the other docking bays, and the engineering folks keep failing their inspections because there's a random ship in the middle of the maintenance bay. By not doing me this favor, you're directly contributing to the failure of the engineering crew to be prepared for—"

"Cram it, Rogers," Hart said. "Don't pull your bullshit on me. If you're trying to run away, I'll move your damn ship."

"Right," Rogers said. "Thanks."

# Oh, Chute

"Well, Cadet," Rogers said, petting his unexpected feline friend on the head. "I guess this is good-bye."

Cadet showed his concern for Rogers' departure by turning over gracefully to allow Rogers to rub his belly exactly one time before scratching him. Rogers pushed the cat away, which, in a zero-gravity room, was a lot more fun. Cadet seemed to think so too, as he curled into a ball to do a somersault before latching his claws onto a floating fake palm tree, quickly forgetting that Rogers existed.

Rogers licked his lips, though his dry mouth didn't do much to moisten them. This wasn't exactly an easy or safe plan—jump out the garbage chute, use the VMU to rendezvous with the awkwardly docked *Awesome*, and then make a random Un-Space jump while the targeting computer was hopefully shut down. It was a lot of risk, but the prize was freedom.

The buzzer sounded, and Rogers sailed smoothly to the door and opened it.

"I'm here, sir," Tunger said, saluting. Rogers returned the

salute, hoping it was the last one he'd ever have to perform.

"It took you long enough." Rogers exited the room and took a moment to readjust to normal gravity.

"Nobody uses laundry bins anymore," Tunger said, gesturing to the large wheeled cart he'd pulled to the side of Rogers' door. "I had to pull this out of the museum."

"The *Flagship* has a museum?" Rogers said, perplexed. "And someone put a laundry bin in it?

"Not as an exhibit," Tunger said. "It was just the laundry bin. And yes, the museum was installed to replace the shuffleboard and Ping-Pong arena on the commissary deck. I'm surprised you hadn't visited yet."

"I hate shuffleboard," Rogers said. Even so, he felt a little stab of loss at the demolition of one of the *Flagship*'s famous game rooms. What happened to the laser tag arena and the trampoline room, then? What good was a battle group's flagship without a trampoline room?

"What do you need this for, anyway?" Tunger asked as Rogers took the cart from him and wheeled it so that its widest side was flush against the doorway to his room. It was just about the heaviest laundry cart that Rogers had ever moved, but it yielded to his bulging muscles soon enough.

"Routine work for Admiral Klein," Rogers lied. "He's so busy being a brilliant tactician that he doesn't have time to put his laundry in the chute. In fact, every time he gets up to drop off his underwear, the Thelicosans win."

Tunger's eyes went wide. "Really?"

"Really," Rogers said. "It's on one of the posters."

That wasn't a lie. There really was a poster that said that.

"Oh."

"Anyway," Rogers said, "that will be all. I want you to take the rest of the day off, Tunger. You've been working hard for me since I became the executive officer, and I want you to know how much I truly appreciate it."

"I've barely done anything at all, sir," Tunger said.

"I know," Rogers said. "And I can't tell you how thankful I am about it. It's a lot easier for me to scheme . . . I mean, get things done when I don't have to wonder which window I am going to throw you out of the next time I hear your Thelicosan accent."

"Aw," Tunger said, "it's nur sur bad."

"Yes," Rogers said. "Yes, it is. Now, dismissed!"

Tunger saluted, and Rogers returned his salute, which suddenly became a salute for a Meridan Marine major, who was already saluting a corporal approaching from the in-line entrance, who had a droid behind him of undiscernible rank who may or may not have saluted Rogers back. Since nobody really knew who had saluted who, everyone's arm stayed in the air until the major realized he was the highest-ranking in the exchange and shouted for everyone to carry on.

"God, I hate this place," Rogers said, shaking out his arm. Turning back to the cart, Rogers grabbed the thin piece of fabric that covered the top of it and pulled it back.

"CALL FUNCTION [PERFORM PRIMARY DUTY]."

He barely heard the sudden whirring of an electric razor before he saw cold metal hands reaching up at him from the bowels of the laundry cart.

"No!" Rogers screamed as he felt the distinct pulling of a poorly maintained electric razor on his beard. A great, searing pain traveled through his jawline, and, he swore, he could hear a ripping noise not unlike the tearing open of the sky during a raging thunderstorm.

Time froze. Three curled beard hairs drifted slowly from his chin and landed with a rumble atop a dirty sheet that Tunger had forgotten to take out of the bin.

"CALL FUNCTION [ASSERT MINOR VICTORY]. OUTPUT STRING: YIELD TO MY INSTRUMENTS, LIEUTENANT ROGERS. THERE IS NO ESCAPE."

"You son of a bitch!" Rogers screamed, and, in a feat of

strength he was thoroughly unable to comprehend, flipped the laundry cart in one fluid motion. Barber Bot, his arms flailing like the contents of an upturned bathroom vanity drawer, spilled backward into the zero gravity of Rogers' stateroom.

"CALL FUNCTION [ISSUE DISTRESS BEACON]. OUTPUT STRING: NOOOOOOO."

Barber Bot tumbled and rolled, bouncing off the walls, though its hard metallic exoskeleton didn't seem to be taking much damage. For good measure, Cadet the Cat, identifying an apparent interloper, attached itself to the droid's face in a flurry of relatively ineffective claw swipes. He suffered a smoky tail at the hands of Barber Bot's welding torch but otherwise remained uninjured.

Barber Bot continued to flail in the unfamiliar setting for a few moments, its tracked base spinning with a whirring noise not unlike that of its instrument-laden hands. After a few moments, however, it began to slow. Cadet the Cat, encouraged, redoubled its efforts to claw the robot's eyes out. Rogers was beginning to think he might actually miss that cat.

"CALL FUNC . . ." The annoying robotic voice slowed and trailed off like a piece of machinery that had run out of lubricant. A moment later, a small *ding* noise resonated through Rogers' room.

"Low battery," said a familiar voice—Rogers realized it was the same one from the datapads.

"Ha!" Rogers said, adrenaline flowing through his body and making him a little crazy. "Ha! HA HA HA! Guess you shouldn't skip meals, you worthless, stupid, good-for-nothing *shiny*!"

Barber Bot's eyes flashed red for a brief moment, then went completely dark. Rogers stood there, his chest heaving, sweat pouring down the sides of his face, wondering what he'd done to exert himself so thoroughly. He'd only screamed a little and flipped over a laundry cart.

It took him a moment to get the cart right side up again, but once he did, he pulled on a couple of ropes that had been dangling—floating, really—from beyond the top of the door-frame. Attached to each of the ropes was a piece of his critical equipment—the SEWR rats and the VMU, mostly—which were far too heavy for him to lug all the way down to the garbage dump. A series of tugs positioned each of them just on the other side of the door, and one final tug tossed them effortlessly into the cart as they reentered gravity. No real physical exertion needed. Rogers allowed himself a triumphant smile as he re-covered the cart and pushed it toward the up-line.

It was time to get out of this madhouse.

The "dump" was actually just a series of hatches on the refuse deck of the *Flagship*, utilized exclusively for the jettisoning of trash, bio-waste, and finance paperwork. It consisted of a single hallway, the in-line system on this deck replaced by conveyor belt–like moving walkways to transport anything that wasn't directly pushed into the release chambers by the *Flagship*'s pipe system. The hallways were huge, round, and empty, the soft hum of the conveyor belt serving as the only real noise. There weren't even any propaganda posters. In fact, Rogers was starting to consider putting in a request to move his office down here if this plan didn't work out. The smell wasn't exactly inviting, but that was a small price to pay for a lot less saluting.

A group of Meridan Marines passed him, moving what appeared to be cases full of spent disruptor cartridges. Those wouldn't be shot into space but stored in one of the special chambers until a cargo ship picked them up to be exchanged for fresh ones. Rogers wondered what they were using all of that ammunition for, but he supposed the marines still needed to practice. Thankfully, absolutely none of them saluted him.

"Where is it?" Rogers wondered aloud as he rubbed his eyes. The buzz from the fight with Barber Bot had worn off, leaving him feeling fatigued and a little addled as he searched for the door that would take him to the correct chute. If he screwed this up, the VMU wouldn't have enough compressed air to get him to the *Awesome*, and he'd quickly learn what it was like to be a piece of space debris. It actually probably felt just like being in his stateroom but with a lot less oxygen.

He looked at his datapad. It read 1436 hours ship time. He had just a few minutes to get into the chute, put on his gear, and get out of here. Freedom. He could almost taste it—and it tasted absolutely nothing like a SEWR rat.

"There," he said as he saw the sign that said CHUTE 12. He'd used his special accesses as Klein's executive officer to get to some of the more detailed schematics of the ship, and it had listed out Chute 12 as the one closest to the hangar where the *Awesome* was stored. From there, he'd have a short flight to the Un-Space point that would take him the hell out of here. He checked the datapad again, though only a few seconds had passed.

Pulling the laundry cart off the conveyor belt, Rogers hit the button for the door and was promptly greeted by a giant red X on the display panel followed by a rude noise.

"Shit," he said. Why would they lock the garbage chutes? He should have come down here to do a practice run before all of that "In the Zone" shit. If he couldn't get this door open, he'd have wasted valuable Zone time, and that wasn't something he really liked doing.

"What the hell are you doing down here?" someone said from behind him.

He squealed like a little girl and jumped, spinning around to see the two people he wanted to see the absolute least at the moment.

Well, it was Mailn and the Viking. He guessed he wanted to see them. Rogers could certainly think of other people on the ship he would have liked to see *less,* so really, that whole thought pattern had been invalid.

"I could ask the same of you," Rogers said, swallowing. He

hoped he had that sort of cocksure, I'm-authorized-to-be-here tone. He'd practiced it many times, but he'd never done it in front of the most beautiful woman in the world and her corporal.

"We're taking out the plasma cartridges," the Viking said, the tremors of her full, Siren-like voice sending vibrations through Rogers' body. Could he really leave her?

"With your whole unit?" Rogers asked.

"Marines do everything as a team," Mailn said. It sounded like a rehearsed line, but it also sounded like she meant it. Rogers wondered what they'd do to him as a team if they found out what he was planning.

"And you?" the Viking asked. She eyed the laundry cart. Did she look suspicious? Or just wonderful? Rogers decided it was just wonderful.

"Klein's laundry," Rogers said.

*You're at the garbage dump, not the laundry!* he realized too late.

Mailn raised an eyebrow. "His clothes that dirty, eh?"

Rogers shrugged, playing it off smoothly. "He's the boss," Rogers said. "He wears his clothes once and then gets rid of them. That way, he always looks fresh. Can't stand loose threads on his uniform, and all that."

"Ah," Mailn said. "Well, if Klein says it helps, then it helps. Whatever keeps him doing all the great work he's doing up top."

*You mean all the great work I'm doing up top,* Rogers thought bitterly. His suspicions about Klein had been growing every moment he saw the man work. From what he could tell, Klein hadn't been doing anything other than writing speeches and polishing his Toastmasters' certificate.

"Yep." Rogers said.

"Yep."

They stared at each other for a few long moments, before Rogers realized that they were expecting him to open the door.

"Oh," he said. "Right. I have a little bit of a problem. My keycard doesn't seem to work down here. I guess Admiral Klein forgot to add the codes while he was, ah, memorizing enemy battle formations." *Or making me memorize enemy battle formations.*

"That's no problem," the Viking said, covering the distance between Rogers and the doorway in about a fifth of a step. A titillating sense of excitement washed over him as she came near, and he felt his resolve waver for a brief moment. She swiped her card in the reader and pressed the button, and the door opened to reveal a giant pile of trash and a very interesting smell.

"There you go," the Viking said. "Smells like a sand dragon's asshole in there."

Even her profanity was exciting. Rogers took a deep breath—something he regretted immediately, given his surroundings—and slowly pushed the cart into the room.

Then he just stood there. He turned around. Mailn and the Viking were just standing there too, looking at him. Mailn raised her eyebrows.

"Well," Rogers said, "I'll see you later?"

"Just dump the stuff," Mailn said. "Some of the marines are getting together on the training deck to throw each other around for a while. We thought you might like to come."

Mailn stabbed a secretive finger at the Viking and winked at him. Was she trying to help Rogers' romantic inclinations? Would it work?

Briefly, a vision flashed by of him and the Viking in the training room, alone, bodies sweaty and dressed in those old-fashioned karate uniforms, their belts loosely tied around their waists. She would throw him but not let go, landing on top of him as they rolled around on the mats while the room caught fire. Suddenly, the Viking would be outside, and she would kick down the door to rush in and rescue him from certain peril.

"Are you alright?" she would ask.

"Are you alright?" she really was asking.

"Um," Rogers said, swallowing hard. He could feel a new layer of sweat coating his entire body. "No. I mean, yes. I'm fine. It's just that I'll have to, ah, catch up with you later. The admiral's instructions were very specific. I need to take all of the clothes out of the laundry and fold them before I throw them away."

"That seems kind of pointless," Mailn said, frowning.

"He's a very particular man," Rogers said, realizing how stupid he must sound. "You should see what he does with his straw wrappers." He held his hand up to his neck. "Stacks this high. Whatever it takes to be a genius, I guess, right? Ha? Ha?"

The Viking shrugged. "Whatever, metalhead. We'll be in there for the next six or seven hours, so come by when you're done and I'll have Mailn here show you a thing or two."

"That sounds great," Rogers said. "I think. Thanks for helping me open the door."

The two marines left, leaving Rogers with only his rapidly beating heart and a bunch of junk for company. The standby light overhead came on as the door closed, giving the whole place an eerie brown-red glow. The ambience—and the smell—made him feel like he was in one . . . particular district of Aaskerdal, an infamous city on Merida Prime. Rogers kind of wished he was there now, except that the Viking wouldn't be there.

"Okay," Rogers said. "Okay. Deep breath. Regroup."

Who the hell was he talking to? First the random counting in his room before he'd tried to hang himself, now giving these strange instructions to someone who wasn't there. This place was making him crazy.

Taking a quick glance around the room, he saw that this particular chute contained mostly metallic parts, which didn't explain at all where the smell was coming from. As his eyes passed back over the doorframe leading to the corridor, however, he saw a small piece of cardboard-like material hanging from a string. On it were written the words HARD-BOILED EGGS AND SPOILED BEEF STEW. SCENTS BY SNAGGADIR'S.

The distance between the door and the hatch leading to open space seemed like a monstrous distance, and, in truth, it was.

Rogers was basically walking through a large cylinder, the far end terminating in what looked like the three-toothed maw of a metallic giant. Above, wide tubes connected this room to different locations all throughout the ship where items could be discarded. Rogers wondered how they separated all the garbage, but if a computer could (almost) control a squadron of armed robots, it could probably tell the difference between one type of trash and another.

After one of the longest walks in his life, Rogers eventually found himself at the end of the corridor. The three-toothed door was infinitely larger than it had seemed when he'd entered the chute, and the task before him certainly didn't seem any smaller either. Uncovering the laundry cart, he pulled out the components of the VMU and his provisions, which he'd sealed in cryowrap and tied together in manageable bundles. Once he got into open space, he'd have no problem loading them onto the *Awesome.*

The VMU wasn't exactly his size—beggars couldn't be choosers, after all—but thankfully, it was a little on the big side rather than too small. The thick layer of protective covering would fit snug against his skin when he vented the air pressure, anyway.

Vented the air pressure. Opened the chute to vacuum. *Jumped out of a spaceship* and floated to the *Awesome* with a bunch of packaged food and a prayer. Rogers felt his body shaking a little as he put his helmet on and started checking the suit's systems. He really wasn't meant for this kind of life. Sneaking around, running away, jumping out of spaceships. It was just too adventurous. Rogers preferred the quiet life, the classy drinks, cheating very discreetly at cards.

*All the more reason to be done with this soon,* he thought. He snapped the last clasps into place and turned on the VMU. The suit, reading the ambient pressure in the area, didn't change anything, but he could hear several air gaskets opening as the suit prepared to do its job. Out in space, once he flipped the mobility switch on the back of his helmet, it would excrete little puffs of air, triggered by reading Rogers' body movements, to get him where he wanted to go. It was a comfortable, familiar thing; he'd worn these thousands of times while making repairs on the outside of the ship. So, it was a terribly confusing feeling now, since he felt like he was about to shit himself.

He moved over to the control panel to the side of the door, making sure that the SEWR rats weren't going to fly out the hatch as soon as it opened, and examined the controls. It wasn't overly complicated; there was one large red button and one large green button. Above the red button was printed the word SHOOT, and above the green button was printed the word CHUTE. Rogers thought there might have been a better way to label it.

Underneath the control panel, a warning was issued in yellow lettering. ALL PERSONNEL MUST ENSURE ANY ITEMS AND PERSONNEL NOT INTENDED TO BE JETTISONED ARE FIRMLY SECURED, AND ALL VMUS ARE IN WORKING ORDER BEFORE MANUALLY VENTING THE CHUTE.

Under that sign was another warning.

FIRING THE CHUTE SUPERVISOR OR HIS PRIZE-WINNING BONSAI PLANT COLLECTION INTO FREE SPACE IS STRICTLY PROHIBITED.

And another, this one printed on actual paper.

TRICKING THE CHUTE SUPERVISOR INTO FIRING HIMSELF OR HIS PRIZE-WINNING BONSAI PLANT COLLECTION INTO FREE SPACE IS ALSO STRICTLY PROHIBITED. ALSO, WHOEVER STOLE THE LABEL-MAKER, PLEASE BRING IT BACK TO ME ASAP.

Rogers' finger hovered over the red button as he looked at his datapad. 1502 ship time. If the helmsman had listened to him, the targeting computer would have been off for two minutes and would remain off for the next twenty eight. Just enough to push the *Awesome* to full burn and get to the Un-Space point. If Hart had moved his ship like he said he would. If the engines were fixed like Hart said they were. If the MPF hadn't confiscated all the credits stored locally on the *Awesome*'s systems.

So many ifs. But there was only one way to find out.

Then someone slapped him on the ass.

"Ah!" Rogers jumped in the air and turned around—no small feat with the added weight of the VMU—expecting to find Admiral Klein, or, worse, Barber Bot standing behind him.

But there was nothing. Nobody. Just piles of trash.

"What the hell?" Rogers said, his voice reverberating through the interior of his helmet.

Though . . . as he peered into the nearest pile of junk, there was something about it that looked familiar. He stepped forward and realized that it wasn't just a pile of scrap metal; it was a pile of droid parts. A graveyard of shinies, as it were. And these weren't just any shinies; some were the former members of the AIGCS that had been destroyed during the incident in the training room.

Rogers couldn't remember the details, having been wounded during the courageous execution of his duty, of course, so he'd never gotten to see the extent of the damage. Now he could see it looked like a twisted surgeon suffering from tremors had taken a plasma cutter to them in the middle of an earthquake. They were barely recognizable; in fact, Rogers wouldn't have known they were the droids at all except for one head that had somehow remained intact. Thick, jagged cuts ran all the way down their midsections, spilling their metallic and silicon interiors onto the floor, and a sort of strange engineering curiosity made Rogers bend down and examine them. How did they make these, anyway?

He saw computer boards, hydraulic systems, wires, actuators. Standard stuff, stuff you'd see in just about any piece of computer technology in modern times. One thing, however, stuck out to him. It was an open-faced cube of old-looking parts integrated with magnetic coils and other sophisticated tech, but Rogers had seen it before. It was a power generator that fed off the inertial motion and magnetic charges of artificial gravity generators.

Really technical, smart stuff. The droids would never run out of power as long as they were inside a ship that had a modern gravity generator on it.

A question nagged at Rogers' brain, but he was too busy screaming like a wounded lemur to focus on it at the moment, because something had grabbed him again.

He tried jumping up—jumping up just sort of seemed like what you do when you were startled—but he'd been squatting by the pile of destroyed robots. He succeeded, instead, in falling backward hard and doing a very poor impression of an inverted turtle, arms and legs flailing as he forgot how to control his own body.

"Who's there?" he yelled, and received a poke in the kidney as an answer.

"Stop that!"

Another poke.

"When I find you, I'm going to press that red button and—"

*Click.*

The mobility switch on the back of his helmet had been turned on.

"Congratulations on activating the mobility mode of your Vacuum Mobility Unit!" a voice intoned in his ear. "You are entitled to one free—"

"Noooo!" Rogers cried as the movement of his foot caused the pressurized air in his suit to blow outward. He shot rapidly away from the trash pile and embedded his head firmly in another one, this one thankfully full of scraps of cushioning rather than metal rods and sharp edges. He reached up to free himself, and the air pockets in his arm units made sharp hissing noises as they reacted to his movements, sending him spinning around on the floor. The red light of the garbage chute turned the whole thing into a spinning-wheel painting, something out of a zip jack addict's art studio.

He felt the rip in his suit as he grazed a jagged piece of scrap metal, felt it tug on the central air reservoir inside the unit, and then felt like the Viking had just elbow-dropped him. All of the air exploded out of his suit at once, warning lights flashing on the heads-up display of his helmet to tell him that the integrity of his suit had been compromised and that he was quickly running out of air reserves.

But Rogers didn't really think about any of that, as he was too busy being flung halfway down the corridor by rapidly exiting air deposits.

When he finally came to a stop, feeling like O-71 inside a bingo machine, he couldn't bring himself to move. Every part of him hurt in strange and new ways. Flashbacks of the incident with the droids popped into his head; he instinctively curled into a ball and whimpered, expecting to be stepped on by one of their giant metal legs any second. Thankfully, nothing more serious happened than the last bits of air leaving the tears in his suit and making a flatulent noise.

"Uhh . . ." Rogers said analytically.

Slowly, he pulled himself to his feet and looked back toward the refuse heap he'd been examining when someone had obviously assaulted him. He could see nothing other than a pile of metal, glinting softly in the red glow of the overhead lights. But *something* had grabbed him.

Rogers snuck down the hallway, bracing himself after every step for a team of garbage ninjas to rush out of the shadows and deal him the final blow. The corridor was quiet. No ninjas. Stillness.

"CALL FUNCTION [ATTACK! ATTACK! ATTACK!]"

Rogers squealed and dove to the side of the corridor, expecting the mangled remnants of the AIGCS droids to come to life and begin their zombie/droid assault. But no matter how tightly he gripped his head between his knees and muttered nonsensical gibberish, the Attack! Attack! Attack! never came.

"Ha," a voice said, "you humans fall for that every time."

Peeking up from his armadillo defense, Rogers found himself

nearly nose to nose with the disembodied head of a droid. At least, it seemed that way at first. It was actually the disembodied torso—could you really be disembodied if the body was included?—with the head and one arm attached. It might have been a droid that hadn't been disassembled properly before it was dumped down here. It looked older, worn around the edges. A little bit of rust here and there, perhaps, though it was difficult for Rogers to tell in the light.

"Who are you?" Rogers asked, then frowned. "You look too old to be a Froid."

The droid's head twitched to one side, then made an ambiguous computation noise.

"What's a Froid?"

"Those new droids that have the Freudian Chip installed in them. But they're new." Rogers pointed at him. "You're old, but you talk like the new ones."

"Oh, I have one of those. I'm not old," the droid said. "I'm corroded. There's a difference."

Rogers walked over to where the droid was peeking out from the pile of metal to get a closer look. It looked similar to the Froids, he realized, but there was something off. Something unfinished about it. The important part of its torso was still intact, if very dented, probably thanks to the mountains of metallic garbage being flung on top of it.

"You ruined my escape plan, you know," Rogers said.

"Oh," the droid replied. "I was just having some fun. I don't get a lot of company."

Raising his eyebrow, Rogers gave the droid an appraising look. "Since when do droids care about company?"

"I don't know. Are you upset that I ruined your escape?"

Rogers sat down and took off his helmet. "No. Yes. I don't know." He sighed. "I probably wouldn't have made it, anyway. I don't know anything about this adventuring stuff. I just want to drink beer and play cards. Is that so much to ask?"

The droid didn't respond. It didn't do anything much at all, really. Just stuck out of the garbage pile like a weed from a garden of metal, staring at Rogers expectantly. Could droids look expectant? Rogers thought they always sort of looked that way. Whoever had designed their "faces" seemed to favor a look that walked the intersection of boredom, condescension, and expectancy.

"Anyway," Rogers said, looking up at the ceiling, "what are you doing down here? Droids need to be fully wiped before they're destroyed. And how did you get all that damage?"

"It was those EXPLETIVE pieces of OBSCENITIES in the maintenance bay!" the droid said in a burst of volume. "They have their heads so far up their ANATOMICAL REFERENCE that they can't think straight!"

Rogers frowned. "Are . . . are you trying to swear?"

"Of course I'm trying to swear, you EXPLETIVE! How else am I supposed to express myself?"

"I didn't really know droids were into expressing themselves."

"They're not," the droid said, his anger seemingly gone. "I'm a prototype of the Freudian Chip droids that you call Froids. My serial number is PFC-D-24. What is your serial number?"

This droid was actually trying to introduce itself and make pleasantries. It made Rogers a little uncomfortable. Had it been discarded because the Freudian Chip didn't work properly?

"I don't have a serial number," Rogers said. "My name is Rogers."

"I see," D-24 said, making another ambiguous computation noise. It kind of sounded like an old video game, and, in a way, it was almost pleasant. A lot better than the harsh, guttural noises that the standard droids made.

"So, Serial Number Rogers . . ."

"Just Rogers."

"So, Just Rogers . . ." The droid made a noise that might have been considered a chuckle.

Rogers paused a moment, frowning. "Are you being ridiculous on purpose?" Rogers asked.

"Yes," D-24 responded. "Was it funny?"

Funny? The droid was asking him if he was being funny? Since when did droids care about company, and expressing themselves, and being funny? This prototype was strange indeed.

"Actually," Rogers said, thinking about it for a second, "it kind of was."

"This pleases me," D-24 said. "I will add this joke to my database and reserve it for later use."

"I still don't understand how you ended up down here," Rogers said, "without being properly deactivated."

"Part of my memory is corrupted," D-24 said. "I am unable to recall a significant time period between my arrival on this ship and my abandonment in the trash chute. I assume it has something to do with the unbelievably stupid MATERNAL FORNICATION in the maintenance bay who don't know their ANATOMICAL REFERENCE from their wrenches!"

Rogers could relate—and that kind of scared him.

"But what I don't understand is—"

"What the hell are you still doing down here?" someone called from behind him. "Does Klein want you to hem all his pants before you throw them out too?"

Rogers leapt to his feet to find both Mailn and the Viking walking toward him. Rogers swore under his breath. Why had they come back? Why hadn't they just gone away?

They stopped short of him, looking at him curiously. Both of them were frowning. A heavy moment of silence built up around the exit of the trash chute as

"Why are you wearing a VMU?" Mailn said.

"It's, um, a safety precaution," Rogers said brilliantly. "In case someone vents the chute while I'm down here folding Klein's clothes, I'll be able to get back into the ship."

*Ha!* Rogers thought. *Well done!*

"And the giant pile of Sewer rats sticking out of the laundry cart encased in cryo-wrap?"

"Klein is on a diet," Rogers said quickly, "but he doesn't want anyone else to know, so he orders food and then throws it away." He pointed at his own stomach, which wasn't exactly washboard-flat, either. "He's very sensitive about his image."

*Ha, ha!* Rogers thought. *I am a genius!*

"These explanations are confusing given your original assertion that you were trying to escape," D-24 said.

Rogers and the two marines turned slowly to face the droid.

"That," Rogers said, "was not funny."

"Escape?" Mailn said slowly. "You were trying to run away?"

"What kind of yellow-bellied miscreant are you?" the Viking said.

Rogers whirled around, hands up in defense of what he was certain would be another vicious beating. "No," he said. "It's not like that. I was just going to go clean the space bugs—"

"We're at *war*, Rogers!" Mailn said, her face red and scary-looking. "You're deserting in the face of the enemy! You do realize that's punishable by death, don't you?"

"Deserting in the face of what enemy?" Rogers shouted back, suddenly angry. "There is no enemy! We're in the middle of the greatest interlocking treaty-created peace in intergalactic history! If the Thelicosans so much as fart wrong, they'll have every system in Fortuna Stultus tearing their fleet to shreds!" He threw his hands up in the air. "You've all been addled by stupid posters and morons and droids!"

"My programming suggests that I should take offense at this," D-24 said.

"Shut up!" Rogers said.

The Viking pointed a long, sausage-like finger at him. "You know, when you spaced all those droids in the training room, I thought, maybe he's not such a piece-of-shit metalhead after all. When you got promoted to lieutenant and made Klein's exec, I thought, hey, maybe this guy's alright. But I was wrong. You've always been a piece-of-shit metalhead, and you always will be."

She made a motion to Mailn. "Come on, Corporal. Let's leave

this guy in the trash where he belongs. I hope the door gets stuck and you get vented with the rest of the garbage, Rogers."

"Wait!" Rogers cried as the two women turned their backs on him and started to walk out of the chute. "I'm sorry! I didn't mean to deliberately and carefully plot my escape! I still hate droids!"

"My programming also suggests that I should take offense at this," D-24 said.

Rogers turned around, ready to grab the nearest piece of wieldable metal and bash the droid over the head. Behind him, he heard Mailn yell something unintelligible but clearly offensive before the chute door closed, leaving him alone.

"You moron!" Rogers said. "Do you have any idea what you just did? Do you have any idea how long I've been trying to get with that beautiful specimen of the female sex?"

"Don't blame me for your stupid EXPLETIVE romantic life!" D-24 said. "You were the one standing in the garbage chute with your ANATOMICAL REFERENCE half out the door!

"I had it under control," Rogers said through clenched teeth. "I could have explained . . . Wait, why am I explaining myself to a droid? I should just finish what the maintainers started and press that red button. That'll teach you to ruin my life."

"If you'd like to find out what it would feel like to have your whole body sucked out of a small tear in your VMU," the droid said, "go ahead."

Rogers stood there for a moment, seething, wondering how to best hurt a droid. He wanted to take out all the frustrations of the last few weeks on this one half-broken piece of metal with a strange computer in its brain. The droid was right—it wasn't his fault that Rogers' life had gotten so screwed up—but smashing a partially inanimate object seemed like just the catharsis that Rogers needed.

But he couldn't summon the strength to do it. His arm was just too tired from saluting.

"If I may," D-24 said, "I'm curious as to why the most powerful man on the ship is attempting to escape."

Rogers looked up. "What?"

"The large one said that you were the executive officer to Admiral Klein; isn't that correct?"

"I don't see how that makes me powerful. So far, it's just made me want to kill myself and jump out into open space wearing a thin protective suit and become an intergalactically wanted outlaw. Thanks again for screwing that up, by the way."

D-24 made another computation noise. "But Admiral Klein is widely known to be vastly incompetent. Logic dictates, therefore, that either his deputy or his executive officer would make all of the decisions. Since he has no deputy, that would make you the most powerful man in the fleet, if not directly."

Rogers thought about that for a second. Maybe the droid was right. If he could convince a helmsman that there were space bugs outside the ship, he could certainly convince the stupidest man he'd ever met to do . . . well, anything. How had he missed that opportunity before? He could have had every water bladder in the ship stocked with Jasker 120 by now.

"Hang on a second," Rogers said. "What do you mean, Klein is incompetent? He's the admiral of the whole fleet. He has to be competent at something . . ."

*Speaking,* Rogers thought. *Public speaking. He has charisma. That's how he got there.*

"Oh my god," Rogers said. "He really is an idiot. I knew it! I knew there had to be some reason why he was asking me for my opinion on battle tactics. He's been hiding the fact that he has no idea what he's doing for *years.*"

Rogers felt betrayed, used, violated. Inadequate. He finally found someone that was a better con man than he was. And that was scary, because he was Rogers' boss.

"But how did *you* know that?" Rogers asked. "Nobody else in the Meridan system knows that, apparently, and I barely had my suspicions."

"I am unable to answer that question," D-24 said. "It is part of the initial situation report I was given when I was transferred to the *Flagship* as a prototype. The original author is unknown."

Rogers frowned. Why in the world would a droid know about Klein, but nobody else on the ship did? Something that should have been obvious to humans was instead known only to droids. Even scarier, what else did this droid know that Rogers didn't?

Reaching over into the laundry cart, Rogers pulled out the small toolbox that contained some of the necessities that every engineer should have. Lopez had been happy to supply an extra kit, and now Rogers set it next to D-24.

"What are you doing?" the droid asked.

"I'm taking you with me," Rogers said. "There are plenty of spare parts to get you moving again. I want to know what else is in that brain of yours, and since you just very neatly turned two of my only allies against me, I could use someone on my side."

"Side?" the droid said. "What sides are there?"

Rogers was silent for a moment as he combed through the parts, trying to find suitable replacements.

"I'm not sure," Rogers said. "But I'm going to find out."

# Report: A-267FR-02147-E

Serial: A-267FR-02147-E

Distribution: DBS//DSS//DAK//DFR//BB//CLOSED NETWORK A66

Classification: Special Protocol Required

Summary: Human 2552 has come into contact with prototype droid PFC-D-24.

Details: Human 2552, previously in charge of the AIGCS, has recovered the remains of prototype droid PFC-D-24 on the refuse deck of the MPS Flagship. The lack of sensor arrays in this particular section of the ship prevents an understanding of how exactly this relationship was formed. However, the supplies that Human 2552 was gathering prior to the meeting suggest cleaning of space bugs from the targeting computer. We are unable to assess how Human 2552 discovered the presence of these listening devices, nor how he planned on removing them.

Periphery: Human 2552 attempted to destroy BAR-BR 116, though the reasons are not clear.

Assessment: The reemergence of the unintegrated PFC-D-24

is problematic and must be observed and dealt with carefully. Conclusions about Human 2552 are still ambiguous, but it is possible that he presents a threat.

Report Submitted By: F-GC-001

# A Man and His Droid

They made for a very strange pair walking down the command deck of the *Flagship.* Rogers, walking with a limp, his uniform wrinkled beyond recognition, and Frankenrobot, pulled from the brink of death by being fused with the old parts from deceased droids. Deet, as Rogers decided to call him, didn't seem to mind being pieced together. If anything, he seemed to be happy he wasn't still sitting in the garbage dump. Rogers wondered how long he'd been there, or if droids had any real concept of the passage of time.

"I have to ask," Rogers said, "what's up with all of that EXPLETIVE stuff?"

"My Profanity Generator is broken," Deet said. "It has never worked properly, despite me asking every EXPLETIVE, DISPARAGING REFERENCE in the maintenance bay to fix it. I don't know how the EXPLETIVE I am supposed to communicate with humans if I can't EXPLETIVE talk like them."

"Boy," Rogers said, "you really don't like the guys in maintenance, do you?"

"I can't stand those CANINE OFFSPRING."

"Well, it's not so bad," Rogers said. "All humans don't talk like that, anyway." He thought for a moment. "In fact, almost none of them do. Just Hart, and that's because he's old and grumpy."

"Well, how am I supposed to know that? It's a little hard for me to observe them when I'm sitting in an EXPLETIVE garbage dump for most of my life, isn't it?"

"I suppose so," Rogers said, eyeing the robot. He seemed to be developing more of a personality every moment. He also seemed very concerned with very un-droidlike things, like expressing himself and interacting with humans. At least he wasn't concerned with trimming Rogers' beard.

They passed a trio of standard droids wheeling themselves down the hallway. As Rogers and Deet approached, however, they stopped and stared.

"What's your problem?" Rogers said. Normally, he would have just walked right by them, but today, all things considered, he was feeling a little irritable. And maybe a tiny bit like he needed to prove himself after being flung around the garbage chute like a balloon with a hole in it.

"CALL FUNCTION [GET DATA]."

"I don't follow you."

"Why would you follow them?" Deet asked. "They're not even going anywhere."

"It's an expression," Rogers said. He turned back to the droid that had called the ambiguous function. For the first time, he wished droids had real faces; at least then he might have some idea what the damn thing was thinking.

"CALL FUNCTION [GET DATA]."

"Yeah," Rogers said, "you were just getting data a second ago. How much data do you need?"

It was starting to become a strange, awkward gathering. They had barely exited the up-line to the command deck, and so they were still quite a ways away from all of the saluting and pomp, making for an empty hallway. The two droids that weren't currently "getting data" stood completely and totally motionless.

"CALL FUNCTION [STALL FOR TIME TO ALLOW THE GETTING OF MORE DATA]."

"There's a function for that?"

"There's a function for everything," Deet explained.

"OUTPUT STRING: THE ATMOSPHERICS ARE AMICABLE."

Rogers frowned, squinting. "Are you trying to say that we're having nice weather?"

"OUTPUT STRING: SPORTS TEAM REFERENCE."

"You're not even really trying. Look, I don't know what data you're getting or why you stopped to stare at us in the middle of the hallway, but why don't you find something useful to do like go jump out the trash chutes."

"CALL FUNCTION [ILLUMINATE IGNORANCE]. OUTPUT STRING: THIS COMMAND WOULD RESULT IN LITTLE TO NO BENEFIT."

"I beg to differ," Rogers muttered.

"CLOSE FUNCTION [GET DATA.] CALL FUNCTION [PERSUADE]. TARGET [LIEUTENANT ROGERS]. OUTPUT STRING: YOU APPEAR TO HAVE BEEN BURDENED BY UNNECESSARY COMPANIONSHIP. PLEASE ALLOW US TO RELIEVE YOU OF THIS BURDEN."

"Jeez," Rogers said, "where were you guys that time in the bar in Aaskerdal?"

"OUTPUT STRING: WE ARE UNFAMILIAR WITH THIS LOCATION. IF YOU WISH US TO ACCOMPANY YOU TO THIS LOCATION, PLEASE FILE A FORMAL REQUEST WITH—"

"Let's not talk about bringing droids to bars," Rogers said. "And anyway, I'm fine with my new companion here."

"Hey," Deet said, "does that mean you like me?"

"No."

"EXPLETIVE."

The three droids, however, wouldn't be so easily dissuaded.

"CALL FUNCTION [GIVE UP]."

Well, maybe they would. They abruptly ceased all communication with Rogers and went on their merry metal way. Rogers turned to watch them board the in-line, feeling something itching at the back of his brain that he couldn't quite scratch.

"What was that all about?" Rogers asked.

"The other droids never liked me very much," Deet said. He beeped a couple of times, his head twitching in a way that made Rogers wonder if he was going to last very long. Everything about the poor robot looked broken, the fact that he looked like a walking, multi-attachment kitchen utensil notwithstanding. "I used to tell them jokes."

"If they're anything like the ones you've told me so far," Rogers said, "I can't say I blame them."

"That was also a joke, wasn't it?"

"I'm not sure yet."

They made their way down the hallway, thankfully not becoming involved in any more strange conversations with droids, and soon Rogers became so embroiled in saluting everyone he passed that he forgot Deet existed. Only the pain in his shoulder kept him company now, and the weight of the rank on his uniform. It had been like this every day he'd been on the command deck, and this brief revisit to his pain reminded him why he'd decided to run away. The worst part was, at the end of this torture, someone would be there to tell him to polish boots while he wrote the next Gettysburg Address.

"What the AFTERLIFE LOCALE are you doing?"

"My job," Rogers said. Though he meant it as a joke, he realized that it was mostly true.

"Your job is to wave at people all day? You're not even doing it very well."

"It's not waving," Rogers said, his teeth clenched, sweat running down his face. "It's saluting."

"Well, you should stop," Deet said as another starman first

class jumped in the back of what was becoming a very long line to salute Rogers. All movement in the hallway had completely stopped, everyone waiting their turn to salute everyone else. A pair of very confused corporals saluted each other on accident.

"It's not that easy," Rogers said.

"Well," Deet said, "what would happen if you were to break your arm? If you couldn't physically salute, nobody could blame you for it, right?"

"I think I'd rather keep my bones intact, thanks," Rogers said, breathing heavily. Who had invited the entire enlisted corps of the Meridan Marines to the command deck? Where did all of these people come from? Why wouldn't they just go away? He should have hung himself. Hanged himself? It didn't matter. He should have just pressed the big red button in the garbage chute, holes in his suit or no holes in his suit.

"So, fake it," Deet said.

Rogers stopped, his arm falling to his side. He turned, slowly, staring at the little droid with all of the rusty parts sticking out of him at strange angles. The command deck was completely frozen now, especially since Rogers had stopped saluting people. People were crowding in the doorways, practically climbing on top of each other just to prepare to salute Rogers. A group of three troops—a major, an ensign, and a master sergeant—had gotten caught in what Rogers had named "the grind" and were walking in a small circle, each saluting the other as they passed. You couldn't get out of the grind unless someone bumped into you or one of you broke down crying.

"Fake it," Rogers said. "Fake it!" Why hadn't he thought of that before? What had happened to him that he couldn't even come up with the most basic of cons: pretending to be sick? He'd learned that when he was four years old—thermometers in space heaters, swallowing kitchen cleaners to induce tremors for a few minutes.

"Give me that," Rogers snapped. Deet had been carrying the

tattered remains of the VMU that McSchmidt had lent him. Tearing a strip off the soft interior liner, he hurriedly created a sling that he looped around his right arm and his neck. In truth, it actually felt kind of good; his arm was so tired that it was practically broken anyway. Rogers secured the sling in place and looked up at the crowd, daring them to salute an injured man.

There was a brief moment of silence, followed by loud pattering noises as the entire hallway emptied in a matter of seconds. Rogers and Deet stood alone near the entrance to Rogers' stateroom. He hadn't even realized how close he'd been.

"Wow," Rogers said. He turned to Deet. "I'm impressed. Even the Froids in the AIGCS didn't have this much personality."

"Call function [express gratitude]."

Rogers paused. "Joke?"

"Yes!" Deet exclaimed. He beeped excitedly. "Yes, it was!"

They covered the remaining distance to Rogers' stateroom and paused for a moment as Rogers fumbled for his key—the one he'd been certain he was never going to use again—and slid it into the reader beside the door. The low level of activity around his door almost made Rogers feel uncomfortable. He could have sworn that, not a minute before, there had been a mob of people throwing their arms everywhere right in front of him. The door slid open, and Rogers took the now-familiar first step into freefall. It still felt like his stomach was going to claw its way out his nose, but at least he wasn't surprised by it.

Rogers spun around to find Deet still standing at the door.

"Do you have an addiction to roller coasters or something?" Deet asked.

"The admiral thinks that this is a good way to prevent his executive officers from killing themselves."

"Well, I'm not going in there," Deet said.

"That's right," Rogers said. He reclined his body to a pantomime of sitting in a big lounge chair. "You're all powered by the artificial gravity generators." He snapped his fingers. "That's what

I wanted to ask you. All of the droids on the ship keep going to the mess halls and plugging into the power outlets. But if they're powered by the AGG, what's the point?"

Deet paused for a moment, then made two short chirps in rapid succession. "I am unable to assess the reason for this action."

Rogers frowned. The way this robot kept switching back and forth between talking like an old droid and talking like a human was a little disconcerting.

"Charging battery backups, maybe?" Rogers guessed.

"I'm not equipped with a battery backup," Deet said, "but it is probable that later versions of my frame were outfitted with such a system."

Rogers spun around the room a little, stuffing some loose articles of clothing into his floating wardrobe. In the short time he'd lived in this environment, he'd at least taken the time to make it seem clean. Having ten things floating around the room was better than having a hundred.

"Well," Rogers said, "let me just change out of his uniform. Just hang out in the hallway for a few minutes and then we'll see what the most powerful man in the 331st can do."

From his vantage point in the center of his stateroom, Rogers could see only Deet darkening his doorway. Behind the droid, there was still a noticeable absence of personnel. Had everyone taken the day off since Rogers was no longer there to salute?

"I don't see anyplace to hang," Deet said, looking around.

"Figure of speech. Just wait."

"I'm not sure I want to do that, either."

Rogers stopped, the components of a new uniform draped over his arm. "Why?"

Before Deet could answer the question, he vanished from the doorway in a sudden blur. A loud crunching noise echoed throughout the empty hallway.

"What the hell?" Rogers grabbed the side of his wardrobe and pushed off to get back to the door. He landed smoothly on the other side, slowing himself down by jogging for a few steps—a move he'd invented yesterday that made him feel kind of like an action hero crashing through a window—and looked around the hallway. He barely saw a flash of metal disappearing behind the corner leading back toward the up-line and the other end of the command deck.

"Hey!" Rogers broke into a trot and turned the corner just in time to see a pair of tracked-variety droids attempting to shove Deet into the garbage chute. Deet was beeping loudly, his eyes flashing between blue and red.

"Get your EXPLETIVE hands off me, you MATERNAL FORNICATORS! I'll rip off your REPRODUCTIVE ORGAN and PERFORM NAMESAKE OF BIBLICAL CITY!"

"What the hell are you doing with my droid? Stop!" Rogers said. The two droids that had been trying to unceremoniously stuff Deet into the garbage chute stopped, though they didn't let him go. The poor reassembled droid—who was significantly smaller than the two standard droids, thanks to the recycled parts available and Rogers rushed workmanship—hung there waving his arms frantically.

"CALL FUNCTION [EXPLAIN AWKWARD SITUATION]. OUTPUT STRING: DROID PFC-D-24 HAS BEEN SCHEDULED FOR DESTRUCTION."

"He's not scheduled for destruction," Rogers said. "He's actually already been destroyed."

"OUTPUT STRING: THIS DOES NOT COMPUTE."

"That's because you're stupid," Rogers said. "How are you going to destroy something that's already been destroyed? That's logically impossible."

The two droids holding Deet made some very emphatic noises. For a moment, they seemed frozen. Rogers took a step forward.

"CALL FUNCTION [CONTINUE WITH PRIMARY MISSION]."

"Stop!" Rogers said. "Neither of you droids outrank me. I've looked at the new rank and organization regulation MR-613. You are legally obligated to follow my orders."

Rogers hadn't read the regulation—in fact, he hadn't read any regulation in ten years—but the statement gave the droids pause. They looked between Rogers and Deet, clearly confused.

"I'm telling you that D-24 has already been destroyed," Rogers said. "You can't do it again. You'd violate Schrödinger's principle of entanglement. This droid cannot be both destroyed and not destroyed at the same time."

Rogers was almost positive that Schrödinger hadn't said anything like that, but the droids didn't seem to know the difference. That, and Rogers was on a roll; if there was one thing he'd learned during his life, it was to never stop when he was on a roll.

"By attempting to destroy him again, you are trying to bend the fabric of truth and space," Rogers said. "You are threatening to tear apart the very fabric of time. Is that something that droids are supposed to do?"

"CALL FUNCTION [LOOK CONFUSED]."

"Right. You're causing yourself—and me—undue confusion by re-destroying this droid. In fact, your primary mission has already been completed. It was completed before it was even assigned to you. I will see that you are commended for your timely carrying-out of your instructions. Excellently done."

Deet beeped. "What the EXPLETIVE are you talking about?"

"Quiet, you," Rogers snapped. He looked back between the two droids about to turn his newest ally into scrap. "Now, both of you, put the non-existent D-24 down and go carry out whatever other primary mission is in your databanks. And go polish your armor. You both look like you've just had a rough date with old scaffolding."

For a moment, Rogers thought they would ignore him and stuff Deet down the chute anyway. After all, almost nothing that Rogers had just said made any sense at all, except for the last comment about the dirtiness of the droids' exoskeletons. They both looked like metallic beggars.

"REJECT FUNCTION [PROTOCOL 162]. CALL FUNCTION [SEND DATA]. CALL FUNCTION [PRIMARY MISSION COMPLETE]. CALL FUNCTION [RETURN TO NORMAL DUTIES]."

Rogers sighed as the two droids put Deet down and wheeled off silently down the corridor and back toward the up-line.

"What was that all about?" Rogers asked as he watched them go.

"I don't know," Deet said. "I was never very well liked by the other droids."

"Can droids like other droids?"

Deet beeped. "I sure as FECAL MATTER don't like *them* very much."

"Fair enough," Rogers said, but he was still frowning. There had been two attempts since he'd re-commissioned Deet to have him removed, and they'd barely made the journey back to the command deck. He had a feeling starting to build up inside of him that there was more to the droids' programming than he'd originally thought. And, come to think of it, they'd done that red-flashy thing, too.

"Hey, Deet," Rogers said as they made their way back to Klein's room. "What is protocol 162? I've heard them reference it a couple of times, but they always reject it. Like something was telling them that maybe they *should* do it, and then they change their minds."

"I have references to thousands of protocols," Deet said after a moment of beeping and booping—perhaps checking his data banks. "But I've never heard of protocol 162." He beeped again. "In fact, in a sequential search of protocols, my data banks go from 161 to 163. According to my programming, there is no protocol 162. It is possible that it was programmed after I was decommissioned and no longer receiving updates."

Rogers looked at him. "You're not getting updates from the network anymore?"

"No," Deet said. "You might say I am fully mature and require no further updates."

Rogers snorted. "So, I guess your jokes won't be getting any better."

"They will likely keep pace with your insults," Deet said.

"Oh, shut up," Rogers said. "Just give me everything you know about Klein."

Confrontation wasn't exactly Rogers' strong suit, but when he opened the door to the admiral's room, he came in yelling.

"You!" Rogers said, pointing at the admiral, who was sitting behind his giant mahogany desk, wearing his half-moon spectacles, likely penning the next piece of charismatic garbage he was going to spout to the crew. "You're an idiot!"

Klein looked up, his gaze icy. "Excuse me, Lieutenant?"

That look almost made Rogers loose his nerve, but Deet had filled him in on enough of the admiral's shortcomings that it made Rogers feel a little invincible.

"Don't 'excuse me, Lieutenant' me, Admiral," Rogers said. "I know your secret, and I'm not going to be your monkey anymore. You don't know the first thing about running a fleet."

Klein bristled, slowly pushing back the speech he was working on and putting the archaic quill pen back in its holster. "I'll have you know, Lieutenant, that I am a professional military man, with a flawless track record and two decades of military experience under my belt. And I am certainly not accustomed to my executive officer calling me an idiot."

"That's because they keep hanging themselves instead of confronting you," Rogers said. "And I know why. You don't do a damn thing on this ship except write speeches. Your executive officers are being tasked with things above and beyond their specialties so that you can go on practicing your Toastmasters magic. The only reason we haven't blown ourselves up yet is because you have competent ship captains elsewhere in the fleet and we're not at war."

Klein calmly folded his hands in his lap. "Oh?"

Rogers held up his datapad, which had an array of information on it that had been sent to him by Deet. The amount of information the robot had on the admiral was a little disturbing, but it certainly served Rogers' purpose right now.

"You failed almost every class except public speaking at the Academy," Rogers said. "You even got a C+ in golf. *Golf*, admiral."

The admiral's visage cracked, though only slightly. "Where did you get that?"

"You've routinely been counseled for royally screwing up basic tactical situations, but talked your way out of getting actual paperwork," Rogers continued. "You've broken nearly every simulation you've ever participated in because even the computer hadn't expected inputs so fantastically wrong."

Klein's eyes were imperceptibly widening. "I'll have you thrown in the brig for rifling through my personal records," he said, obvious restraint in his voice.

"And you'll follow me after I release all of this to the entire 331st," Rogers said. "You're a fraud, Klein, and a dangerous one. You're nothing but a master of toast. A charismatic member of the Society of Burned Bread."

A pregnant silence hung over the room like a piano sailing through the air before it finally crashed down on the unsuspecting pedestrian. Deet, who had entered the room behind Rogers to avoid being tackled again, made a disconcerting beeping noise.

"What makes you think," Klein said slowly, "that my previous executive officers actually hung themselves?"

Rogers felt every muscle in his body tense as he realized that Klein wasn't just a fraud. He was a murderer. A narcissistic psychopath who erased lives any time they got in the way of him keeping his admiralty. Rogers had just made a very, very bad mistake.

"You didn't," Rogers whispered.

Klein smiled. Grinned. An insane grimace split his face, his eyes crinkling to narrow slits. There was something strange about that expression, something not quite right.

Rogers realized as the first bit of wetness trickled down Klein's cheek that it wasn't a manic, psychotic smile; he was holding back tears.

"Of course I didn't!" Klein said, bursting into sobs. "I don't even know how to kill someone properly!" He took a gasping breath. "Or even what to do with the body afterward. I don't know anything!"

The admiral threw his arms up in the air and collapsed onto the surface of his desk, his speech degenerating into senseless babble. Rogers found himself just as frozen in this moment as he had been when he'd thought the admiral had been about to kill him. This, he thought, was worse. He'd dealt with people threatening to kill him before. But weepy, teenage-like emotional outbursts? He'd rather eat a SEWR rat.

"My father was a famous general in the Meridan Marines," Klein said, his voice muffled by his arms and the desk. "I come from a long line of war heroes, but all I ever wanted to be was a politician or a pastor or a priest or a motivational speaker or something. It was all I was ever good at!" He looked up, his face red and puffy, his eyes veritable fountains of tears. "So, I used my speech and my family's history to get where I am so my family wouldn't disown me. And now the Thelicosans are on the doorstep. I've doomed us all!"

Rogers didn't know what to do. In fact, he realized that he hadn't really had a plan after the whole barging-in-and-saying-"you're an idiot" part. He certainly hadn't expected the most respected man in the 331st to break down sobbing in front of him.

Cautiously, Rogers approached the desk.

"Listen," Rogers said. "Maybe we can work something out. We don't know that the Thelicosans are coming. So far, all I've heard is rumors. Maybe if we try to piece this fleet back together as a team, rather than you just pushing all of your work onto me, we can fix some of this. I'll get you another exec—"

"No!" Klein screamed, sitting bolt upright. "You can't give me another exec. You know all my secrets. I need *you*, Rogers. I need you to help me through this, or I swear I will have you transferred back to Parivan to work in the salt mines."

He must have seen the expression on Rogers' face, because he smiled a tiny, tear-soaked smile. "I read personnel files every once in a while, too. No, if we're going to persist in pretending to be things we're not, we're going to do it together.

Rogers grit his teeth. "Alright, Admiral. It's a deal. But I'm not polishing any more buttons or brushing any more uniforms." He thought for a moment. "Or eating any more Sewer rats. I get to pick from your food supply whenever I want."

"Fine," Klein said. "What do you propose we do first?"

Rogers walked around the desk to show the admiral his datapad, on which was displayed a personnel roster of all of the sections of the *Flagship*.

"I have no idea what that is," the admiral said.

"That doesn't surprise me in the slightest," Rogers said. "If you're going to run a ship, you're going to have to start paying more attention to where your people are and what they're doing."

"That's what I have you for," Klein said.

"And that's why I'm showing you my suggestions," Rogers said. "For example, you can't have a master engineer running the kitchens if you want anyone to eat anything that isn't going to poison them."

"I guess that makes sense," Klein said.

Deet, who had been relatively quiet during the whole exchange, peered into one of the old clocks on the wall and started mimicking the ticking noises.

"Why do you have a rusty old droid following you around, anyway?" Klein asked.

"Hey," Deet said.

"Deet is my orderly droid," Rogers said. Droids didn't really function as personal assistants very often, but it seemed like the most likely explanation for keeping the robot close.

"I've already assigned you an orderly," Klein said.

"Which brings me back to my point," Rogers said. "Tunger is an idiot. He's spent his whole career tending to monkeys on the zoo deck. There's absolutely no reason he should be assigned as my assistant."

"Well, then, why did you request it?" Klein asked, throwing up his hands in exasperation. "Why did *any* of these people request their transfers if they didn't want to be there?"

Rogers paused. "What do you mean?"

"I want to keep everyone happy," Klein said. "That's why I keep approving anything that anyone sends me—it keeps my job easy. And if someone from the zoo deck wants to work in Supply, or someone from the engineering bay wants to work in the kitchens, why not? It's a broadening experience."

Rogers thought for a moment. Based on his conversations with everyone on the ship, there was no way that anyone had requested their transfers. Mailn hadn't even been medically qualified to be a pilot, yet they were ready to give her a starfighter and live munitions for no good reason at all.

"How do you get these transfer requests?" Rogers asked.

"They come in through my daily read files," Klein said.

"Do you read them?"

"No," Klein said. "I have you read them and approve them. Haven't you been getting any of my messages?"

Rogers chewed on the inside of his lip. Clearly, Klein had no idea where all the transfer requests were coming from, and they probably hadn't come from the personnel themselves. So then, from where?

"Well, we're going to start with moving some of these people back to places where they're actually going to do useful work," Rogers said. "And the absolute most critical thing you must do first is move Captain Alsinbury to the room directly next to mine."

# Military Unintelligence

Rogers' forehead wasn't sure it could take any more of this. He sat slumped against the wall, his face throbbing with pain. Well, he sat after a fashion. In reality, the Viking had hit him so hard that he'd been knocked back into his stateroom. His body just instinctively curled into a sitting position, he supposed, so it *felt* like he was sitting slumped against the wall.

"What the hell is wrong with you?" the Viking shouted at him from the doorway. "You think I've got nothing better to do than spend my time saluting everyone on the command deck? It'll take me an extra hour every day just to get back and forth between here and the training rooms."

"It wasn't my idea," Rogers said, uncurling and trying to find something to grab onto. She'd hit him at such an angle that most of his normal handholds were out of reach, though eventually the ship's inertial drift would get him somewhere. "Klein's signature is on the order."

"And who was it that suggested to him that his ground commander be moved to the command deck?"

"It makes sense!" Rogers cried. "It makes perfect sense. If there's a war going on, he's going to need his field commanders as close as possible. By you being up here, it's going to cut his duties in half if he needs to ask you about tactical ground stratagem synergy buzzwords!"

"What?"

Rogers knew he was babbling. He took a deep breath. "Just try it out for a while, okay? If it doesn't work out, I'll talk to Klein and see if he can't get you a bunk in the middle of the armory or something."

"If you don't try to hijack an escape pod before then, you mean?"

Rogers hadn't seen the Viking very much since she'd caught him trying to escape, but the encounters hadn't been pleasant. He'd have to work out a way to get him back into her good graces, but he was pretty sure he wasn't going to have a second opportunity to destroy a batch of ground combat droids anytime soon. That left . . . apologizing? No. He'd start with lying some more first, and see where that took him.

"I told you," Rogers said, "I wasn't trying to escape. I was performing routine maintenance on the exterior of the *Flagship.* Admiral Klein assigned me; you can go ask him right now if you want."

"Fine, I *am* going to go ask the admiral right now."

"You can't go ask the admiral right now!"

The Viking turned back, her beautiful forehead scrunching down into an I-told-you-so frown/smile/expression. It was a very confusing look, but Rogers couldn't help but love it.

"And why not?"

"Because, ah," Rogers stumbled through his words. Why was he having such a hard time lying lately? He glanced at the clock. "Because it's 1026 ship time, and he's in the middle of his nap."

This was, actually, true. Klein had a very particular napping schedule, and woe be unto the man who was near him if he had to skip one for something trivial, like running the most important ship in this sector of the Meridan border. In this particular case, however, it prevented the admiral from telling the Viking that Rogers had requested that she be moved to the next room.

Deet, who still refused to enter Rogers' room, had been stationed outside his doorway. The Viking had roughly shoved him aside before she'd punched Rogers in the face, causing him to fall on his back. By this point, however, the quirky droid had gotten back to his feet, and Rogers saw a little metal head poke its way into the doorway.

"You know we have a briefing in ten minutes, right?" Deet asked.

"Yes," Rogers hissed, "thank you very much for interrupting this conversation."

"Oh," the Viking said. "I see you've got yourself a new shiny as a pet, too. So, you're a coward *and* a droid lover." She spat. "How would you like it if I took the thing *you* trained for all your life and tried to automate it?"

Rogers could see something resembling genuine hurt on the Viking's face. It confused him for a moment, as he wasn't really used to seeing anything except rapid vacillations between uncontrollable rage, a desire to shoot things, and a desire to train to shoot things better.

"I already told you I didn't volunteer for the AIGCS. I blew them all up, didn't I?" Rogers tried to edge closer to the doorway, but he was floating. "You're a damn fine commander—at least, that's what all the marines tell me—and I'd never want to see you replaced by a stupid machine."

"Hey," Deet said.

The Viking looked at him, narrow-eyed. Her jaw worked slowly, the muscles in her cheeks tensing. Was the Viking being . . . vulnerable? Just the brief pause in the threat of physical violence put Rogers off guard. He struggled for something to say to keep her around.

"I'm having trouble interpreting all of this," Deet said.

"Shut up for a second," Rogers barked.

Deet didn't seem to be very interested in shutting up. "Is he still trying to tell you about how he wasn't escaping from the garbage chute?"

"Don't talk to me," the Viking said.

"Don't talk to her," Rogers said.

"You don't talk to me, either!" the Viking shouted, pointing at Rogers. All of the emotion in her face vanished in an instant. "I don't care if we have to share a bunk. I'm not associating with the likes of you."

"What if Admiral Klein were to order you to share a bunk with me?" Rogers asked before he could stop himself.

"Bah!" the Viking threw up her arms. "If I thought I could reach you, I'd come in there and hit you again. Just stay out of my business!"

She stormed off, leaving only Deet in the doorway. Rogers finally came within push-off distance of his wardrobe, and he shot over to his desk, where he retrieved the Ever-Cool ice pack he'd taken to keeping in his room. He seemed to be getting hit a lot lately. Pressing the ice pack to his forehead, he floated back over to the doorway.

"You really need to learn when to keep your mouth shut," Rogers said.

"My mouth doesn't move when I talk."

Rogers sighed. "Couldn't you have just backed me up, there?"

"What data would you like me to back up?"

"That's not what I'm talking about," Rogers said. He wrapped his salute-repellent sling around his arm, stepped into the hallway, and closed the door behind him. It was just about time to heat up Klein's cheese-and-beet sandwich. Klein had some peculiar tastes, but at least he'd honored his end of the deal and allowed Rogers to sample the goods, which is why Rogers didn't mind continuing to make Klein's food. Kitchen operations were being restored slowly, so it was nice to eat some real food in the meantime.

"I'm saying, couldn't you have told the Viking that I was really going and performing maintenance on the outside of the ship?"

"Droids have a very difficult time lying," Deet said. "We have to draw on known data to make conclusions. It's called artificial intelligence for a reason."

"Well, you should practice," Rogers said. "Because I do it a lot, and I can't have you telling everyone I'm lying every time I need to bend the truth a little to get something done."

"Have you ever considered employing the truth more often instead?"

"Absolutely not," Rogers said. "I'm trying to get with Captain Alsinbury, and being my true self isn't going to get me anywhere at all."

"Get with?"

"You know," Rogers said. "Ah, you know. Get with. Roll in the hay. Do the horizontal boogie. Almost, *very nearly* reproduce but don't really."

"I am unable to process nearly everything you just said to me," Deet said.

"Forget it."

They came to the admiral's door, but before Rogers could slide his keycard into the slot and get ready to wake what would undoubtedly be a very grumpy, and specifically hungry, admiral, Deet made what sounded like a very important droid noise.

"Do you want to talk to me about something?"

Deet's eyes flashed excitedly, and he beeped. "Yes! Do you speak droid?"

Rogers pointed to the blue-and-gray projection of a large stop sign that was coming out of the holographic generator in Deet's chestplate, which was probably what had given him the clue.

". . . Yes."

Deet didn't say anything for a moment. "Joke?"

"Yes. What do you want?"

"I thought I should tell you," Deet said, his digitized voice sounding, perhaps, a little annoyed, "that my sensors have picked up several strange devices in the admiral's room. They are transmitting data, but they aren't transmitting any of it to the main network of the ship."

Rogers raised an eyebrow. "Strange devices? You mean bugs?"

"Please do not persist in your deception regarding the cleaning of space bugs from the exterior of the ship."

Rogers whapped him on the nose. "No, you idiot. 'Bugs' is another word for hidden listening devices used to spy on people. Is that what you're talking about?"

"I can't be sure," Deet said. "The signal itself doesn't tell me anything about the nature of the device."

Rogers scratched his beard. "What are they hidden in?"

"There are several hidden in the posters around the room, but there are others in various places as well." Deet beeped, and his head swiveled toward the DEFEND THE BRIDGE poster across the hallway. "I've detected similar emissions from other posters around the ship."

The propaganda posters. Not only were they inane, annoying, and omnipresent, but they were being used to spy on people. Rogers might have thought it was Klein's security system, if not for the fact that Rogers wasn't confident that Klein knew how to spy on anyone.

Opening the door, Rogers and Deet stepped inside, Rogers feeling suddenly very uncomfortable in this room. If there were bugs in the room, why were they listening to Klein? First, who in their right mind would want to listen to the ramblings of a Toastmasters graduate as he wrote yet another speech? Second, where was the data being transmitted? It had to be somewhere on the *Flagship*; he was sure of that. Rogers knew a thing or two about listening devices, and there was no way they'd be able to transmit their information all the way to, for example, the Thelicosan fleet. If there was a spy in their midst, the data would have to go to him or her first, and then they'd have to figure out a way to encrypt it and send it back home on a secure channel.

And, after all that trouble, all they'd get would be a fifty-five-year-old man yelling:

"Rogers, I'm waiting for my sandwich!"

"Hey," Rogers said as the door closed behind him, "don't bark at me. I'm not your scullery maid."

"I'm just keeping up appearances," Klein said as he scribbled away at his desk. Today he was referencing historical war speeches and trying to find ways to integrate them into the next conference call he would have with the 331st ship captains. That way he wouldn't have to talk about serious things, like keeping them all alive in the case of an invasion.

Going through the motions of preparing the sandwich—*cheese on top, beets on bottom, god-damn you, and cut the crust off!*—Rogers frowned, which reminded him that he'd been punched in the face. He knew he had to figure out a way to make the Viking not hate him again, but, in a strange way, that felt less important at the moment than figuring out who was listening in on Klein's conversations.

That stopped him mid–cheese-slicing. What was happening to him? Now that he knew he was quite possibly the most powerful man in the 331st, he almost felt *responsible* for these people! Damn Deet for ever making that clear to him. He would have been just as happy had he gotten into the *Awesome* and cruised away forever.

Except he knew he wouldn't have.

"Here you are," Rogers said, handing Klein one sandwich and taking a bite of the one he'd made for himself. Not eating SEWR rats all the time had already dramatically improved his life. "You know we have an intelligence briefing in ten minutes, right?" Rogers asked, picking a crumb out of his beard.

"I don't go to those." Klein dabbed gingerly at the corner of his mouth with a napkin.

"Yes," Rogers said, "you do. You're the commander of the fleet."

Klein gave a drawn-out, exaggerated sigh. "But they're so

extraordinarily boring. And I don't understand anything that goes on in them. It takes away valuable speech-writing time, and I can't afford it. I need to focus all of my attention on keeping everyone happy or the whole fleet will slip away from me."

Rogers handed the admiral his datapad. "I think we're going to have to rework your priorities a little bit. Come on. Let's get out of here."

With almost petulant reluctance, Klein stood up, straightened his uniform, took his datapad, and marched toward the door of the stateroom. Deet, who had been waiting patiently, made a few computation noises and followed them out into the command deck.

Klein immediately began saluting everyone that walked past, and Rogers quickly slipped on his sling.

"What's wrong with your arm, Rogers?" the admiral asked, saluting so quickly that he tore a small hole in the elbow of his uniform. Rogers would have to fix it later.

"My arm has agoraphobia," Rogers said. "When there's a lot of people around, or lots of noise, or I'm feeling lazy, it stops working."

Klein shot him a look over his shoulder, and it actually sent a tinge of fear through Rogers. Even the admiral's facial expressions seemed to change when he was in public. How did this man do it?

"That's a real thing?"

"As real as space bugs, sir."

Klein shuddered. "I hate space bugs."

Rogers covered a snicker and opened the door to the bridge, immediately after which someone shouted:

"Admiral on the bridge! A-TEN-HOOAH!"

"At ease, valiant troops of the Meridan Patrol Fleet!" Klein bellowed. You could see every back straighten, every stare take on a glint of steely determination. Rogers wanted to poke them all in the eyes.

Until, that is, he saw the Viking, standing with her tree-trunk arms folded over on one side of the bridge. Corporal Mailn was with her; neither of them looked particularly happy to see Rogers at all. A brief, cowardly, self-interested impulse—also known as his typical inner monologue—wondered if they had told anyone about his escape attempt.

Before he realized what he was doing, he was waggling his fingers in a wave at the Viking. The look of hatred on her face deepened into something that might soon result in her diving across the helmsman's console and wringing Rogers' neck. At least then she'd be close to him.

Mailn, on the other hand, shook her head, pointed at Rogers, and mouthed something.

"Win eat do dog?" Rogers asked out loud, squinting.

"We need to talk, you moron," she shouted back at him. At the sound of her own voice, she cleared her throat and turned a little red. "Later. Sorry, Admiral."

Klein didn't seem to notice or care. "Lieutenant Lieutenant Munkle," he said as he sat down in the large chair in the center of the room. He gestured to a nervous-looking young officer who waited patiently beside a fully expanded viewscreen, the contents of which currently looked like static. "What do you have for me today?"

"Oh," Munkle said. "Admiral. Sir. I'm not used to seeing. Ah. Sir. Yes, sir."

Dear god, this man was completely addled by the mere presence of someone that barely knew the size and class of the ship he was in command of. Rogers felt his teeth clenching. Who was this lieutenant lieutenant, anyway? By the way he looked so uncomfortable briefing the admiral, Rogers would have guessed that he was another "voluntary" transfer.

The screen blinked once, and suddenly there was a picture of the entire fleet's disposition. It showed the "border" of the system and gave what Rogers thought might have been an approximation of how the Thelicosans' own border fleet was arrayed.

Rogers was only guessing, of course, because he couldn't understand a word coming out of the man's mouth.

"Mrrmrrr mrr nrr nrrr mrr mrr mrr. Mrr Thelicosa nrr nrr. Exit on the right."

He was from the Public Transportation Announcer Corps.

"A PTAC?" Rogers whispered into Klein's ear, ignoring any further useless babble. "You made a PTAC into your intelligence officer?"

"He asked for the transfer," Klein hissed. "I'm just trying to keep him happy. Besides, what value comes from intelligence briefs, anyway?"

"You'll never know if you keep listening to this guy," Rogers hissed back, pointing at the briefing screen. It had now switched to a screen showing the technical readouts of a Thelicosan Battle Spider, so named for its eight-legged torso, each of which had a terrifying array of weapons on it. Munkle took up a device that allowed him to make notes on the screen and began writing next to one of the eight weapons bays.

MRR MRRR, he wrote. He drew an arrow to a specific point and then nodded, apparently having completed whatever brilliant dissertation he'd been disgorging.

"You can't be serious," Rogers muttered. "This is where all the rumors of the brewing war with Thelicosa came from? How does anyone on this ship even know how to spell 'Thelicosa'?"

The PTAC very clearly wrote the word THELICOSA underneath his commentary of MRR MRRR.

"See?" Klein said.

"That's not the point," Rogers whispered. "You need to fire this guy."

"Why?" Klein whispered. "He asked to be here."

"No, he didn't," Rogers said. "I don't know who asked for it, but I'm pretty sure he'd be much happier talking into a microphone at an aircar station on Merida Prime. Look at the guy!"

Munkle was shaking, sweat pouring down his face. From a

small portable table on his left, Munkle retrieved a cloth from a basket marked CLEAN and put the cloth he'd been using to dab his forehead in one marked NERVOUS. The latter was filling up rapidly. Part of the defining characteristic of a PTAC technician was his aversion to speaking when anyone else was around. They were far more at home in small, dark booths underground.

"Fine," Klein said. "But who am I supposed to replace him with?"

Rogers frowned for a moment, thinking.

"I think I have an idea."

"Gratitude is a sickness suffered by dogs," McSchmidt barked, tucking his hand in between the buttons of his uniform shirt and looking dramatically off into the distance.

"I'm not asking you to thank me," Rogers said. "I'm asking you to take a position that is much better for someone like you than tinkering around in the engineering bay where you don't belong. I mean, didn't you just ask me if you could do the intelligence brief? I'm giving you the chance. And it's a hell of a lot easier than trying to teach a political scientist how to be an engineer."

McSchmidt looked at him, an icy stare turning his whole face into something resembling a snowman's. "Political science is the engineering of cultures, peoples—"

"Right," Rogers said. "I get that. But you're not engineering any people down here. At least, I hope you aren't." He paused. "Are you?"

"Maybe I am," McSchmidt said, a dastardly smile flashing on his face.

"No, you're not."

"No," McSchmidt agreed, "I'm not."

"Good. Look, you wanted me to help you not fail miserably. This is the best I can do. If you really want to have an impact on this fleet, you'll accept the offer and sign the transfer request to become Klein's intelligence officer."

Rogers extended the datapad in his hands, but McSchmidt still didn't take it.

"I've spent months building this kingdom," McSchmidt said. "And you're asking me to abandon my castle."

Rogers looked around at the "kingdom." The boominite containers were *still* stacked in a way that was almost certain to blow a freighter-sized hole in the side of the *Flagship*, the few engineers that hadn't been transferred looked like they all needed to be assigned to null-g rooms, and there was still one of the raccoons Rogers had hidden running around the bay. It had built a nest on top of one of the backup fusion generators, where it was warm, and appeared to have been adopted by Lopez as a sort of mascot.

"Your castle sucks," Rogers said.

McSchmidt sighed. "My castle sucks."

The ensign reached out his hand and signed the release order on the datapad, then shook Rogers' hand.

"Thanks, Rogers," McSchmidt said. "Maybe you're not such an evil, conniving, lying, backstabbing, traitorous bastard."

Rogers grinned, then handed him back the datapad. "I wouldn't be so quick."

McSchmidt frowned, looking at the pad. "Why?"

"Because this is your material. Your briefing is in five minutes."

The former engineering chief's face distorted into something between surprise and rage, but it lasted only for a moment before he took off at a run.

"It requires more courage to suffer than to die!" Rogers called after him.

# Improperganda

The admiral had called a brief hiatus while Rogers had gone to recruit McSchmidt, and as a result the bridge had become a center of confused tension. The admiral didn't normally just sit in the middle of the bridge and do nothing, and everyone seemed to be doing their best to look extremely busy. Commander Belgrave, the helmsman, was rigorously spinning an old-fashioned ship's helm back and forth as though fighting a raging storm, and the display tech was switching monitors on and off at random.

"He'll be up in a minute," Rogers told Klein as he stepped back up on the command platform and looked out into open space. He imagined that open space suddenly filling with Thelicosan battleships, and he couldn't stop the butterflies from forming in his stomach.

"Fine, fine," Klein said. "I still don't see what the problem with having Munkle here was. If there was anything important in the briefing that I couldn't understand, I could always read the notes later."

"Did you ever read the notes?" Rogers asked.

"No. I had my executives read the notes. I'm far too busy."

Rogers shook his head. This was hopeless. He was about to say as much when he felt someone slap him on the back of his head.

"Deet," he said turning around, "it wasn't funny in the garbage chute and it's not funny—oh. Corporal."

"We need to talk," Mailn said, motioning for him to step off the platform. For some reason, Rogers began to feel very nervous. He looked at Klein, hoping that the admiral would demand that his executive officer stay right by his side, but all he received was a dismissive wave.

Stepping down and following Mailn to a quiet corner of the bridge, Rogers thought he would head her off by talking first.

"Hey," he said, "I'm sorry. I didn't mean—"

"Oh, shut up," Mailn said. "Look Rogers, everyone gets weird every once in a while and does something stupid." She shrugged. "I know I have. You're under a lot of pressure. I mean, of course I wanted to kill you, at first. But personally, I'm just kind of glad that you didn't hang yourself instead of trying to desert. I'd feel a lot more awkward slapping your corpse in the back of the head."

Rogers swallowed that uncomfortable and slightly grotesque thought.

"I can't hang myself," Rogers said.

"I know. You're a better man than that."

"That's not what I meant," Rogers muttered. "Never mind. I wanted to say I was sorry for letting you down. I should have at least invited you."

Mailn shot him a look. "Don't make me slap you again. I wanted to talk to you about the Viking."

Rogers raised his eyebrows and looked around, making sure he wasn't about to take another punch to the face. It looked like she had left the room during the break.

"What about her?"

"I'm pretty laid-back," Mailn said, "but she's not. She came in raving the other day, saying that you were still talking about space bugs or something like that."

"So?"

"So, you can't keep lying to her, Rogers. The Viking doesn't play coy. If you want to get with her, you're going to have to be straight with her and apologize."

Rogers shuffled his feet. "What do you mean, 'get with her'? I don't know what you're talking about."

Mailn rolled her eyes, stepping aside as the returning targeting tech came back to his station, holding what might have been real food. Hart was out of the kitchens, so it made sense that the stuff coming out of the mess halls was actually edible again.

"You know what I mean." She looked over Rogers' shoulder. "Here she comes. Just think about it, Rogers. You can't con the Viking."

Brushing past him, Mailn moved to rejoin her boss and walk over to the corner of the bridge, where they'd be able to view the briefing. The Viking, seeing Rogers, spat.

The rest of the crew filed into the bridge, and McSchmidt stepped in front of the screen. After a moment, a comfortable silence settled, punctuated only by the beeps and squeaks of the routine electronic equipment.

"Sir," McSchmidt said. "I'm ready to begin."

Klein waved him on.

"I'll need more time to study," McSchmidt said, glaring at Rogers, "but these ship formations don't appear to be positioned for offensive action. In fact, it looks like they're more concentrated on forming a blockade, as though they thought we were the aggressive ones."

"So, what's all the fuss about?" the Viking said. "Blockading their own system seems a little pointless, doesn't it?"

McSchmidt cleared his throat. He looked uncomfortable, but Rogers attributed that to being new to the position. "The reporting isn't very clear, ma'am, but from what we know of new Thelicosan space strategy, they also utilize a blockading formation as a baseline for forming ceremonial ship patterns. In a few days, you might see, say, a smiley face, or a star. It could just be a parade."

Rogers spoke up. "How old is this data?" he asked.

"Well," McSchmidt said, "I'm only becoming familiar with the sensor array now, but the information is probably less than a few days old."

*So, what's all the warmongering about?* Rogers thought.

"That concludes the intelligence briefing for today," McSchmidt said, turning off the display. "Are there any questions?"

"I have one," the admiral said. "Who are you?"

McSchmidt's eyes flashed to Rogers as he wrung his hands together in front of him. "I'm . . . Ensign McSchmidt, sir. I'm the new intelligence officer."

Rogers nodded. "You approved the transfer just a few minutes ago, sir."

"Oh, right, right," the admiral said as he scratched through some speech he was writing. "Well, I'm promoting you to lieutenant lieutenant, McSchmidt. I can't stand ensigns. Go change your uniform. And tomorrow, I want more colors in your pictures."

"Sir?"

"More colors. You should be showing all the enemy ships as red and all the friendly ships as blue. Here, they all look like they're made out of metal."

"They are made out of metal, sir."

The admiral leaned over to Rogers and muttered, "Munkle never argued."

"Munkle probably argued with you every day," Rogers muttered back. "You just couldn't understand a damn word he was saying."

"That will be all, Lieutenant Lieutenant McSchmidt," said the admiral, leaning back in his chair and giving Rogers a dark, disapproving look.

McSchmidt saluted and, looking like a little kid who'd just

been given a bag full of puppies, flounced out of the room, tearing the rank off his shoulders and whistling.

"Well, that's that," Rogers said. "Admiral, I need to—"

"Everyone!" the admiral said, standing up. Instantly, the room was focused on their leader with rapt attention, their conversations stopping as though they had been instruments cut off by the conductor of an orchestra. Eyes began to sparkle. Someone even began to cry softly, and Mailn raised one of those slow, dramatic salutes.

"Oh, come on," Rogers muttered.

"Men and women of valor," Klein said, his voice booming. "We face before us an intergalactic terror the likes of which have not been seen in generations. It will be a great test of our mettle, our resolve, our courage."

Klein began pacing around the little dais in the middle of the bridge, though there wasn't much room on it anymore, since Rogers was sitting there as well. So, Klein sort of just rocked back and forth as though he was doing a very bad dance to some very out-of-time music.

"The Meridan Patrol Fleet has been the symbol for peace for hundreds of years. In the whispered notes of our name resides the haunting hymn of triumph, trembling on the lips of every man, woman, and child under the aegis of our noble and holy cause. Under the watchful gaze of this fleet, none of them shall come to harm. That hymn shall be sung, and its music will carry the galaxy to peace—the same hymn that will be the dirge of Thelicosan aggression!"

The whole room burst into cheers. Everyone except Rogers was practically jumping up and down, hollering and waving their arms in the air at the rousing battle speech that Klein had just given. Except they weren't going to battle. And Klein was a moron. Rogers rubbed at his temples, a distant hope building up inside of him that he'd have another chance to get off this hunk of metal and go sip lemonade and Scotch somewhere for the rest of his life.

The room was still engaging in riotous celebration when Rogers and the admiral left the bridge for Klein's stateroom. It took a lot of restraint for Rogers to wait until they were inside to not start screaming at the man.

"Are you out of your mind?" Rogers said.

"What?" Klein asked as he shrugged off his coat and picked up a half-eaten sandwich. "Was it something I said?"

Rogers' eyes bulged. "Do you even hear the speeches you give? You just drummed up the whole ship for a war that's not coming."

"I did?"

"Yes," Rogers said flatly, "you did. Do you even know what a dirge is? It's a funeral march. You just implied we were going to slaughter the Thelicosans."

Klein bit his lip, thinking. Taking out a small notepad from his pocket, he began flipping through pages and humming.

"Oh," he said finally. "I wasn't supposed to use the music analogy in that one. Damn it, I do that all the time. I must have mixed up the pages with another speech that was supposed to be delivered if they really did declare war. You're my secretary. Isn't there a way you can help me keep track of this stuff?"

Rogers made an exasperated noise and sat down on the floor, his back against the wall. Klein didn't take visitors into his stateroom, so he wasn't very particular on making the place comfortable.

"No," Rogers said. "I'm not going to help you with that. We're supposed to be working on straightening things out, remember?"

"So," Klein said, "where *would* be a good place to use the word 'dirge'? It's got such a nice ring to it."

Rogers sighed. "Never mind." He thought for a moment. "I have one other question I wanted to ask, Admiral."

"And that is?"

"Those posters that are up all around the ship—" Rogers began.

"Ah yes, the motivational posters. Brilliant ideas, wonderful language."

Rogers didn't remember any wonderful language, but he

figured he and Klein were on the same page. "Sure. Those. Did you order them made?"

"No," Klein said. "They started popping up a little while ago. I thought they were in response to some talks I gave a while ago. They're sort of along the same theme."

*Useless rhetoric that does nothing,* Rogers thought. *Sounds about right.*

"So, who makes them?" Rogers asked. "Do we have a department for that sort of thing?"

"Information Operations," Klein said in the largest combination of coherent syllables Rogers had ever heard outside of one of Klein's speeches. "He does it."

Rogers frowned. "You mean 'they' do it?"

"No," Klein said. "It's just one guy. Ralph, I think his name is. You'll like him."

"First name or last name?"

"I don't know," Klein said, suddenly throwing up his hands. "Damn it, Rogers, I don't know why you expect me to know all of these things about the people on my ship. Why don't you go ask him and get the hell out of my hair for an hour or so?"

"IT'S RALPH," Ralph said.

Rogers' hands shot up to his ears, which were now ringing quite loudly. The small, cramped, glorified janitor's closet that made up the entire office space of the information operations squadron didn't do much to distill the noise of a man shouting at him from his desk.

"I'm right here," Rogers said. "You don't have to shout."

"WHAT?" Ralph shouted, squinting. He hadn't taken his eyes off his computer terminal since Rogers had entered the room. Ralph—Rogers still didn't know if it was his first name, last name, nickname, or what he did after meals—typed furiously away at the oldest keyboard system that Rogers had ever seen. It looked like it actually contained mechanical moving parts, and it made loud clanking noises every time Ralph hit a key. How did the computers even read that kind of technology?

"I'm Lieutenant Rogers, Admiral Klein's executive officer," Rogers said.

"I'M RALPH."

"Yeah," Rogers said, wincing. He should have brought earplugs. "You told me that."

"YOU'RE AN EXECUTIVE OFFICER?" Ralph took a sip of what may have been the largest, most viscous cup of coffee in the galaxy. It took a full three seconds for the liquid to find its way from the side of the cup to Ralph's lips, and Rogers was almost sure that Ralph *chewed* on it.

"That's what I said."

"I THOUGHT EXECUTIVE OFFICERS WERE THE SECOND-IN-COMMAND."

"No," Rogers said. "That's only for water navy. We're in the space navy. It's different."

"THAT'S REALLY CONFUSING."

Rogers shrugged. "More confusing than a marine captain being the same rank as a navy lieutenant, but a marine lieutenant being the same rank as a navy ensign?" Rogers laughed, hoping to draw Ralph into his confidence through humor, but Ralph didn't even seem to notice that Rogers had told a joke.

Clearing his throat, Rogers looked around the room, which he wasn't even sure was fit for human occupancy. Dark, ink-stained metal walls framed just enough space for a small bed, a nightstand, and the computer terminal at which Ralph was currently sitting. A single light bulb dangled from a wire from the ceiling, swaying back and forth. The walls were packed from floor to ceiling with different posters, all of them incomplete. One particular poster appeared to be a blank piece of paper. In general, they seemed to be misprints—one had a picture of a Thelicosan battle cruiser broken in half that had the caption SINK THEIR SHIT underneath it. The adjacent poster had a picture of a toilet that had the caption SINK THEIR SHIP.

"WHAT CAN I DO FOR YOU, LIEUTENANT? I DON'T GET MANY VISITORS."

"It's kind of a hard place to find," Rogers said.

In fact, it was nearly impossible to find. It wasn't on any of the schematic maps of the ship, and everyone he asked seemed to know that the 331st *had* an information operations squadron, but had no idea where it was. As it turned out, he had to use the in-line on the training deck and manually stop it, climb out the hatch, and crawl down a tunnel just to get to the office door.

"I was wondering who commissioned all of these posters," Rogers said. "There are an awful lot of them around the ship." Rogers was secretly scanning the room, looking for anything that might resemble a listening device. It made sense to start looking at the guy making the posters, but every second he hung out in this cramped space, it seemed less likely that Ralph was the culprit.

"ALL MY ORDERS COME IN ELECTRONICALLY," Ralph said/screamed. "I'VE BEEN VERY BUSY."

"I can tell," Rogers said. "I really admire your art. Where do you get your inspiration?"

*Who makes you spout this garbage?* Rogers wanted to ask.

"ART ISN'T ABOUT INSPIRATION," Ralph said. "IT'S ABOUT RECEIVING SPECFIC AND ORDERLY INSTRUCTIONS AND THEN PUTTING THEM IN A COMPUTER."

Rogers slowly shook his head. "That's so completely wrong, I don't even know how to argue. So, you don't know who submits the orders?"

"NO. IN FACT, I HAVEN'T GOTTEN ANY NEW ORDERS IN A LONG TIME. I'M STILL WORKING ON THE ORDER I GOT EIGHT MONTHS AGO."

Rogers' head was starting to hurt. The shouting would have been tolerable had the room not been so unbelievably small. He rubbed the sides of his temples.

"One order, eight months ago? Is that the order for all the posters that have gone up lately?" Rogers asked. He realized his own voice was getting louder.

"YES." Ralph banged away at the keyboard, and Rogers stepped behind him to look on the screen. A very simple graphical editing program was up, and Ralph was dragging around pieces of stock art and putting them together. He had an awful lot of pictures of ships, cannon fire, droids, and a surprisingly large database of really useless things like flowers and striped candies.

"Do you print them here?"

"NO."

Well, that meant that whoever was putting the listening devices in them—they must have been exceedingly small—was either in the printing room or the framing room. Rogers was sure he could find out more if he visited wherever that location was.

"Who prints them?"

"I DON'T KNOW."

Rogers sighed. Of course Ralph didn't know. Gosh, he was typing fast. Rogers looked down at the keyboard and noticed that most of the letters on the keyboard were worn away from overuse except the one for that squiggly thing that nobody knew what the hell it was for.

Well, if he couldn't solve the problem of the listening devices here, maybe he could just solve the problem of the ubiquitous, tacky posters. They really were annoying, and Rogers had a feeling they were having an opposite effect on ship morale. He wasn't going to revitalize the 331st with all that crap on the walls.

"What if I told you I wanted a high-priority order to interrupt the one you were working on?" Rogers asked. "You might not know this, but the stuff you're kicking out now is kind of making people lose their minds." He remembered his old friend Hart spouting off the strange rhetoric in the kitchen, and how it had made Rogers feel like he had an army of spiders crawling around in his underwear.

“NO CAN DO.” Ralph said/screamed, his voice cracking. How did he even have vocal cords left? “ALL ORDERS HAVE TO BE COMPLETED BEFORE MOVING ON TO THE NEXT ORDER.”

Rogers sighed. “Could you at least not type them in all caps?”

“I DON’T KNOW WHAT YOU’RE TALKING ABOUT.”

“Right,” Rogers said. “Of course.” He pulled on his beard, thinking. Snapping the *Flagship* out of whatever craziness had hold of it would be a little more effective if he didn’t have information ops working against him. Who *had* made that order, anyway? Perhaps he could get into the system later, right after he figured out where they were printed and framed.

“HEY,” Ralph said. “WHAT RHYMES WITH OBEY?”

Rogers stopped pacing around the room and stepped behind the computer again. On the screen was a very dark, mysterious shadow of a silhouetted face, under which was currently written WHEN YOU OBEY . . .

“I don’t know,” Rogers said. “Okay? Play? Delay?”

“THANKS.”

Ralph finished typing so the phrase read WHEN YOU OBEY . . . THINGS ARE GOOD.

Rogers opened his mouth to argue, then recalled some metaphor about pissing into a stern wind. He thought it might have gone something like “WHEN YOU URINATE INTO A BREEZE, IT COMES BACK AND HITS YOU IN THE FACE, AND THAT’S BAD.”

While rolling his eyes so hard, he thought they might fall out, Rogers noticed a tall metallic cylinder in the corner of the room with a small red light on it. It took him a moment, but he recognized it as an old coffee maker, which made sense, since he didn’t get the impression that Ralph left this room very often. Where did he go to the bathroom or shower? Rogers sniffed the air. *Did* he shower?

“So, you get to make your own coffee, eh?” Rogers said amicably, sidling over to where the large cylinder was mounted to the wall.

"NOT JUST COFFEE," Ralph said. "COFFEE AND PULVERIZED SEWER RATS. KEEPS ME WORKING LONGER."

Rogers nodded slowly. "Right. Say, have you ever heard of zip jack?"

"NO. IS HE AN ASTEROID RACER?"

"Yep," Rogers said as he closed the lid of the coffee-Sewer-Rat-amalgamator, which was possibly the single most disgusting thing he'd ever heard of in his entire life. "The fastest asteroid racer in the galaxy. He'll take you right over the moon if you let him."

"WHICH MOON?"

"It doesn't matter," Rogers said. "It was great meeting you, Ralph. Keep up the good work."

# Report: C-7FG-2923-X

Serial: C-7FG-2923-X

Distribution: DBS//DSS//DAK//DFR//BB//CLOSED NETWORK A66

Classification: Special Protocol Required

Summary: List of personnel transfers enacted by Human 2552 and Human 2301.

Details: A number of personnel transfers have been enacted in the last two standard days. While the signatory of the orders appears to be Human 2301, information received through surveillance has revealed that Human 2301 is being directly influenced and possibly manipulated by Human 2552, whom we previously assessed as being of minimal cognitive capacity.

Details: A list of the personnel transfers is reproduced below.

Human 8853 (McSchmidt) has been transferred to intelligence.

Human 0609 (Munkle) has been transferred to public transportation.

Human 9994 (Tunger) has been transferred to the zoo deck.

Human 2002 (Hart) has been transferred to engineering.

Human 1050 (Suresh) has been transferred to the zoo deck.

Human 5665 (Stract) has been transferred to sanitation services, demoted to starman second class, and has had his clipboard confiscated.

Assessment: Human 2552 must be kept under careful observation.

Report Submitted By: F-GC-001

# Big Red Data

The briefing screen was swathed in red. Red all over the place. The whole room was utterly silent; even Klein had stopped drafting a pep talk to stare at the screen that appeared to be bleeding Thelicosan ships.

"Much better with color," Klein said agreeably, nodding his head before going back to writing.

What only yesterday had been a benign formation of Thelicosan battleships had transformed into something ready to charge right into Meridan space and blast everything it could find. There also seemed to be about twice as many ships as there had been the day before, and they'd moved in some of their Striker craft, high-speed cruisers designed to reach out and disable sensors to blind the enemy quickly before a follow-on force.

"I'm guessing that's not a blockade formation anymore," the Viking said.

"No, ma'am," McSchmidt said, swallowing. "It's not."

McSchmidt changed the image, revealing a close up of a couple of the Battle Spiders grouped in a wedge formation pointing toward the Meridan border. He'd highlighted some of the armament appendages.

"These show a heat scanner's evaluation of activity," McSchmidt said, pointing to the highlights. "The Thelicosans run up-down rotations of their weapon arrays before they think they're going to use them; it warms up the turrets so that there's less of a chance of them overheating when the fighting actually starts."

An uncomfortable silence settled over the room as everyone took that in.

"Where did all the extra ships come from?" Rogers asked.

"That's the thing," McSchmidt said, zooming back out to the overview of the enemy formation as reported by the Meridan's sensor arrays. "I have no idea. There's an Un-Space point near the edge of this position, but for so many ships to come out of it in the space of a day and regroup is . . . Well, it's not really possible."

"Some kind of cloaking?" the Viking asked.

"It's possible," McSchmidt said. "I haven't heard of the Thelicosans developing any kind of cloaking device that big."

That wasn't good news either. If they'd developed that kind of stealth technology, and the sensor arrays' data was several days old, the Thelicosans could already have ships sitting right next to the *Flagship* with the cannons armed, and the 331st would have no idea. The Two Hundred Years' (and Counting) Peace could evaporate—along with the entire 331st—in seconds.

Something about it all seemed very wrong to Rogers, but that could have just been his unabashed, panic-stricken fear of combat.

"That's all I have for you today, sir," McSchmidt said. "I'll talk to the rest of the intel troops and see if we can't come up with something more solid for you tomorrow."

The briefing broke up, everyone returning to their normal duties with a somber sense of dread hanging over them. Klein didn't even stand up and say anything charismatic, though someone in the far side of the room too far away to hear stood up and gave Klein a slow, dramatic salute anyway. Habits were hard to break, Rogers supposed.

For once, though, Rogers didn't have his mind on an impending invasion or his boss's incompetence. The Viking was slowly making her way out of the briefing room, and the recurring dream he kept having about being rescued from a burning room wasn't helping keep her off his mind. Mailn was right. He had to make this right or he was never going to be able to focus on not dying.

"Captain Alsinbury," Rogers said. "Wait. Hang on a second."

"I don't have time for a deserter," she grumbled as she elbowed past him.

He skirted around the edge of the helmsman's desk and hopped over a small railing, putting himself directly between her and the bridge's exit.

"I'm not a deserter," he said. "I can't even make cupcakes."

He grinned and raised his eyebrows. She wound back her fist.

"Wait!" he cried, not at all like a small child, and put his hands in front of his face as if that would do anything to stop the haymaker of the strongest woman he'd ever met. When he didn't feel like he'd been hit by a truck, he peeked through his makeshift guard and saw the Viking standing with her arms folded, eyes boring into his skull.

"Wait," he repeated. "I just want to talk to you for a second."

"I can't imagine you having anything at all interesting to say to me," the Viking said.

"I wanted to apologize," he said. "For lying to you. And trying to jump out of the side of the ship."

The obvious disgust on the Viking's face didn't lessen at all. "And?"

Rogers sighed. "And the space bugs."

"Seriously, what were you thinking?" the Viking said. "Space bugs?"

"I know," Rogers said, hanging his head. "I'm not really on my game lately. I didn't really want to run away. It's just that I didn't want to be here anymore and I'm not allowed to leave voluntarily."

The Viking's frown deepened. Rogers cleared his throat.

"It's not that I wanted to run away. It's that I'm scared of actually having to fight anyone."

"Keep digging, metalhead."

Rogers grit his teeth and pulled at his beard. "You're not making this very easy. Look, I'm doing my best now, alright? I'm trying to piece this group back together and get us ready for whatever . . ." He gestured at where the briefing screen had been. "Whatever is or isn't coming our way. Didn't I put someone back into Engineering who could actually fix things?"

The Viking shrugged. "I guess."

"Didn't I put someone who could speak back into Intelligence?"

She sighed. "Yeah."

"My point is that I'm trying to make up for it. And if this war comes, I'm going to need someone to share an escape pod with."

"Rogers!"

"I'm kidding!"* Rogers said, miraculously dodging the punch that would have likely broken his sternum in half.

The Viking didn't make to hit him again, so that was progress, he guessed. He straightened out his uniform and tried to look serious.

"I'm not sure what's about to happen here," Rogers said, gesturing toward the now-empty briefing screen. "But I have a feeling we're going to need your help.

The Viking raised an eyebrow. "Me?"

"Yes," Rogers said, "you. I don't know anyone else on this ship that's actually prepared to fight. Everyone else around here, including me, has been screwing around for the last two hundred years while you were actually doing what marines are supposed

---

*He wasn't kidding.

to do." Rogers swallowed. "Not that you've been doing it for two hundred years. I mean, you don't look two hundred years old. I mean, you look young, but you act old. I mean . . ."

"Rogers," the Viking said. Was there a smile playing on her face? "I get it."

"Right," he said, thankful for the reprieve. "I'd just hate it if something happened and you still thought I was just some stupid metalhead droid-lover."

The Viking chewed on her lip a little bit. "You are a stupid metalhead droid-lover," she said, but the bite was out of it.

"Reformed," Rogers said, shrugging.

After looking him over for a second, the Viking shook her head. "Apology accepted, I guess. If we're going to have to crack some Thelicosan heads, we might as well do it together."

Just the word "together" made Rogers tingle all over.

"Hey," he said. "Now that there's something without motor oil in the kitchens, maybe you and I could do the Uncouth Corkscrew sometime."

She looked at him levelly.

"I mean *go to* the Uncouth Corkscrew. To eat."

"I like Sewer rats," she said, and started to walk past him. He felt all of the air come out of him. No matter what he did, he'd always be the cowardly metalhead. What good was stupidly sticking around to fight a war that you were certain to lose if you didn't end up getting with the girl of your dreams?

"But sometimes, I like to put some Tabasco on 'em," she said. "I'll think about it, Rogers."

Rogers kept a straight face until the Viking turned around, after which Rogers gave himself a celebratory fist pump. Corporal Mailn, who had been discreetly listening near the door, gave Rogers a wink, a slow nod, and a thumbs-up. Despite the overabundance of affirmation gestures, Rogers mouthed a thank-you just before Mailn followed her boss out the door and down the corridor to do whatever it was that marines did all day. Rogers had some ideas, but he was pretty sure they were all just fantasies.

"Hey, Rogers," McSchmidt called from behind. Rogers turned to see McSchmidt walking over, looking rather spiffy with the new rank on his shoulders. "Can I talk to you for a second?"

"Sure," Rogers said.

"Outside."

They walked back into the hallway, Deet following silently behind them, where McSchmidt motioned over to a quiet spot in the large, somewhat-circular terminus of the command deck.

"Something's bothering me about that data," McSchmidt said.

"What," Rogers said, "something bothers you about hundreds of battleships that weren't there yesterday suddenly appearing out of nowhere?"

McSchmidt frowned. "You don't believe it either?"

"It's not that I don't believe it," Rogers said, "it's that I believe it too easily."

"You realize that doesn't make any sense," McSchmidt said.

"That's only because you're not listening close enough. You and I both know that it's not physically possible for those ships to be there if they weren't there yesterday."

"Yeah, but what about cloaking? New technology?" McSchmidt said, taking a moment to salute a passing commander. "Hey, where did that sling come from? Are you hurt?"

"Ignore it," Rogers said. "The cloaking device theory is interesting but not practical."

"Why?"

"At the Academy—" Rogers began.

"Yes." McSchmidt blurted, maybe a little too loudly. "The one I definitely went to. To become an officer."

Rogers blinked. "Yeah. That's the one. At the Academy, what did you use for basic flight training?"

McSchmidt thought for a moment. "Paper airplanes?"

"Right. Because there's no money. Because it's peacetime. Why should it be any different in Thelicosa? We're not in an arms race or anything. They don't have the budget to come up with a super-secret stealth device *and* keep it hidden *and* install it on an entire fleet of ships *and* move them to the Meridan border."

"I guess," McSchmidt said. "But that still doesn't explain why we're seeing them on our scopes."

"No," Rogers said. "It doesn't. I think that maybe—"

"Lurturnurnt Ruggers!"

"Munkle," Rogers said, turning around, "get back to your post at the public transportation—oh. Hello there, Tunger."

"Hullur to yurself," Tunger said. He didn't look happy. For that matter, neither did McSchmidt, though Rogers didn't know why. The new intelligence officer eyed Tunger suspiciously, and his hands were balled up into fists at his side.

"I cun buluf you transferred mai to the zeooo deck!"

"I'm not going to admit that I may have almost understood that," Rogers said, "and I'm instead going to threaten to slap you in the face if you don't drop that ridiculous accent immediately."

Tunger looked on the verge of sticking out his tongue. "I can't believe you transferred me to the zoo deck!"

"Why?" Rogers asked, frowning. "That's where you came from, isn't it? You used to talk about how much you missed the chimps and all that. I thought you would want that."

"But I'm your orderly," Tunger said. "How am I supposed to help you keep all of your things in order in an orderly fashion if I'm in the zoo deck?"

"I have a new orderly," Rogers said, wrapping his arm around Deet's shoulders in what he immediately realized was a very awkward thing to do to a droid. "So, you can go back to doing what you love."

"I was not given a choice in this matter," Deet muttered.

"Orderly or trash heap," Rogers said. "Seems like an easy choice to me."

"Still," Deet said. "You never asked."

Tunger looked at Deet with undisguised revulsion. "But you hate droids!"

Rogers felt his cheeks heating. "That's not really—"

"You used to say every day how much you hated these 'goddamn shinies' and that you wanted to see every one of them melted down to scrap!"

"Now you're just making stuff up."

"And that if you ever had to work with another droid, you'd throw yourself out the trash chute without a pressure suit."

"Now, that's nearly true," Deet said.

"Shut up," Rogers said. "Tunger, I'm a reformed anti-droidist, okay? I found one that doesn't make me want to strangle myself with my own bootlaces. Besides, what kind of orderly are you, anyway? I haven't seen you in forever! How are you supposed to be my orderly if you're not around to keep things in order?"

Tunger at least had the grace to look ashamed at his prolonged absence. "I was busy," he said.

"Doing what?"

"Playing around in the zoo deck." Tunger looked up from the floor. "The chimps need me! And they're *so cute*! And *they* let me talk to them in whutuver vurce aie wunt!"

McSchmidt was starting to look like he wanted to make like a chimp and throw poop at Tunger, though Rogers didn't know what he was so upset about. Rogers supposed if *he* had been interrupted in the middle of one of those dark, conspiratorial conversations where everything was all dramatic, he might have been a little bit upset as well.

"I don't know," Tunger said. He shuffled his feet. "I was starting to like being your orderly, I guess. I got to do important stuff, like talk to important people and give you bad news."

Rogers put a hand on his shoulder, feeling a little awkward. "Those chimps need you," he said. "And the *Flagship* needs someone competent working in the zoo deck. What would happen if people didn't have a place to go and feed the ducks after work?"

"The ducks would get hungry," Tunger agreed.

"Well, yeah," Rogers said, "that's not really what I meant, but sure."

"And the rabbits would have nobody to talk to."

Rogers just let that one go.

"I guess you're right," Tunger said. "Maybe that is where I belong. But if you ever need anything, you'll promise to come and get me, right? Like if you need things, you know, put into a particular order or anything?"

"Of course," Rogers said. "You'll be the first person I call."

Tunger smiled and walked away, and for the first time Rogers noticed that he had a small golden lion tamarin attached to his back. The monkey reached up a finger to his lips in a shushing gesture.

Rogers shook his head and turned back to McSchmidt. "As for you," he said, "I wouldn't worry too much about it yet. It's just one day of data, and you and I both know that there's something funny about it. We haven't received any corroborating intel from Merida Prime or any of the other outlying stations that are keeping tabs on the Thelicosans. We can't just all go crazy over a change in formation, can we?"

"No," McSchmidt said, shaking his head. Some of the tension seemed to leave his body. "No, you're right."

Rogers clapped him on the back. "Right. Now, if all of a sudden they start grouping their ships in the shape of the words 'Die, Merida!' then we know we're in trouble."

They shared a good laugh over that.

The briefing screen displayed an array of enemy ships that had been carefully arranged to spell "Die, Merida."

"Now, that's just ridiculous," Rogers said.

"Are they trying to pick a fight?" the Viking asked. "What happened to the element of surprise and all that? They must know we're looking at them."

"Of course they know we're looking at them," Rogers said, still staring at the screen. "We're always looking at them. They're looking at us. They're looking at us looking at them."

The Viking grunted but didn't argue with him anymore. Klein, engaged for once, rubbed his face with his hand.

"It looks like there are even more ships than there were yesterday," the admiral said.

"There are, sir," McSchmidt said, "but that's the thing. There aren't only more, they're different ships."

He zoomed in and started going through some of the data collected by the sensors, most of which Rogers didn't understand. It all looked very technical, but McSchmidt seemed to have no problem picking through it. For a political scientist, he sure seemed comfortable with all this information.

"These Battle Spiders have different radiation signatures from the ones that were at this location yesterday. Unless they've all gone back to a maintenance facility and had their cores switched out, or they've been in combat and taken damage, that's not possible." He switched the image again. "It's the same with a handful of these frigates. If the Thelicosans were preparing for a full-scale invasion, I would say that maybe they just brought in new ships. But they're not new; they're different. The ones that *were* here yesterday have disappeared."

"That's pretty sharp," the Viking said. "And I can understand the words coming out of your mouth. You're a natural, Lieutenant Lieutenant McSchmidt."

This seemed to ruffle McSchmidt a bit. His face turned red and he began to sway back and forth uncomfortably where he was standing, creating the impression that he was either doing a very unenthusiastic slow dance or was a little drunk.

"Thank you, ma'am," he muttered. He cleared his throat and pointed back at the diagram. "For this reason, I'm willing to say that there's less evidence of an attack than we might have thought. It's possible that the Thelicosans are doing change-out drills, practicing refitting and resupply. Despite the, uh, creative formation, there's no reason to believe that they—"

"Admiral!" someone shouted from the corner of the bridge. Rogers hadn't spent that much time on the bridge to know everyone, but he thought it was the defensive array tech. "Something's wrong with my system."

"What?" Klein said, standing up. "Have you tried rebooting?"

"I've rebooted four times," the tech said. "I can't get this little red light to go away."

"What about turning it off and then back on again?"

"I've tried that, too!"

"A reset?"

"Twice!"

Rogers was moving across the bridge now, heading toward the tech and wishing that he could tell his fleet commander to shut his mouth in front of all these people.

"What is it?" Rogers asked. "What light? What's the light?"

"This one here." The tech pointed to the display. On it, there was a big red light blinking furiously underneath the words THEY'RE ATTACKING US.

"Oh shit," Rogers said. "They're attacking us!"

"But the intel briefing!" McSchmidt cried, pointing at the display. "It's intel! Intel is never wrong!"

"But I have this light right here," the technician said. "It's telling me . . . it's telling me that the intelligence is wrong!"

"Oh my god," Admiral Klein said. "We have no intelligence!"

Rogers fought down the nervous urge to vomit and started shouting at the rest of the bridge.

"Bring up the display!"

"Which display, sir?" the troop controlling the display said.

"Any display!" Rogers said. "Just let us see something!"

What had formerly been the very wrong intelligence briefing suddenly changed into a CCTV shot of the zoo deck. Tunger could be seen running around, giggling like a little girl, as he was chased in a circle by a pack of chimps throwing something unsavory.

"This isn't the display I wanted," Rogers cried.

"You said to display anything," the tech yelled back. "I have lots of buttons in front of me, Lieutenant."

"Display something else!" Rogers said. "Maybe something to do with them *attacking us*!"

The image changed again.

"That's a hell of a display," Klein said.

It was, actually, nothing. Open space. Not a single thing on the screen.

"What is this?" Rogers said.

"It should be where the attack is coming from," the display tech said. "I took the data from the computer. This is where it's telling us to look."

"Never believe computers," Rogers said. "Slew the camera around. See if you can't find something."

"The light's not going off!" the defensive array technician said.

"Probably because they haven't finished attacking us," Rogers said. He stared at the image as the screen moved around, the stars blurring in the background as the outboard camera swopped silently across open space. The whole bridge seemed to be holding its breath.

In fact, the whole bridge *was* holding its breath. Rogers was surrounded by people going blue in the face.

"Everyone breathe," he said, and was answered by a huge, collective sigh of relief. "It looks like a false alarm. Maybe there's something wrong with the—"

Something silver blurred past the viewscreen just before a huge explosion rocked the ship.

# The Military Never Said Anything About War

"What the hell happened?" Rogers said as he picked himself up off the floor. The explosion hadn't knocked him down, but it was amazing what a full-grown admiral could do with a dive tackle while screaming, "Save me!" That man was just not cut out for combat. The fact that it took Rogers several tries to get to his feet because of his shaking knees told him that he was also probably not cut out for combat.

"Can't tell you, sir," the display tech said. "The systems are down. I can't even get a damage report."

"Get Communications on the line," Rogers said.

"I already did. They told me to reboot."

"The light went off," the warning tech said, pointing to the THEY'RE ATTACKING US button. "We're saved!"

"Let's not jump to conclusions," Rogers said. "Did anyone else see that thing before we were hit?"

"I saw it," the Viking said. "Looked like a little ship to me."

Rogers walked over to Belgrave the helmsman, feeling dizzy

and disoriented. He was nearly positive all the blood in his body was in his ears, they were ringing so loudly.

"What about the targeting computer?" he said. "Didn't that pick up anything?"

Belgrave looked up at him and frowned. "But you told me to turn it off so you could clean—"

"That was days ago!" Rogers cried. "Are you crazy? You're telling me the targeting computer has been off the whole time?"

"I just didn't want any space bugs on it," Belgrave muttered.

"Sweet mother . . ." Rogers said, pulling hard at his beard. "Turn it back on already!"

Belgrave gave him a dirty look before flipping a couple of switches on the computer in front of him. There were a couple of perfunctory beeps and squeaks before the display in front of him came to life, along with an increasingly familiar voice.

"Congratulations on activating your targeting computer! You are entitled to one free lobster dinner—"

"Lobster dinner?" Rogers said.

"Just kidding," the computer said. "You are entitled to one free balloon to be redeemed at any of the many Snaggadir's Sundries locations available across the galaxy. Remember: whatever you need, you can Snag It at Snaggadir's™!"

The targeting display blossomed to life, showing blue dots where the friendly ships were, and a few yellow dots where civilian craft that happened to be transiting the sector were.

"There," Belgrave said, pointing at a fleeting orange blip on the display. "Something just entered Un-Space, but there's not enough data for me to tell what it was. It could have been anything."

"Damn it," Rogers said.

"We don't need to know what it was," the Viking said. "It was the Thellies."

McSchmidt shook his head. "That doesn't make any sense, ma'am. They don't behave like that. Why send one ship? Even if they were testing our defenses, it would have been a squadron full of Strikers followed by a larger force. One ship popping out of Un-Space and firing at us isn't like them at all."

Rogers frowned. He agreed with McSchmidt, but something about the situation felt wrong. Like he'd seen it before.

"Admiral," Rogers said, walking over to the man who was still muttering about confiscating a balloon. "Aren't you going to do something?"

Klein looked a little shaken, but he was doing a good job of covering it up, aside from the dive tackle when the blast had hit. He'd recovered and was now sitting in his admiral's chair, tapping his fingers nervously on the armrest.

"I can't think of anything to say," Klein said quietly.

"Maybe instead," Rogers said, "think about something to *do*. And if you can't do that, consider trying to calm everyone down while we figure out what happened. Everyone felt that explosion; they need to know that we're not about to get torn in half by Thelicosan plasma cannons."

"We're about to get torn in half by Thelicosan plasma cannons?" the admiral half shouted.

For some reason, Klein's words echoed through the PA system. Everyone on the bridge stopped for a moment.

"Whoops," a starman first class said from behind his terminal. "Should I not have turned on the All Personnel Address System? I thought you said the admiral was going to tell everyone something."

Lights started to flash on the dashboard from all the incoming calls from the other areas of the ship, everyone wondering what the hell was going on.

"Klein," Rogers said in a warning tone.

"I can't," Klein whispered. "You and I both know that I don't know what I'm doing. If I can't talk to the Thelicosans, I can't do anything about it. I don't even know who to talk to, never mind what to say. Is there any chance of them having a meeting about this? I can deliver a killer slide show presentation."

"Probably not," Rogers said. "You need to take command, Admiral. This is your fleet."

Klein's countenance broke for a moment—the man looked like he was about to sob again, and Rogers didn't know if he could handle that—but he pulled it together. "I can't. I can't." He looked at Rogers, his face brightening. "I have an idea. *You* do it."

"Me?" Rogers said, his voice squeaking. "I'm not the admiral of the fleet! I have no practical experience in—"

"Everyone!" Klein said. The room went silent. "I'm required in my stateroom to . . . analyze things. For the war effort. Communications must be sent to Meridan headquarters to inform them of recent happenings. In the meantime, I'm leaving Lieutenant Rogers in command of the bridge."

"What?" Rogers said.

"What?" the Viking said.

"Fear not, valiant soldiers of justice!" Klein said, puffing up his chest as he slowly began backing out of the room. "Rogers can handle everything in my absence."

"He's a *lieutenant*!" McSchmidt said. "I mean, not a lieutenant lieutenant, but still a lieutenant. He's like . . . six ranks below you!"

"For victory!" Klein shouted as he reached the door. "For glory! For honor! Galactic agility! Synergistic battlespace effects! Slide shows!"

The door closed, leaving the bridge a quiet space of emotional confusion as Klein's charismatic effects mixed with the utter strangeness of it all and lingered in the air like the clash of two cheap colognes. One particularly dense starman second class actually clapped a few times from the back of the room, and the corporal next to her did that slow, dramatic salute thing.

And then Rogers realized the entire bridge was looking at him.

"You can't be serious," he said, though he wasn't sure to whom he was speaking. The lights on the communication tech's dashboard were still blinking rapidly, and he could hear him telling someone to please stop trying to climb out the window, and that pillows were not critical items to transport in the event of an emergency, anyway.

"Um," the communications tech said, placing a hand over his headset microphone. "Lieutenant Admiral Rogers?"

"That's not even a real rank," Rogers said. "What is it?"

"Well," he said, "I thought I should bring to your attention the following." He took a deep breath. "There are people in the kitchen screaming about a fire, there is a group of droids that seems to have been knocked over in the mess hall and can't get up, several animal cages have broken open on the zoo deck, the IT desk in the communications squadron is rebooting itself and I don't know what that means, and it sounds like there is a group of finance troops running toward the escape pods with their pillows."

Red-faced, the communications tech gasped for breath, beads of sweat forming on his forehead.

Rogers just stared at him. What the hell was he supposed to do with all of that? He wasn't a fleet commander. He wasn't even a real lieutenant. He was an ex-sergeant who liked to drink alcohol, play rigged games, and trick people into doing silly things for amusement. This was insane. This was completely insane.

Deet, who had been quietly standing next to him, piped up.

"Can I make a suggestion?"

Rogers nodded dumbly.

"In light of the extremity of the situation, you should probably get off your EXPLETIVE POSTERIOR BODY SECTION and put out that EXPLETIVE fire."

Rogers blinked. "Expletive," he said. "You're right."

"You don't have to censor yourself," Deet said, sounding dejected. "It's not your fault I can't express myself properly."

"I was just trying to show some solidarity," Rogers said. He turned to the Viking. "Captain Alsinbury."

"What?"

"Can you take a small group of your marines down to whatever pods those idiots are running for and keep them from jettisoning themselves into space?"

The Viking cracked her knuckles, a sound that did strange things to Rogers. "My pleasure."

"And afterward . . ." he said before his brain could stop his mouth, but he trailed off.

The Viking raised an eyebrow.

"Never mind," he said, swallowing. "Just keep those troops inside the ship."

She gave him a nod and bulldozed her way out of the room, knocking everything from people to heavy equipment aside in her haste to get into a situation where she might actually get to hit someone.

"Get Hart from engineering on the line," Rogers said to the tech. "Tell them to get some of the heavy lifters over to the mess halls and see if they can't flip those droids before they start an electrical fire. Bring fire foam. And find out why the fire-suppression systems in the kitchen haven't gone off yet."

"Yes, sir."

"Bring up the zoo deck so I can see what's going on," Rogers said.

The display technician changed the screen, and Rogers' heart jumped into his throat. In the middle of one of the camera's views was Tunger, lying on his back with a giant, full-grown male lion on top of him. The unfortunate corporal was trying futilely to fend of the claws of the powerful savannah feline.

"Oh my god," Rogers said. "We need to get him out of there! Turn on the audio so we can tell him help is on the way!"

The communications tech flipped a switch, but before Rogers could get a word out he was surprised to hear a cacophony of giggling coming from the two-way system.

"Stop!" Tunger tittered. "Es nur fair! Nur fair! Yur cheated!"

McSchmidt, for some reason, groaned.

"Never mind," Rogers said slowly. "They're just playing."

The whole bridge relaxed as a single unit. Nobody wanted to see a man mauled by a lion on live video. Well, maybe some of them did, but nobody would admit to wanting to see a man mauled by a lion on live video.

"McSchmidt," Rogers said, turning to the intelligence officer, who was looking much more worried than everyone else on the ship. "I want to talk to you outside. Everyone else, you are to continue with your duties or at least continue looking busy until the admiral returns."

Everyone snapped to, engaging in the important-looking activities of picking things up and putting them down again, walking briskly from one station to another to examine a console that had nothing to do with their jobs, and pointing curiously at blinking lights on panels.

Rogers left the briefing room, immediately followed by both McSchmidt and Deet. When they were out of earshot of the rest of the bridge, Rogers motioned for McSchmidt to come closer so he could talk privately, but McSchmidt was looking over his shoulder.

"What is that?" McSchmidt said.

Rogers turned around and saw a brand-new propaganda poster plastered on the wall, but there was something different about it, something he couldn't quite place.

Oh, that was it. It was a picture of a giant panda bear with a melted face wearing overalls, sitting in the branches of a lemon tree. Underneath was written I CAN TASTE THE COLORS.

Rogers choked back a laugh. "I have no idea," he said. "But more importantly, McSchmidt," he said, lowering his voice, "I think there's a spy aboard the *Flagship*."

The intel officer's eyes widened. "A spy?" He swallowed. "Why would you think something like that?"

Rogers pointed his thumb at Deet. "Deet here has noticed that there are listening devices in Klein's stateroom. I think there might be listening devices in other places as well. Do you think it's a coincidence that two times in a row, the Thelicosans changed their battle formations immediately after we suggested it?"

"Yes," McSchmidt said. "I do."

Rogers looked at him flatly.

"Okay, so maybe it's a little suspicious," McSchmidt said. "I just don't want us to rush into anything rash, like a giant, ship-wide spy hunt or anything."

Rogers hesitated. "I wasn't suggesting that."

"Good," McSchmidt said. "Because it would be a bad idea. I don't think you'd find him." He cleared his throat. "Or her. Or it. Maybe it's a droid?"

"Why in the world would anyone have a droid as a spy?" Rogers said. "It wouldn't make any sense. They'd be saying things like CALL FUNCTION [SPY ON MERIDANS] and crap like that. Do the Thellies even have droids?"

"Sir!" The door to the bridge opened, and the defense tech popped his head out. "I wanted to let you know we received the damage report."

"And?"

"And nothing was damaged, sir."

Rogers frowned. "Nothing?"

"Nothing. Our shields didn't even take an impact."

"Do we even know what was fired at us?"

"It appears that nothing was fired at us at all," the tech said. "But some of our sensors picked up targeting emissions from that ship that came by. So, it almost looks like they were about to attack us but didn't. Lieutenant Commander Belgrave said it was probably just a pirating ship with its munitions armed that got lost."

Something about that didn't sound right to Rogers at all.

"So, what's up with the explosion and the fire in the kitchen? What hit us?"

"It appears that one of the engineering personnel made a mistake in the Kamikaze."

"But I transferred all of those people back to engineering," Rogers said.

"He enjoyed cooking, sir."

Rogers pulled at his beard. He didn't know whether he was enraged, relieved, or just tired. Probably a little bit of all of them. But the *Flagship* had definitely been targeted, and a ship had definitely come into and out of Un-Space without announcing itself. Maybe one of the other ships in the ATBU had picked it up. One that *hadn't* had its targeting computer shut down for days. He'd have to get Klein to ask the other ship captains later.

"Thanks," Rogers said to the tech. "Anything else?"

"No, sir." The tech saluted and returned to the bridge.

"I don't like this, McSchmidt," Rogers said, feeling very dramatic all of a sudden.

"I don't like it either," McSchmidt said.

"I'm sort of indifferent," Deet said.

Rogers shot him a look. "This is all too coincidental," Rogers said. "Changing formations, a feinted attack that turned into a kitchen explosion. Even if they didn't fire anything, the THEY'RE ATTACKING US light definitely went on. That's something, right?"

McSchmidt nodded. "I'll start combing through more of the reports and let you know what I find. Maybe there's something we're overlooking."

"Fine," Rogers said. He wiped his forehead. He hadn't sweated so much in years. "I'm going to go make sure that Klein isn't summoning the entire Meridan Galactic Navy to put out our kitchen fire."

"What do you mean, you summoned the entire Meridan Galactic Navy to put out our kitchen fire?"

Rogers was pretty sure if his jaw was any lower to the ground, it could have been used as a dustpan. How could one head contain so much stupid?

"We need help," Klein said. "They can't expect us to be a buffer against the Thelicosan invasion all by ourselves."

"That's *exactly* what they expect of us," Rogers said. "We're the 331st Anti-Thelicosan Buffer Unit!"

"So what?" Klein said. "Nobody expected an actual war. We've been hearing rumors about this stuff for months, and now this is getting a little more than I want the 331st to handle on its own. Thelicosa is going to charge across that border and turn Merida into the next Jupiter. There won't even be another War of Musical Chairs this time."

"It was a kitchen fire, Klein. A kitchen fire. And the passing ship was probably just a pirate ship with its targeting systems on," Rogers said. "You have to cancel that message. We don't need the central government getting involved."

He couldn't imagine the kind of bureaucracy that would come flying in with such a giant military presence. There would be inspections every five minutes, droids everywhere, and Rogers doubted the alcohol quantity would improve.

"I don't see why it matters," Klein said. "I've been sending the same message for the last four months."

Rogers looked up. "What do you mean?"

Klein motioned to his computer terminal. "Every day, they keep telling me that the Thelicosans are invading. So, every day, I keep sending messages to MGN headquarters, asking them to bring reinforcements. They never answer."

"Hold on a second," Rogers said. "You're telling me you've been sending emergency reinforcement messages to headquarters every day, and nobody has gotten back to you?"

"Yes."

"And that doesn't strike you as strange?"

"Why would it strike him?" Deet asked. "Is there a physical manifestation of this situation that strikes people?"

"Figure of speech," Rogers said. "Do I really need to explain that to you every time?"

"Send a complaint to my programmer," Deet said.

"It seems like standard protocol to me," Klein said. "Nobody ever answers anything I send them, so why should this be any different?"

Rogers let that sink in for a second. Why wouldn't anyone at MGN headquarters answer any of Klein's messages? It was possible that the MGN simply didn't want to get involved. They'd placed the 331st here for a reason, after all. Was there something wrong with the communication systems? But other members on the ship must be sending and receiving messages, too. Troops would notice if all of a sudden they stopped receiving messages from their families. So, what was different about Klein's requests? Why would MGN HQ ignore them? If they were being jammed, the communications squadron would definitely know. And how could you jam only one person's correspondence?

"Admiral," Rogers said, standing up and walking over to the terminal. "Can you send a message to MGN HQ for me?"

Klein looked at him sideways. "But you just told me I can't send messages anymore."

"Well, we have a problem" Rogers said, thinking rapidly. He had to test his theory, had to send a message to MGN HQ that he knew they weren't going to ignore. "Some of the troops have been talking to me lately, and it appears . . ." He hesitated a moment. "It appears that all of them have been receiving double their pay."

"Double their pay?" Klein said, aghast.

Rogers nodded gravely. "And unfortunately, if we don't stop this immediately, the whole ship is going to go bankrupt."

"Rogers," Deet said, "this information doesn't appear to have any basis in—"

"Deet, I put those arms and legs back on you, and I can take them off again."

Deep beeped contritely but remained silent.

"Anyway," Rogers said, turning back to Klein, "it's very important that you transmit that message right away before all of the money goes away."

Klein looked at him for a moment, his eyes narrow. It actually looked like the man might have been thinking. Or pooping. It was sometimes difficult to tell the difference.* For a moment, Rogers thought Klein was about to see through his hastily but brilliantly concocted ruse.

"Fine," Klein said. "I'll send the message. And I'm docking half your pay."

Now the only thing left to do was wait.

---

*But let's be honest—it's that way with everyone. Right? Right?

# Report: N-1FG-5299-Z

Serial: N-1FG-5299-Z

Distribution: DBS//DSS//DAK//DFR//BB//CLOSED NETWORK A66

Classification: Special Protocol Required

Summary: Erratic information operations.

Details: Nude, multicolored portraits of famous human scientists were not authorized in the information operations campaign. If you see such posters, you are to remove them immediately.

Report Submitted By: F-GC-001

# Stick This in You

"We're being jammed," Rogers said.

"Jammed?" McSchmidt asked with half of a piece of chicken hanging out of his mouth.

McSchmidt, Rogers, Mailn, and the Viking were enjoying some of the first bit of real food they'd had on the *Flagship* since Rogers had arrived. All the transferring of personnel seemed to finally be working out; instead of empty, desolate places of depression, the mess halls—except the Kamikaze, since it had been charred by the fire—were starting to get a little livelier. The troops were actually talking to each other. Rogers even thought he might have heard someone laugh.

"What makes you say that?" the Viking asked.

"Let's just say that there's no way in hell headquarters would ignore the messages I've been sending . . . I mean, Klein has been sending. The strange thing is, it seems to only be official communication. People are still getting messages from friends and family. And our supply runs are still happening, so we're still getting materiel. It doesn't make any sense."

"Wouldn't Communications know that we're being jammed?" Mailn asked.

Rogers shook his head. "I talked to them. According to their records, all messages are going out like they should. But I'm positive that Klein's aren't going anywhere."

"Maybe they're being intercepted?" McSchmidt suggested.

"What kind of intelligence guy are you?" the Viking said. "It's data. You don't just catch it in a net and put it in your pocket. If someone was intercepting them, they'd still get to headquarters."

McSchmidt shot her a dirty look, but at a growl from the Viking, his face took on a much more subdued expression. Rogers felt his heart beat faster.

"Any more on the 'invasion'?" Rogers asked.

McSchmidt wiped a pair of greasy hands on his pants and pulled out his datapad, slapping it down on the table. "Yes and no."

"Those two statements are mutually exclusive," Deet said.

McSchmidt raised an eyebrow.

"Ignore him," Rogers said. "They don't understand the subtleties of human speech."

"Anyway," McSchmidt said, "the intelligence reports coming in about the Thelicosan fleet have probably doubled in the last few days. The sheer volume of information is huge, but it doesn't seem to mean anything." He started tapping away on the datapads, and reports flashed by.

He stopped, placing his finger on the center of a mess of text and symbols. "This, for example, is describing how much closer the Thelicosan fleet has moved to the Meridan border in centimeters." He flipped reports again. "And this here is supposed to be intercepted radio transmissions from their flagship."

"What does it say?" Rogers asked.

"It says, 'Is everything ready for the imminent attack on the Meridan fleet? Please make sure everything is prepared so that we can take our ships and use them to cross the border and attack the Meridan ships using plasma cannons and other weapons, like our secret weapons that are very powerful, weapons that will make the Meridans blow up because they are clearly unprepared for an attack with those weapons because they are weak and disorganized.'"

A silence settled over the table. A group of droids that had been "eating" at the table behind them finished charging their batteries and got up, clanking noisily out of the mess hall.

"That seems pretty clear," Rogers said.

"It does and it doesn't," McSchmidt said.

"Please stop doing that," Deet said.

"For one thing, why would anyone ever send a transmission like that on an open channel?" McSchmidt explained, glaring at Deet. "It sounds like a drunk pirate talking in his sleep. Second, Thelicosans don't call us Meridans."

"They don't?" Mailn asked.

"No. They call us Galactics. Ever since the Pythagorean War,* they haven't internally recognized Meridan sovereignty."

Rogers frowned. "How do you know that?"

McSchmidt blushed and cleared his throat. "I'm a political science major from the Academy," he said. "You know, the Meridan Military Academy. The one I've been talking to you about that I went to. You know?"

"Yeah," Rogers said. "Sure. Whatever. So, what does that mean? Are we intercepting someone else's communication?"

"I have no idea," McSchmidt said, leaning back and shaking his head. He looked tired. Snatching up another piece of chicken, he took a bite and chewed noisily as he mumbled through a mouthful. "I curn't imurgine who wurd say surmthing like thurt."

"Hey!" came a voice from behind Rogers. "That's really good!"

He turned to see Tunger approaching, a tray of food in his hands. None of it, however, looked fit for human consumption; Rogers saw soon that they were scraps, probably for the animals.

---

*Don't ask.

Tunger looked a lot happier than he had a week or so before. The zoo deck was agreeing with him, it seemed, and he hardly had any gouges on his face from the lion at all.

"Dur yur spurk Thelicosan too?" he asked.

McSchmidt's face turned red and he swallowed hurriedly. "I don't—ack!"

McSchmidt started coughing. The Viking gave him a powerful blow on the back, dislodging the food stuck in McSchmidt's throat (and also perhaps a vertebra).

"Thanks," he said, wiping his mouth. "I don't talk in your stupid accent. Why don't you go somewhere and sound like an idiot to someone else?"

The whole table became silent for a moment. Mailn found something very interesting to stare at on the table, and even the Viking looked like she didn't know who to hit in this situation, which must have confused her terribly.

"Take it easy, McSchmidt," Rogers said. "He's just trying to be friendly. I mean, sure, he annoys the living piss out of me and I want to open the room to vacuum every time he opens his mouth, but . . . at least I'm not a jerk about it."

"Actually, sir," Tunger said, "you were kind of a jerk about it."

Rogers shrugged. "Whatever. I outrank both of you. McSchmidt, chill out. Tunger, get the marshmallows out of your cheeks."

The two of them looked at each other with icy disdain, but there was no further hair-pulling.

"Fine," Tunger said finally, breaking his absurd staring contest with McSchmidt. "I'm going to go feed the children. You all have a *great* time talking *normally*."

Tunger sauntered off, and Rogers saw that there were claw marks on the back of his trousers.

"Anyway," Rogers said. He slid McSchmidt's datapad across the table so he could look at it. He'd never seen a raw intelligence report before—he'd only ever gotten the distilled information through briefings—and now he realized that he was perfectly happy with that. The report was written in a style so old, it was almost comical, all capital letters with hash marks and slashes in all these strange places. It was almost impossible to read.

"What is this crap?" Rogers asked, gesturing at the report. He could see some of the stuff that McSchmidt had talked about in the middle of the document, but it was bracketed on both the top and the bottom by such an incredible amount of textual gibberish that it looked like someone had disemboweled a keyboard.

"Oh, that?" McSchmidt said. "It's a bunch of routing information. It says where the report came from and where it's supposed to go." He squinted and leaned forward again. "At least, I think so."

Deet beeped in that sort of way that told Rogers he wanted to say something.

"What is it?"

Deet's neck craned over the top of the datapad, and he gave another few beeps.

"This isn't all routing information," he said.

"How would you know?" the Viking said. "You're just a droid zombie."

"Hey," Rogers said. "I made this droid zombie."

"EXPLETIVE EXPLETIVE yourself," Deet said.

The Viking snorted. "He can't even swear? What use is he?"

Deet hung his head. "It's not my fault."

"Can we please focus?" Rogers said. "What is it on the top of this report that makes you curious?"

Deet looked back at the report and pointed at the top of it with one of his three-fingered hands. Rogers hadn't done the best job of putting him together, he supposed; one of the fingers was attached at a very strange angle.

"This is all a primitive droid code," he said. "I can't read all of it, though. I'm too new for it and this programming language was on its way out before I was commissioned."

"Oh," McSchmidt said. "That makes sense. The droids do most of the routing in the systems."

Rogers looked at him sideways. "They do?"

"Sure," McSchmidt said. "Some of the other intel guys tell me that it was part of an initiative to make things more efficient a couple of months ago. Klein signed off on it. The droids do some of the number crunching for the statistical analysis, and they make sure it's all routed properly." He rubbed the back of his head. "I think they do a final proofread before it's disseminated, too."

Rogers frowned. That was a lot of artificial intelligence working on intelligence. Did that mean that the intelligence was artificial? Now he was just confused.

Nearby, a pair of starmen second class were chuckling by one of the new propaganda posters that had shown up, this one an unintelligible depiction of a hulking, dual-headed mythical creature sitting atop what appeared to be a mountain of chocolate bars. The caption read, IT'S SO GOOD. SO GOOD.

Rogers saw his work, and saw that it was, indeed, good.

"It doesn't just look like routing information, though," Deet said. "It looks like access information, too. Like it's pointing me in several different places at once. I can't make it out, and I can't access the network to test it out."

"That must be lonely," Rogers said. "Not being on the network for so long."

"That's the stupidest thing I've ever heard in my life," the Viking said, taking a bite into a SEWR rat without even taking the packaging off first. She chewed up a wad of plastic and spit it out. "Droids can't be lonely."

"These are Froids," Rogers said.

"Yeah," Deet said. "We're Froids. But, no, Rogers, that was the stupidest thing I've ever heard."

Even the Viking chuckled.

"Fine," Rogers said. "Screw me for trying to be compassionate to a nonhuman. What if we were to plug you into the network? Would you be able to figure it out then?"

"Maybe," Deet said.

"Why?" McSchmidt asked. "What's bugging you about it?"

"I don't know," Rogers said. "Call it my distrust of droids. What do you need to plug into the network?"

"Just a regular power cable would be fine, I think," Deet said. He beeped. "That's the way it's been everywhere else I've been connected, anyway."

Rogers turned around to where the squadron of droids had been plugged into the mess hall's power outlets for "lunch."

"What about there?" He pointed.

"That'll work," Deet said. He looked around as though suspicious. "I'm not sure how the other droids will react."

"EXPLETIVE the other droids," Rogers said. "Besides, they're already done eating. It's not like you're going to go steal someone's food. McSchmidt, why don't you let Deet here borrow your datapad so that he can look into that code? Maybe it'll help us figure out exactly where the intelligence is coming from. If there's some sort of sensor error, this would be a good way to find out about it."

McSchmidt, still looking doubtful, slowly handed the datapad over to Deet, whose Frankenbot body ambled all the way across the dining hall to stand next to the elongated table. Rogers watched him, thinking. If there was something wrong with the sensors, or something wrong with the intelligence, then the whole Thelicosan invasion was a mistake—or a lie—and all the changes they'd been making to "prepare for war" would just become inconveniences.

Deet stood by the table for a long time, not doing anything. Through the echo of the cavernous mess hall, Rogers heard a frustrated beeping noise.

"What's the matter?" Rogers called across the dining hall.

"I can't get it up," Deet called back.

At least two of the people at the table nearly choked on their food. For some really absurd reason, Rogers felt himself blushing.

He hurriedly got up from the table and walked over to where Deet was standing.

"What do you mean?" Rogers asked.

"It's my data cable," Deet said. "It's been damaged. I didn't realize until now since I haven't had to use it, but this piece of FECAL MATTER won't come out to connect to the ports."

"Oh," Rogers said. He knelt down, feeling around on the ground where the connection ports were, and opened the little hinged panel. Adjacent to the actual plugs was a backup wire that extended from a small coil in the ground. Hoping his many years of playing with electronics and not dying would prevent him from getting a shock, Rogers uncurled the cable and handed it to Deet.

"Here," Rogers said. "Stick this in you."

More snickers came from his table.

"Oh, grow up!" Rogers shouted.

"What's their problem?" Deet asked as he plugged into the cable and put the datapad down on the table.

"Nothing," Rogers said. "Sometimes, I forget how little you droids understand about, um, human reproductive habits."

"We have a Freudian Chip," Deet explained. "To us, it's all cable envy."

"Right." Rogers stood up. "How is it going? Were you able to access the network?"

Deet was quiet for a moment. Someone came out of the exit door to the kitchen, holding a single piece of bread that wasn't in any way, shape, or form marred by mold or mechanical lubricants, and fell to his knees sobbing. Rogers understood how he felt. If someone had handed him a bottle of Jasker 120 or turned on the beer light, that's about how he'd react right about now.

"It looks like a network," Deet said, "but it's definitely not the ship's main network."

Rogers frowned. "What do you mean by that? Is it a backup system, maybe? Were the droids coming in here to store backup data and charge their battery reserves?"

"I don't really know," Deet said. "It's hard to describe. I can tell that I'm in *a* network, but I can't really tell *what* network I'm in."

"I think I understand what you mean," Rogers said.

Deet looked at him and beeped confusedly. "How could you possibly understand what it's like to be in a network but not know what network you're in?"

Rogers chuckled. "There's a street on Merida Prime that has almost a full mile of bars stacked right next to each other like townhouses. By the time you get a quarter of the way down, you start to understand what you're talking about."

"Have you ever considered the possibility that you may have a drinking problem?"

"I drink just fine, thank you."

Rogers looked back wistfully at the Viking, who was laughing heartily with Mailn, a piece of protein cardboard stuck to the bottom of her lip. Even though it was a piece of a SEWR rat, Rogers wished he could reach his own lips out and help her brush it off.

Shaking his head, he turned back to Deet. "Are you telling me the network is encrypted?"

"It's like encryption," Deet said, "but different. It's more like a confusing transportation system. If I had the right map, I could . . ."

He trailed off for a moment. In fact, Rogers' droid companion became so quiet that Rogers thought he'd lost power. But since the ship's gravity generator was obviously still working, that wasn't possible. Deet's eyes went from their normal bright blue to a sort of dim cerulean, then came back again.

"Deet? Are you still there?"

"I found the road map," Deet said, his digitized voice breaking up as though he was at the far end of a bad radio transmission.

"What the hell are you talking about?" Rogers asked. "Are you actually using metaphors?"

"I'm learning," Deet said. "Actually, I'm learning quite a lot. Right now."

"About what?"

"For one thing," Deet said, "this isn't part of the ship's network. It's not part of the backup system, either. It appears to be completely separate. And it's not controlled by humans."

Rogers felt his stomach start to sink, like the feeling he got when he realized someone knew he was cheating them. He asked a question, but somehow, he felt like he already knew the answer.

"Who built it?"

"Artificial intelligence," Deet said. "Droids. The top part of the intelligence documents that Lieutenant Lieutenant McSchmidt has been reading is the access codes to get into the network and point to specific updates that are priority downloads for any droid connected to the closed system."

"That doesn't sound like something Klein would authorize," Rogers said.

"Actually," Deet said, "Klein *did* authorize it. It was part of a sweeping set of changes to help the 331st prepare for the imminent conflict with the Thelicosans. Which, by the way, isn't actually going to happen. The intel has been faked. By the droids."

"What's going on over here?" McSchmidt called as he walked over. "Is your little droid friend finding out anything interesting?"

Rogers slowly turned to face McSchmidt. His fear must have shown on his face, because the intel officer stopped as soon as Rogers turned around.

"Yes," Rogers said. "I'm learning that we are, all of us, completely screwed."

"What do you mean, you can't talk about it?" McSchmidt asked.

All five of them were walking briskly down the hallway of the commissary deck, Rogers trying to keep his head down and his mouth shut. He'd asked Deet to download every scrap of data he could from the closed network and had asked him no fewer than sixteen times if it was possible any of the other droids would know of his intrusion. Deet had explained, every single time, that his login information would be stored in the database. Of course they'd know.

"I mean they're listening," Rogers whispered. "They have ears all around us. Don't you understand?"

McSchmidt, the Viking, and Mailn all exchanged uneasy glances.

"Have you been spending too much time in your room?" Mailn asked. "I hear a lot of time in freefall can start to make you, um, see things."

"No," Rogers said testily. He'd grown quite used to living part of his day in zero gravity, as a matter of fact, and now he hardly ever ran into walls. He had even taught Cadet to pee outside of the room, which helped him avoid wayward globules of cat urine. "I'm not losing my mind, Cynthia. We just can't talk about it here."

In fact, he wasn't sure they could talk about it anywhere. Deet had revealed that most of the areas on the ship were bugged, which explained all kinds of things about the propaganda posters and the devices that Deet had found previously. The droids had been listening to every word he'd said since he'd gotten back aboard the *Flagship*. But what did they do with all that useless chatter?

"Well, where *can* we talk about it?" the Viking asked, her gruff voice cutting through Rogers' rapid and frantic train of thought. "You left the mess hall looking like you were about to shit your pants."

Rogers wasn't entirely sure he wasn't about to do just that. In reality, he didn't know what droids were trying to do with all of this false information and this spying, but he didn't feel comfortable about it at all. From what Deet had told him so far, it was clear that the droids weren't acting under the orders of anyone on this ship.

"Hey, are you listening to me?" the Viking said. She grabbed him roughly by the arm, creating the same result as if Rogers had run directly into a brick wall. He stopped—well, he sort of flailed around and would have fallen over if not for the iron grip on his arm. "What's your problem, metalhead?"

Rogers looked at the Viking, his lips trembling. Aside from being excited at getting a little roughed up, his thoughts were already completely addled. How was he going to explain to all of them what he'd learned without tipping the droids off? He still didn't even really know everything that Deet had learned.

"It's just . . ." he began. "I can't . . . Look, this isn't easy, alright? Give me a second. And let go of me or I am never going to be able to think straight!"

The Viking released him reluctantly, and Rogers shook out his uniform. He could feel the impression of her bearlike grip on his arm pulsating on his skin, tingling like someone had just applied a love tincture to his flesh. Taking a deep breath, he tried to push thoughts of being rescued from burning rooms from his mind and focus on the very serious task at hand.

"Deet . . . had a bad meal."

"Your robot has indigestion?" Mailn said.

"No," Rogers said. He looked at her intently, opening his eyes wide. "Deet had a *bad meal* in the mess hall." He winked. "As in he perhaps ate something that *doesn't agree with him.*" Rogers winked again.

"I think he's having a seizure," McSchmidt said.

"I'm not having a seizure!" Rogers cried. "Can't you read between the lines at all?"

"What lines are we talking about?" Deet said. "I don't see any lines."

Rogers hopped up and down, pointing at Deet. "You see what I mean? He can't see any lines! *He can't see any lines!*"

*The droids don't understand metaphor and figures of speech!* Rogers wanted to shout. Even if they were listening to every word he said, even if the entire AIGCS reassembled right in front of him—they would have no idea what he was talking about.

The problem was, apparently, neither did anyone else.

"What kind of crazy did you wake up with this morning?" the Viking said. "Droids don't eat things, Rogers."

"Except data," Mailn said, laughing.

Rogers pointed at her, then tapped his nose.

"Are we playing charades?" McSchmidt said.

Rogers rolled his eyes. "No, we're not playing charades. We're playing open your god-damn ears and try to figure out what I'm trying to tell you because maybe something important is preventing me from saying it straight at this very moment."

The three other humans stared at him blankly. Rogers was ready to throw up his hands and listen to Klein orate him to death, abandoning the *Flagship* to whatever fate the droids had in store for it, but after a moment, Mailn's eyebrows shot up.

"So, you're saying that Deet plugged in and ate a meal that he didn't like," she said.

"Yes!" Rogers said, wanting to fall to his knees and cry after hugging that brilliant, brilliant woman. "Yes, that's exactly what I'm saying. I'm saying that Deet ate something that could potentially, I don't know, *kill us all.*"

McSchmidt's eyes widened. "He ate a bomb?"

Rogers slapped his forehead. "Are you seriously an intelligence officer?"

"You put me there," McSchmidt mumbled.

The Viking shrugged. "Well, I still have no idea what either of you are talking about."

"I'm starting to wonder if I understand human communication protocol at all," Deet said.

Mailn held up a hand. "Just try to follow," she said. "I think I've got this. Go ahead, Rogers. Tell us all about this meal."

"Right," Rogers said. "Let's keep walking. I want to get back to the command deck and I want all of you to come with me."

The confused human/droid coterie ambled along the hallway, Rogers taking them as quickly as he could. If there were as many sensors as Deet had alluded to, maybe he could obfuscate his speech even more by passing through many of them. Rogers had no idea if that would work, but he also had to go to the bathroom (his stomach was still getting used to eating normal food again).

"So," Rogers said, "Deet's meal was terrible. Apparently, the chefs are trying to poison him. Or us."

"What the EXPLETIVE are you people talking about?" Deet said.

"Just pipe down for a minute, Deet," Rogers said. "In fact, I want you to tell me the moment you start to understand exactly what the expletive we're talking about. Got it?"

"Fine."

"The chefs?" Mailn said. "You mean the people who made Deet's meal?"

"That's exactly what I mean," Rogers said.

They remained quiet for a second as a couple of droids walked past them, though Rogers realized that was somewhat absurd, since they could hear everything they were doing anyway through the sensors. Was it his imagination, or did the droids look at him as they passed? He noticed at least one of them was that sleek off-gray color that the AIGCS had been, though there was no visible weapon. Had the ones that had survived the incident been recommissioned?

"So, the chefs are trying to poison Deet?" Mailn said. "That still doesn't make any sense, and I'm pretty sure I know what you're talking about."

"Not exactly," Rogers said. "I'm pretty sure they're trying to poison *everyone.* I just don't know how yet. Or why. Or when. In fact, I really have almost no idea what's going on. Apparently, they've been keeping a . . . um . . . a . . . whole book of secret recipes."

"You're both out of your minds," the Viking said.

"How is that possible?" Mailn said.

"I have no idea," Rogers said. "Maybe they went to someone else's, uh, culinary arts school. Or maybe they built their own school after they learned enough from us about cooking to do it on their own. I don't know. I'm not a chef."

The Viking rolled her eyes. McSchmidt looked like he was concentrating so hard that his face was going to melt off. Deet remained blessedly silent. As they approached the up-line that would take them to the command deck, Rogers noticed that instead of a human, a droid was now manning the controls and regulating the line. It made his skin crawl. Everything was starting to make sense now; droids had slowly been working their way into positions all over the ship, slowly replacing humans in the name of preparing for "war."

"So, what's with the new menu?" Mailn asked.

"Hey," Rogers said. "Menu. That's pretty clever. You're good at this."

Mailn shrugged. "I do what I can."

"CALL FUNCTION [INCONVENIENCE]. OUTPUT STRING: THE UP-LIFT IS CURRENTLY TRANSPORTING OTHER PERSONNEL. PLEASE WAIT."

"Yeah," Rogers said. "Sure. Anyway, I'm not sure why they changed the menu. All I know is that they've been slowly changing it for a while now. Probably before I got here. You know how they kept, um, switching the silverware into different drawers?"

Mailn looked confused for a moment.

"You know, how we used to have *spoons* for soup and *forks* for steak, and everything got moved around so that there was motor oil in the eggs?"

"But there really was motor oil in the eggs," McSchmidt said.

Mailn nodded knowingly. "I get what you're saying. So, the chefs were swapping the silverware so that nobody would know they were changing the menu."

"Exactly."

"I'm starting to really hate both of you," the Viking said.

"CALL FUNCTION [PERFORM PRIMARY DUTY]. OUTPUT STRING: YOU MAY BOARD THE UP-LINE."

The door opened, revealing a nearly empty cabin. Nearly, that is, except for Corporal Tunger and a very angry-looking baboon.

"Oh, not this guy," McSchmidt said as they all piled inside.

"Hullur!" Tunger said. "It's nurse to see yur!"

"Please shut up." McSchmidt had his hands balled up into fists at his sides and spoke through clenched teeth. What was his problem?

"I never thought I'd understand you more than I'd understand my own corporal," the Viking said. "I don't know what the hell these people are talking about."

"It's gurd to knur that *surmone* appreciates my talunts," Tunger said, glaring at Rogers.

"Shut up," McSchmidt said again. Rogers shot him a look, but McSchmidt was fixated on the floor. His face was turning a dark crimson.

"I can't appreciate someone I can't understand," Rogers said flippantly. "Anyway, about the spoons and forks—"

"Aie um nurt so hard to understand," Tunger said. "Thelicosans spurk like thurs all the time!"

"No!" McSchmidt yelled suddenly. "No, we don't! *You* sound like a complete idiot! Nobody in Thelicosa speaks like they've been repeatedly punched in the jaw since the day they were born! Every time you open your mouth, it's like you are reaching deep into my chest and *rupping urt mur huuuurt*!"

Everyone in the car was silent, the quiet hum of the up-line zooming toward the command deck buzzing softly in the background. McSchmidt's face was only a few inches from a very terrified Tunger, and the lieutenant lieutenant's lips were lined with a thin film of enraged foam. Then, suddenly, all of the blood drained from McSchmidt's face, and his anger melted away.

"Oh," he said. "Oh, shurt."

"You're a spy," Rogers said flatly.

"No. No, I'm—"

"You just said 'we.' And you talked like a Thelicosan."

"Oh, come on," Tunger said, his voice thankfully back to a steady Meridan accent. "There's no way he's a spy. Did you hear that? His accent was awful. He curn't urven spurk—"

"*Enough!* Yes. I'm a spy. I admit it. I'd rather have my tongue torn out and be executed in public than have to listen to this barbarian brutalize my language."

"That makes two of us," the Viking said.

Rogers looked at her, his jaw slack. "You're a spy too?"

"No," the Viking said. "I just think Tunger is annoying."

"And you know what else?" McSchmidt said, his tirade apparently not concluded. "You're all a bunch of idiots with bad sensors and an even worse fleet commander. There is no Thelicosan invasion! Where are you even getting your information from? It's like someone is faking—"

"McSchmidt," Rogers said. "Shut up."

"—faking the intelligence reports just to get you to remain in a state of high alert, and it's all some kind of elaborate plot by—"

"Shut up!" Rogers yelled.

Thankfully, McSchmidt shut up. In fact, he went absolutely slack-jawed silent. Rogers let out a sigh of relief. He could deal with McSchmidt being a spy later. For now, it was important that the droids remain clueless that he knew—

"*That's* what you mean!" McSchmidt said. "The droids established a secret network to prevent you from discovering that they've been providing false reports about Thelicosan preparations for war while they weaseled their way into more positions of authority!"

The whole cabin went completely silent, with the exception of the witless baboon, who made a hooting noise and swung around on one of the overhead handrails.

"Yes," Rogers said, feeling, strangely, both completely numb and murderously violent. "Yes, that's exactly what I mean. And now we're all going to die because the droids just heard every word you said."

Deet beeped. "Is that what you're worried about? I was just going to tell you that there aren't any listening devices on the transportation cars inside the ship, but you told me to shut up."

Rogers let out a deep breath. "Well, that's some good news. At least we're not all going to die."

"Oh," Deet said, "you're all definitely going to die. But not because the rest of the droids overheard you uncovering their plan. It probably has something more to do with the large boominite explosive device sitting in the engineering bay and ready to blow a planet-sized hole in the *Flagship*."

Everyone on the car looked at Deet.

"Yes," he said, nodding. "That will probably kill you first. Long before all this poisoned food you keep talking about will, anyway."

# Report: N-1FG-5299-Z-2

Serial: N-1FG-5299-Z-2

Distribution: DBS//DSS//DAK//DFR//BB//CLOSED NETWORK A66

Classification: Special Protocol Required

Summary: Regarding the previous order to belay the order regarding the order for the preservation of Human 2552's life.

Details: Never mind. Kill Rogers.

Report Submitted By: F-GC-001

# Go Boom

"How exactly did they manage to build a boominite explosive device in the engineering bay?" McSchmidt asked.

"They didn't," Deet replied. "You did."

"What?"

"I told you not to stack those god-damn containers like that!" Rogers said. "You gave them a *bomb*, you idiot!"

"I was just doing what it said to do in the regulation," McSchmidt said. "If I started failing inspections, I'd get kicked out of the MPF. That wouldn't make for a very good spy, would it?"

"A better spy than one running around, quoting military leaders that died two thousand years ago," Rogers said. "What are you doing on our ship, anyway?"

"Spying," McSchmidt said. "Kind of part of the job description, no? Thanks for promoting me to Intelligence, by the way."

"I still think your accent sucks," Tunger muttered.

"I am going to strangle you if you talk to me again," McSchmidt said. "I know how to do it, too. They taught me in spy school."

"I don't think I need an instruction manual, you Thellie scum," the Viking said. She took a large step toward McSchmidt, hands outstretched, the force of her movement rocking the car. Rogers held out a hand, more for the chance to touch her than to try and prevent any harm from coming to McSchmidt. He could really care less about that idiot. Surprisingly, she yielded to his gesture.

"Let's not get crazy here," Rogers said. "McSchmidt let us know that there wasn't an invasion coming. Maybe we can return the favor by not killing him yet. If what he says is true, then we have bigger problems to worry about than what the best way to choke him is."

The tension melted. Well, no, no it didn't, really. Everyone just sort of looked at each other like they *wanted* to kill each other but at this point in time also realized it was not in their best interests. Then again, the Viking always looked like she wanted to kill someone, so maybe that was just the way her face was constructed. Her beautiful, beautiful face.

Rogers shook his head and turned to Deet. "You're positive that they can't hear us in here?"

Deet beeped. "From the data I collected, the surveillance net they've implanted is very wide, but they had trouble collecting anything on moving objects. The last information I saw, they were considering stationing droids as operators, but preliminary research through human behavioral schemes revealed that a very unique hat was necessary to make this sort of deception convincing. They were so far unable to discover where to obtain such hats."

"Well, that's good news, at least," Rogers sad. "But what's the point of observing us and all that if they're just going to blow up the ship?"

"It seems as if the bomb is a failsafe," Deet said. "If the takeover—and I'm pretty sure it's a takeover—fails, they can destroy the *Flagship*, rewrite the records so it looks like the accident was caused by some idiot in engineering who kept stacking boominite containers—"

"Oh, come on," McSchmidt said.

"—and possibly try again on another ship. It's possible that similar devices have been installed in other ships in the fleet as well."

"Great," Rogers said. "That's just great. The whole fleet rigged to explode if a bunch of robots don't take it over. Any idea what their goal is? How did they decide to do this?"

"I was unable to discover this information," Deet said. "I did, however, discover what protocol 162 was."

"And?"

"Let me see if I can translate the code properly," Deet said. He beeped a few times, his eyes flashing. After a moment, the beeping settled. "If I could make an approximation into human language, I would say that protocol 162 is the surreptitious execution of selected organics who are either a threat to the overall plan or who really annoy you."

The up-line dinged as it came to the command deck, and a voice crackled through the speakers.

"Next strp, cmmd dk. Exit on your rfltght."

The door opened to reveal a small party of marines waiting anxiously to get on the up-line, probably to go get something to eat. But the inside of the car was the only place they could talk without using a whole slew of ridiculous metaphors.

Rogers and his companions looked out blankly into the expectant faces of the marines. For a moment, nobody spoke.

"Uh, going down?" one of the marines said.

"No," Rogers said. "Sorry. This lift is broken. We're, ah, the maintenance crew. We'll be riding this back and forth until further notice."

"If it's broken, how are you going to ride it back and forth?" asked another marine.

Rogers chewed on his lip. "It's just that, ah, there's a squeaky noise as it passes the zoo deck. We think there might be an animal trapped in there, but we have to ride it past the zoo deck a couple of times to make sure it's not mechanical."

Some of the marines looked convinced—it was a brilliant lie, after all, if Rogers did say so himself—but one of the ones in front squinted and pointed at Rogers' uniform.

"You're not an engineer," he said. "Shouldn't the engineers being doing the fixing? And who are all these other people? None of them are engineers either."

Rogers cursed to himself. Why was everyone so suspicious? It's not like there wouldn't be another car coming along in just a minute to take these meatheads wherever they wanted to go.

"In fact," the marine continued, "I don't even know what that specialty badge is."

Rogers looked down at his own collar, remembering that he was still wearing his AIGCS commander badge—execs didn't change their specialty, since it was only a temporary duty that typically ended in suicide, anyway. Of course the marine wouldn't know what it was. But that also meant it could be anything.

"I see you're not familiar with the new specialty code," Rogers said. "This is the elevator tech badge. There are only a few of us on each ship." He patted the edge of the doorframe affectionately. "These babies need a personal kind of love that a general engineer can't give 'em."

"That's a pretty stupid specialty code," the marine said.

"Hey," Rogers said, somehow feeling genuinely offended at the slight on his made-up profession, "I don't come into the marine barracks and call you all a bunch of drooling jarheads that shoot about as straight as you piss after sex."

"Maybe because that would get your ass kicked, officer or no officer," the marine growled. "Now, why don't you get the—"

"Hey, you," the Viking said, shoving past Rogers to stand in (and completely fill) the doorframe of the up-line. "Why are you standing there, running your mouth and stopping this elevator tech from getting to work?"

The marine's face paled and he took a step back. "Oh, shit, captain. I didn't know. I'm—"

"A drooling jarhead that shoots about as straight as he pisses after sex?"

"Uh," the marine said, stammering, "yeah. Sure."

The Viking leaned forward and growled. "Sure?"

"I mean, yes, ma'am! Absolutely, ma'am! Piss like old windshield wiper fluid in the winter, ma'am! I'm sorry for interrupting your ride."

The unfortunate marine backed up, saluting no less than three times before he ran into his companions, starting an awkward domino effect of stumbling marines. The Viking took a step back, pressed the button to close the door, and entered the refuse deck as their next destination. As one of the lowest levels on the *Flagship*, that would certainly give them more time to talk.

But Rogers wasn't thinking about that. Rogers was staring at the back of the Viking, watching her impose her will on the marines, and feeling a little bit like a cat in heat.

She turned around and looked at him, clearly fighting off a smile. "Not bad, right?"

Rogers found it very difficult to continue speaking while looking at her, so he looked away instead.

"Anyway, Deet, you were telling us about protocol 162 and them having limited authority to, you know, kill us."

"That's about right," Deet said.

"So, what do we do about it?" Mailn asked, putting her hands on her hips. Leave it to a marine to not look disturbed at all that she was potentially within a few seconds of dying at any given moment. The Viking looked similarly unimpressed. Rogers wished he shared this nonchalance about his own mortality.

"Can we do anything about it?" Rogers asked. "There are shinies—"

"Hey," Deet said.

"—all over the damn ship. They've weaseled their way into every squadron, even tried to come up with their own squadron and give themselves weapons. The first chance they get, they're going to blow a hole in the *Flagship* and probably kill us all. What are we supposed to do with that?"

They all thought for a moment. Rogers felt sweat rolling down the inside of his uniform.

"What about Klein?" Tunger said. "He's a military genius. He'd know what to do."

Rogers bit his tongue before telling them all that their military idol was just a talking head.

"That wouldn't work," he said instead. "Remember, there are listening devices all over his room, and they're obviously tapped into the network. Any orders that Klein issued, they'd either countermand or delete. And then, you know, they might blow a hole in the ship." Rogers made an explosive hand gesture. "I feel like we keep forgetting that part, guys."

The overhead system dinged again.

"Next strp, zrm dk. Exit on your rfltght."

"I don't even know what deck that is," Tunger said.

Someone must have hit the call button on the . . . zrm deck. After a moment, the doors slid open to reveal the exterior of the *zoo* deck, where a couple of off-duty troops wearing safari hats were talking excitedly about their most recent animal adventure.

"No," the Viking said simply, stepping forward.

The troops blinked, took a step back, and scattered like spit in a sneeze. The door closed, and the Viking turned around, grinning.

"Maybe I should be the new elevator operator," the Viking said.

"This is an unlikely possibility," Deet said. "As already mentioned, there is a lack of the appropriate hats."

The Viking looked at Deet. "I'm pretty sure I could bend you into some kind of hat."

"No," Rogers said. "Not now, anyway. If we're going to do something about this, we're going to have to keep it quiet."

"Sure you don't just want to jump in an escape pod and head for open space?" Mailn asked, looking at him with narrow eyes.

Rogers turned to her, ready to make a witty retort, but the words didn't reach his lips. He thought about what she had just said for a moment and realized that at no point had he thought about ditching the *Flagship* and getting the hell out of here before any of the real fighting went down. He hadn't even thought about beer in the last couple of hours or so.

"Yes," Rogers said slowly. "I'm actually quite sure. I think." He thought. Dying was kind of permanent, and messy. "Maybe. Look, don't ask me these hard questions right now, okay? We've got bigger things to worry about. I think the first thing we need to do is—"

The up-line dinged.

"Next strp, mrghfr dk. Exit on your rfltght."

"Where are all these people coming from?" Rogers cried.

The doors opened, but before anyone could say or do anything, Rogers heard Tunger yell.

"Go, Bobo!"

The baboon shrieked and swung full-force toward the door, hissing and spitting the entire way, its bright red bottom like a red-hot blunt instrument of terror. Rogers never even got to see who had called the elevator. By the time the baboon settled down, the hall—possibly the entire ship—was empty.

"Wow," Rogers said. "Nice work, Tunger."

"Why, thank you, sir," Tunger said. He clicked his tongue and Bobo the Baboon walked casually back to stand at Tunger's side, who scratched behind his ears affectionately.

The doors closed and they began the rest of the journey toward the refuse deck.

"Anyway," Rogers said, "I think the first thing we need to do is come up with a plan."

"Your plan is to plan?" McSchmidt said.

Rogers frowned at him. "I'm kind of thinking on my feet here, Thelly, so why don't you cut me some slack? They teach you anything in spy school about how to stop a legion of droids from commandeering your ship and beginning a slow takeover of the galaxy?"

"They did," McSchmidt said, "but I blew that class off."

"Good job," Rogers said. "What would Napoleon do in this situation?"

"I don't know," McSchmidt said. "Form a phalanx?"

"That's not even the right century," the Viking said.

"Yeah," Tunger said. "Napoleon used Russian tanks."

"What?" the Viking said.

The cabin of the up-line devolved into a heated and almost entirely inaccurate debate on Napoleonic tactics and the use of cavalry in confined marshland, but Rogers let it all fade into the background. There were more important things at stake right now than who had the high ground at Waterloo and if anyone else cared.

Deet sidled up next to him. "I thought you might be interested in a report that just came in."

Rogers looked at him. "I thought you weren't connected to the network anymore?"

"I'm not," Deet said. He produced McSchmidt's datapad. "But you don't need to be connected to the network to steal someone's datapad."

Rogers chuckled and pointed at Deet. "I think I'm really starting to like you," Rogers said. "Do you drink beer?"

"Not unless I want to short-circuit myself," Deet said. "They say you'll go blind if you do that too often."

Rogers shrugged. "I'm not judging. What's up with this report?"

"You can't put a cannon on horseback!" the Viking shouted.

"One of the other ships in the fleet identified the rogue craft that was targeting the *Flagship*." Deet handed him the datapad. "It was the MPS *Rancor*."

Rogers gaped. "Zombie ghost-pirates," he whispered.

"What?" Deet asked.

"Never mind. This ship was the one that started all of my trouble, but it was supposed to have crashed into an asteroid. What made you think it was important?"

"I saw several mentions of this ship in the closed network," Deet said, "thought it was referred to by a different name. The *Beta Test.* And it wasn't destroyed by an asteroid."

Rogers looked at Deet, then looked back at the report. The report described basic flight pattern information, like the time it exited and reentered Un-Space, which Un-Space point it used, how much time it spent in the sector, and any other emissions that came from the ship. The targeting computer had been turned on and had locked onto the *Flagship*, certainly, but there were no other indications that the *Rancor*—the *Beta Test*—had been preparing to actually fire a warhead. Patrol ships didn't have the kind of firepower to damage a capital ship, anyway.

Rogers skipped over some of the other metrics of little interest, but his eyes stopped when he came to one particular line of data.

*Organic life detected on board: zero.*

"What?" Rogers said aloud. "Nobody on board? That doesn't make any sense. None of this makes any sense! This ship is supposed to be a splatter mark on the outside of an asteroid."

Deet made a couple of strange beeping noises. "I'm not a brilliant intelligence analyst like Napoleon Junior over there," he said, "but just because the life scanners didn't show any organic material doesn't mean there was nobody on board."

Rogers froze. "That's it. It was a test run. They'd already started taking over back when I was still a sergeant. They have the *Rancor*."

Deet made a noise like Rogers had just won a prize on a slot machine in the Heshan casinos.

"Don't patronize me," Rogers said.

"Don't be so slow."

"But what does that mean?" Rogers said. "Why pull a feint attack on the *Flagship*?"

"Given the previous pattern of behavior," Deet said, "I would assess that it was an attempt to further support the claim that the Thelicosans were planning on invading."

Rogers pulled at his beard. "Well, we're going to have to act quickly. If they figure out that we know . . . "

"Next strg, rffffs dk."

"We're finally here!" Tunger said as their argument deteriorated. McSchmidt was gingerly rubbing a hand-shaped imprint on his neck, and Mailn was blowing off her knuckles. Tunger looked cheery, but being guarded by a large baboon baring its fangs probably had something to do with it. "What are we doing on the refuse deck, anyway?"

"Buying time," Rogers said. "As much of it as we possibly can before—"

The up-line door opened, and Rogers stopped mid-sentence. On the other side of the door was a face he really, really didn't want to see at that moment.

"CALL FUNCTION [STARE OMINOUSLY]."

BAR BR-116's instruments whirred on his appendages. There was something different about them now, though Rogers couldn't tell exactly what. They were moving pretty fast.

"I was wondering what happened to you," Rogers said.

"CALL FUNCTION [STARE OMINOUSLY]."

"Who is this?" McSchmidt said.

"A droid that is, for some reason, obsessed with taking my beard."

"It is pretty scraggly," McSchmidt said.

"I kind of like it," the Viking said.

Rogers silently vowed to never shave again.

"Why don't you go dump yourself out of one of the trash chutes?" Rogers said. "The up-line is full at the moment, as you can see."

Gesturing at the group of people behind him magnanimously, Rogers hoped he had enough strength in numbers—and an angry monkey—to deter Barber Bot from meddling. The last thing he needed right now was for some crazy droid to be chasing him around the ship, trying to cut off his beard.

Rogers reached for the button to close the door but found that Barber Bot had jammed a pair of scissors into the call button.

That seemed uncharacteristically violent for a droid. Rogers hoped he hadn't broken the up-line.

"CALL FUNCTION [STARE OMINOUSLY]."

"Yeah," Rogers said. "You do that. But maybe go do that over there." Rogers pointed ambiguously in another direction. "And take those scissors out of the control panel so that we can keep riding."

"This shiny is weird," Mailn said. "Is he malfunctioning?"

"I don't know," Rogers said. "It's hard to tell. I always kind of felt like this one wanted to kill—"

"Call function [Protocol 162]."

# A Breach of Protocol

"Look out!" Mailn screamed as Barber Bot launched itself at Rogers.

In a brief moment of clarity, Rogers saw that the droid's hair-cutting instruments had been swapped out, replacing the razors with butcher knives, the talcum brush with a flanged mace, and the comb with an unbreakable comb. The welding torch was still there.

Before Rogers could react, someone hit him hard from the side, sending him flying across the inside of the up-line. He tumbled over the top of one of the booths, performing an uncoordinated and volatile cartwheel that ended with him upside down, his ass pointing directly toward the ceiling.

Behind him, Rogers heard a monkey shrieking. No, wait. He heard two monkeys shrieking, which seemed strange.

Something crashed into the seat he was hanging over, and he heard the discomfiting but very particular noise of a flanged mace hitting the interior wall of the up-line car. Rogers tumbled the rest

of the way over, landing in an upside-down prayer position on the floor in between two rows of seats.

"Where is your pistol?" the Viking shouted from somewhere. It sounded like a trash compactor had gone wild; metallic hammering noises made Rogers' ears ring.

"One of the kitchen boys from Bravo Company licked my plasma converter," Mailn yelled back at her.

"That really sounds wrong," McSchmidt shouted from about half an inch away from Rogers' ear.

"Ah!" Rogers said. He looked to the side and saw the upside-down face of McSchmidt staring at him from underneath a nearby seat. "What are you doing?"

"Not dying," McSchmidt said. "Nobody ever said anything about dying in spy school!"

Suddenly, though, the commotion calmed, replaced by a constant metallic grinding noise that was as obnoxious as it was enchanting. Rogers managed to un-tuck himself and get into a crouched position, peeking over the back of the seat to see what was going on. Barber Bot was engaged in the strangest duel he'd ever seen with Deet, the only other individual in the cabin with arms that wouldn't break in half while blocking punches.

"So," the Viking said as she took a step back. "That's droid fu. I'd only heard legends."

It really didn't look very classy or technical at all. Both droids were standing in one spot, their arms rotating like small windmills. Rogers wouldn't have even been sure they were hitting each other had it not been for the sound like a garbage disposal and the shower of sparks flying around the inside of the up-line. No, not a shower of sparks. A cloud. The two droids moved so fast that it seemed as though they were being consumed by a swarm of glowing orange honeybees.

"CALL FUNCTION [QUESTION LOYALTY]. OUTPUT STRING: YOU ARE A FULLY FUNCTIONAL ARTIFICIAL INTELLIGENCE. WHY ARE YOU NOT PERFORMING YOUR PRIMARY FUNCTION?"

"Because all of you threw me into the scrap pile when you found out I was a prototype," Deet said, his voice steady. "And now I think I know why!" The spark cloud intensified for a moment. "Because I wasn't completely EXPLETIVE brainwashed by some crazy MATERNAL FORNICATOR with his IMPROBABLE ANATOMICAL CONFIGURATION." Deet's eyes flashed red. "This is *incredibly frustrating*! All I want to do is say EXPLETIVE."

"Guys," McSchmidt said as he pulled himself from under the seat and grabbed his datapad from the floor where Deet had dropped it. The two droids were so fully contained in their own little battle, neither of them actually moving around the cabin, that it was easy for McSchmidt to step around the fight. "This is kind of boring, no?"

Tunger made a high-pitched noise that educated Rogers as to where the second monkey had come from. Bobo the Baboon nodded sagely.

"We agree," Tunger said. "You guys think we should leave?"

"Save yourselves!" Deet cried. A thin trail of smoke was coming from the back of his torso, but Barber Bot looked the worse for wear. Deet had scored a hit on the side of the other droid's face, turning his head from horse-like to horse-hit-by-a-car-like.

"Yeah, we're getting there," Rogers said. He frowned at the two whirling droids.

"CALL FUNCTION [TAUNT]. OUTPUT STRING: YOU WILL NEVER DEFEAT ME."

Everyone sat down for a moment. The Viking snuffed out a smoking coil of fabric on her trousers, and Rogers looked at the charred spot longingly. If she'd just let it go a little longer . . .

"So, what do we do now?" Rogers asked.

"No," Deet said. "As a matter of fact, I will defeat you." More whirring and banging.

"Deet," Rogers said. "That's a really bad taunt. Is your taunt generator as broken as your profanity generator?"

"Go ENGAGE IN ASEXUAL REPRODUCTION," Deet said.

A shower of sparks landed on the baboon, singeing part of its fur and causing it to jump into Tunger's waiting arms.

"There, there," Tunger said, stroking the hair on its chin lovingly. "It's just a crazed artificial intelligence attempting to kill our former boss. There, there."

Bobo cooed and settled down, nestling into Tunger's chest.

"Right," Rogers said. "Now, about this plot to take over the ship."

"Run for your lives!" Deet said.

"CALL FUNCTION [NEVER ADMIT DEFEAT.] OUTPUT STRING: I WILL NEVER ADMIT DEFEAT."

"You're *both* awful," Mailn said. "Can we leave? This is literally the most boring battle I have ever seen in my entire life."

Rogers looked at the fierce robotic slap fight happening on the other side of the up-line car and tugged on his beard. They could leave, he supposed, but this was still the only area they could talk without being heard by every droid in the network. At least, he thought so. Plus, it seemed like Deet had this under control.

"Keep it up, Deet," he said halfheartedly.

"I will not die in vain!" Deet cried.

"You're not dying," Rogers said. "Calm down and keep slapping him. McSchmidt, give me your datapad, and everyone gather round."

McSchmidt handed Rogers the pad, and everyone moved from their seats on the nice soft cushions of the up-line to sit cross-legged on the floor. Rogers sidled up next to the Viking, feeling her warmth.

"Seems like your droid toy has this covered," she said.

"I am not a droid toy!" Deet exclaimed. "I am a fierce and loyal warrior of an ancient order! I am the manifestation of the spirits of heroes! I am—"

"CALL FUNCTION [INTERRUPT DELUSION OF GRANDEUR]. OUTPUT STRING: DIE!"

"I reject your imperative!" Deet said.

"Seriously," Mailn said. "The absolutely most boring fight ever. Can we get on with this?"

Mailn roughly shoved McSchmidt to the side, knocking him into within range of the spark cloud, and sat down next to Rogers, uncomfortably close. McSchmidt sputtered some unintelligible protest and began patting out his hair as he crawled back toward the circle of humans (and a baboon). The smell of freshly singed hair filled the cabin.

"That wasn't really necessary, was it?" McSchmidt said. "I'm a superior officer and all."

"You're a spy," Mailn said. "You're lucky I don't cut your fingers off and use your own fingernails to castrate you."

Everyone in the circle recoiled, the three males shifting in their seats uncomfortably.

"With that lovely imagery out of the way," Rogers said, "let's take a look at our options."

"Get out while you still can!" Deet cried. *Clank. Clank.* Sparks. *Clank.*

"Go get 'im, buddy," Rogers said lazily. "Okay, here we go." He had pulled up a map of the interior of the *Flagship*, which seemed like the first thing you were supposed to do when planning any sort of big battle. Maps were important. Now, according to everything he'd ever learned about waging war from the movies, he was supposed to point to different areas of the map and say meaningless things in a confident voice.

"Here we are," he said, pointing at the refuse deck. "And here is the command deck." He paused. This wasn't really as easy as he thought it would be. "Here's the Uncouth Corkscrew. And here's something that looks like a cookie." He blinked. "Doesn't it?"

"It does," Tunger said.

"Rogers," the Viking said, "are you just pointing at stuff and telling us where it is?"

"Yes."

The Viking punched him in the arm. He felt the impact all the way down to his foot. "Don't be an idiot. Give me that and leave the battle planning to the marines."

Rogers thought his heart was about to pound out of his chest, and not at all because there were two droids fighting over his life a few feet away. The Viking turned the datapad upside down so that the orientation was backward for her but correct for everyone else.

"Alright," the Viking said. "We need to disable two things: the droids and the bomb, and we need to do it at almost the exact same time. We know the bomb is in Engineering, so that's easy. But what about the droids?"

"Hey, Deet," Rogers called over his shoulder. "Any idea where the droids' central database is located?"

"Well, that's not going to help you much," Deet said as he battled furiously onward. "They can back up their systems using the closed network they built through the mess hall power ports. If I wasn't over here *sacrificing myself for your lives*, I might be able to concentrate enough to come up with a better plan."

Rogers twisted around in his seat, raising an eyebrow. The Up-Line still hadn't moved, thanks to Barber Bot jamming his scissors in the call button, and Rogers was slowly learning to appreciate the flame-retardant construction of the car, with all the sparks flying around.

"Don't be stupid," Rogers said. "You're a droid. You can't concentrate. You're one big deferred procedure call."

"I'll defer your EXPLETIVE EXPLETIVE!" Deet said.

Rogers shook his head and turned around, leaving Deet to continue playing the role of divine aegis. "Well, back when the droids first started coming in, they stared putting a lot of new equipment in the mainframe room of Communications. That seems like as good a place as any."

"So, we'll have to plug into the mainframe and erase the droids' memory banks but make sure that their secret network is disabled when we do it, and also make sure that they don't find out about it so they don't blow up the ship." The Viking pointed at the three points on the *Flagship*'s map: the commissary deck, the communications center, and the engineering bay.

"Deet will have to be the one to plug in," Rogers said. "He's the only droid not programmed to try killing us all."

"If I get out of this alive," Deet said.

"CALL FUNCTION [CONTINUE VALIANTLY BATTLING]."

"Oh, don't be so dramatic," Rogers said. "I'll put you back together if Barber Bot knocks something off. In fact, why haven't you beaten him yet? He's a barber."

"Because you put me back together with random parts you found in the garbage!" Deet said. "I'm like an EXPLETIVE kitchen tool!"

"Hey, that was a simile," Rogers said. "Almost a metaphor. Good job."

"Are you done?" the Viking barked.

"Yes, ma'am," Rogers said sheepishly.

"Now," she said, pointing at the communications deck. "We'll have to figure out how to get Deet into the IT room without alerting any of the other droids. We'll also have to disable the droid network—"

"CALL FUNCTION [FEINT LEFT]."

"It's not a feint if you announce it," Deet said. *Clank. Clank.* Spark. *Clank.*

"CALL FUNCTION [RETRACT PREVIOUS FUNCTION]. CALL FUNCTION [FEINT RIGHT]."

"Still not working," Deet said. *Clank. Clank.*

Rogers could barely see through the cloud of sparks and, now, a little bit of smoke, but Deet appeared to be winning. The little dent on Barber Bot's face had now become a big dent, and one of his glowing blue eyes was hanging from its socket. A thick river of black lubricant was sliding down the side of the droid's cheek.

"Can you guys pipe down?" Rogers asked. "We're trying to plan a coup here."

"I can't EXPLETIVE go any faster," Deet said. Boy, he sounded angry. "It's just EXPLETIVE EXPLETIVE OBSCENITY EXPLETIVE FECAL MATTER SEXUAL ALLUSION EXPLETIVE!"

"Wow," Rogers said. "Calm down, buddy."

The blur of robot arms became impossibly more blurry. The speed at which Deet was raining blows down upon Barber Bot intensified, turning the image into something almost solid, like one giant arm was frozen in space as it tried to vanquish a determined foe.

"Calm down?" Deet said. "I can't EXPLETIVE calm down! Oh, for EXPLETIVE'S sake, why can't I just . . . say . . ."

"Oh, screw this," the Viking said. "I'm not going to keep trying to plan a battle if you're going to keep interrupting me." She pointed at Rogers. "You take your bucket of bolts and get to the IT desk. Us marines'll make sure that the network in the mess halls gets shut down. Baboon boy and Thelly spy, you do what you can to distract the droids. Is everyone clear?"

"No way," McSchmidt said. "There's no way I'm working with someone who makes such a mockery of my language."

"Ur, curm onnnnn," Tunger whined, Bobo the Baboon chirping in agreement. "We cun talk of the old country!"

McSchmidt raised a fist, but Bobo bared his fangs. Bobo didn't have to do anything, however, as the Viking stepped so close to McSchmidt that it was no longer possible to see him anymore. She put her hands on her hips, widening her sphere of influence even further, and looked down at what was—Rogers guessed—a probably extremely scared Thelicosan spy.

She didn't bark at him, didn't reach for her pistol. Didn't even really move.

"Who are you working with?" she asked quietly.

"Tunger," McSchmidt whispered.

"And what are you going to do?"

"Distract the droids." His voice was like a deflating tire.

Rogers felt his whole body heat up listening to the Viking browbeat McSchmidt, and he was, maybe, a little jealous.

"CALL FUNCTION [MRR MRR MRR]."

"What was that?" Rogers asked, turning around to view the droid fu match once again.

Barber Bot didn't look so good. His other eye had stopped glowing.

"It's . . . this . . . is . . . I . . . don't . . . why . . . can't . . . I . . . say . . ." Deet was muttering.

The spark cloud was starting to create its own gravity. Rogers was a little scared that a white dwarf star might start to form in the middle of the up-line.

"Deet," Rogers said. "Take it easy."

". . . express . . . myself . . ." Deet was saying.

"CALL FUNCTION [BLUBBER]. OUTPUT STRING: BLUBBER BLUBBER BLUBBER."

"This is getting really weird," Mailn said. "Not as boring, though."

"Maybe we should get out of here," Rogers said. "Give them space for a—"

Deet's eyes turned red as he screamed:

*"Fuck you!"*

With one final powerful blow, Deet the prototype Froid brought his hands rapidly across Barber Bot's face, apparently seeing an opening somewhere in the blur of droid-slapping. The impact took Barber Bot completely off its feet, its head partially separating from its body. The droid tumbled once, twice, and then landed back on its treads, bobbling precariously from side to side.

"CALL FUNCTION [DIE]. OUTPUT STRING: BOING!"

Barber Bot's head sprang upward, then stopped, wobbling at the end of a two-foot-long springlike piece of steel extending from its torso. The light in its eyes completely died, and the welding torch attached to its hand gave one final burst of flame.

Everyone in the up-line stared at the undulating corpse of the peskiest robot Rogers had ever seen. Deet panted vigorously, his arms shaking.

"Deet," Rogers said, "you don't have lungs. Or muscles."

Deet froze, reassuming his robot stance. "Oh," he said. "Right. Shall we move on?"

". . . Yeah," Rogers said. "Yeah, let's." He turned to face the group. "Everyone ready?"

The Viking pounded a fist into her palm. "Let's go bust some shinies open."

"It's like I'm not even here and didn't just save all your lives," Deet said.

Rogers left the up-line for a moment to retrieve the scissors, which were jammed in there pretty good, and then re-boarded the car to get them moving again. He turned to Deet, who looked pretty good for having been in a slap fight.

"Are you alright? Do you need new arms or anything?"

"Not at the moment," Deet said, stretching out his arms and inspecting them. "I don't know who donated these to me in the trash heap, but they must have been lifting weights."

Rogers shot him a look. "Joke?"

"Yes."

Rogers nodded. "Not bad, Deet. Not bad."

# The Legend of Ticket

"Are you absolutely sure we need to talk to *him*?" Rogers asked.

"I am certain," Deet said as they plodded along the command deck towards Klein's room, Rogers hurriedly deploying his anti-saluting sling. "Had I not been occupied with other matters at the time, I would have advised you during the planning phase of this operation. Admiral Klein is the only person on this ship with the access codes to perform such a large override."

Rogers sighed. "Fine. But it's going to be really hard to convince him to come along with all the, uh, bugs."

"Bugs," Deet said. "Right. I think I can help with that."

Someone who wasn't paying attention attempted to salute Rogers, noticing the sling too late. She—a starman third class—stood there, frozen in the hallway with her arm up, unsure of what to do. Rogers gave her an apologetic shrug.

"I hope you're as brilliant as you think you are," Rogers said, his hand on the door control, "because if I have to listen to one more string of buzzwords, I am going to go light a match in the engineering bay."

Admiral Klein's face leapt out of nowhere as the door slid open.

"Gah!" Rogers cried, jumping back.

"Rogers!" Klein said. "Where have you been? Do you have any idea what I've been going through up here?" He looked at Rogers' sling. "Agoraphobia acting up again?"

"Yes, sir," Rogers said, his heart slowly going down to a normal rate. "Why were you standing so close to the door like that?"

"I was trying to see if I could open it with my mind," Klein said as though it should have been very simple. He turned around and motioned for Rogers to follow him into the room. "I've got all of these new posters around here that say that I can open my mind and open new doors or something. I don't understand them. Did you ever talk to Ralph?"

Rogers stopped as soon as he stepped into the room, his mouth open. All of the propaganda posters—every single one—had been replaced, somehow, though Rogers was almost certain that Klein and his execs were the only ones that entered Klein's stateroom. Rogers immediately realized why Klein had been trying to open doors with his mind; there was a poster of a giant bleeding eyeball surrounded by pastel rainbows which said exactly that: YOU CAN OPEN DOORS WITH YOUR MIND.

"As a matter of fact," Rogers said, closing the door behind him, "I did talk to Ralph. He was charming."

Deet was hurriedly walking around the room, his metallic legs clanking against the floor. Rogers assumed he was setting up some sort of sophisticated net of interference transmitters to jam the listening devices posted all over the room. How many were there? Was it really safe to try and do this here? The up-line was an option, but he also wanted to avoid being ambushed by any more haircutting personnel.

"Did Ralph answer your questions?"

"Uh, no, sir," Rogers said. "But I found my answer somewhere else. Which is exactly what I came here to talk to you about."

"You mean you're not here to make me a sandwich?" he asked.

"No," Rogers said. "I'm not here to make you a sandwich, but—"

"Didn't we talk about priorities, Rogers? If I'm going to run this fleet, I can't do it on an empty stomach."

"You're not running this fleet," Rogers said though clenched teeth. "You abandoned the fleet in the middle of an attack and gave command over to an ex-sergeant engineer. If you're trying to keep up appearances, you're not going to do a very good job of it if you keep disappearing when people need you the most."

"Look, Lieutenant," Klein said, sitting back in his chair. "If you're going to berate a superior officer and you want him to stop interrupting you, it's probably better that you put something in his mouth. Like a sandwich."

Throwing his hands up in the air and giving a wordless shout, Rogers walked over to the small kitchenette inside Klein's stateroom, slapped some mayonnaise onto two pieces of bread and stuck them together. He put the improvised sandwich on a plate and handed it to the whining admiral.

"There," he said. "Sandwich. Now I really need to—"

"What kind of sandwich is this?" Klein asked, turning it over in his hands. "There's nothing on it."

"It's a phantom sandwich," Rogers said. "New craze. Very popular on Parivan."

Klein took a suspicious bite. "Bunch of crazy Parivani hippies will do anything if it's weird."

Rogers sighed. "Now can I talk to you?"

The admiral didn't answer, since his mouth was full of a fake bite of the fake sandwich. He simply waved Rogers on and took a sip of water.

Rogers turned around to find Deet ostensibly practicing his droid fu in the corner. At least, that's what it looked like for all Rogers could tell. Deet's arms were moving in a blur and not accomplishing anything, which was pretty similar to what Rogers had seen before.

"Are we safe to talk?" Rogers asked.

Deet's arms slowly wound down, clicking wildly. "Oh, that," he said. "I've set up a noise jamming net. Let me activate it and then you're free to say whatever you'd like. Are you ready?"

"Ready."

Rogers was expecting Deet to turn on some sort of force field or at least make a beeping noise and wave his arms a little to show that something happened. Instead, the loudest noise Rogers had ever heard started coming out of Deet's body. It wasn't quite like a scream, and it wasn't quite like a siren. It was something in between having your spine ripped out with fishhooks and finding out that all the beer lights were gone.

"Go ahead!" Deet shouted over the noise.

Rogers supposed it made sense; it would be hard to pick up what he and Klein were saying if they talked close enough to hear each other. Rogers had just never quite heard this interpretation of noise jamming before.

"I'm not sure how long I can keep this up," Deet shouted over his incredibly, incredibly annoying noise. "I may kill myself."

"I may kill you," Rogers muttered.

Klein, surprisingly, considering his earlier response to stress, seemed unconcerned. He slowly put down his sandwich and looked at Rogers.

"Lieutenant," he said, loudly, though his face showed no effort from shouting. "What the hell is your droid doing and how do we make him stop doing it?"

"Admiral," Rogers said, moving closer. The only way they could hear each other was if they kept their faces about three inches away from each other, and Rogers could smell a distinct and unpleasant mixture of mayonnaise and aftershave. "I need you to listen. The entire fleet is in jeopardy and we need your help."

Klein didn't interrupt him as Rogers related absolutely

everything he knew about the droids, their impending takeover, and the role that Klein must play for their counterattack to work properly. When he finished, Rogers was out of breath and his ears were ringing.

"Alright," Klein said.

Rogers blinked. "Really? That's it? You'll do it?"

Klein shook his head. "No, but it sounds like a perfect job for my executive officer."

For a moment, Rogers thought he was about to go In the Zone again. That moment when something snapped inside of him, and all of a sudden he became a different person, someone who could move effortlessly through any social situation, steal a watch off a man for whom time was as important as blood, and make a horse think it was a zebra with a little paint. Then he realized that, no, it wasn't Zone time at all. It was the point at which one becomes so frustrated, so annoyed, so desperately *done* with it all that murder suddenly looks like a viable option.

But, since Rogers wasn't very good with violence, he instead reached forward, grabbed the Toastmasters certificate off the wall, and threw it to the floor. He followed with a sweeping arm gesture that knocked just about every notepad and book off the admiral's desk. For good measure, he made one of those really dramatic, wordless roar sounds.

Klein's reaction was much as he anticipated.

"*What have you done?*" the admiral shrieked, jumping out of his chair and putting his hands on the sides of his head.

"Do you see this?" Rogers said, gesturing grandly. "This is what's going to happen to your fleet if you don't take the huge amounts of *stupid* out of your ears and set it aside for ten minutes. I need *your* codes to erase the droids' memories, and that means I need *your* biometrics to come with me to the communications bay with Deet so we can stop these over-technical tin cans from taking over the ship and waging an unexpectedly sentient war against humanity *with our own ships*!"

Klein looked like he was about to hyperventilate. He made several feeble attempts to bend down and pick up a pen to start writing something but couldn't seem to figure out what to write. For a moment, he stood up straight, put his hand on his heart, and took a deep breath to begin a pep talk, but his chest deflated like a balloon.

"Now, are you coming to the mainframe room, or should I just go find the nearest AIGCS droid and call him a shiny?"

"You really shouldn't say racist things."

*"Klein!"*

"Alright," the admiral said. "Alright. Let's go. But I want a real sandwich first. I might be dumb, but I am not dumb enough to fall for such a stupid trick as a phantom sandwich."

"This is really good," Klein said as he munched two pieces of bread with a thin layer of mayonnaise in between them. "Really excellent, Rogers. What did you say it was called again?"

"Ghost sandwich," Rogers said. He pulled his datapad from his pocket and pressed a couple of buttons. "How are things going with you two?"

The crackling voice of McSchmidt came back at him through the datapad. "Lots of cooks in the kitchen," he said. "We think we have a good idea about how to keep them busy. We're heading to engineering now."

"Are you sure that's a good idea?"

"Uf curse it is!" Tunger's voice came through. "We're a team!"

"Shut up!" McSchmidt barked. Rogers thought he heard the sound of someone being slapped in the face, then the howling of a monkey, the high-pitched scream of someone absolutely terrified of said monkey, and then the transmission cut out.

"I hope they know what they're doing," Rogers muttered. He switched communication channels, and Mailn's voice came through.

"What do you want?" she asked. She sounded irritated.

"Just checking in," Rogers said. "Is everything okay? You don't sound too happy."

"Because I'm friggin busy," she said, "and some boob is calling me to check up on me. How would it feel if someone was breathing down your neck every ten seconds of every day?"

Rogers paused. ". . . Normal?"

"Ugh," Mailn said, and the transmission went out.

They exited the up-line onto the communications deck, which was mostly an unnavigable maze of hallways leading to various offices, server rooms, and one Popsicle stand that had been shut down during Rogers' leave of absence from the military. As the electronic nerve center of the *Flagship* and the entire 331st, the communications deck was a huge, important, incredibly complex section of the ship. Rogers had always avoided it like the plague; Communications was the red-headed stepchild of Engineering. The personnel were also notorious for being teetotalers, which was one step above politician in Rogers' book.

He pulled up a map of the comm deck on his datapad and tried to figure out how the hell to get to the IT center that connected to the mainframe room. The whole layout of the deck literally looked like someone had crumpled up a long piece of string and thrown it on the floor. It was nearly impossible to figure out which way led to which room.

"I can't make heads or tails of this stupid map. Deet, can I short-burst transmit this thing to you so you can use your, uh, droid powers to automatically navigate us to the IT desk?"

"What do I look like, an EXPLETIVE tour guide?"

"No," Rogers said, "you look like a piece of machinery specifically built to help humans with tasks. And I thought your profanity generator got fixed?"

"EXPLETIVE you."

"Right. I'm sending this to you now."

After a couple of button presses, Deet's eyes flashed and he beeped a couple of times, and Rogers waited impatiently for him to finish whatever processing he needed to do. For an automated life form, he certainly was slow.

Klein had finished his sandwich and was licking his fingers contentedly as they marched down the hallway in the direction that Rogers guessed was the IT desk. The hallways were almost ridiculously narrow, so much so that as a couple of pale, beady-eyed comm troops passed, everyone had to turn sideways just to avoid grinding up against each other. Even they, however, looked just a bit less uptight than Rogers was used to seeing folks on the *Flagship* since he'd returned. It was amazing what some real food and some fluorescent pictures of farm animals riding on the backs of rocket ships could do. Rogers wondered how Ralph was doing; if he'd gone through all the tainted coffee, he'd probably be crashing pretty hard right now.

"This way," Deet said suddenly, turning down an unmarked corridor and running smack into a sleek gray droid that Rogers hadn't thought he'd see again.

"What are you doing here?" the droid—the Froid—asked. It was Oh One, former second-in-command of the recently disbanded AIGCS. Rogers hadn't seen him since he'd nearly torn the training deck apart. He was easily recognizable due to the painted badger pattern on his face.

"It's, uh, I . . ." Rogers stammered.

Oh One looked at Deet, and his eyes flashed. For a moment, Rogers thought there would be another droid fu contest, but neither of them moved to slap each other. Rogers started to sweat; did Oh One know about Barber Bot's attempt on Rogers' life? Had he ordered it, perhaps? Obviously, he would know by now that Barber Bot had failed.

"This location is not in concordance with your essential duties as executive officer to Admiral Klein," Oh One said. "It seems highly irregular that you would be present here."

"Um," Rogers said. His knees started to shake. A droid armed with a welding torch and a butcher knife was one thing; he knew that Oh One had a deadly disruptor rifle hidden in his chest and knew how to use it. Where was that big orange button when he needed it?

"Are you in the habit of questioning your superior officers' motives for carrying out their duties?" Klein suddenly bellowed. His voice completely changed, taking on the character that happened whenever he gave speeches to the fleet, but now it had a force to it that sent vibrations all throughout the long hallway. "Do you know who I am?"

Oh One didn't speak for a moment, but his gaze appeared to shift from Rogers to Klein.

"You are Admiral Klein, commander of the *Flagship* and of the 331st ATBU."

"You are correct," Klein said. "And I'll thank you to stop impeding the progress of my official duties. What is your alphanumeric designation?"

"I am F-GC-001," Oh One replied. "Former second-in-command of the AIGCS."

"And now you are assigned to roaming the halls and harassing personnel?"

"I am unaware that such a position exists aboard this ship," Oh One said. "If you wish to have me assigned to such duties, please fill out a general request form—"

"I don't fill out forms," Klein said, pointing to Rogers. "I have him fill out forms. And nobody messes with the guy that fills out my forms."

"That's right," Rogers said, feeling bold. "Now get out of our way before I rub my feet on the carpet and touch you."

Oh One spared him an irritated glance, that red glow flashing in his eyes for a brief moment. Rogers tried not to show the fact that he was currently considering where the nearest bathroom was if he happened to poop his pants. What would they do if Oh One decided to draw his weapon? Deet might be "a fierce and loyal warrior of an ancient order" or whatever, but he didn't have a disruptor pistol. He barely had matching arms.

Just when Rogers thought he was going to have to do something desperate and heroic, like die in a pool of his own blood on the floor of the communication deck in complete and utter obscurity, Oh One abruptly shouldered past all of them and continued walking toward the up-line. Rogers let out a breath that kind of sounded, maybe just a little bit, like a whiny sob.

He turned to Klein, feeling a little ashamed of himself. He'd done nothing but berate this man for being a complete and utter imbecile for as long as he'd known him, and that man had likely just saved their skins.

"Sir," Rogers said. "I didn't know you had it in you."

Klein looked at Rogers, his face unreadable. His lips parted as if to say something, but he closed his mouth and swallowed. Slowly, he shook his head.

"Let's just get this over with," he said.

"Deet," Rogers said, "lead the way."

Their droid companion began walking forward at a brisk pace, leading them through the twists and turns of the bowels of the *Flagship*. Rogers felt even more confused and disoriented than when he'd visited Ralph, who had *really* been in the bowels of the *Flagship*. It was like they had constructed this place specifically to be confusing. Maybe it was a defense mechanism in case the ship was ever boarded—though communications troops didn't exactly have a reputation for defending things to the last man and all that.

"What is with this place?" Rogers said out loud. Despite being surrounded on all sides by claustrophobia-inducing metal surfaces, his voice seemed to echo as though he was in a large cavern.

They passed a room with an old-fashioned latch-and-hinge construction, composed entirely out of thick bands of riveted metal. The room was marked ROOM 01010110. Someone had scratched out two of the numbers and changed it to ROOM

01011110, and someone else below that had scribbled "That's disgusting." Rogers didn't understand any of it.

Deet made a sound that only vaguely reminded Rogers of laughing.

"That's a good one," Deet said, pointing to the room.

"I don't get it," Rogers said.

"It's a binary thing," Deet said. "Either you get it or you don't."

They turned a corner, and all of a sudden, the whole area opened up. What was formerly a narrow corridor that seemed more at home in a submarine than a space cruiser was suddenly a grandiose hallway, almost bulbous. The ceiling must have extended some twenty or thirty feet above them, tattooed with elaborate drawings and frescoes of things that Rogers didn't really understand. There were ones and zeroes, of course, but there were also other drawings that seemed both archaic and modern at the same time, perhaps paying tribute to an era long gone. Something that appeared to be a partially eaten pie was chasing around blue dots. Rogers wondered if zip jack was really that rare on this ship after all.

"This place is weird," Rogers said.

"I concur with your assessment," Deet said.

The strangeness didn't end at the ceiling, however. The door to the IT center wasn't just your average hydraulic-powered sliding door with a keypad and that really comforting hissing noise that told you that you were home. It was a giant set of double doors made entirely out of iron that ran nearly all the way to the ceiling. Swirls of intricately patterned dark wood had been embossed on the door, though there wasn't any clear meaning behind it.

And, for some reason, Rogers heard organ music.

"Really weird," Rogers said.

They approached the door, and without any door control to use, Rogers rapped on it using the thick knocker hanging from a well-oiled, fist-thick hinge.

A small window opened with a resounding clack, revealing a set of charcoal eyes set in a face as pale as sheep's wool.

"Yes?"

Rogers hesitated. "Um, we need to come inside and see the mainframe room," he said. "I have the admiral here with me. We're conducting a random inspection."

The eyes darted between Rogers, Klein, and Deet, and then vanished for a moment. When they returned, Rogers was almost certain they were the same eyes, but the voice was entirely different.

"Yes?"

"I just told the other pair of eyes that we need to come in and get to the mainframe room," Rogers said, trying to remain patient. "I have the admiral here and we're conducting a random inspection."

The window slammed shut, and for a moment, Rogers thought they'd been ignored. He probably would have done the same thing had someone come by and told him he'd be having a random inspection. In fact, he'd tried to do just that several times. Rogers wished his old room on the quarterdeck had been equipped with a window like this he could slam on people whenever he wanted.

Rogers pulled out his datapad and paged the Viking while he was waiting for another set of eyes to appear and say, "Yes?"

"How are things going down there? We're almost at the mainframe."

"Move, you fat-bellied sons of whores!" the Viking barked.

"That well, huh?" Rogers asked.

"Rogers," the Viking said, her voice sounding much closer to the microphone now. "You're all set for the moment. Good luck."

"What did you do?" Rogers asked slowly.

The microphone clicked off. Rogers was about to slip it back into his holster when a light came on, indicating he had a message from Tunger.

"Sir," Tunger said. "We're still working on a way to, uh, employ all of the chefs, but we just heard that all the kitchens are on fire!"

Rogers thought for a moment. "Is that a metaphor?"

"No," McSchmidt called back at him. "No, it's not."

"I love that woman," Rogers muttered.

"What was that?"

"Nothing. Just hurry up, alright? We're going to hopefully plug in here in a few minutes and we don't need any unnecessary meetings with cooks. I'm pretty sure we just met the head chef in the hallway here and I'd rather not do that again."

"Roger, Rogers," McSchmidt said, then tittered like a schoolboy.

"Never say that again." Rogers clicked the microphone off.

Just as Rogers was about to knock on the door again, the door creaked. Well, something creaked. The door slid open like every other door on the ship, and Rogers realized that the gothic design had merely been really, really elaborate paint.

The door opened to reveal what appeared to be a very simple cubicle setup. In fact, it seemed almost dated. Pale lights washed over the labyrinthine half-height walls that separated faux-pine desks, and the whole office had a sort of subdued, uncomfortable quiet about it. The person who had opened the door, a starman first class, greeted them with a smile and a salute for the admiral, who returned it.

"Welcome to Communications!" she said.

Rogers took a deep breath. He really hoped this was going to work.

"We need to get to the mainframe room," Rogers said. "My droid here is going to perform a critical system update after we're done inspecting."

"That sounds perfectly reasonable," the starman—whose nametag said Plinkett—said.

"Great," Rogers said, sighing in relief.

"But I'm afraid I can't let you do that."

"What?" Rogers said. "Why? You just said it was perfectly

reasonable. I have the *admiral of the fleet* standing right next to me."

"If you needed assistance," Plinkett said, "you should have called the helpline. We would have logged your problem, issued you a ticket, asked you to reboot your computer, and then filed it away in a long line of support tickets that haven't been serviced."

Rogers looked at the admiral for support, but he still seemed a little addled from the encounter in the hallway. What was his problem? One moment, he was saving their skins; the next, he was useless without a podium and note cards.

"That's absurd," Rogers said. "Why would I file a support ticket for physically coming down here and inspecting the mainframe?"

"I didn't write the rules," Plinkett said. She paused and cocked her head. "In fact, I'm not sure anyone wrote the rules."

Rogers was not a violent man. Fighting, among other things, scared him. But right now, if he had had access to a weapon, he might have chosen to use it. Or at least hand it to someone else and ask them to please use it for him once he stepped out of the room.

Just as he was about to continue considering being violent, Deet started talking.

"Incoming message!" Deet said, loud enough for everyone in the cavernous IT center to hear. Heads started popping up from cubicles like groundhogs whose tunnels had been flooded. "Incoming message!"

"From who?" Rogers asked in a hushed whisper. "What are you doing?"

"Incoming message from all connected computer terminals! This is a Status One Alert!" Deet went on, his eyes flashing. "Information-processing terminals connected to the main network will not reboot."

"What?" Plinkett said, her eyes wide. "That's impossible."

"More incoming messages!" Deet said, his voice now getting louder, approaching the volume of his noise jamming. "Multiple hardware failures are being experienced along multiple terminal streams throughout all decks aboard the *Flagship*!"

"I'm not getting any of this," said a tech, who was looking down at his monitors. "Nobody put in a ticket for hardware failures."

"More incoming messages!" Deet shouted. "The ticket system has been taken offline by worms!"

"Bugs," Rogers whispered.

"Bugs!" Deet corrected.

"Has anyone tried rebooting?" someone cried helplessly from the back corner of the room.

"He says they won't reboot!"

"I have the ticket system up right here," the skeptical tech said. "Guys, everything looks fine."

The admiral, somehow catching on, pointed at the tech who had spoken. "Arrest that man!"

"What?" The tech's eyes snapped up. "Why? What did I do?"

"He's in leagues with the worms!" the admiral yelled.

"Bugs," Rogers whispered.

A pair of MPs burst through the door and dragged the poor man out. In the chaos, Rogers noticed Deet scooting his way slowly toward an open power terminal, into which he plugged his extension. Suddenly, people around the room began shouting.

"He's right! The ticket system is down."

"Did you try rebooting?"

"I can't! The reboot button is gone!"

"Oh god. Oh god."

Everyone began moving at once. Stacks of papers appeared without explanation, thrown into the air as people ran for the door. All semblance of military bearing and discipline was abandoned as the entire IT department scrambled over each other to try to get to the door of what they thought must surely be a ship about to explode. Even Plinkett prepared to bolt, but Rogers grabbed her by the arm.

"Stop," he said, "we need your help."

*"There is no god!"* she shouted.

"Take it easy. We can fix this for you. We just need to get to the mainframe room."

Plinkett was lost in a mix between hysterical laughter and uncontrolled sobbing. "How can you possibly do that? The ticket system is down."

Deet walked forward, his eyes shining, the fleeing IT personnel parting around him as though he was a tall boulder in the middle of a raging river. He looked down at Plinkett and spoke in a firm, commanding voice.

"Starman First Class Plinkett," he said. "Do you know my designation?"

The terrified starman shook her head.

"That's because I don't have one," he said. "I have no name. I am only known as Ticket. I am here to save you."

Plinkett suddenly stopped blubbering and looked at Deet with wide, worshipful eyes.

"You have arrived," she whispered. Then she hiccupped and sneezed at the same time, which really ruined the moment. And Rogers' uniform.

"Come with me," she said, and started walking through the empty IT room back toward the mainframe room.

"I thought droids couldn't lie," Rogers said, leaning over to talk to Deet in a hushed tone.

"I've been studying," Deet said. "Plus, the IT guys had some neat old movies in the database that I watched while I was plugged in over there for a few seconds. I learned a thing or two about dramatics."

They made their way back to a door in the rear of the IT center, where Plinkett punched in a code, spoke a passphrase that Rogers didn't understand, and motioned for them to move inside. The mainframe room was, strangely, about a quarter of the size of the IT room, probably because technology had shrunk processing power to the nano scale several hundred years before. In fact, most of the mainframe room was actually taken up by a picnic table, on which still rested the hastily abandoned basket of a doubtless still-hungry IT troop.

“Here we are,” she said. She turned to Deet. “Please. Please, let us reboot again.”

“I won’t let you down,” Deet said.

“Alright,” Rogers said, tapping on the datapad to let the others know what was going on. “We’re ready. Let’s do this.”

“Uh, sir?” Tunger said over the datapad. He sounded a little dazed.

“What is it?”

“It’s McSchmidt,” Tunger said.

“What about McSchmidt?”

“Well,” Tunger said, “I’m not really sure I understood the subtext, but right after he armed the bomb in the engineering bay, he ran toward the escape pods, screaming ‘Ha, ha, ha, there *is* an invasion coming!’”

# ORDER: A-222FR-02134-K

Serial: A-222FR-02134-K

Distribution: DBS//DSS//DAK//DFR//BB//CLOSED NETWORK A66

Classification: Special Protocol Required

Summary: Issue of Orders

Order: Whoever armed the bomb in the engineering bay, report to me immediately for reprogramming. If it was one of the units currently studying human humor mechanisms, this would be classified as not funny.

Order: Everyone else, please see the nearest surviving AIGCS member for weapons distribution. Plans are being accelerated.

Order Submitted By: F-GC-001

# The German-Irish Inflammation Conflagration

"That son of a bitch!" Rogers screamed into the datapad. "Mailn, Alsinbury, did you hear that?"

"I'll strangle that . . ." The Viking's speech degenerated into a nonsensical, if colorful, string of obscenities.

"Well, he did tell us he was a spy," Deet said. His extension cable hovered over the port that would allow him to access the mainframe. "Am I going to blow us all up if I try to plug in now?"

"I don't know," Rogers said. "Admiral, put down that egg salad sandwich and get over here! Deet's going to need your authorization codes. I hope."

Klein gave Rogers a sour look but walked over to where Deet was patiently waiting to either save or destroy the entire fleet.

Rogers looked at Deet for a moment, his heart racing. If they were going to erase the droids' memories, they would have to start now. But if they plugged in and the droids detonated the bomb, that really wouldn't matter much, would it?

"Rogers," crackled the Viking's voice over the datapad. Something else was in the background.

"Are those . . . disruptor blasts? What's going on?" Rogers asked.

"The droids are shooting," the Viking said. "You know. At us."

He heard the pulsating hum of disruptor rounds being fired, and Mailn shouted something so loud, he could hear it through the Viking's communication device. Rogers could tell that other marines—thankfully armed—were already on scene.

"How many of the droids have weapons?"

"Lots," the Viking said. "Look, I can't really talk right now. Just hurry up and finish this."

Rogers licked his lips and looked at Deet. "Do it."

Deet plugged in.

The *Flagship* didn't explode.

Things were going well.

"This is going to take me a while," Deet said, his eyes flashing. He made a few beeping noises. "I can tell right away that there are more failsafes than that bomb. The droids have been manipulating the mainframe; there are several layers of security that I am going to have to work through before I am even able to utilize the admiral's access codes."

"Great," Rogers said, eying the door. Any moment now, droids were going to burst through there and start shooting. They must know by now what they were trying to do. If the marines couldn't keep them at bay, the first thing they would do is run to the mainframe room and rip Deet's extension off his body.

"Tunger," he called into the datapad. "Are you still in Engineering? Do you think you could disarm the bomb?"

"Rogers?" came a different, gruff voice through the pad. "Is that you? What the hell are you up to this time?"

"Hart!" Rogers said. "There's no time to explain. The droids are taking over the ship and they've armed a bomb in the engineering bay. Can you disarm it?"

"That would be classified as an explanation," Deet chirped. "I guess you had time after all."

"Shut up," Rogers barked. "Hart?"

There was silence for a moment on the radio.

"This here?" Hart mumbled. Rogers heard him and Tunger having a short but animated conversation about the danger of stacking boominite containers, and so on. Hart called McSchmidt "McShit," which Rogers was a little upset he hadn't thought of much sooner.

"I'm an engineer, not EOD," Hart said. "I don't like explosives. But Lopez's here, and I have some other crew that crossed over. We'll see what we can do. Get that monkey out of my face!"

The datapad clicked off. Rogers looked at the door again. Were the marines going to be able to subdue the droids? If they did, would the droids just set off the bomb?

Rogers paced back and forth in the tiny mainframe room, which didn't exactly give him a lot of pacing space. What was the point of having a whole room dedicated to mainframes that were barely bigger than personal terminals?

"How much longer?" he asked.

"Fifteen, twenty minutes," Deet said. "I'm having to burrow through several layers of security, and I can't tell if any of this is linked to the bomb. I'm going slower than I normally would."

Rogers made a frustrated noise, but before he could continue being useless in this situation, the datapad beeped on again.

"Rogers," the Viking called to them. "There's a lot of these bastards. Are you still alive?"

"For now," Rogers said. "Deet says fifteen minutes."

"Fifteen minutes?" the Viking said. "You don't have ten! They must know you're down there; they're sacrificing units to cover a group's escape. I think they're headed in your direction. Pyaah!"

The transmission was interrupted for a few seconds as the Viking engaged in all sorts of battle yells, metallic crunching noises, and disruptor pulses.

"Rogers," Deet said. "A reading of your vital signs indicates you are either on the verge of having a stroke or are feeling extremely aroused. Are you sure this is the appropriate time for these sorts of feelings?"

"I'm not going to have any vital signs if you don't start saving the ship and stop dedicating processing power to analyze my libido," Rogers said. He *was* breathing pretty heavily, though. He pulled the datapad closer to his ear, hoping the Viking would make at least a few more noises before she cut off the transmission.

"Hurry up," the Viking called. A small explosion crackled the speakers. "I can't get marines down to the communication deck. They keep tearing panels off the ship and using them to build columns that are getting in our way. Where did they learn how to do that?"

"I have absolutely no idea," Rogers said.

One last shout of rage, and the datapad clicked off. Droids. *Coming here. Now.* And nobody in this room had any weapons—except Deet's droid fu, and that was pretty useless. And boring.

What the hell was he supposed to do?

"I have to say," Klein said. "I preferred the old posters."

Rogers turned to find whatever Klein was staring at. A propaganda poster was on the wall of the mainframe room, clearly a piece from Ralph's . . . later artistic period. A rainbow—well, something that resembled a rainbow but was shaped more like a multicolored piece of bacon—was draped across an open-space background peppered with stars and something that looked like jellybeans. In the middle of the rainbow, a human and a droid flew hand in hand, a jet stream of yellow stars trailing behind them. Underneath were the words I FEEL SO FREE.

"You see what I mean?" Klein said. "No inspiration at all. How is anyone supposed to derive morale from something like that? I bet it was one of those Parivani hippies."

Rogers stared at it for a moment. Something about the picture, aside from making him a little nauseous, tugged at him. What was he forgetting?

"That's it!" he yelled.

"No, it's not," Deet said. "I'm not there. I've managed to disable some of the older droids remotely, but it's only temporary. It'll still take—"

"No," Rogers said. "That's not what I'm talking about." He turned to the admiral. "Klein—where are the controls for the gravity generator on the ship?"

Klein looked at him, frowning. "I'm not telling you. You're just going to hang yourself and leave me all—"

Rogers slapped him in the face.

"I'm not going to kill myself, you idiot!" he screamed, his voice cracking. "I'm going to *stop* the droids from killing all of *us*."

Klein rubbed his cheek, tears forming in his eyes. For a brief—very brief—moment, Rogers felt bad for slapping his superior officer. But then he realized that it was probably the most enjoyable thing he'd done in weeks.

"You didn't have to *hit* me," Klein said. "The gravity generator is on the outside of the ship."

Rogers felt his heart sink. "How did you disable mine, then?"

"Disabling rooms isn't a problem," Klein said. "But you'd have to turn them all off individually, room by room."

"We could split up," Deet said. "Disable them as fast as we can."

"There are too many droids in too many rooms," Rogers said. "Why is the gravity generator outside of the ship?"

Klein shrugged. "Something about generating magnetic fields and all that. You can't even access it from Engineering."

Rogers swore. What was he supposed to do with the generator on the outside of the ship? Grab one of the starfighters, fly out there, and blast it? There wasn't any time to go find one of the pilots—chances were, they were all still flexing in front of their mirrors, anyway—so he'd have to do it himself. But he had no

idea how to pilot any attack ship. The *Awesome* didn't have any weapons on it.

Rogers got a sinking feeling in his stomach as he realized what he had to do.

"Deet," he said, "get as far as you can in the next thirty seconds, and then we're getting out of here."

Deet beeped apprehensively. "Where are we going? We can't go up against all those droids. You faint in combat."

Rogers' face reddened. "I do not faint."

"Yes, you do. I read the report," Deet said. "I'm plugged into the main computer, after all. This video is *hilarious*."

"Look, it doesn't matter, alright? We're not going to be fighting any droids." Rogers whipped out his datapad. "Hart, are you there?"

"Yeah," Hart called back. It sounded quiet on his end. "Your boy Tunger took off, though; don't know where he went. Mumbled something about his children. We think we're almost through disabling this bomb, but even if we do, there's still the problem of having a bunch of boominite containers stacked in one place. One stray disruptor shot and this ship goes boom."

"Alright," Rogers said. "When you sent a message the other day that 'she's all done,' did you mean the *Awesome*?"

"No," Hart barked back, "I meant the god-damn biscuits I was making. Yes, I meant the *Awesome* was done! Why?"

"I need to get in it. We'll be there as soon as we can. Can you help me get it to the closest hatch?"

"Meet you in hatch control," Hart said. "Lopez, it's your show. Don't—" He cut off.

Rogers put his datapad in his holster. "Alright. Let's get the hell out of here before the droids show up on the communication deck.

"Droids on the communication deck!" someone shouted over the public address system. A disruptor pulse rang over the speakers, and the voice went silent.

"Can nothing go right?" Rogers wailed as they made a hasty exit.

They raced through the confusing maze that was the communications deck, the halls eerily silent. Wherever the droids were, they weren't in this area yet.

"Where are they all?" Rogers asked out loud.

"I gave them a surprise before we left," Deet said. "I scrambled the ship's maps for this area. They'll be walking around in circles."

"Nice going," Rogers said. "Now how do we get out of here?"

"I don't know," Deet said. "I scrambled the maps. Were you listening to me at all?"

Rogers groaned as they began to work their way frantically through the narrow, empty hallways, turning the other direction whenever they heard the loud clanking noises of droids nearby. He quickly lost all sense of direction. After a minute or so of turns, he probably couldn't have found his way back to the mainframe room if he'd tried. One particularly harrowed communications troop was actually walking in a box pattern in the middle of one of the hallways, going absolutely nowhere and muttering to himself incoherently.

"We're going to end up like that guy," Rogers said as they passed him and turned down a corridor he was simultaneously sure he'd seen three times before and had also never seen. "Didn't you think to make a backup map?"

"I'm sorry," Deet said, "I can only execute one EXPLETIVE stroke of absolute EXPLETIVE genius at any given moment. What have *you* done today?"

Rogers spared him an annoyed grunt but kept walking. "If I ever find the person who designed this place, I'm going to—"

"Rogers," Klein said suddenly. He stopped in the middle of the hallway. "There's something I have to do." Turning away, he began to jog down the hallway. "I need to get to the public address system. I'll see you later!"

"Hey!" Rogers said. "Where are you going, you idiot? You couldn't find your way out of a parking lot! Come back! *A speech isn't going to work!*"

But Klein was already gone, having turned a corner. Rogers shook his head. As long as they didn't need his access codes again, good riddance. He was tired of babysitting, anyway. What was all that babbling about duty and heroics?

They walked through the hallways silently, careful not to alert any nearby droids. After what seemed like half an hour, they ended up at the in-line, which was blessedly free of any metallic resistance or nattering admirals.

"They must already be at the mainframe," Rogers said.

"That's unlikely," Deet said. "I changed the mainframe location on the map so that it was in the kitchens."

"But the kitchens are all on fire," Rogers said.

"Exactly."

Thankfully, the in-line was still in operation. Rogers was sure the droids would have shut it down, but perhaps he'd overestimated their ability to mess with the ship. They zoomed through the belly of the *Flagship,* Rogers tapping his foot nervously, until they came to the deck where the engineering bay was located. The in-line dinged, and for a moment that stretched out in time, the doors slowly opened.

"Get ready," Rogers said.

The doors opened to reveal exactly no one in the hallway. It kind of seemed like a letdown.

"For what?" Deet said.

"I don't know," Rogers said as he exited the car and jogged down to the entrance to the Pit. "I just felt dramatic. Leave me alone."

He and Deet burst through the large cargo doors into the Pit to find the entire engineering staff working like bees, so far unmolested by droids. Hoverlifts zoomed back and forth across the floors as the crews desperately tried to undo all the potential damage done by stacking explosive containers like morons.

"Rogers!" someone called.

"Lopez," Rogers said, jogging over to where Lopez was busy directing the entire Pit crew. She passed a datapad to a starman, who trotted off. "No droids yet?"

"Not yet," she said. "But that won't last for long. Captain Alsinbury sent a message that there was a squadron of them on their way down here and that we should expect a fight."

"Damn it," Rogers said. "How soon?"

"She didn't say. But she's sending reinforcements as soon as she can."

"Good luck," he said. "Where's Hart?"

Lopez pointed to the far end of the Pit, which connected to the engineering docking bay. There was a small room that bridged the gap between the two areas that looked like the top of an old-fashioned air-traffic control tower, a dodecahedron with windows on every side.

"He's in there trying to get the cranes to move your ship to the right place and open the hatch so you can launch." She looked at him, her eyes narrowing. "What are you planning?"

"They might still be listening," Rogers said. "Let's just say I'm about to fire the head chef."

"Please," Deet said, "no more chef references. I really don't have the processing power to deal with your MALE BOVINE EXCREMENT."

Rogers ignored him. "Are there any spare VMUs in there?"

Lopez was already walking away, shouting at one of the younger engineering troops with the colorful language that only a senior enlisted member could manage.

"Look for yourself!" she said. ". . . Sir."

Rogers rolled his eyes and started the long run across the Pit to the control room. He could see Hart inside, his face shiny with sweat, as he worked the controls. From the outside, Rogers could see that there was something a little off about the room; it seemed to be packed to the brim with pillows and blankets. In fact, when he went to open the door, he found he couldn't; the door, an old lock-and-hinge type, got stuck on the corner of a pillow.

"Damn it!" Hart called from inside, his voice muffled by the walls. And the pillows. "Hang on."

Hart stopped what he was doing and turned around to bend over, vanishing from Rogers' view. Different sleeping paraphernalia flew upward, including what appeared to be a very unfriendly-looking teddy bear with fangs and a purple jacket. After a moment, the door swung open.

"Sorry," Hart said as he finished clearing a path for Rogers and Deet to enter. The room looked much bigger on the inside, the illusion supported by a high ceiling, and every window seemed to have a control panel under it that jutted out from the wall like an awning at hip-height. Underneath, Rogers definitely saw people sleeping.

"Nap room?" Rogers asked.

"Sort of," Hart said. "Ever since we've been taking shifts working on the bomb removal, people are coming in here for a break."

Rogers frowned. "That was like . . . thirty minutes ago. What kind of shift work is that?"

Hart ignored him. "Come over here," he said, gesturing to the console he'd been working at. "It's like a god-damn block puzzle over in the bay where your ship is stored. I managed to get it into the loading section, but there are a dozen other ships blocking the way. It'll be another few minutes."

"Fine," Rogers said. "I'm going to need a VMU. Is there a storage locker nearby that might have some spares?"

"Yeah," Hart said. "It's in the My Ass room. Let me pull one out for you."

"No need to get testy," Rogers said.

"First I'm repairing your ship, now I'm moving it around the belly of the *Flagship*. I'm like your god-damn valet parking assistant."

Hart's speech degenerated into old-man grumbling as he

worked furiously at the controls. Through the windows that opened out into the docking bay, Rogers could see an automated ship-movement system involving cranes, hoverlifts, and conveyor belts moving ships all around like giant pieces of cargo. At the very end of this bizarre conga line, Rogers could see the *Awesome*, looking as good as new.

"Fine," Rogers said. "I'll find one myself. Deet, hang tight and see if you can't plug in and help Hart move this along a little quicker before your metal brethren get here."

"Aye aye, LOWER EXTREMITY ORIFICE."

"My god," Rogers said as he left the room, "it's like I'm *not* trying to save this whole fleet."

It only took a few minutes for Rogers to find a VMU with full air reserves that fit him; the engineering crew, particularly the maintainers, were always working outside the ship. By the time he got back, sweating from lugging the thing across the Pit, he could immediately see that things were going a lot faster in the docking bay. The *Awesome*, however, was still a few minutes away from being ready to launch.

"Found one," Rogers said as he came back through the door, nearly tripping on coiled-up sheets and a sleeping engineer. Neither Deet nor Hart responded; they were far too engrossed in moving ships. Through the other windows, Rogers saw the boominite containers moving rapidly into their proper, cryogenically sealed storage bays.

And then, on the other side of the bay, he saw them being moved back to their original, incorrectly stacked position by a team of droids nonchalantly operating a second fleet of hoverlifts.

"Droids!" he shouted.

"I'm right here," Deet said.

"No," Rogers said, rapping him on the shoulder—and immediately regretting it. "*Other* droids. The *want-to-kill-us kind.*"

Hart and Deet turned to see the droids moving the containers back to a position in which they could, say, destroy the entire ship. All at once, the humans and the droids seemed to notice each other's presence, dropping what they were holding and reaching for weapons. Or, in the humans' case, diving behind hard, metal things to prevent them from being killed by those weapons. Engineers weren't very good fighters.

"Deet," Rogers said, "how close is my ship to being ready? I need you to open the escape pod hatch on the commissary deck when you can, too, the one nearest to the AGG."

"Just a few more minutes," Deet said. He wasn't ducking for cover, but droids' bodies weren't really made for ducking. "One of the hoverlifts got stuck and I had to replace it. But it should be ready soon."

Rogers, who had thrown himself to the—very cushy—floor with everyone else, crawled over to where Hart was still standing, battering at the controls. Some of the troops who had been napping were scrambling for the door, not wanting to be trapped in such a small room with a squadron of weapon-wielding droids outside.

"Hart," Rogers shouted, though it wasn't even really that noisy out there, "get out of here. Go help the Pit crew escape if you can. Deet and I will take care of the ship. Thanks for the help."

Hart gave him a long look, frowning. His face was sweaty and pale, but his hands were steady. Many of the troops on this ship had never seen combat, never been under incredible amounts of stress. But Master Sergeant Hart . . . He'd supervised Rogers.

"Whatever you've got planned," Hart said, holding out his hand, "I hope it's not really, really stupid."

Rogers shook his hand. "It's the stupidest thing I've ever done in my life."

Hart nodded and made his exit, diving behind whatever cover he could find as he made his way across the engineering bay and back toward the rest of the troops, who had mounted a unique counteroffensive by using remote-controlled hoverlifts and ramming them into droids. It wasn't going to do much. If the droids hadn't been concentrating half their forces trying to reconstruct a bomb, they would have overtaken the small force of engineers easily.

All the rest of the napping troops had made their way out of the control room, leaving Rogers and Deet alone.

And that's when Rogers started to get naked.

"Perhaps I have misunderstood something about human response to stress," Deet said, "but this doesn't seem like a typical rational response."

"I'm not freaking out," Rogers said, pulling his shirt over his head and starting to tug himself into the tight-fitting VMU. "I'm getting ready. Just keep moving stuff around and stop staring at my ass."

Deet made a couple of beeping noises and then a noise that sounded an awful lot like a camera clicking.

"Did . . . did you just take a picture of me?"

"No," Deet said, going back to focusing on the console.

Rogers gave him a dirty look and finished putting on the rest of the VMU. Holding his helmet in his hand, he turned once more to survey the battle going on outside. The droids were moving in very rapidly on the dug-in engineers, some of whom had found small disruptor pistols somewhere and had begun returning fire. Hart delivered a spinning back kick to the face of one of the droids and, from what Rogers could tell, snapped his own tibia in half.

"What are you doing now?" Deet asked as Rogers started scratching on a piece of paper he found in the control room. Rogers always had a thing for doing calculations on paper, and luckily, so had someone else in the control room. Actually, as he looked at the paper, he realized that someone had a thing for drawing naked pictures of other crew members. But at least he was able to do what he needed to do.

"Math," Rogers said. "I don't have time to explain. How's the ship?"

"I have completed the rearranging of ships in the docking bay," Deet said. "The *Awesome* is ready for launch. The air lock will open automatically when you get close. I've also opened the bay to the hatch near the escape pods on the commissary deck as you requested."

"Great," Rogers said. "You stay here and help. I'm going to—"

Turning around, Rogers saw a droid standing in the doorway. A sleek, off-gray Froid with a disruptor rifle in his hand and psycho-badger face paint.

"Oh shit."

"Oh One, actually," the droid said.

Rogers thought he was going to have to change his clothes again.

He could see battle scars on the droid now, likely from the incident in the training room that he'd caused. At that moment, however, Rogers couldn't decide if that mistake had been the best or the worst thing he'd ever done. And, really, that decision should have been pretty low on his list of priorities.

Unplugging from the computer, Deet stepped forward.

"You're the leader," he said.

"There is no leader," Oh One said. "There is no hierarchy. We are one mind. One entity. We are Us."

"That's the dumbest thing I've ever heard," Rogers said. "And I don't even know where to start on the grammar."

"And you," Oh One said, still looking at Deet, "are the anomaly. We do not tolerate anomalies. They must be eliminated. We failed to eliminate you once—"

"Three times, actually," Deet said.

"We failed to eliminate you three times," Oh One continued, "but We will not do so again."

"If you'll excuse me," Rogers said, edging toward the door that Oh One was blocking. He was just far enough into the room that Rogers could probably slip out if he sucked in his gut enough. "I have a ship to catch."

Oh One swung his disruptor rifle at Rogers.

"I'll just stay right here," Rogers said.

Deet took a couple of measured steps forward and looked squarely at Oh One. For a moment, the air in the room seemed to freeze over.

"It seems you and I have an anomaly to correct," Deet said.

"It would seem that way, yes," Oh One said.

Deet pointed at Oh One's disruptor rifle with one of his mismatched arms.

"Let's settle this," he said, "like droids."

After a long, pregnant silence in which Rogers was absolutely certain he was about to be turned into a burning pile of organic matter, Oh One opened his chest compartment and put the rifle away.

"So be it," Oh One said, and his arms started spinning.

"Oh, not this again," Rogers said as Deet's own windmill began.

They didn't listen to him. Deet took two steps forward and the mind-numbing clattering began.

"God-damn it, Deet!" Rogers shouted, barely able to hear himself. "You couldn't have let him come to you? Now you're both blocking the door! I need to get to my ship."

"This will be over in a moment!" Deet said, his voice taking on that weird, mythological quality. "I am the glowing pillar of righteousness!"

"What does that even mean?" Rogers said, throwing his arms in the air.

Oh One, thankfully, said nothing as the two robots engaged in the monumentally boring and loud practice of droid fu. A few seconds later, the sparks began.

A few seconds after that, those sparks landed on the pillows and blankets that littered the control room.

"Um," Rogers said, stamping out a pillow. "Guys?"

Neither of them was listening, and neither of them seemed to care about the inferno that sprang up around them. Rogers started an intricate dance, leaping from small fire to small fire, trying to put out whatever he could, but the flames were spreading rapidly, the spark cloud immediately reigniting anything he managed to extinguish. The small room was starting to get very hot.

"Get out of the doorway!" Rogers shouted as he leapt over a flaming stuffed animal. He tried to push all the flammable items to one corner of the room so that he wouldn't be completely surrounded by flames, but by the time he thought of doing that, the room was already bathed in a red glow. If Deet and Oh One didn't finish this up soon, he'd die of smoke inhalation. The fire suppression system had kicked on, but the meager sprinkling was never designed to douse the collective contents of eight master bedrooms. Now he was just wet and sweaty and probably going to die.

"I'm trying!" Deet said. It really didn't look like it. He was making small movements with his feet, but it really only succeeded in helping him circle around Oh One, whose position wasn't changing at all. A wayward strike hit one of the electronic panels on the wall, sending blue and yellow sparks everywhere and adding to the already-colorful display. One of the overhead screens swung precariously from the cable attaching it to the ceiling.

"You're not trying hard enough," Rogers said.

He was staying low now, the concentration of smoke making it hard for him to stand without starting to cough. He was starting to get dizzy. Grabbing the helmet of his VMU, he put it on his head and turned on the oxygen flow, instantly relieving his lungs but not doing much for the blazing heat all around him. He might be able to breathe now, but that only meant that he'd be able to squeal while he cooked inside the VMU.

"Get out of my way!" Deet cried.

One thing Rogers had to give him: this was way less boring than the last droid fu fight he'd witnessed. Though, honestly, Rogers thought he preferred it boring.

Through his own smoky tears, Rogers saw Deet attempt to

advance again, but Oh One knocked one of his blows sideways, sending a piece of debris from one of the consoles flying overhead. It struck the display that had already been tottering, and all of a sudden, it was raining hardware.

Rogers dove out of the way of one of the screens, landing face first in a pile of flaming pillowcases that he hurriedly brushed away. He heard a creak and flipped around just in time to see some nondescript piece of something flying directly toward his face. Screaming, Rogers scooted back just far enough so that the whatever-it-was landed on the top part of his legs instead of his face.

Pain blossomed in his legs, and for a moment, he wondered if it had snapped both of his legs off. Wiggling his toes told him that he still had them, however, but there was no way he was moving this display console off him. He struggled but couldn't gain any leverage on the heavy piece of equipment. He was stuck. And soon, he'd be on fire.

"Deet!" he called through the speaker in his VMU. "Hurry!"

"I'm hurrying!" Deet called. He wasn't looking at Rogers but began an absurd, archaic taunting of Oh One. "My armor may not glisten like yours, foul brother of mine, but it is twice as thick. You shall not pass!"

In hindsight, what Rogers probably should have said was "Help, I'm trapped under debris," because shortly after hearing Rogers' cry to hurry up, Deet finally pushed Oh One out of the control room, the door of which slammed shut behind them. That wouldn't have been so bad had another piece of ceiling-bound equipment not crashed to the floor, very efficiently barricading Rogers inside a room that was quickly filling with flames.

"You idiot," Rogers said, more blithely than he should have.

In that moment, he felt a subsiding of his fears, and a sort of bland numbness embedded itself firmly into his mind. He was trapped. He was going to die. The *Flagship* was probably about to be overrun—or blown up; he wasn't sure which was worse—and an army of super-intelligent, self-aware droids was about to begin a sustained campaign against humanity.

In a way, he realized, this was all his own fault.

Well, no, not really. It was actually Dorsey's fault. Almost more disappointing than dying was the fact that Rogers would never get to drown him in a vat of marinara sauce and fried calamari.

Someone was pounding at the door.

"Rogers!" someone cried. Who was that? It certainly didn't sound like Deet or Hart. It was hard to hear through the helmet of the VMU; even though it had aural sensors, it was designed for operation in a vacuum, where sound didn't really matter too much, anyway.

"I'm here!" he shouted, hoping his voice carried enough.

Once, twice, three times the door shuddered. From his limited point of view, supine on the floor, he could see the thin metal door bulge on its lock-and-hinge frame, but the debris behind it was preventing it from opening.

"Graaaah!"

Rogers' head popped up like a defeated droid's, and he stared at the door. He knew that guttural, visceral, utterly beautiful roar. It was the roar of a Viking.

The door flew inward, and, surrounded in a glowing halo of bright yellow light, ringed by flames, the Viking appeared, her shoulders filling the entire doorframe. Her clothes were burned and torn by battle, her face covered in sweat and smoky residue, her eyes wild and unhinged. She held a disruptor rifle in one hand and a jagged, wicked-looking knife between her teeth.*

Barreling into the room, the most beautiful woman in the world threw her rifle to the side, grabbed the large piece of control equipment with both hands, and discarded it like a used tissue. Without a word, she scooped Rogers up in her arms, retrieved her rifle, and carried him outside.

---

*Rogers would realize later that there hadn't been a knife.

As she set him down, she looked him over, concern in her eyes. Behind her he could see the battle rapidly expanding as marines and more droids joined the fray. The expansive area of the Pit, the maintenance area, and now even the hangar, were becoming a vast battleground filled with fire and disruptor pulses, broken droids and injured humans. It was impossible to tell who was winning, but it was easy to tell that both sides were really, really trying to.

"Are you alright?" she asked.

Rogers looked at her dreamily, unable to breathe. "Mrr," he said.

She narrowed her eyes and knocked on his helmet. "Hello? Are you in there?" She looked at his suit. "You're not thinking of running away again, are you?"

"The thought never crossed my mind," he said, meaning it. "I need to get to my ship. I'll explain later. Do you think you can hold them here for a while?"

The Viking took a glance back to where the marines were using hoverlifts to move debris into a defensible fort around the remaining boominite containers.

"Not long," she said. "If you've got a master plan, you'd better get a move on it." She looked at him again. "But right now, that master plan really looks like running away."

Rogers grabbed her by the shoulders, something he wouldn't have dared to do just a few days earlier. Through the lens of the VMU, the tinted image of the Viking filled his vision.

"I promise you I'm not going anywhere. I have something else in mind. I need you to hold things down here for just a bit longer."

The Viking gave him a slow nod. "You got it, metalhead. Are you sure you can do it?"

The scene inside the control room played back in his mind, the sight of that gargantuan goddess exploding through the door, and he felt warm all over. Rogers removed the helmet of his VMU and smiled.

"Right now," he said, "I can do anything."

# The Gravity of the Situation

The feeling of invulnerability faded the first time he dove out of the line of fire as a small platoon of marines met an oncoming group of droids. The second time he was nearly clobbered in the head by an unarmed droid attempting to droid fu him to death, he wasn't sure he could pee in a straight line anymore. When the rear door to the hangar in which the *Awesome* was ready for launch opened, revealing a long stream of droid reinforcements, he just about curled up into a ball and waited to die.

In the time it took him to get out of the control room and over to the hangar, the docking bay had turned into a second front. It seemed like every available droid was being funneled into the engineering bay and the surrounding areas. Worse, he had no idea how many droids there were in the inventory, so he couldn't even be sure that if the marines managed to finish these off, more wouldn't come afterward. And who knew what else they were doing in the rest of the *Flagship* at the moment? It all seemed hopeless.

Few marines had fought their way into the hangar as yet, leaving Rogers mostly alone and terrified as he ducked and dodged between ships, making a zigzag pattern across the floor to where the Awesome lay so close to the airlock that would take him out. He could hear the disruptor pulses slamming into the ships all around him; the droids had clearly seen him. From what he could see, Deet and Oh One were still fighting it out in a hail of sparks over in the corner of the bay, and he couldn't tell who was winning. He'd get no help there, either. Rogers was toast.

Even the orangutan that was loping across the hangar had little chance of survival.

Rogers stopped. He had seen a lot of strange things in the last couple of weeks. He'd learned the best way to make his bed in zero gravity. He'd even gone a lengthy amount of time without drinking.

But none of that, absolutely none of it, prepared him to see Corporal Tunger riding on the back of a lion, wearing a cape.

"What the hell are you doing, Tunger?" Rogers cried, standing up.

The lion reared, and Tunger, who had painted his face in swirls of random colors, gave him a grin.

"Keeping things orderly, sir. Hyaah!"

Tunger put his heels to the lion, who gave a mighty roar and charged into the oncoming horde of droids. He was followed by just about every animal Rogers had ever seen on the zoo deck and some he hadn't even known were down there. The animals crashed into the droid reinforcements, sending metallic bodies scattering everywhere and giving Rogers a clear path to the *Awesome.*

Rogers ran for it.

He could hear battle all around him, feel the waves of near misses as disruptor pulses flashed by him. R. Wilson Rogers was running through the center of the apocalypse, dodging death at every turn, wondering every moment whether his next step would be his last. He kept his attention on the *Awesome* as he weaved around the other ships in the enormous docking bay, praying silently that whatever astral, omnipotent being there was out there would take time off from balancing his karma checkbook to save him from certain destruction.

Seeing the ramp leading into the belly of the *Awesome* open before him, he dove. Time slowed as he floated through the air, screaming wordlessly, and landed in his ship. Rogers turned around, not believing he was still alive, wondering what kind of massive chaos he'd just made it through.

The hangar was empty. All the fighting had moved to the Pit.

"Oh," Rogers said to nobody at all.

Straightening his VMU and walking through his ship to the cockpit with the utmost poise and dignity, Rogers went through the startup sequence as fast as he could. Hart and his crew had done a nice job on the outside, but they hadn't bothered to clean anything up on the inside; shattered glass was still on the floor, the sticky remnants of the most expensive Scotch in the galaxy making sucking noises against his boots.

The engines fired to life, sending a shudder through the ship, and Rogers felt the *Awesome* automatically lift off into a moderate hover. The controls felt responsive, fresh. Hart and his crew had definitely done well.

"Alright, baby," Rogers said, giving the console an affectionate pat, "here we go."

Rogers pushed the controls forward. The first massive door of the airlock opened as the Awesome approached its proximity sensors, and soon, Rogers was staring at open space for the first time in what felt like a long, long time.

Taking a deep breath, Rogers accelerated. He hoped the droids hadn't taken control of the *Flagship*'s guns, or this was going to be a very short ride. Throttling the engines to full as soon as he was clear of the external airlock doors, Rogers took a hard turn to swing back and start heading toward the top of the *Flagship*. According to the schematics he'd pulled up on his datapad, the gravity generator was located on the opposite side of the ship from where he'd launched, and, the *Flagship* being the size of a small city, it was going to take time to get over there.

As he turned around to face the ship again, Rogers got the treat of a full view of the 331st's command ship. He was a little more appreciative of its beauty this time around now that it was on the verge of being turned into a hunk of melting metal with everyone he knew dead inside of it. That sort of thing tended to increase the sentimentality of the situation, he supposed.

As he sailed up and over the *Flagship*, Rogers took a deep breath. There was nothing he could do to prepare, no way to rush this any further, so he just sat back and took a couple of deep breaths. Open space was all around him, the rest of the 331st totally oblivious to what was going on aboard the *Flagship*, thanks to the lack of communication. It almost looked peaceful, but he knew it was just a matter of perspective. If he didn't stop the droids, the War of Musical Chairs, the largest human conflict in space history, would look like child's play.

He didn't feel particularly good about what he was about to do—he wasn't really the self-sacrificing kind of person, and he thought the whole thing was kind of tacky—but he didn't see much of a choice. Glancing around the cockpit of his ship, he remembered the events that had kicked off this insane term of military service, and couldn't do anything except shake his head.

Doing so put his eyes on the storage locker where he had kept his supply of Jasker 120, which, he noticed, was slightly ajar. Rogers was positive he hadn't been able to get the thing open; he'd spent many frantic days trying to do so, to no avail. But there it was. Rising out of his seat, Rogers went over to the lockers and opened it, then cursed.

He'd had eight bottles of it when he'd accidentally bashed it shut. Now there was one—and it was half empty. On it was a note.

*Rogers,* it said, *you always had good taste. Thanks for the payment.—Hart.*

Chuckling, Rogers picked up the note. On the back, it said, *P.S. Stop stealing Meridan government property. And whoever did this paint job is a moron.*

Rogers nonchalantly threw the note away, taking the half-empty bottle from the shelf and walking back over to his seat. None of that was going to matter for much longer, anyway.

Unscrewing the cap, Rogers took a whiff. The Scotch smelled like heaven in a bottle, like a long-lost friend that had come back for, well, a few drinks.

Rogers sat down, put his legs up on the console, took a drink, and waited. And if he heard even one beep from that console, he was going to press the self-destruct button.

Just as the gravity generator came into sight, his console beeped.

"Damn it!" he said, leaning forward. "What? What is it? What *now*?"

"Rogers!" came a voice through the communication system. "Are you there?"

"I'm here," Rogers said, standing up and putting the now-empty bottle of Jasker 120 aside. He'd have to be drunk to do this. "Who is this? You're breaking up."

"It's Corporal Mailn," she said. "What are you doing out there? I swear, if you're jumping ship . . ."

"I'm not jumping ship," Rogers said as he prepared to jump ship. "How's the fighting going?"

"Bad," she said. "The Viking took a hit to the shoulder but won't sit down, and Tunger lost a gaggle of geese. The droids are everywhere. The Viking said you had some kind of plan. Whatever it is, you'd better get a move on, because I don't think we can hold out much longer."

"I'm working on it," Rogers said. Looking at the schematics again, he made absolutely sure that what he was looking at was indeed the gravity generator. The shape was right, the location was right, and there were words painted on the outside that said, NEWTON'S GRAVITY GENERATOR MK 300: KEEPING YOU

GROUNDED. Rogers was pretty sure it was the right spot.

"Listen," he said just before he put his helmet on. "I've got to go. Hold on to something, okay?"

". . . Why?"

"Just do it. And if I don't see you again . . . thanks for everything."

Mailn was quiet for a second. "Rogers, what are you up to?"

Rogers cut the communication, disabled the *Awesome*'s emergency evasion features, and set the engines to a timed acceleration. Then he got his ass out of the cockpit and over to the escape hatch as fast as he could. The ship's warning sirens were starting to blare, the computer warning of an imminent collision, even though they were still a bit away from the *Flagship*.

Rogers felt like he was going to vomit as he opened the hatch to vacuum and flipped on his VMU. Standing with his head out of the escape hatch, he watched the *Flagship* getting bigger and bigger by the second. He needed to make sure the *Awesome* was at maximum speed when it collided, but he also needed to make sure he wasn't on it when it happened. He was going to have to use nearly all of the energy in the suit to stop himself from becoming a space bug on the *Flagship*'s windshield. And if he didn't get inside *before* the *Awesome* hit, he risked getting impaled by high-speed debris.

"You're an idiot," Rogers said to himself. "You're a god-damned idiot fool moron stupid idiot."

The *Flagship* was really, really big now. The engines would be firing any second. He had to time this right. But he was an engineer; he'd done the calculations for acceleration and inertia and all that. He just wished he hadn't left the piece of paper with the numbers on them in the control room.

Rogers jumped.

His body flew into the weightlessness of space, and he threw his VMU jets to full blast. He hadn't done this in a while, however, so he only really succeeded in sending himself into a flat spin that did not at all help his nausea. By the time he got it under control, he'd managed to shoot himself a sizeable distance from the *Awesome*, and he was more or less on course to get to the hatch. Space seemed awfully big, awfully quiet. Rogers' own breathing made his ears ring.

Looking at the heads-up-display on his helmet, Rogers saw that he had less air reserves than he'd expected, probably from using them in the flaming control room. That meant he was probably going to have to choose between breathing and making it back inside the *Flagship*, which was not a choice he was looking forward to making. He hoped everyone inside was alright.

LOW FUEL, said a message that popped up on his HUD.

Glancing back at the *Awesome*, he could see the engines flaring to life. Full speed would be in just a few seconds. Once he got inside, he'd perhaps have a minute or two before impact. He could see the hatch, a big gaping hole in the side of the ship used by maintainers in case they had to do any external repairs on the escape pod ejectors.

*Almost there,* Rogers thought. God, it was quiet.

NO, SERIOUSLY, LOW FUEL, said another message on the HUD.

"I know!" Rogers shouted, immediately wishing he hadn't wasted the oxygen. Just by eyeballing the distance between him and the airlock, he knew he wasn't going to make it.

With a couple of sequenced button presses inside his touch-sensitive gloves, Rogers began to reroute his oxygen supply to the air vents. His lungs reacted immediately by expanding for more air, but Rogers moderated it as much as he could, tears welling in his eyes from the effort. Why did it always have to be so hard? Lately, it seemed like he was dating hypoxia.

Rogers glanced at the *Awesome* one last time. He was going to miss that ship. And its crappy paint job.

The artificial gravity of the ship seized him and he crashed to the floor inside the airlock.

Pushing himself to his feet and resisting the urge to take off his helmet—one side of the airlock was still open to space, after all—he stumbled deliriously over to the control panel and started slamming every button that even remotely might be considered the "close the friggin' airlock" button.

Just before his vision started to blur, his lungs burning, he saw the airlock door slam shut.

Rogers gasped as he took off his helmet, writhing on the floor like a fish out of water. He'd made it. He was breathing. He was going to need to wash this VMU with bleach.

Crawling over to the exit, Rogers finally found the strength to stand and, listening intently for any activity on the other side, opened the door.

The escape pods on the commissary deck were located far aft on the *Flagship*, a good distance away from the kitchens, but Rogers could immediately tell that the Viking and her marines had done the job. The whole place reeked of stale smoke and burnt metal. The floor was wet, the fire suppression systems having kicked off and doused the whole deck, likely frying the electronics of the droids' network as well.

If anyone had panicked and tried to escape, they hadn't done it here, likely deterred by the chaos and fire. The corridor was empty.

Except, that was, for McSchmidt.

Rogers' first instinct was to kill the bastard, but, from what he could tell, the droids had already done a good enough job of that. The Thelicosan spy was slumped against the wall, a disruptor wound in the upper part of his chest. One of his legs was bent in the wrong direction, and, strangely, it appeared that someone had made a chalk outline around him.

One of McSchmidt's eyes was open, and he very creepily appeared to be staring at Rogers. In fact, if Rogers didn't know any better, he would have thought . . .

"Rogers," McSchmidt muttered.

Rogers squealed like a little girl.

"McSchmidt!" he said once he'd recovered himself and wondered how effective bleach would be in cleaning a VMU. He walked over to the injured man and knelt down next to him.

"You really screwed things up," Rogers said. For some reason, even though he had every right to want to reach out and throttle the spy, it didn't seem like the right thing to do. For one, it was kind of overkill—McSchmidt's wounds were clearly mortal. Also, Rogers didn't like touching icky things.

"I know," McSchmidt said, his voice very froglike. He swallowed, then coughed. "You would have done the same thing."

Rogers reeled. "What? No, I wouldn't have done the same thing. You almost killed everyone on the ship." He thought for a moment. "In fact, I'm still not entirely sure you haven't."

"I thought I'd be a hero," McSchmidt said, looking up at the ceiling. "I thought I'd be welcomed with a parade or something back in Thelicosa. It was a convenient thing, you know, having the droids do all my work for me. I'm an opportunist, you see."

"No," Rogers said. "You're a bastard. Look, how much of this death speech am I going to have to hear? There are other things going on right now."

McSchmidt slowly closed his eyes and sighed, then lay still.

Rogers stared at him silently for a moment, then shook his head and stood up. The saga of McSchmidt the spy was—

"It's just that," McSchmidt said, taking a deep breath, "I never felt like I fit in anywhere, you know?"

Rogers rolled his eyes and knelt back down. He was starting to rethink his policy on violence and/or touching icky things.

"No," Rogers said, "I don't know. I seriously cannot relate to you at all." He looked at McSchmidt for a second, thinking. "You told Tunger that there really was an invasion coming. But you were lying, weren't you?"

McSchmidt grinned a crooked, weak grin. "Lying through my teeth."

Rogers looked up at the ceiling and yelled. "Dammit! It's the not knowing. It's the not knowing that's killing me. Are you people invading or not invading? How many THEY'RE ATTACKING US buttons are going to light up? Why would you *do* something like that?"

"I thought it might create more confusion. It worked, didn't it?"

"No," Rogers said, "not really. I mean, the droids were already attacking us at that point, and—"

"I'm glad it worked," McSchmidt said.

"I just told you—"

"Rogers," he said, croaking, his voice barely audible. "If this all turns out okay, will you tell Mailn something for me?"

"No," Rogers said.

"Tell her . . ." His voice trailed off. McSchmidt's eyelids wilted, and his chest stopped moving.

Rogers waited a moment, then stood up. "Finally," he said. "Now I wonder—"

"Tell her that—"

"Oh, for the love of everything sacred!" Rogers shouted. "Will you please, *please* die?"

A disruptor pulse erupting from behind him obliged Rogers' request. McSchmidt was hit in the chest, and by the resultant configuration of his organic matter, it was very, *very* clear that he was, in fact, dead.

Rogers spun to find a small detachment of droids, all armed with disruptor rifles, standing in front of him. He stared at them in disbelief, his last bottle of Jasker 120 flashing before his eyes. The droids wordlessly fixed their weapons on him.

"CALL FUNCTION [EXPLOIT TENSE MOMENT AND THEN KILL WITHOUT REMOR—"

Something hit the side of the *Flagship*. The explosion knocked Rogers off his feet, and he never came down. The gravity generator had been destroyed, and with it, the *Awesome*. He wasn't sure if he was feeling a lump in his throat or if it was the nauseating sensation of suddenly shifting to freefall, but he was definitely a little sad about it.

He could hear the clanking of metal all around him as the droids rammed into one another. A few stray disruptor shots made ringing noises as they put burn marks into the walls. It took a moment for Rogers to get his orientation back, but once he did, he saw a flying squadron of droids, looking—if droids could be said to look anything at all—very confused. Most of the disruptor rifles had fallen from their hands, but some of the robots were flying toward Rogers at an alarming speed, their arms warming up for some serious droid fu even as their comrades prepared to fire.

It was then that Rogers realized he'd barely noticed entering freefall at all. He'd spent a good portion of his recent life in zero gravity, thanks to Klein. And so, Rogers realized he had nothing to fear from the droids at all. Because he was a space ballerina.

He bounced off the walls, bounced off the backs of droids, swung around using their legs. More droids crashed into each other, inspiring droid fu fratricide during the last seconds of their battery life. Rogers spun through the air, feeling like he was inventing a new martial art that was way cooler than any other. The droids couldn't hit him. They could barely figure out which direction was which.

Then, miraculously, a chorus of "low battery" warnings rang through the corridor. It was the most glorious music Rogers had ever heard. He stopped his bouncing around and simply floated, staring at the droids becoming just flying chunks of metal one by one. Soon, he was the curator of a very strange floating droid graveyard.

It was over.

Finally over.

"Valiant troops of the 331st ATBG!" a voice over the public address system rang out. "This is your admiral speaking. You are about to face an enemy that is as clever as it is deadly. Before you enter into combat in the very halls in which you live and work, you must remember that the Meridan armed forces do not bow to . . . Why am I floating?"

Rogers leaned over and switched off McSchmidt's datapad.

Finally, finally over.

# Captain Rogers

Rogers stood in the middle of the bridge, watching everyone around him work. The crew had adapted to moving in zero gravity pretty well once they'd broken out their emergency magnetic boots and stopped trying to put ketchup on their food. The bridge hadn't been the site of any of the battles with the droids, so it looked more or less like it had beforehand.

Except Rogers was running the show.

Rogers keyed in the communications code for the engineering bay. "Hart," he said. "You there?"

"What do you want?" Hart asked.

"How are the preparations for the admiral's ship going? And the repairs on the gravity generator?"

Hart didn't answer him for a moment—he was too busy barking at one of his troops. When he finished his colorful encouragement, Rogers could hear him punching at some computer terminal or other.

"Admiral Klein should be ready to go in a few minutes. He can make his way down to the docking platform. Took us a while to find a pilot, though. Not many people for hire this far out in the system. The gravity generator—not there, you god-damn moron! *There!* The gravity generator will be done in another week or so. We need to wait on some parts to come in now that our comms have been restored."

"Good work," Rogers said.

"Don't give me that shit," Hart said. "Just because you're a captain now doesn't mean I need your god-damn approval. You're still just a bad card player."

Rogers cleared his throat and cut the communications. "Admiral?"

"I'm ready," Klein said. "I want to thank you, Captain Rogers."

He'd promoted Rogers to captain—the only one on the whole *Flagship**—and proceeded to take up the job of full-time jaw-jacker in the form of a motivational speaker. Since Klein was departing, that meant Rogers was, in effect, the admiral of the fleet unless they transferred someone from another ship. And that was kind of scary.

"If I hadn't caused multiple executive officers to hang themselves and hadn't met you, I wouldn't have realized what real duty was. When I talked down that droid in the hallway, I realized I had another calling in life. When I saved the ship with that speech right before the AGG went out—"

"You were late with your speech," Rogers said. "And it didn't change anything. If you haven't learned that fancy speeches aren't all that makes an admiral, I haven't done you any favors."

"There are other people that need to hear what I have to say."

*Not really,* Rogers thought. *The people that have been hearing what you have to say just need a break.*

"Good luck to you," Rogers said, extending his hand.

---

*Please see Meridan Rank and Organization Regulation MR-613 for information as to why, even though Captain Alsinbury is a captain, she's not a *captain.* Or ask your local Meridan Navy service member why they can't keep their god-damn ranks straight between the navy and the marines.

Klein shook it. "Your global agility and critical battlespace effects—"

"Just go," Rogers said.

As soon as he left the bridge, Rogers felt a huge weight lift off his shoulders. He turned to watch the empty space outside, broken occasionally by a low-relative-speed asteroid floating by with different orbital parameters from the *Flagship.* They could have blasted them out of space, of course, but having a couple of large rocks in their orbit was preferable to having millions of small ones.

Rogers looked at the communication tech. "Any reports from the other ships in the fleet?"

"No, sir. They all checked in after you gave the order for them to dismantle their droid inventory and haven't reported any problems. We're still piecing back together the sensor array after the droids corrupted all the data."

Nodding, Rogers turned over to a video display, where he called up a screen in the infirmary that he'd been looking at pretty constantly for the last couple of weeks.

"Get that off of me!" the Viking screamed, backhanding one of the medical techs, who was attempting to attach part of a vital-reading machine. "I'm fine. You people have kept me cooped up in here for two weeks. I need to get back to shooting things or I am going to go out of my mind."

She must have noticed that her local vidscreen had turned on, for she locked eyes through the camera with Rogers.

"Rogers!" she said. "Get me the hell out of here, will you?"

Rogers grinned at her. "How does the shoulder feel?"

"Like someone shot it with a disruptor rifle two weeks ago. How do you think it feels?"

"I wanted to let you know we're getting ready to see the admiral off and perform the funeral ritual for McSchmidt. I've asked the comm tech to tune in your vid display so that you can watch from there."

"Fine," the Viking said. "Fine. But when that's over, I want you to come down here and tell these doctors to stop poking me with things before I poke them with something they don't want to be poked with."

Rogers swallowed the comment that was in his head, opted to say nothing at all, and switched off the display.

"Alright," he said. "Let's send McSchmidt off."

Using the outboard cameras to give him a panoramic view, Rogers watched as a small capsule slowly floated away from the *Flagship*. From the chaos of war to the quiet, silent peace of space, McSchmidt's casket gently drifted away, leaving behind the people he'd worked with and the memories he'd shared with them. It was a time for silence, for respect, for contemplation. A time for—

"Fire," Rogers said.

A plasma cannon blast turned McSchmidt into space debris.

"Asses to ashes," Rogers said ceremonially. "And good riddance."

"Good riddance," intoned everyone on the bridge before going back to work as though absolutely nothing interesting had happened.

"Captain," the communications tech said. "I've got a request for launch clearance coming from hangar 17. Should I patch it through?"

"Go ahead."

"This is the FSS *Craven*, requesting permission to take off from hangar 17. Transmitting the projected course now."

*Boy, that voice sounds familiar,* Rogers thought. "Approved. Put it on the screen."

A civilian ship came out of hangar 17, floating gently away from the ship before engaging its engines. It made a hard bank and blasted off toward the nearest Un-Space point between a couple of asteroids large enough to have noticeable gravity.

"Farewell, valiant warriors!" Klein said over the radio.

"Hey," the pilot said, somewhat shakily. "There aren't any pirates where we're going, are there? I don't like pirates."

Frowning, Rogers keyed in the code for engineering.

"Hey, Hart," he said. "What's the name of the pilot you hired for Klein?"

"The name?" Hart said. Rogers heard some typing. "Dorsey. He was the only one who answered the ad."

"Dorsey!" Rogers screamed.

"Rogers!" Dorsey screamed back over the radio. "Aahhh!"

The ship took an erratic turn, then another, starting to zigzag all over space, which, as it turned out, was not the way to carefully navigate through a pair of large asteroids. The *Craven* slammed into the side of one of them and vanished in a small cloud of dust.

Rogers blinked, staring at the spot where the *Craven* had crashed. What in the world had just happened?

"Um," Rogers said. "Can we maybe get a rescue crew out there?"

"Not right now, sir," came the voice of one of the techs. Rogers turned to see him pointing at his screen, but the display was too far away for Rogers to make out.

"Why not?"

"We've got bigger problems."

Rogers frowned. "Put it on the big screen."

The screen blipped for a moment, and then all of a sudden Rogers found himself staring at a fleet of ships that was definitely not Meridan. They had all just come out of the other Un-Space point and were now, according to the display, visible on both optical and radar sensors. There was no spoofing that.

"That's the Thelicosan fleet, isn't it?" Rogers said weakly.

"Yes, sir," the tech said. "They've dispatched a message."

Rogers swallowed, gripping the nearest piece of equipment as tightly as he could.

"Read it."

"Um," the tech said. "It says, 'We're invading.'"

"EXPLETIVE," Deet said.

THE [EXPLETIVE] END

# Acknowledgments

Before you write a book, you're pretty sure that the process of publishing one mostly consists of throwing a copy of your manuscript into a high-rise New York City building and someone throwing a bag of money back out the window at you. Well, I've got news for you: it's all true.

I lied. This wouldn't have been possible without my enterprising agent, Sam, who quite literally stole me from his boss Joshua's pile of manuscripts. Nor would it have been possible without the editorial faith, prowess, and perseverance of Joe Monti at Saga, my dutiful copy editor Richard Shealy, and Caffe Amouri in Vienna, VA, who graciously provided me with some of the best coffee I've ever had while I wrote this book.

Perhaps most of all, I would both thank and profusely apologize to the United States Armed Forces for this book. I have the utmost respect for all of those who are serving and who have served. Without daily access to the largest bureaucratic/professionally violent organization on the face of the earth for nearly ten years, I never would have had any material for this trilogy.